Jacob

Battle for Olympus

EAMON BLAKE

ISBN: 978-1-9191643-1-1

Acknowledgements

Book 5

This book, **Jacob - Battle for Olympus**, is the fifth and final book in the Jacob series. It tells the story about a battle between the Gods and the one known as Shadow. For me, authoring the books was a labour of love that began in 2016. Little did I know that over time, it was to grow into a story to be told in a series of five books.

Book 1 - Jacob - Journey of a God

Book 2 - Jacob - Walk of the Messengers

Book 3 - Jacob - War of the End Times

Book 4 - Jacob - Children of the Gods

Book 5 - Jacob - Battle for Olympus

These books would never have been written if it weren't for the support and encouragement of my amazing family and friends who listened to my relentless telling of the stories and the ideas I had. A special 'Thank You' to you all, you know who you are.

I would like to take this opportunity to thank those who took the time to read and proof-read this book in a genre that, in a lot of cases, is alien to them. They were the ones who particularly encouraged and cajoled me into taking this epic story to its conclusion. Thank you, a million times, to Teresa Carroll, Rita Foley, Sean Blake, Tom Lillis, Vincent Reynolds, Eamonn Maguire, Raymond King, Vanessa Keogh and Thérése McGarry.

To my friend Damien Carroll: What can I say. Your regular emails and phone calls were a great help in getting some of my Dublin 'isms' out of the story making it a far better read. I am filled with gratitude.

I am eternally grateful to a very special group of people, the Poets, and Authors in the 'All About Writing Group'. Thank you for assisting me in getting my book to print ready; this would not have been possible without your valuable critique and editorial assistance, especially with grammar, layouts, and storylines.

To my amazing niece, Niamh Blake, thank you so much for your wonderful cover designs.

I would also like to acknowledge PerpetuityPublications.com for their assistance in formatting my books and getting them ready for release. Thanks again Perpetuity Publications.

And finally – A special thanks to Blake's Transport for their kind sponsorship of this book.

Author's Profile

Eamon Blake is from Crumlin, a Southside suburb of Dublin, Ireland, a place he still has a great love for. It was there, between 1970 and 1975, where he attended the local secondary school, Meanscoil Naomh Colm. During fifth and sixth year, he had the pleasure of being taught English by the late Michael Condon, an inspirational teacher who had an amazing teaching technique commanding the greatest of respect from his pupils. Eamon believes that as a result of that teacher's style and perseverance he developed an interest in writing. It was in that same school where he developed his passion for real and classical history. *The history and mythology learned during that time lingered in Eamon's mind and those early influences only resurfaced in recent years, inspiring him to pen a series of five fantasy novels recounting the tale of a Dublin schoolboy discovering his extraordinary powers, and who he actually was.*

A widower with one son, Eamon, over the years, has successfully navigated various employment roles involving procurement, sales and marketing. His professional journey included delivering marketing presentations to major wholesale and retail chains, as well as participating in monthly sales and planning meetings. He believes the wealth of experience garnered during those years helped him develop his own writing style, ultimately leading to the Jacob series.

Eamon's first foray into writing began with him researching and publishing a book detailing the history and genealogy of his own family in central Dublin, dating back to the 1780s. Motivated by a desire to share this heritage, he produced and published enough copies exclusively for his extended family.

The idea for the Jacob series came to Eamon in the late summer of 2016 after he witnessed a charming yet humorous incident in Temple Bar, Dublin. This event led to the realisation that a fantastical story could be crafted by intertwining major historical events from Africa, America, Europe, the Far East as well as the Near East, linking them, and drawing inspiration from worldwide mythological realms featuring Centaurs, Dragons, Elves, The Gods, The Little People, Mer-Peoples, The Yeti and Wizards.

Contact author:

Email: thejacobsaga@gmail.com

Table of Contents

Prologue

After accessing the aftermath of what was supposed to be the War of the End Times, Jacob began enjoying the calmness all around him. He loved having his friends share in all Olympus had to offer, in particular the excitement brought about by the number of toddlers that had arrived at the temple. Those same youngsters began their journeys as babies, all born across different centuries, but when they arrived in the temple, for them everything changed. As the days passed their ages aligned, in some cases they went to bed as two-year-olds only to awaken the following morning as five-year-olds, some already showing their powers.

Jacob had become the God of Gods and was anxious to take total control, this only happened after the departure of the senior Gods. It was also around that time when Jacobs friends left to make their way back to their own realms, leaving him, Eala and their three children as the only occupants of the temple.

Peace reigned for the next eleven years while the Children of the Gods grew into sixteen-year-old youths whose powers were increasing and needing refining. This especially applied to Jacob's son, Obelius, who was believed to be out of control, prompting Jacob to propose he establish a school, tutored by the wizards, and assisted by several of the War Gods. He sent messages across the universe and within days, much to the relief of many drained parents, pupils began arriving.

Just before the school opened, the first signs of a new menace showed itself, at first in the east, then in the dragon realm. It was after the menace arrived in Olympus when Jacob placed all realms on alert. He insisted on the school opening as soon as possible, training for war being its sole purpose.

The school initially opened with sixteen pupils, split evenly between War and Mystic Gods. This changed with the return of Lord Magni, bringing with him two sons no one knew about. They too were to be trained as War Gods.

The training was intense and done with a sense of urgency. It was a training that paid off when all eighteen found themselves at war when the temple came under attack. Hemish took control whilst Drayce and Galyna used their dragon powers, Aria became the Lioness of the Gods, Viktor became the Nineth Archangel and Maximus shared his power to be in two places at once, allowing the five War Gods to increase their numbers to ten. The Mystic Gods used their magic to seek the assistance of the Earth Mothers, while the Goddesses of the Light summoned all their powers to finish off the attackers.

Even though the attack on the temple failed, Shadow was making its presence felt as the danger intensified. For Jacob, fear was never too far away and even thought he was happy with the progress for the young gods, he concluded that the momentary calmness he felt while sitting alone on his throne wasn't to last, he knew it was a false calmness.

Jacob and the Attack on Olympus.

Jacob – Battle for Olympus

Chapter 1

The false calmness bothered him causing a feeling of dread to develop especially while looking out across the meadows and imagining they were still under attack, but they weren't, they were safe and looked to be once again at their radiant best. While still standing on the highest step he closed his eyes and allowed the sun to cast its warm glow across his worried face. He kept his eyes closed and listened to the light breeze dance through the vibrantly coloured wildflowers, encouraging their intoxicating scent to reach his nostrils. He tried to relax while taking in the melodious sound of birdsong and the rustling of grasses as industrious creatures scurried through the undergrowth. He opened his eyes to again look out across the meadows, hoping the sea of green, interspersed with its carpet of blooms, would cheer him up, but it didn't. It seems nothing eased his fears. He was interrupted when Odi entered his head.

"Brother," he said, "come and enjoy the celebration, come and meet my granddaughter."

"As much as I'd love to," replied Jacob, "I'm troubled. I promise to soon give her all my attention but not just yet. I need some time alone, too much has happened, and I need to understand."

He returned into the temple, wanting a quiet time, hoping not to be disturbed, but it wasn't to be. He was soon interrupted, it was Demetrius.

"Father, today I used all my powers and this time, it was without fear of letting you down. With Gaia by my side, I was in total control. We sensed all of nature work through us and, at times, I thought of you and hoped you'd be proud of me."

"Proud of you!" exclaimed a surprised Jacob, "I've always been proud of you, what made you think I wasn't?"

"You always hug and encourage Obe, always doing things together, always bringing him on your trips, never me. Do you love him more? Even Helena noticed."

"Just so you understand," said Jacob, stretching across to embrace his son, "when your mother and I first met, we were inseparable and soon after we became one. Before too long our hearts were split, one piece was given to you, my amazing boy. Another went to Obelius, and the third to Helena. We've always loved you equally. I fear you have confused love with attention."

"I'm sorry father," said Demetrius, feeling ashamed, "it was selfish of me to trouble you."

"The last thing that anyone could accuse you of is being selfish," said Jacob, "you're not. You've never needed my attention; throughout your short life, your powers continuously grew, and you quickly learned to be their master. Those times when you were struggling didn't you notice your mother and I were always watching? We never doubted you and that's because we saw how you were always in control. We knew you were a master when flowers bloomed as you passed. We knew when the white horses bowed as you approached, and we knew when all of nature thrived just because of your presence. Your sister controlled the light from an early age and was fiercely independent; we didn't have to worry about her either." He then raised his arms and threw his eyes to the heavens as though in despair. "Obe!" he exclaimed, with his hands now covering his face, "he was, and is still a nightmare. He's constantly and inadvertently making a fool of himself. He's only now learning to control his temper and his powers; that's why I gave, and still give him so much attention. Apollo remained behind when the senior gods left, not just to support me, it was so he could keep an eye on your brother. The gods saw in him a new, and more out of control Magni, they are terrified of the damage he could do. Remember the stories about your uncle and how, when he was three years old, he brought down one of the four pillars that kept the sky separate from the earth; Magni has been hiding from that Titan since soon after the beginning of time. The Gods feared Obe was much worse but trust me he's not. He's a powerful War God with a great respect for all those he loves; do you ever notice how he's forever watching out for you?"

"I'm sorry for doubting you father," replied Demetrius, lowering his head, "but even with all you say; there are times I too need a hug. The battle has taken a terrible toll, and I feel unnerved. My dreams are showing me something more sinister lurking out in the cosmos, and already I feel tension rising."

Jacob again embraced his son, holding him until his need passed. What they didn't realise was Obelius was close by and heard everything; he approached and said while moving to sit with them. "Am I really that bad?"

"I got off lightly," laughed Jacob, "if you actually turned out anything like Magni, I think I'd be in an early grave. Now, both of you; out to the meadows, have some fun and leave me in peace."

Demetrius stood to leave, he then hesitated. "During the battle," he said, "when I dipped my hands into the soil, my visions showed me why your decision to move Olympus back to earth was so important, I don't know why but its message was clear. All of nature trembled in fear when Olympus was out among the stars."

"Father," said Obelius, "he's right, I too felt something, it said we should be where all other pantheons can find us, I was surprised when I felt the tremors but now I think my visions are at last starting to make sense." Jacob nodded then gripped both their arms.

"It seems my sons are now truly powerful gods of Olympus," he said, "I'll sleep soundly this night. Now, please go and leave me to think."

They left and were walking towards the doors when Obelius enquired, "Demy, did you see me fight?"

"Obe," replied Demetrius, placing his arm across his brother's shoulder, "I was really impressed, you looked to be in your element, and you definitely were in total control of your powers, Shadow didn't stand a chance."

"It felt great," continued a chuffed Obelius, "but I can't take all the credit. Lovisa was ruthless, she took the lead. She will, one day, be the greatest Asgardian of them all, and the boys? They focused on protecting Thora while at the same time they fought so valiantly: Did you see how we worked as a proper team?" Demetrius just nodded.

"Viktor," said Obelius, getting more serious, "can you imagine? He becomes a father and an Archangel, all on the same day. Who would have thought?"

"Yes," agreed Demetrius, "what a sight? Magni and Apollo said what we saw was very rare, he's only the ninth Archangel to have been created since the beginning of time."

"I hope he won't be leaving us," said Obelius, getting concerned, "he's good fun. He and I are back to the way we were when we were toddlers, really close friends."

Demetrius went quiet for a moment, struggling to find the words, and when he did, he said, "Obe, I need to ask you something, something kind of personal? It's important to me so please don't tease." Obelius was intrigued and just nodded.

Chapter 2

Demetrius was still hesitant but soon found the courage.

"When I was with Gaia, that time we were calling for the Earth Mothers. I got an urge, a stirring, more intense than the stirrings I get when I think of girls. I like her, I really do. Do you think she'd be interested in me? I'm not like you, all strong and powerful. I'm not a War God; you gods have all the luck."

"We," laughed a surprised Obelius, "we have all the luck? Are you mad? What luck? I've never been touched by a girl; the only stirring I get is out in the dunes, then there's a mess. We War Gods always think it's you sensitive and nature loving types who have all the luck."

"In the dunes!" sniggered Demetrius. "You're a perv,' you could be caught. At least mine happens in the Dreamworld."

"The Dreamworld?" said Obelius, while swiftly turning back and placing both hands on his brother's shoulders. "You've got to take me there! Are there girls? Is Aria there?"

"There's no way I'm taking you there," snapped Demetrius, while forcibly pushing Obelius's hands away "it's my Dreamworld, find your own."

"Take me there," threatened Obelius, attempting a headlock on his brother, "or I'll make your life miserable."

"There's no way you are entering my Dreamworld," sneered a more assertive Demetrius, much to Obelius's shock, "they're my fantasies and anyway, nobody there would be able to cope with your fat arse and dangly bits."

"I'll have you know," replied an insulted Obelius, "there's not an ounce of fat in my arse. It's pure muscle, big and very firm, and just for the record - if you have a big nail, you need a big hammer."

"So, we're a comedian now?" laughed Demetrius, "you forget, I'm your brother and I've seen you naked, trust me, you've a fat ass and your 'nail' is not that impressive."

Demetrius backed away, expecting a painful kicking but there was no kicking. He ran, not noticing Obelius had frozen on the spot, he was being disarmed by a warm and moist tongue seductively teasing his earlobe while a hand gently caressed his lower back, causing his heart to race.

"He's right about one thing!" she whispered while allowing her warm breath travel across his neck, and using her hand to gently massage his backside. "Em, for the record, it's certainly big, but it's definitely not fat. It's muscular and, let me just check again. Ah, Just as I remember, still a pleasure to touch."

"Aaaaria," stuttered Obelius after turning, "where did you come from, did, did… did you hear everything Demy and I talked about?"

"Yes," she replied, while gently kissing his neck, "I heard everything, and again, for the record, I also heard what you said when I first arrived at Olympus. You seem to forget that I'm the Lioness of the Gods. I silently crouch then pounce, my prey never sees or hears my approach, and like all lioness's, I've perfect hearing. By the way, those scratch marks, are they still hurting?"

"How do you know about them?" asked a bewildered Obelius.

"You don't remember?" she enquired, "I feel insulted."

"Aah, one of my scratches," she continued while getting closer and gently moving her hand along his inner thigh, "I too can walk in the Dreamworld."

"I can't," he said, looking totally confused, "I've never been there. Did you attack me while I slept?"

"Attack you?" she exclaimed, "as if I would."

She increased her teasing by extending her index fingernail to gently scratch her way up his back, trying not to tear into his flesh. All she wanted was to send intense and unceasing tremors through his body. When her finger reached his neck he leaned his head forward in anticipation of her tongue being used to part his lips. He was beginning to receive flashbacks of being in the Dreamworld, but he wasn't sure.

Her sweet scent was so intoxicating it was totally disarming him, drawing him in much deeper. Beads of sweat gathered, and the closer he got to losing control the more his breathing intensified.

"Trust me," she whispered, sensuously nibbling on his ear, "you were definitely there, and there was no attack. You gave as good as you got, you knew what to do and how to bring a smile to my face."

"Ah, another scratch mark?" She said while moving her hand back under his tunic to feel his toned and muscular chest. "Is it painful?" she asked, pretending to be concerned, "should I be insulted that you don't remember?"

He just shook his head, unable to speak. His rapid breathing had turned to pleasurable gasps as wild sensations continued cascading through his body, he knew something was getting closer and didn't want this magic moment to stop. She did stop, smiled, and said before walking away,

"I can't believe you've no memory of us being together in the Dreamworld."

He backed away to rest against the nearest pillar hoping to prevent himself from collapsing from the continuous pleasurable sensations travelling through his body. Aria was now the centre of the relentless erotic thoughts swirling around his head, and he knew the slightest hint of friction would cause one hell of an explosion. He momentarily opened his eyes and saw his uncles were close by and knew if they noticed him he risked being ridiculed for the rest of his life. His worst nightmare came to pass when they approached. "Please don't come near me," he prayed, "please, please." It wasn't to be,

Magni and Modi acknowledged Aria as she walked away, they then saw how flustered Obelius was, especially when he tried to discreetly cover his crotch. They decided to have some fun. On reaching him they rested a hand on each side of the pillar, planning to totally humiliate their nephew. Modi moved closer sensing his chance for revenge. "Was it good for you?" he asked, enjoying Obelius's discomfort, "or is it about to be good for you?"

"Piss off," demanded Obelius, still gasping for breath.

"I don't think so," smirked a delighted Modi, "remember how revenge is best served cold? Remember that kick you landed on my very special place?"

"For Zeus's sake," cried Obelius, his knees about to buckle, "I was only five!"

Modi smiled and moved his hand to gently caress his nephew's neck, "Are you still thinking of Aria? Are there any extra stirrings?"

Obelius couldn't get Aria from his mind, it was as though she had enchanted him. Nothing, even the thoughts of having sex with the Gorgon Medusa, could shift her from his thoughts. His knees continued to weaken, making him more distressed; his breathing was now so rapid, even the notion of how embarrassing his situation was failed to kill his passion. The teasing was now a nightmare.

"We've had our fun," said Magni, taking pity, "and it's best to leave him be. I fear he's about to experience his first knee trembler."

"What," asked Obelius between breaths, "what's a knee trembler?" Magni just shook his head.

For Obelius the pressure deep within had welled up waiting for his mind and body to explode. At that very moment in time, without even touching himself, every nerve in his body electrified, lighting him up from the inside. The contractions were at breaking point and his knees were losing the strength to keep him standing. He took one last deep breath and then everything happened almost at once beginning with a shallow pleasurable moan escaping his lips. A temporary paralysis prevented him from processing what he was experiencing, and by wedging himself tighter against the pillar he prolonged the release, before enjoying an amazing relief. His eyes remained closed while savouring the warm cascading sensations travelling through his body to eventually buckle his knees, causing his legs to weaken. When it was over, and his strength returned to his legs, he thought, "so that's a knee trembler?"

He opened his eyes to find Aria standing before him, her arms folded and her foot loudly tapping. "Something made me return sooner than expected," she said while seductively smiling, "tell me, was I there?"

"You were being a very bold girl," he replied, "but I forgive you. I know what you did, that was sneaky. Releasing the pheromones of a lioness into my face as you walked away was… there are no words."

"As if," she said while taking his hand, "I imagine you need to go to the lagoon and have a wash."

"A wash?" he exclaimed. "After what I just experienced I'm ready to go again."

"Now, now," she said, pinching his backside, "don't be greedy."

They walked towards the lagoon and found a semi-secluded sandy spot where they sat and just enjoyed each other's company. The conversation between them flowed and they became much closer.

"Don't you think you should go for that wash?" she asked.

"Yeah right," he laughed, deciding not to move, "you're only after my body."

"So?" she said, standing to walk towards the water's edge. "Wow, the lagoon is warm today." She bent forward in a most provocative way before slowly disrobing and then sauntering into deeper water. When she looked back she was delighted to see him standing there, naked as the day he was born.

He looked nervous, unsure if he wanted to enter the water. "I, I, I," he stuttered, "I don't know what to do. I think I; I need to leave."

"There's something very attractive about a War God of Olympus who's afraid of a woman," she said, encouraging him to join her.

"Give me my sword and my shield," he responded, "and nothing will stand in my way, but a beautiful woman like you? It seems that's something I just can't handle."

"I appreciate the compliment, thank you," she replied, "you do realise I'm a goddess of the five sacred mountains and like goddesses all across the cosmos I too have needs. Us goddesses dream of meeting a Greek God and right now, standing naked before me is the most handsome of them all, and he's afraid? Get in here and take me to places I can only dream of."

Her words touched a nerve and he, without further hesitation, walked into the water. He reached in, raising his arms to surround her shoulders, and said before softly kissing her, "This isn't the Dreamworld so I might need you to be gentle with me, I've a lot to learn."

"Excuse me," she said, "what do you think I am? Be careful where you go with your comments, I've never been with a man in the real world. The Dreamworld doesn't count; it's just our imagination. Let's learn together."

They weren't as secluded as they thought. On the patio Obelius's three uncles were enjoying the quietness of the mid-morning when Modi caught sight of movement near the dunes. "Would you look at that prick!" he said, "first he gets a knee trembler and now he's about to get the real thing."

Magni and Odi leapt up to watch prompting Odi to say, "There's something perverse about three uncles watching their nephew ..." He was interrupted by Jacob arriving.

Magni grabbed Jacob in a tight hug and turned him to face back into the temple, but Jacob freed himself just as his view of the lagoon was blocked by Modi who, at the same time, said, "We need to go back into the temple."

"Forget it. No! I want to sit in the sun." He was still being blocked by Modi who was now joined by Odi, but they were unable to prevent a glance towards the lagoon. A glance that was just long enough for Jacob to ask, "Is that my son?"

Odi grabbed him and jokingly pushed him back into the temple, "There are some things a father shouldn't see.

Chapter 3

In the meantime, Demetrius had plucked up the courage to ask Gaia to join him on a walk through the woodlands. She agreed, and they made their way across the meadows to a pathway, taking them to the foothills of the snow-capped mountains. Others had the same idea, Hemish and Sunniva were just ahead of them. They too seemed to be finally getting to know each other.

Gaia paused, stared into his eyes, then offered her hand. He responded, slowly raising his to rest on her cheek.

"Don't be so nervous," she said, "I'm not going to bite."

"I'm not nervous," he replied, "I just don't know how to act when alone with a girl. Here in Olympus, Obelius and I led a very sheltered life."

They continued their walk, taking in the beauty all around them, the majestic trees, the vista of colourful wildflowers - behind them the sounds of the woodlands, before them the silence of the snowfields.

Demetrius picked some scented, white daisies, placing several into Gaia's hair. "I'll never forget the stirrings I felt that first day you arrived in Olympus," he said, "they were much stronger when we plunged our hands into the soils, that time when we summoned the Earth Mothers. In my dreams I see us with a chance for the kind of love the great stories are written about."

"For me arriving in Olympus was magical," she said, moving closer, reaching across to kiss his cheek, "never before did I have anyone look at me the way you did. Your eyes, those deep and inviting brown eyes, your smile, the way your hair fluttered in the light breeze, the way you were so striking. I too dream, and it's always about us sharing our bodies, but most importantly it's about us sharing our souls."

They continued walking and soon reached the snow line from where they made their way up to an ice ridge taking them deeper into the mountain. Their shy smiles became almost permanent as their voices softened to a whisper. It was the way they gazed at each other, gazes that soon became long and lingering.

It wasn't too last. As soon as they reached the next ridge Demetrius froze.

"I feel it too," said Gaia, gripping his hand tighter and moving her head from side to side, "Hemish is being attacked, he's defending an injured Sunniva; we need to go to them."

"Obe," said Demetrius raising his fingers to his forehead, "can you hear me? Answer me."

"Don't be so nosey," replied Obelius, still on a high, "yes, Aria and I have been together, and it was mind blowing; go away."

"Obe!" cried Demetrius, getting more desperate, "listen carefully, Hemish and Sunniva are being attacked; we need you here now,"

"I hear you brother," said Obelius, quickly dressing, "do nothing until I get there, Maximus and Isidra are close by, we'll be there at the blink of an eye."

"You might be too late," replied a panicking Demetrius, "I'm going into battle. Hemish is in real trouble and Sunniva seems to be injured. Stay linked to me, it will help you find us."

Demetrius and Gaia were on a ridge giving them a view across the vast plateau that should have been a vista of pure white snow, but this day it was stained with the blood of the almost totally defeated Yeti army. In the centre of the battlefield were two beams of light fighting off Shadow Riders. One of the beams was strong and the other showing worrying signs of rapidly weakening. All over the plateau the riders were targeting the wounded Yeti soldiers, quickly dispatching them before attacking any Yeti still strong enough to fight.

Demetrius and Gaia blinked themselves to join Hemish and Sunniva, and their arrival gave the remnants of the Yeti army a slight reprieve. Within seconds Obelius, Aria and Maximus arrived. Isidra was sent to the temple to alert Jacob. Odi gripped Modi and Jacob gripped Magni and together they blinked their way to arrive just behind Obelius. Magni immediately assessed the situation and then took control. The Yeti nation now had seven War Gods and three Mystic Gods by their side.

It didn't go well, the Shadow Riders avoided the gods and continued to target the Yeti, the annihilation of the Yeti seemed to be their objective, and it was going on at such a pace it seemed it would soon be completed. Aria was first to detect the strategy and decided on a solo run, telling Magni to trust her; he was concerned but agreed, knowing she had been trained by the best. She swiftly leapt into the midst of the Shadow Riders and shape shifted into being a very large lioness. She released her odour causing alarm, but when she roared, the horses reacted by rearing and bolting, throwing their riders. The riders panicked, never having seen a lion before. It was then when the War Gods attacked, all except Jacob.

Jacob levitated himself high above the ground to scour across the plateau, he was searching for Yaz. He soon located the royal standard lying shredded on the ground with an aged Yeti body lying beside it, he knew it was Yaz. He rushed to assist and was horrified to find this head partially severed, but he was still alive. Jacob loved Yaz and was devastated to see his condition, knowing a partially severed head was enough to ensure immortality was lost, with no coming back.

"Why? Why us?" whispered Yaz. "Who is this Shadow?"

"I wish I knew," replied Jacob, leaning in closer, struggling to hear Yaz speak.

"My friend," said Yaz, trying to breathe, "protect the last of my people. Listen carefully, I used an ancient magic to shield the elderly, the younglings, and their mothers. Two of my sons are with them, they are their guardians and will be my successors. All others had to fight for their survival, and we lost. I can't say where they are for Shadow is everywhere and listening." He gripped Jacob's tunic trying to lessen the pain. "I've hidden my people," he continued as his eyes began closing for the last time, "where the shadow of the four mountains never reaches." He then passed away.

Jacob stood, gritting his teeth, and clenching his fists as his temper rose, at the same time his eyes narrowed and every muscle in his body tightened. When he turned all saw the fire in his eyes, and they knew the rage had taken him. He raised his hands and using an unseen force he pulled the remaining Shadow Riders closer; he also used his power to capture the bolting horses. Magni and Modi backed away; knowing it was unwise to interfere when the rage was present. Odi didn't know. "Brother," he said, entering Jacob's head, "let go the rage, you're better than that."

Demetrius also entered his head. "Father," he pleaded, "your face has changed, and your eyes have darkened. You're frightening me, let go the rage, it will destroy you."

Jacob pushed them both from his head and, using the power of his Light, he produced two swords. He then created a large circular cocoon, big enough to imprison the Riders and their horses. He waited a few moments before walking the circumference of the cocoon, and as he walked he scraped one of the swords against the light-filled walls causing a screech that spooked the horses into stampeding. They had nowhere to run other than in a circle, and as they ran they trampled the Riders, killing many as the minutes passed, those that survived now had to face molten lava. Jacob had commanded the sun to send its liquid fire which he funnelled into the cocoon incinerating everything, ensuring nothing made its way back to Shadow.

He deliberately held one Rider aside, the one he felt was in charge, the one that showed the least empathy. He ruthlessly tortured him using degrees of pain unbecoming of a god, let alone the God of Gods. He wanted the identity of Shadow so badly he was prepared to do anything, including using his mind to inflict a level of pain never used before. His strategy was working, the commander's perseverance was weakening, and he began spluttering incoherent words. The words were beginning to make sense when from beneath the snows an ice spear emerged, skewering the commander, and just to ensure no information was imparted his head exploded sending what was left of his brains in all directions. Jacob was so furious; he used his magic to throw what was left of the remains into the cocoon to be incinerated with his comrades. For a while he said nothing, such was his anger, that was until Obelius stood before him, blocking his attempts at walking away. He just kept staring until his father showed signs of calming.

It took some time but when he calmed he used his Light to remove all traces of the cocoon and its contents. He then looked out across the battlefield at the number of Yeti Warriors that were left, some injured, many seriously. He sensed their grief and gestured for the Mystic Gods to assist those suffering the most. They worked their magic, taking away the pain and saving the lives of well over two hundred warriors.

Jacob still hadn't spoken; he was embarrassed by his loss of control and needed more time. He moved further out on to the plateau and while on his way he reached Sunniva who was still lying in the snow, badly mauled. He knelt beside her and used his powers to quickly heal her. He walked further away while watching the sun pass the mountains of the south. They were high mountains and as the sun passed behind them a shadow was sent to a point halfway across the plateau. He summoned Maximus and pointing to the centre of the plateau he said, "Send an arrow to land where the shadow meets the light, wait for two minutes and do it again, and again, and again until I tell you to stop."

"Uncle," replied Maximus, "Obelius is the greatest archer; he should be the one to complete this task."

"Do not miss," he said, showing he was still furious and didn't want to be questioned.

Maximus raised his bow and fired, but the arrow landed slightly further into the shadow than he intended. "Relax," said Jacob, placing his hand on Maximus's shoulder, "you are a warrior of Asgard, concentrate."

His next arrow was more accurate, as were all subsequent arrows. The sun was now reaching the west, sliding behind the mountains casting its shadow towards the centre of the plateau.

"You know what to do," continued Jacob. Maximus fired his arrows and never once did he hit the light. Darkness then fell.

Jacob and Maximus stood all night, facing the east. In fact, the remaining gods and the last of the Yeti warriors also stood facing the same direction, no one saying a word. At daybreak the sun began sending the shadow of the eastern mountain towards the centre of the plateau and as before, Maximus fired his arrows until the sun reached the south. What Maximus had created was an almost complete circle of arrows where the shadow of all mountains could never reach. Jacob called on the now healed Sunniva.

"My Sun Goddess," he said, "ask the sun for assistance, use your power and ignite the arrows." She raised her hand and turned her palm facing the sun, she called on its fire and it came to form a flame that flickered above her hand, a flame she then blew towards the arrows; they immediately ignited, preventing any shadows from forming.

Jacob walked to the gap in the circle and called out, "Children of the Yeti; rise up and answer my call, come back into the Light."

From within the burning arrows ice crystals shimmered and glowed. The two nearest enlarged to become fully armed and crowned Yeti warriors. As they approached Jacob, they grew taller to stand at over seven feet tall, and although looking formidable, they were inconsolable after looking around to see the decimation of their kin. Jacob helped bring the calmness, but their grief was too deep. "Sons of Yaz," he said, "I understand your grief, but everything has changed. Time is not on our side. We must leave before darkness again takes this place. Allow me to awaken those who are still hidden, I promised your father safe passage for all the Yeti."

"Who are you?" asked one of the warriors.

"I am the God of Gods," replied Jacob. Both warriors bowed.

"Our father tasked us to protect our women and younglings," said the second warrior, "we don't know who to trust."

Jacob backed away and called Odi to join him, he hoped what he was about to do would help. He and Odi closed their eyes, bowed their heads, then arced their right arms. The other gods instinctively knew to raise theirs. The yeti warriors then felt an urge to do the same. They all faced the west, and it was as though they had all become one. Jacob and Odi then said,

"Warriors of the Yeti, Elysium awaits, answer its call. Rise up and go rest among the blessed kings and heroes of old. Your place, sleeping among your proud ancestors awaits. Go now to be with your fathers."

Within seconds the Yeti dead levitated to rest six feet above the ground, when all had risen they began floating towards the west. It was a sad sight to behold with no one to grieve or shed a tear except for the two sons of Yaz and the few remaining warriors, but no tears were shed, they were only too aware of what lay ahead. When the last body had departed they turned back towards the circle and released a terrifying roar, a roar that echoed off the far mountains. It was then when many more tiny ice crystals began shimmering and shaking, releasing a procession of almost six hundred younglings, their mothers, and the elderly. Under the protection of the remaining warriors, they briskly made their way towards the ridge circling the plateau. No words were spoken, absolute silence was required, just in case.

On reaching the Olympus shield the procession was ushered through to great relief. It was then when Yaz's sons approached Jacob.

"I am Cetan," said the older one, "they call me the Hawk of the Mountains, and this is my brother, Yeshe. He is known as the wise one. My father spoke of your visit to our homeland many years ago. He also spoke of your compassion and wisdom."

"On the brightest of nights," said Yeshe, "from high on the summits we watched the lights of your temple shine brightly and wondered about its grandeur. Little did we know that we would be refugees seeking its protection?"

"You are welcomed guests of Olympus with the right to stay as long as needed," replied Jacob, resting his hands on their shoulders. "My visions show you both leading your people back to their homeland, a place you are destined to rebuild. Be assured we will assist in every way."

The strangest thing happened as the Yeti walked deeper into the Olympus realm, they transformed from being very tall, white apelike creatures, into humanlike beings with the palest blue eyes, and the whitest hair. They were safe and given time to begin grieving.

Chapter 4

Although everyone was rattled after the attack on the Yeti, it was time to continue with Magni's plans. HeeHe had already identified those whom he wanted to send to the Fair Lands and told them to prepare to travel immediately. He decided Demetrius and Gaia were the appropriate ones to travel, with Magnar as their escort. Jacob conjured up modern clothing, helping them blend in with those they met.

Demetrius and Magnar left for their room and while changing they were joined by Jacob who called Demetrius aside. "Deme, son," he said, "this is your first trip outside of Olympus and I'm worried, all I ask of you is to be careful. One other thing, it's most important you do this for me. Look after Magnar; he's going to need you before your trip is over."

He then called Magnar to join them. "Remember," he said, "think of St Stephens Green, and the power of Olympus will take you there. Everything else will fall into place."

When Demetrius arrived back to the Great Hall, Gaia was waiting. On seeing her he was awestruck, having difficulty averting his eyes from her inviting cleavage. She stood before him wearing a brilliant white figure-hugging blouse over very tight ripped jeans and to him, she looked amazing.

"I'm not sure you and I should travel together," he whispered after taking her hand, "I mightn't be able to control myself."

"When it comes to control," she replied, moving her arm around his waist, "trust me, you wouldn't be able for me."

"Is that a challenge?" he nervously asked,

"When we're in the Fair Lands," she said while slipping her finger beneath his t-shirt, gently teasing him, "how do we get rid of Magnar?"

"Trust me!" he gasped, "the way you are making me feel right now; that'll be easy. Shit, these jeans are too tight. Stop teasing me."

Just then Magnar arrived at the far end of the hall.

"Look at poor Magnar," said Gaia, "he seems to have the same problem, he's struggling to walk, I think his are also a bit too tight, they're showing everything he has."

"This is ridiculous," said Magnar, trying to fix himself, "Jacob calls them skinny jeans, they feel like vice grips; they're squeezing the living daylights out of me. My 'Boys' are not a bit happy."

"I know exactly what you mean," said Demetrius, while adjusting himself. "I think it's time to go."

"Not so fast," it was Magni. "It might be wise not to mention your encounter with Finn; Jacob wants to handle that himself." All three understood. They linked, then blinked, to arrive near the lake in St. Stevens Green. There they found a safe location to materialise before making their way down the now completely restored Grafton St, where Gaia thought she was in Heaven. She spent much of her time window shopping, admiring the clothing and shoes on view. Demetrius was soon bored.

Magnar walked ahead, revelling in the admiring glances he was receiving. He noticed one girl in particular who deliberately bumped off him as she passed, he walked a few more paces and then noticed her again. She walked by; this time smiling at him. He continued walking to soon reach Wicklow Street, she was again walking towards him. 'What!' he thought, getting suspicious, 'how is she doing that?' He then went on alert. She touched him and said as she passed, "War God." and by the time he turned she was gone. He rushed back to join Demetrius and Gaia.

"We're being watched," he said, showing his agitation. "How many can you see?" he asked.

Demetrius had already noticed and was looking at their reflections in the window. "Five are watching us from those shops opposite," he said.

"There are four more," said Magnar, "two on our left and two on our right."

"We hear you," said a female voice, "two Earth Gods and a God of War walking uninvited through the sacred lands of Danu. Do we have something to worry about?"

Demetrius swiftly turned to face her. "I'm Demetrius," he said, offering his hand, "God of Olympus; this is Magnar of Asgard, and Gaia, Goddess of the Indus. We seek audience with the Lady Danu."

Magnar moved his hand closer to his side, preparing for battle. "Tell me My Lady," he said, showing his readiness to fight, "why are nine warriors surrounding us? I see their luminous weapons." He then moved to stand before Demetrius and Gaia. "It's unacceptable for armed warriors to threaten Earth God's," he hissed, "especially when they're under my protection."

"Our weapons," said Gaia, "are made to be luminous, it's what hides them from the gaze of mortals. They can see us but not our weapons."

The lady moved closer to be almost in Magnar's face. "This is the realm of the Little People, it's my domain, and you are the intruders; if you seek audience with my mother you cannot enter this sanctum while armed."

Demetrius placed his hand on Magnar's shoulder. "Relax cousin," he said, "there's no danger here." But Magnar was having none of it.

"If I must hand over my weapon," he replied, turning back to face Demetrius, "the least she can do is give us her name."

The lady was joined by two warriors from the opposite side of the street; they were getting impatient with Magnar's reluctance.

"I am Aoife," said the lady, "daughter of Danu and Faer. These are two of my brothers, Lir, and Aodh; I think you may have tried their patience."

"Magnar," said Gaia, "they are of this realm, and we must respect their laws. Give them your weapon."

Magnar said while reluctantly handing over his sword, "There are no other weapons; Earth Gods don't need weapons. Just be aware, I'm breaking the sacred laws of Asgard by giving you this sword. I'm not happy about this."

Demetrius went very quiet; he had his eyes closed and was moving his head from left to right. "My father and uncle Odi fought somewhere near here," he said, "I sense their essence, it's everywhere. I also sense the great pain visited upon this city, we're close to where the first battle between the gods and the Dark Angels was fought."

"That battle happened not too far from here," said Aoife, "I can take you there."

"Sister," said an agitated Lir, "don't you smell it? The smell of death, and it's getting stronger."

"I too smell death," said Magnar, "return my weapon."

Aoife returned his weapon, much to the ire of Lir and Aodh. Magnar then moved to the centre of the street, followed by Lir, one checking south and the other, north. They found nothing to worry about.

"The scent has faded," said Magnar.

"I agree," replied Lir, "but, just because I agree doesn't mean I'm comfortable with you being here."

"You have nothing to fear from me," said Magnar, "we've been sent by the God of Gods, you need to relax. Our task is too important."

"Well then," said Aoife, turning to her brothers. "Panic over, return to the Fair Lands and prepare for the arrival of our guests."

Lir, Aodh and the other seven warriors shrunk to no more than four inches, before growing translucent wings. They then took to the sky, circled for a few moments, before flying towards the Wicklow mountains.

"Wow, can you do that?" asked an amazed Magnar.

"I can grow wings while standing before you as human," she replied. "I, like my brothers, can shrink to four inches; it's our greatest power. It's why the Irish know us as the Little People; we're also known us the Fairy Folk." She then suggested they move on.

She brought them down Grafton Street towards College Green before turning up Dame Street to arrive on Fownes Street. It wasn't unusual to see striking people on those streets but to see four together attracted a lot of attention, especially when they reached Temple Bar Square, there they noticed hundreds of eyes staring back at them.

"You two," said a concerned Magnar, "hold hands, act like lovers, too many people are looking, and I see lust in the eyes."

"I'd gladly use any excuse to hold your hand," sniggered Gaia, while quickly stretching across to kiss Demetrius's cheek, "never did I expect I'd be ordered to by a War God."

"This is one order I'm happy to obey," laughed Demetrius, returning the kiss, "but I have to say, us being so close, my jeans, they're getting tight again."

Gaia closed her eyes and listened to the thoughts of all those who were staring, she then reached across to Magnar, "Relax, War God. From the girls I detect some jealousy but mostly there's admiration, from the boys I do detect lust, again directed towards myself and Aoife, some is directed towards you, they speak of your big arse. I imagine it's the same thing the goddesses have admired about you since that day you first walked into the temple."

"Magnar," laughed Aoife, "it's the first thing I noticed when you materialised. Some say it's what gets us girls going."

Magnar had no idea what they were talking about but accepted it as a compliment, he was chuffed; he began swaggering and pretended to walk an invisible catwalk. "I think we should stay here for a while," he suggested, hoping they'd all agree. They did, they felt safe, then separated while taking in the amazing atmosphere.

Demetrius and Gaia found a quiet fish cafe and were happy in their own company. Magnar and Aoife walked the cobblestones enjoying the buzz that was all around them. For Magnar, he had feelings he didn't understand, considering he only met Aoife less than an hour earlier. Every time he glanced at her those feelings intensified, all he wanted was to get to know her much better. When she walked a few steps ahead of him his mind played tricks. At times he saw her in modern clothes, not dissimilar to his, blending in with those around them, other times he saw her as she truly was - tall and very striking, dressed in a full-length figure-hugging gown that was a shade paler than mint green. It was a dress not that unlike what high ranking lady elves wore. On her head was a crown holding her soft copper blond hair in place, hair that was enhanced by a smattering of tiny white flowers. From her back, full length translucent wings appeared, emitting a kaleidoscope of colour that shimmered as the sun shone through. The subtle smile that broke through her luscious lips and the depth of her soft blue eyes looked so inviting he became more besotted. He knew then he was looking upon one who was protected by the sun and was bursting with so much magic, she could only be a creation of the Ancient One.

He closed his eyes for a moment and when they reopened, she was again in modern clothes. They coyly smiled at each other knowing they both felt the same way but didn't know what should happen next, no one had ever told them. They instinctively moved their hands together before slowly finding their way to one of the quieter side streets where they found a recessed doorway. There they just held each other.

"I've never kissed a boy, have you?" said Aoife after detecting his fears, "I mean, have you ever kissed a girl?"

"No," he replied, "I never knew what a girl was until I arrived in Olympus." His face bright red, betraying his innocence and his embarrassment.

"There's always a first time," she whispered after raising her hands to gently touch his face.

He slightly turned his head, and their lips touched before developing into what at first was a bit sloppy, before becoming passionate and fiery. The sensations swirling around their bodies took them both by surprise, it was a nice surprise that was filled with a mixture of fear and excitement. As the moments passed their passion grew unleashing a primal desire that threatened to explode. Their hearts skipped beats, causing their breathing to become rapid and shaky. Occasionally, when he'd open his eyes, he'd see a beauty he somehow knew one day would all be his, just like he knew everything about him was soon to be hers. They stopped kissing, and staring deep into each other's eyes, they began to share their future. It was a future with some pain, but it also showed them together for eternity. He moved to kiss her neck and was taken aback at how she let out soft whimpers. This encouraged him to start using his hands to explore her body, but he was soon stopped when she froze. She was troubled.

"Something's wrong," she said, stepping out on to the cobbles.

"Yes, I feel it too," he replied, joining her on the road, "it's the same smell both Lir and I got when we first met, but this time its stronger." He paced back and forth for a few moments. "I don't believe it," he said, raising his hands to bury his head, "I've neglected my duty; Demetrius and Gaia must be in danger."

"No, it's not them," said Aoife, moving her head from side to side, "it's something else."

She grew her wings and shrunk in size before taking to the sky giving her a panoramic view across Temple Bar. From her vantage point she soon saw a troubling sight. She returned to Magnar and told him of a roof terrace where a girl was been attacked by two hooded beings.

Magnar immediately went into invisibility, and when he reappeared, he materialised as a God of Asgard, fully armed and ready to go into battle. He then used his magic to reach the terrace hoping not to be too late. He wasn't too late; the hooded beings were distracted, sharpening their knives, giving him time. He waited for Aoife, feeling she would insist on protecting her own realm, and when she arrived, he knew he made the right decision.

It was the way her hair was held back using a thin silver band, revealing a face full of anger, showing she was ready to do her worst. In those few moments, his eyes travelled down her body, taking in her short and tight mint green dress that revealed her long and slender legs. He noted her feet hugging leather shoes, shoes that legend said gave maximum protection to anyone wearing the knee high laced up version. When he saw her quiver and arrows, shield, and sword, he recognised them to be of a quality that could only have been made by the hand of Lugh.

The two hooded beings had no idea what was coming. They were moving to do their worst when they suddenly stopped and looked down to see the tips of sharp swords tear through their bodies. Aoife and Magnar had silently attacked, quickly vanquishing the demons. As they turned to dust, there was just enough time for Magnar to see their distorted faces, confirming Shadow was now in the realm of man. It was then when they realised a portal had opened on the roof of the building opposite, and from the portal a rasping voice was heard. "Ah, how wonderful. Lord Magni! God of Asgard, we're back!"

Magnar was about to respond but was stopped by Aoife. "Say nothing," she whispered, "let them think you are Magni, it will mislead them and might keep them away from us."

Just as the portal disappeared the injured girl regained consciousness, screaming in terror, seriously traumatised, especially after witnessing the battle robes and armour of two warriors transform into modern clothing. Magnar rushed to cover her mouth, hoping to calm her, but was having difficulty until Demetrius and Gaia arrived. Gaia used her powers to bring the calmness.

"What happened?" Gaia asked, "where did they come from?"

"I've no idea," replied the still sobbing girl, "There was a god-awful smell. I opened the door, and they were there. They barged through, violently pushing me against the wall. Although semi-conscious, I did hear them talk of a doorway to a place called the land of Danu, the land of the young. They spoke of the Cave Fairies and then said their armies were ready to destroy Tír na nÓg."

"Tír na nÓg?" asked a confused Magnar.

"It's my homeland, and is a most sacred place," said a panicking Aoife, "it's the last refuge of the Goddess Danu and our people. It was created thousands of years ago to become our final home after we migrated from the lands of Olympus. Our people are the healers, the seers, the guardians of the

Celtic nations, but we now spend our time protecting all of nature. We don't know of Shadow. Why would Shadow want our realm?"

"They spoke of revenge," said the girl, "they mentioned a guardian named Faer."

"Why are they after my father?" asked a now very distressed Aoife.

Demetrius crouched next to the girl who was now very calm.

"What happened to you today is too much for any human to bear," he said, "allow me to erase the memory of these sad events, this will ensure you move on. It will also protect you from further attacks, but you must leave this place."

He slowly moved his hands across her head and soon the bad memories faded, eventually to disappear. She felt safe even with four strangers in her apartment, Gaia's calmness was still assisting. She quickly packed her belongings and as she was leaving she threw her keys across the room.

"We too need to leave," said Demetrius turning to Aoife, "it's now a good time for you to show us the way."

Demetrius moved to the centre of the terrace, insisting all four quickly link. He blinked and using his power they arrived on the old Military Road close to the village of Laragh. They then made their way to Glendalough.

On reaching the round tower they were met by the guardian wolfhounds, the very ones tasked with protecting the spirit of the monk, Kevin. "My friend Aoife!" he said on seeing her approach, "what tribulation have you brought upon us this day? Oh, I see a Shadow and it's close by. You must hurry into the protection of your mother's realm."

"Only once before did I meet with Gods of Olympus," he continued after turning to greet Demetrius, "one was your mother, another a dragon, and the third was one who became a God of the Fair Lands. I also met you when you were no more than a toddler. It pleases me to see how you've grown to be a powerful Earth God."

"My mother speaks fondly of this sanctuary," said Demetrius as he bowed, "I have only vague memories, but they are good memories. It's the calmness I remember."

"Quickly, go now. Aoife knows the way," replied Kevin, pointing towards the mountain, "follow the deer-worn path into the woods. The gateway into the land of Danu is there. The white stags will be watching."

They followed the pathway before making their way deeper into the forest and higher up the mountain. Using their acute hearing they took in the cacophony of birdsong unknown this late in the season. As they climbed they listened to scurrying mammals foraging among the first fallen leaves. The higher they climbed the purer and richer the air became, an air that was filled with all kinds of leaf and earth fragrances, all telling them they were close. They were now in an ancient forest, teaming with songs and tales to tell.

They left the forest and soon reached a dense woodland of old oaks, trees that were in full leaf, creating a canopy so thick not much light reached the forest floor, but their colour was changing. Their boughs were thick, supported by twisted and worn roots, ensuring they were still strong. In the middle of the great oaks were two much younger trees and those trees attracted their attention.

"Is this the gateway?" asked Demetrius.

"Yes," replied Aoife.

A mist formed between the two younger oaks, and its arrival was followed by a whispering. Aoife walked through and they all cautiously followed. When they reached the other side they were mesmerised by what greeted them. It was another woodland; light filled with magical walkways and byways. Every tree brimmed with leaves shimmering and shaking as though dancing to an inaudible symphony of the most enchanting music. Even with the dense canopy, the sun beams always found a way through to brighten the array of colourful wildflowers growing along the passageways. The rivers and streams glimmered in the relentless light of the welcoming sun. All around them they heard the sweet sound of the numerous birds who called this place their home. There was no mistaking it; they had entered the realm of the Goddess Danu.

They now had escorts, hundreds of armed fairy folk, who brought them to an ancient, moss-covered stone grotto, one that was set in a clearing and bathed in brilliant sunshine. The clearing was a grass covered meadow filled with the most vibrant coloured flowers, watered by a trickling stream that gently flowed over lichen covered cobblestones. The surrounding willow trees draped their leaf-filled branches providing protection from prying eyes while the taller trees enhanced that security using mosses, algae, and ferns.

They followed a narrow pathway that brought them before two thrones where Danu and Faer were waiting. Faer was first to react.

"Deme," he said, leaving his throne to embrace Demetrius, "how you've grown, you were a five-year-old when we last met, now look at you, so tall. Your father told me you were to become an Earth God, welcome into the domain of the Little People."

"You are most welcome," he said turning to greet Gaia, "I don't think we've ever met."

"We haven't my lord," she said, "I'm Gaia, daughter of Manasa and your good friend, Girish."

"I didn't know he had a daughter," said Faer, getting emotional, "but you're right, your father is one of my dearest friends. We played together as children and worked together as teenagers, he's the greatest. I only met your mother once; it was after the great battle. How are they?"

She didn't get a chance to answer, Danu interrupted when she saw Magnar.

"For days I've been watching," she said, taking his hands into hers, "my visions showed two very distressed boys walking into Olympus, they then showed you walking into my domain, and I wondered as to who you were. Your modern clothing didn't fool me; I knew you were a disguised War God. In you I see the face of Magni, Lord of Asgard and now as I see you more clearly, I also see a sister Goddess, Medeina. She told me of the birth of twins. Are you one of those twins?"

"You knew my mother?" he gasped, getting excited. "How? When? Tell me, where is she?"

"She's not too far from here," replied Danu, "always remember, she never left you; she was always close by."

"She did leave us," he said, raising his voice as his excitement quickly turned to anger, "she said she'd come to us when we needed her the most, she didn't. We needed her while watching Marduk being torn asunder by the forces of Shadow; we were only twelve-year-old boys. We needed her during those times when our father's heart sunk so low we feared for his life; we wanted her to come to us while watching him fall in and out of grief."

He raised his voice even higher forgetting to whom he was speaking. "Have you any idea what it feels like to see someone you love in so much despair? She never came; she didn't care."

Danu felt his pain and moved to comfort him, but he backed away, looking on her with contempt. He then ran off into the forest. Faer gestured for Aoife to follow.

"That was impressive," she said after reaching him, "I've never seen anyone get away with shouting at my mother. She brings the calmness to all she meets; your pain must run very deep. Can I help?"

"What would you know?" he yelled, still showing aggression, "you've had your mother all your life, I didn't, she never came for us; she abandoned us."

Aoife took his hand, drawing him closer. "The hand of a warrior," she softly said, "brave and strong. So much anger, trust me it's misplaced. Walk with me and see where the path takes us."

They walked deeper into the forest, all the time holding hands with no words passing between them. Feeling her hand in his, and the occasional touching of their bare arms, brought back memories of their first kiss and the passion that followed. His innocence and inexperience troubled him especially after seeing how masterfully Viktor made love to Thora. He put those fears aside very time he caught her scent, a timeless aroma, taken from a multi-coloured rose. It was a fragrance he didn't recognise but he liked it, and it drew him closer. Occasionally when she squeezed his hand he felt intense and wonderful sensations race through his body.

On seeing a stone archway up in the distance, she stopped and reached in to hold him tighter. "I know where your mother is," she said, hoping he wouldn't lose his temper, "I can show you the way, but I must warn you, you'll not like what you find, do you want me to show you the way?"

"Why didn't you tell me this earlier?" he demanded, showing his aggression again, then he relaxed, "anyway, I'm not sure I want to meet her now. I'll only get angrier and that's something I'm not comfortable with you seeing. Since meeting you I've never been so happy. You've brought the calmness to me, something I didn't expect."

During a single, light gust of wind, another whispering was heard. A second gust came and as it rustled its way through the tall grasses, the whispering got louder.

"For crying out loud," it said. It was Demetrius, and he was in Magnar's head, "let her show you the way, you've wanted to find your mother for as long as you can remember."

"Where are you?" yelled Magnar, looking around and showing his annoyance. "Prick, what the fuck! Are you in my head? I'm going to break your neck. If you tell anyone what you saw, trust me, I'll kill you."

"Now, now, cousin," replied Demetrius, "I'm only looking out for you, anyway there's no way I'd tell the gods what I saw; they wouldn't believe me. Seriously though, remember the calmness has taken you so don't ruin the moment. Let Aoife show you the way."

Aoife's powers allowed her to hear everything Demetrius said so she took Magnar up to the old moss-covered stone arch. "Go," she said while gently encouraging him through, "seek your peace. Step into the realm of a goddess, one who is your mother."

He went through and was taken aback at how day turned to night in just two steps. His jaw dropped and he had difficulty taking in all that was before him. He was in the Ice lands and whatever light there was presented as either subdued blue or misty white. There was a frosty chill, but he didn't feel cold. He looked ahead at a long colonnade of frozen trees, standing like sentinels, as though guarding the way to a sacred place. As he looked around, it was the silence that got to him. There was no scratching of tiny claws searching for food, no warm breaths from bears or squirrels as they hibernated, there was nothing. There were no sounds echoing in the cold and frosty night air. He placed his finger to his temple. "Max," he said, "can you hear me? Brother, I need you, there's something you need to see."

Back in Olympus, Maximus was out training with Obelius, Zane, Drayce, and Viktor when he became motionless. "I hear you," he said. "Why do I feel so cold? Where are you?" He moved away from the others and continued. "What do you want me to do?"

"Send your spirit to me," replied Magnar, "come quickly,"

He had barely finished his sentence when Maximus's spirit appeared alongside him. Maximus had difficulty finding the words but when he did he said, "Wow, this place is exactly as father described. See how every branch, every twig and every blade of grass is sprinkled with ice crystals. Is she here?"

Magnar placed his hand beneath some icicles hanging from a drooping branch and collected some cool droplets to rub into his eyes. "I don't know," he said, "I'm not sure I want to meet her. Think about it, when we needed her she never came, and I'm beginning to wonder if there's any point?" He didn't get an answer.

Maximus moved his arm across his brother's shoulder. "Strange how right now I'm a spirit, yet I feel your warmth, this place is amazing, let's keep walking."

As they walked Maximus became aware of being followed by hundreds of tiny, winged creatures. "They are the Fairy Folk," said Magnar, "guardians of this holy place, see how they swoop down behind us and sprinkle their magic into our footsteps. Soon there will be no evidence of us ever having been here."

"One thing about being a spirit," said Maximus, "is I'm very aware of all that's around me. One of the Fairy Folk seems to be shadowing you. She's very beautiful." Magnar's face reddened; he looked at Maximus and just smiled.

"Aaaaaah," said a trilled Maximus, "You're in love. You found someone to love you?"

They continued walking and soon reached a curved passageway leading to a small wooden bridge, its balustrades covered in ice white sparkling snow dust. It was lit by a spectrum of colours shooting from two ice prisms resting on nearby wooden posts. The colours, red, orange, yellow, green, blue, indigo, and violet emitted their light in all directions, highlighting the flowers and shrubs frozen in time.

On the other side of the bridge the blanket of snow was thicker, pristine, and so white it reflected the beams of the now high moon. Up ahead were more trees, older and wiser, their branches reaching across to greet each other, creating a covered passageway that seemed dark and foreboding, but in this place there was nothing to fear.

The boys continued walking and soon reached two, eight feet tall stone pillars, holding ancient wrought-iron gates. The gates magically opened allowing entry to what they thought was an ornately decorated temple, its roof held up by twelve large marble columns.

It wasn't a temple; it was a baldachin covering an ice encased stone sarcophagus upon which lay the effigy of a beautiful woman. At the foot of the sarcophagus stood two stone cloaked Pleurants as though weeping and mourning someone much loved. Maximus looked at their faces and recognised them to be images of him and Magnar, he closed his eyes and inhaled the cold air, his heart was beginning to struggle; he knew what was coming. He slowly began fading away. Magnar was much slower.

In the meantime, back in Olympus many gods had gathered on the terrace, watching the lone figure of Maximus, his eyes closed, his mouth slightly opened, exhaling what seemed to be very cold air.

"How unfair is this," said Eala, moving closer to hold Jacob's hand, "everything for Maximus and Magnar is about to change, their hearts are again going to be broken, they're about to learn the truth."

Baldor and Magni arrived. They stood next to Jacob, and they too watched Maximus. Magni moved to go to his son but was stopped when Baldor placed his arm across his shoulders.

"There's no need to go to him," said Baldor, "the light came to me this day and it said we should look to the north. Maximus will be fine. Stay and watch." Magni furrowed his brow and, although drawn to his son, he felt Baldor should be trusted. For the first time since his beloved Marduk was murdered it felt comfortable to have someone's arm supporting him, he just never expected it to be Baldor's.

Back in the Ice lands, Magnar stretched forward and gently scraped the ice crystals from the engraved name on the sarcophagus. He revealed an E, followed by the letter I and then N; it was dawning on him as to what was coming. He continued to scrape and soon revealed the full name, M E D E I N A - Earth Mother. He stumbled backwards as the shock took him, crossing both arms over his chest. He fell to his knees and let out a most heart wrenching cry of despair.

In Olympus, at the very same time, Maximus also fell to his knees, and his weeping was heard all across the meadows. There was no consoling them, they both had a pent-up desire to meet their mother and realised it would now never happen.

Magni made another attempt to go to his son, but Baldor tightened his grip, "Trust me, something magical is about to happen, keep watching. Look north and wait."

Maximus's distress reached Isidra who immediately made her way to the meadows. On seeing him on the ground she ran to be with him but was stopped when she felt Jacob in her head. "Wait a few moments," he said, "you'll know when the time is right."

At the sarcophagus, Magnar was still sobbing, his forehead resting on the cold snow. He failed to notice a shimmering mist rising close by, the mist thickened and formed into the image of the beautiful lady.

She bent forward to gently assist him to stand; he did, but because of his tear-filled eyes he couldn't see her clearly. She moved her thumbs to wipe away his tears then said, "My beautiful and handsome boy, you found me. There's no need for tears, I'm here to help you move on."

"You never came for us," he yelled as his anger returned, "all those times when we needed you, you stayed away. Time and time again we saw terrible things and there was no mother to tell us all would be well."

She gently kissed his forehead only for him to aggressively rub the kiss away, and then he looked confused. "I felt that kiss before," he said, putting his hand back on his forehead, "I felt it many times before."

"Try to remember," she said, gently rubbing his forehead, "those kisses are special. Every night, without fail, I visited both of you, waiting until you closed your eyes, then I'd kiss your foreheads just like I did now, even in death I found a way to be with you."

She pulled him closer, embracing him before moving her hands back to his face so as to soothingly rub away the last of his tears. He reciprocated, and she held him until his grief passed.

At the very same time the light from the north had arrived to surround Maximus, and from that light a lady appeared and helped him to his feet. She softly whispered in his ear then quietly rubbed his tears away. "My beautiful boy," she said as she embraced him, "I've always watched over you, even during the bad times." She reached up to kiss his forehead.

"I know that kiss," he said, "my dreams always began with that kiss." It was then when Isidra joined him.

"This is my mother," said Maximus. Isidra bowed.

"Your story is written in the stars," said Medeina. "It's the story of a Warrior God of Asgard rescuing a Dragon Queen. A love story that's destined to last for all time." She then disappeared.

Back beside the sarcophagus, Magnar's eyes were still closed, he was happy to be finally held in his mother's embrace. What he didn't realise was that she was gone, and he was, in fact, being held by Aoife. When he opened his eyes he was startled. "I don't understand," he exclaimed.

"It seems your path and mine has always been destined to cross," said Aoife, "your mother can be very persuasive; she's been in my head for some time now, showing me our future. Like Maximus and Isidra, we're destined to be together for all time. Look on the stone face of your mother; see how she now smiles. She has gone to her eternal rest knowing that her boys have found happiness. You must let that rest be a peaceful one."

"You know of Isidra?" asked a surprised Magnar.

"Yes," she replied, "the universe knows of Isidra and how a valiant War God of Asgard came to her rescue. It's spoken of as one of the greatest love stories of all time."

Through all of this drama Demetrius and Gaia dined with Danu and Faer. The main topic over dinner was Shadow and how it was manifesting itself throughout all realms. They discussed Magni's request that they travel to Olympus, a request that visibly upset Danu.

"Does Olympus not realise how vulnerable my realm will be if I leave?" she said, stretching her hand across to grip Faer's, "you must understand, there's only one way I'll consider leaving - my people must also be allowed to travel. They too will need refuge."

"How many?" asked Demetrius, shocked by the idea.

"There are five thousand living in the Fair Lands," replied Faer, "and twice as many scattered throughout the Celtic lands."

Demetrius never expected such a request, especially for so many to seek refuge, his instincts were telling him it was the right thing to do. He prayed Magni and his father would respect any decision he made. He left the table and paced for a few moments.

"Olympus is vast," he said after returning to his seat, "we can accommodate all your people, make the arrangements. I'll contact my father and ask him to prepare the meadows for your arrival."

That night the trumpeters sent out the call and they came from everywhere. In their thousands they came, answering the call of their goddess. The following morning what left the Fair Lands was a vast procession of Fairy Folk; they were led by Aoife and Magnar. The rear flanks were guarded by Lir and Aodh. It was an exodus bathed in light yet shrouded in mist, a light and mist that magically protected them from prying eyes. They followed a pathway that took them through an old forest to a winding trail that led to another tree canopied walkway. They passed under the canopy to reach a concealed cave where a wide portal had opened. On passing through the portal, they found themselves under the protection of Olympus.

From the steps of the temple, it was an amazing sight to witness. Thousands of Fairy Folk, all walking in their human form, while at the same time displaying their shimmering translucent wings. There were hundreds of carriages drawn by powerful winged unicorns each carriage carrying the history and the wealth of the Fair Lands. The royal carriage was surrounded by hundreds of fully armed palace guards, all wearing the white armour of their rank.

On reaching the steps, Danu and Faer were greeted by Jacob and Eala, Magni was also there.

"I had no choice," said Demetrius, "Shadow lurks behind every tree, every stone, and every mound; it watches our every move. It was in Dublin, it thought Magnar was Magni and said, 'we're back.' It left thinking Magnar was Magni, we didn't enlighten it."

"On both counts, you did the right thing," replied Jacob, "I would have done exactly the same."

"For me alone to leave," said Danu, "would mean my people lose the protection of the gods, I could not allow that happen again."

"I understand," said Jacob, "you, and your people, will always be welcome in my realm."

Faer embraced Jacob and all could see the affection that existed between them. It was also noted how Faer was distracted, he kept looking through the doors. "It's really him," said Jacob, "he's been living for this day, he missed you too."

Faer rushed into the temple unable to contain himself. "Is it really you," he asked, on reaching Fafner, "I couldn't believe the rumours, but now I see you, I still feel I need to pinch myself."

Meanwhile Demetrius briefed Magni and his father before going in search of Obelius who was conspicuous by his absence. He didn't have to search for long when from beside a pillar in one of the annexes he was grabbed from behind and slammed against the wall.

"Have you lost your mind?" screamed Obelius, "there must be at least fifteen thousand Fairy Folk! How many of them are checked and armed? You were sent to fetch Danu, and you bring back her whole nation. I could kill you because of this carelessness."

Helena and Drayce arrived just in time to calm things down. "Obe," yelled Helena, "leave him be. He did the right thing; there's no danger from the Fairy Folk; I would have detected it. There is fear, some of them have never been away from the Fair Lands and are terrified. You, acting like a deranged god, will not help."

Obelius let Demetrius go and said as he stormed off, "When I was five years old I learned I was to become our father's protector; I was also to become a guardian of Olympus. Too much is happening, things are becoming unsafe, and Magni's decisions are alarming me. No one is listening to my concerns."

"Tell me of your concerns," said Helena. He continued walking away while at the same time despairingly throwing his arms into the air.

Helena was furious at being ignored, she sent a powerful beam of light sending Obelius tumbling to the floor. He wasn't happy, clenching his fists and blaspheming. Helena wasn't finished with him, she retracted her Light, painfully dragging him across the floor, back into her presence. She was glowing, and he knew it would be best not to react. She then took his hand and entered his head; she stretched across and took Demetrius' hand, all three closed their eyes and began sharing their thoughts. They soon found themselves travelling through the future and they were not happy with what they saw.

"I'll tell father." said an alarmed Helena.

As she walked away Drayce caught up with her, "Remind me never to get on your wrong side."

Out in a hollow, close to the lagoon, there was a gathering of the oracles, and it was presided over by Fitch who, since arriving at Olympus, had magically grown from being a twelve-year-old boy to being a young adult. He was sitting facing the lagoon with the Sybils to his right and Mug Ruith,

Mirembé, Mieko, Tayanna, and Hyacinthus on his left, all were sitting in such a way so as to form a perfect circle.

Fitch clicked his finger to ignite a small sanctuary fire. From among the flames a mist wafted to rise up and form a magical shield that no evil could penetrate. When it reached Fitch his angelic looks changed, and he transformed to become more powerful, especially when the visions came. He announced reminded all that he was the Arbitrator to the Gods and asked the gathering to share their visions. When they did, they were all seeing the same thing – an attack on Olympus, and how vicious it was going to be. There were many other visions all of which needed to be shared with Jacob, but there was no need, Jacob was well aware of what was coming, Helena had reached him, he too also had the power of the Oracle.

Chapter 5

While the oracles were meeting, Fafner, and his family, including Galyna, were preparing their journey to the Dragon Lands. Fafner was not only bringing news of his and Heulwyn's resurrection; he was also bringing Isidra home to her family. Apart from the good news, he was tasked with bringing reports of the rise of Shadow, and its constant probing of the various realms. Olympus hoped King Derwyn stuck to his original plan - keeping the dragon army constantly on alert.

Maximus arrived just as Jacob prepared to open the portal. "Uncle," he said, "have you forgotten? We discussed this; Isidra is to be under my protection. I must insist on going."

"How could I forget?" said Jacob, failing to hold back a smile, "Eala would make my life a total misery if I stood in the way of true love."

"I knew you'd understand," replied Maximus, reaching in for a hug.

Jacob opened the portal allowing the dragons to arrive close to one of the three gates into their homeland.

"Grandfather," said Drayce, as the gate opened, "it's best that Galyna and I meet with father alone, explain all that has happened. You, grandmother, and Isidra just appearing would be a huge shock to him."

There was no reply from Fafner, he had frozen, his mouth open, his eyes widened such was his pain.

"What is it?" asked an alarmed Drayce.

"Don't you sense it?" replied Fafner. "Don't you smell it?"

"I can smell it," said Galyna, "it's the foul scent of burning flesh."

Drayce looked at his grandmother and saw how distressed she had become; he turned back towards the entrance and then panic set in. He ran through to the other side and all he saw was devastation. He fell to his knees and on moving his hands to cover his face he let out a most sorrowful and distressing roar. His shock was so bad he found he couldn't take to the sky.

Fafner arrived and while placing his arms around Drayce's waist, holding him firmly, he said, "You are in shock, you won't be able to fly until you calm down. Take a deep breath, now another, and again, again, relax. When you're ready we'll fly together."

Maximus then joined them. "The city," he said after looking towards the horizon, "it burns, what evil is this? Allow me to use my powers, I'll soon discover what we're dealing with."

"What can one God do against such evil?" yelled Drayce grabbing Maximus's tunic, "Look at my homeland, the army of the Dragons is decimated."

"You forget who I am, friend," replied Maximus, "I can be in two places at once."

Maximus leaned against the cliff face and closed his eyes, allowing his spirit to leave and move through the city undetected. Within moments he reached a group of fifty young dragons, fighting for their lives against terrible odds. On seeing how they were being eliminated, he immediately acted, protecting them by creating a cocoon.

He moved deeper into the city and established it had fallen to the forces of Shadow. He again extracted his staff and used it to call on the Light and when it came he sent it in all directions, locating all remaining dragons. He used its power to create more protective cocoons, saving many lives and giving the dragons a much-needed reprieve.

When the cocoons were secure he made his way back to the palace gardens where he found the protective cocoon almost depleted, and the royal guards being taunted by sack clothed skeletal beings. They were targeting an incapacitated King Derwyn and a lady whom Maximus surmised could only be Queen Isabella, she was very distressed while cradling a dead dragon.

"My Lady," he said, trying to get her attention, "he's gone. Leave him and move to be among the guards. Move away from the shield, my magic may not last for long."

"He's my baby," she cried, tears rolling down her face, "my youngest. They've taken him just like they took Isidra. I can't leave him."

"My Lady," he replied, with a sense of urgency, "Isidra lives, she's with Drayce and Galyna, they're close by. Please move. My power wanes as each moment passes. Trust me."

Isabella moved to be among the guards, there she immediately knelt and took her husband into her arms. Maximus again called on the Light and just like before, he used its power to enhance the shield hoping to provide extra protection. He was about to leave when a very weak and seriously injured Derwyn opened his eyes. "Tell me warrior," he asked, "who are you?"

"I am Maximus," he replied, "God of Asgard. Son of Lord Magni and the Goddess Medeina." He then left and used his powers to strengthen more of the cocoons, protecting numerous dragons from certain death.

It was on reaching the kinder garden when he again witnessed the real savagery of Shadow. All but four teachers were dead, their corpses being feasted on by hooded demons and by the hounds of Hell. The remaining teachers were frantically trying to calm the youngsters, but their efforts were being thwarted by the constant howling from outside the cocoon. The wailing of the young dragons broke his heart and reminded him of the terror he and Magnar suffered that time when Marduk was killed. Controlling his rage, he prayed the Light would again come to assist, and it did. He closed his eyes and before long, his arm involuntarily raised itself as a warm sensation gripped him. When he opened his eyes there was a shaft of bright light, shaped like a sword, resting in his hand.

Without delay, he attacked, targeting any Shadow warrior he encountered. Shadow had no chance, it was up against an invisible War God seeking revenge, one who was using a weapon they painfully felt, but were unable to see. He was determined to ensure the last sound they heard was the swishing sound of a sword of light. For the remaining dragons who were still fit to fight, hope had arrived.

All around the cocoons the forces of Shadow gathered sensing the shields were weakening again, and it was only a matter of time before they could be breached. What they didn't allow for was the arrival of four powerful dragons, whose arrival was drowned out by the constant chattering and screeching around the cocoons. It was Fafner, Heulwyn, Galyna and Drayce and they were ready to release their fury.

Maximus could do no more and chose to return to his body. There he found a totally distraught Isidra. "Why would they attack this peaceful land?" she asked as her tears fell, "what have they to gain?"

"There's no rhyme or reason to their actions," replied Maximus, "I saw their power when I was a child and today I again witnessed their savagery, especially after they attacked the kinder garden. It was then when the Light came and gave me a new power. Look."

He stretched out his arm and opened his fist, immediately the sword of light reappeared. He placed two fingers at his forehead and closed his eyes.

"Magnar, he said, hoping for a quick response, "can you hear me? Answer me brother, I need you."

In the temple Magnar was sitting with the young gods. When happy, he was the joker, the storyteller, the prankster, the one to have everyone in stitches, and that evening was no exception. He suddenly quietened, placing his hands on the table. "Yes brother," he said, "I hear you. What's wrong? Why do I smell burning flesh? Why do I smell 'Them', and why do I feel so much pain?"

"The dragon realm has been destroyed," said Maximus, "thousands of dragons are dead. King Derwyn is dying. We need the power of Olympus."

Magnar stood and then stumbled; his eyes still closed. He made his way towards his father with the help of Zane and Hemish.

"Father," he said, "Maximus is in my head, he says that the dragon realm has been destroyed."

Jacob and Odi leapt to their feet and placed their hands on Magnar's head. They were immediately in contact with Maximus. "Show me the city," demanded Jacob.

Maximus opened his eyes and showed him the burning city. "Uncle," he said, "my cocoons are protecting the last of the dragons, but they're weakening. Olympus needs to mount a rescue as soon as possible."

"Agreed," replied Jacob, "consider it done."

"It's not that simple," continued Maximus, "you can't allow the dragons enter Olympus without ensuring there's no Shadow among them. Ask yourself, how did Shadow enter the dragon realm? Was it a traitor? Can they shapeshift? There are so many questions. You, and Uncle Odi, are twins and have the power to tap into the powers of all the gods, tap into mine and create a cocoon in the meadows of Olympus. Use the cocoon to filter any evil that may travel with the dragons. Trust me, Shadow is powerful, it can get in anywhere."

"Fear not," said Jacob, "Odi and I will ensure Shadow doesn't use the dragons to attack us."

While Maximus was speaking with Jacob, Drayce and Galyna had taken their human form and were using their Light skills to protect as many cocoons as possible. They were swift and ruthless and took no prisoners, giving hope to the dragons they were protecting. Meanwhile, Fafner and Heulwyn were flying high above the dragon realm, searching for survivors, especially their sons and daughters. There were survivors, many of whom were seriously injured. From their great height they released a roar so loud it woke those who were unconscious; their roar also rallied the wounded dragons giving them the strength to heal themselves, and when healed, they quickly took to the sky to gather behind their Emperor. Four of the recovered dragons were Fafner's missing sons and daughters.

In the palace garden King Derwyn drifted in and out of consciousness and after opening his eyes for the last time, he said, "It seems my time is up. I've just seen my long-departed parents and they're calling out to me." He struggled for a few more moments, then passed away.

All dragons sensed his passing and in unison released a most mournful roar. Isidra collapsed into Maximus's arms and then fell to the ground, sobbing uncontrollably. Suddenly she quietened, before tearing at her skin. She rolled around on the ground, gasping for breath. Wisps of smoke escaped her nostrils, and she began breathing fire; she was changing. Maximus knew to back away and wait. Soon she totally transformed and took to the sky to join her grandfather.

Heulwyn was already searching for her children, hoping all had survived the attack, but her hopes were dashed when she reached the cocoon near the palace. There she saw Isabella cradling the body of Derwyn and was devastated. She attempted to enter the cocoon, but Maximus had it totally secured, or so he though.

All over the dragon lands the Shadow army began disappearing, and when they were gone all that was left was one very tall and hooded figure who appeared at the palace side of the cocoon. He was ecstatic when he looked across to see a frantic Heulwyn trying to get to her son. "Ah, the Empress of the Dragon's," he said, failing to conceal his delight, "you may have escaped the poison of Asmodeus, but believe me this time your pain will last forever." Using his extended finger, he sliced through the cocoon without much effort, smirking as with one quick flick of his hand, he subdued the guards, leaving Isabella as the only person still alive.

Drayce arrived at the palace gardens to find Bryn, one of his younger brothers, lying dead against the palace walls, his body had been savaged and given no dignity. When he reached the cocoon he was devastated to find the body of Steffan, his youngest brother, lying alone just inside the cocoon. His heart lifted when he was joined by his last remaining brother, Osian, who valiantly fought off an attack near the kinder garden. Together they quickly made their way along the rim of the cocoon to where tall shrubs were burning, and there they saw their mother, looking terrified and unprotected. They then saw Shadow.

"Mother," yelled Drayce, "mother," he continued, frantically pounding his fists off the protective shield. At the same time the spirit of Maximus arrived, and using his powers, he enabled Jacob and the Gods of Olympus to witness all what was before him.

Shadow slightly raised his head but still didn't reveal his face. "Ah, grandmother and grandsons," he rasped, "An audience, how wonderful, I have an audience! Oh, I also see the spawn of Magni, this gets better."

He stretched in and gripped Isabella by the neck, squeezed tightly, before raising his sword to decapitate her, he used that same sword to mutilate the body of Derwyn. He then approached the rim of the cocoon to stand within inches of a numb Drayce.

"Now you know real pain," he said, turning to face Heulwyn and Osian, "but there's worse to come." He turned back to taunt Drayce before slowly disappearing, "The terror I'm about to unleash has no bounds."

Drayce collapsed to the ground in disbelief, his grief being felt all across the cosmos, including in Olympus, where Helena was preparing to travel with her father in the hope of helping the one she loved.

For Galyna, her grief was waiting. She frantically searched for her father and when she found him she knew by the look on his face that her heart was about to be broken. He was so numb; all he could do was shake his head. It took some time for him to find the words. "She fell when they first attacked," he said, choking as he thought of his loss, "it was with such stealth they attacked, we never saw them coming. Her light never got a chance to glow."

Maximus's spirit rejoined his body, and he raced to be with Drayce and Isidra. On his way he was met by an unsettling eerie silence, showing how all remaining dragons were in shock. It was the kind of quietness that was known to descend upon a battlefield before total grief sets in. When he reached the palace he took control. "You are a son of a great warrior," he said as he insisted Drayce hide his grief and stand proud. "You are the heir to the dragon lands, don't allow your people see tears. Take control and lead your people to Olympus. I've arranged everything, they will need to recover and where better than in the meadows of Olympus."

Jacob, Odi, and Helena arrived just in time to hear what Maximus said.

"Maximus is right," said Jacob, "after what's happened, your people will need the protection and healing powers of Olympus."

Drayce, although still numb, managed to nod his agreement and without delay, a wide portal was opened, allowing Andres, and Fafner's two daughters, to lead the remnants of the dragon nation through.

While the dragons were leaving their homeland, Jacob and Odi took Maximus's advice and used their powers, ensuring Olympus was fully protected.

"Look out at the fallen," said Jacob, after the portal closed, "there's so many. We can't leave until they've all been given the dignity in death they deserve."

He was joined by Odi, Helena, Maximus, Galyna, and Fafner's family, and together all twelve lowered their heads and raised, then arced their right arms as he said,

"Fallen of the Dragon lands, hear me, rise up and answer the call of Elysium. Your day is done, your battle over. Go now and rest among the heroes and blessed dead of old, go to where your ancestors wait to guide you to your resting place. Go and be with those who have gone before you. Rise up now."

All across the dragon lands silence descended, not an insect, bird, or mammal made a sound as a gentle breeze rose up to assist the bodies begin their journey into the west. It was a solemn sight to see so many float by and never once did Fafner, Heulwyn, Drayce, Isidra, Osian, Evan, Efan, or Galyna avert their eyes until all had passed. For Drayce, Isidra, and Osian, watching their parents and two brothers pass, broke their hearts.

When the last body faded out of view Jacob insisted everyone leave for Olympus immediately. Drayce refused, indicating his intention to remain behind to search and secure the city.

"No," said Jacob, trying to be considerate, "we must all leave, the city can be secured at another time. Trust me, we must leave immediately."

A portal was quickly opened and when it closed it was soon realised that Drayce and Maximus hadn't come through. They had ignored Jacob's decision, but he didn't seem fazed by this. He trusted his young gods and knew if they had taken a different path there had to be a good reason. Viktor was first to notice them missing and approached Jacob. "Something tells me they're going to need my help; may I go to them?" Jacob agreed and sent him on his way.

On arrival in Olympus Fafner decided to remain in the meadows with his people, sharing their grief as like so many of them, he too lost family members - his son, his daughter-in-law, two of his grandsons, and many of his friends. He grieved with Heulwyn, his two remaining sons, his daughters, and his grandchildren. Their grieving, along with that of the entire dragon camp, went on until dawn. Fafner then joined Jacob on the patio.

Drayce will wreak a revenge on Shadow like no other," he said, "when I saw the blank expression in his face, I sensed his anger. I pray his judgement won't be impaired and I hope Maximus is strong enough to stand up to him."

"Fear not, my friend," said Jacob, attempting to reassure him. "Drayce is in contact with me, reporting back everything he finds. He's in the realm of man and feels the answers to our many questions just might lie there. He has a War God of Asgard, and a powerful Archangel by his side. Viktor left to join him last night. Archangels have breathtaking powers and even Shadow should fear them."

They were joined by the wizards. "We fear there's more bad news," said Merlin, showing a pained expression, "nothing has been heard from the realm of the Elves. It's as though a veil has been drawn to smother all vestiges of their existence. Around the great waterfalls the grasses wither and die. It's now high summer and the trees are already shedding their leaves; it's as though late autumn has arrived. No younglings have been born to rabbits, deer, birds, or bees. Is it possible nature is closing down."

Jacob turned to Apollo, Magni, and Athena who had just arrived. "Have any of you ever heard of nature closing down," he asked, "the wizards fear it has. Tell me, has this ever happened before, even around the times of the great floods?"

"I've lived in many places, both here and across the cosmos," said Apollo, "and I've walked through all lands since the beginning of time. I remember 'The Fall', that first battle between the forces of Heaven and those of Hell. I also remember the Floods and even with all that destruction, never once did I see anything like what the wizards describe. Nature was created to be resilient and will always find a way." Magni and Athena agreed.

"It's really troubling me as to who Shadow is," said Jacob as be began pacing, "Drayce, Osian, and Heulwyn are the first to come close to seeing him, or is it her? And still, we're no closer to grasping as to who or with what we are dealing. Maybe nature was created to find a way, but what if nature is exhausted and has reached her end? What if she has no reserves and just wants to go back into the nothingness?"

"Relax brother," said Magni, "I too have walked the cosmos since soon after the beginning of time. I've seen many changes and never once did I sense nature giving up. She always found a way and the one thing she did to secure her future was create the twelve Titans. Remember brother, the Titans came from the union of Father Sky and Mother Earth, Ouranos and Gaea. Somehow I feel our answers just might lie there."

"I appreciate your comments," replied Jacob, "remember what Eala told us when she returned from her visit with the Ancient One, 'I am The Ancient One; it takes a lot for me to waken. You and the gods have done well. Jacob has proved himself as having been well chosen. Peace will reign for just a few years, but you are right, 'The Darkness' will again seek allies. All must understand that where there is light, there is always darkness; where there is goodness there will always be badness, where there is love there will always be hate. The challenge for this age of man is to follow the laws already set by the gods.' Is it the Darkness we are dealing with or is it something else?"

"After you were created God of Gods," continued Magni, "you spoke of the Ancient One's warning. You spoke of real evil that will return time and time again. Is it possible this warning also hides the answer?"

"I've no idea," replied Jacob, "those warnings swirl around my head and like so much given by the Ancient One, they are riddles, and I often wonder - why bother?"

"Let's wait until Drayce reports back his findings," said Fafner, "many of us are still grieving, and we're all confused. We seek answers, yet we don't even know what the questions are. Tomorrow is a new day, maybe a warm and fresh sun will help?"

Jacob left and went for a walk along the lagoon; he reached the reeds and gently glided his hands only for his palms to be tickled as he brushed against them.

"Tell me, mother-nature, is it true?" he asked, "Have you lost the will to live? Can't you find a way? Is there anything I can do to help?"

He walked from the lagoon up into the dunes and then felt a warm and soothing sensation. He quickly turned and saw the very same light that shone behind the spirits of Zeus, Odin, and his mother.

"Who are you?" he yelled, "what are you trying to tell me?"

The light slowly faded and then shot out into the cosmos leaving Jacob baffled. He then heard a familiar voice.

"That was some bright light," it was Odi, "it's the same one we saw in the temple. My instincts tell me it's a source Light and it's our ally. We will find out soon enough who it is we are fighting.

Chapter 6

The devastation in the dragon lands was too much for Drayce to bear, the loss of his parents and two of his brothers was still playing on his mind. He was very quiet and every now and again, he'd clench his fists as though ready to explode. Maximus noticed but decided to say nothing, he planned to just be there when he was ready to talk.

They continued walking through the battlefield and were sickened by the many hundreds, possibly even thousands of bloodstained spots, showing where valiant dragons had fallen. Drayce wondered whose life each spot represented and soon realized that the spots were all that was left of some of his closest friends, and this broke his heart even further. He thought of all that was lost and then thought of his sister.

"Maximus," he said, when finally able to speak, "there's no more you can do. Go to Isidra, it's she who needs your protection. I can do this alone." Maximus was having none of it.

"You forget," he replied, determined to stay, "I saw them in action. I watched them kill Marduk and break my father's heart. I too want revenge. Imagine? You and me together; we'll be unbeatable."

They soon realised they were not alone; from behind they heard footsteps and initially prepared for an attack.

"Relax," it was Viktor, "it's only me. Remember how they tried to take my baby; that's unforgivable." He embraced both of them, then continued,

"I too seek revenge. You are now King of the Dragons, and the way I see it you are strong enough to carry both of us. We will be your Dragon Riders."

"There's no need to fly," replied Drayce, "follow me."

They walked towards the cliffs to reach an exit into the realm of man, and were taken aback by where they ended up. They thought they should have been high in the Welsh mountains, not in a very scenic part of Ireland, a place dotted with many secluded lakes.

After getting their bearings, they cautiously made their way along a narrow ridge to find a safe location set deep in the mountains, a clearing hidden among high banks of red sandstone rocks that had a strong resistance to weathering, showing the antiquity of the land. The nearby dense shrubs formed natural wind shields, their height ensuring night-time light would be well camouflaged. Just next to the clearing was a pristine and totally calm, mirror-like lake, and from its shores they had a panoramic view across to one of the last remaining primal forests, a forest they planned to investigate later that day.

As War Gods their instincts were acute, and they were very aware all wasn't right. They thought it strange that the sun's position high in the sky suggested it was early to midsummer, but the leaves were telling them something different, many had already fallen, creating what looked like a rustic carpet as far as the eye could see. They also noted how there were no nesting birds or foraging bees, even butterflies failed to show themselves, now they were worried.

They remained on alert, keeping their weapons close, hoping to relax and enjoy the quietness, but it wasn't easy. It was a pervading odour that unsettled them, all three recognised the stench, and it seemed to be everywhere. It was also noticed how every now and again, a deep sadness crossed Drayce's face.

"Drayce," said Viktor, hoping to cheer him, "the pain you're carrying might be relieved if you tell us about your brothers, you never spoke of them, and maybe remembering them will help."

Drayce agreed but took his time, it was as though he was trying to put some order into the story he wanted to tell.

"My three brothers, Osian, Bryn, and Steffan were amazing, they had no fear and as soon as they changed they became really powerful dragons. They never teased me, just encouraged me, included me in everything." He grinned while turning to Viktor. "That's how I was able the beat the crap out of you when we fought in the dunes." Viktor bit his lip, choosing not to respond. "I was with them when the change came, it happened to all three at the same time, which was unheard of. Osian is very close to me, he immediately retook his human form and sat with me, knowing my feelings were tearing me apart. When the other two took to the sky, they were ecstatic and their prowess as dragons became evident while we watched, I was so happy for them. Bryn soon became a general in our father's army, a powerful leader. Steffan was too young to join the army, but he was a brilliant tactician, called upon many times for his opinion. That's why I find it difficult to understand how easily they fell. Osian went down the mystic route yet held on to his strength and survived the attack. It's strange how Shadow didn't target him, are mystic gods protected against the power of Shadow? Sometimes I think it's he who should be king, not me."

Drayce's grieving was waning, and he was beginning to enjoy the efforts to cheer him up, Viktors suggestion for him to talk about his brothers worked. The banter between them increased almost to the point of insulting each other showing they were true friends and could get away with saying anything. During all this time they never let down their guard, always keeping their weapons close, and that applied even while walking, swimming, or fishing. They lit a campfire and cooked the days catch still unable to fully relax, the stench was ever present. After lunch Maximus and Viktor again went swimming, they found the depth and the temperature of the lake invigorating, they also felt safe knowing Drayce was close by and keeping an eye on them. While Drayce was clearing up he was surprised by the arrival of a group of teenagers who were part of a mountaineering group of exchange students. They arrived just before Viktor and Maximus exited the lake.

The girls in the group were mesmerised by the sight of two over six foot tall and naked, blond Adonis-like youths walking towards them, causing them great difficulty in averting their eyes. Their boyfriends were not in the least bit impressed and showed it, they felt threatened and insecure, and as the afternoon progressed they got more hostile, so much so, arguments began. For Drayce, the tension was getting to be too much, he was still grieving and was itching to let off some steam.

One of the boys saw Maximus looking at his girlfriend and challenged him, lashing out with a powerful punch only to find his fist stopped in mid-flight by a much faster defence. The other boys leapt to assist and found they too were up against three powerful youths who were ready and willing to defend themselves. The boys soon realised they were in a 'no win' situation and chose to leave, calling the girls to join them. They left and made their way down the mountain.

No more than thirty minutes had passed when Viktor said, "Something's burning and it's not too far away."

"I hear crying," said Drayce, getting to his feet and glancing through the trees, "I feel fear, terror, we need to investigate."

All three went into invisibility before briskly moving along the lake shore to reach a clearing where they hid behind a fallen tree. They had just stumbled upon the students, who were being terrorised by a scouting party of around twenty Shadow Riders. What troubled them the most was the number of riders watching from the ridge opposite, there seemed to be hundreds.

"So, this is why I felt the need to remain behind," said Drayce, "and why a portal opened near these lakes. The Ancient One has guided us to where Shadow was next going to attack." He looked up at the ridge and whispered, "I promise Shadow will pay for what it did to my homeland."

"Forget revenge," said Maximus, "assess the situation and prepare a rescue. Look what they're doing."

In the centre of the clearing a roasting rack was built and placed across a campfire lit in a hastily prepared pit. The students were tightly bound to nearby trees, and the boy who earlier challenged Maximus, was singled out, stripped naked and was being savagely beaten. A six-foot skewer was being sharpened; they were preparing to feast on him by spit-roasting him above the pit. The screams of the boy as the skewer approached will forever be implanted in all their memories.

Viktor took the lead; he moved closer and then materialised in a flash of pure light. He was fully armed and wearing the white armour gifted to him by the Ancient One.

"Release him," he yelled, using a strong and thunderous voice, "release him now or face the wrath of an Archangel."

Maximus remained invisible, waiting for the signal to attack. He too was fully armed, protected by the bronze armour of an Asgard God. Drayce, also invisible, moved towards a high bank of rocks from where he planned to launch his attack.

The Shadow Riders found Viktor's demand amusing and when they settled, their commander asked, "Who challenges the power of Shadow?"

"A God of Asgard challenges Shadow," replied Viktor. "I say again, release him now or face my wrath."

"One young and inexperienced god against so many soldiers of Shadow is no match," sneered the commander, "you will be our dinner this night." He raised his bow and released his arrow.

The arrow, although travelling at a great speed, didn't get very far. It was deflected by something much faster, another arrow that seemed to come out of nowhere. Viktor smiled, knowing exactly who fired the arrow and was happy to have another warrior by his side. At the same time the hidden warrior used his stealth and skills to unbind the captives while telling them to seek protection behind a close-by tree trunk as soon as an opportunity arose.

Viktors concern for the injured boy grew while watching him fall in and out of consciousness. He used his staff to release a sustained and powerful light, hoping to temporarily blind the Shadow Riders, which it did. With his free hand he used his magic to levitate the boy and float him to rest behind nearby boulders where a materialised Maximus was waiting. While the riders were blinded, the captives got their opportunity to seek the protection of Maximus by hiding behind those same boulders.

On seeing the injured boy, Maximus felt there was no hope unless Olympus intervened. "Magnar," he said, placing his index finger against his forehead, "we're in battle with Shadow Riders and many more are approaching. We can deal with them, but we're also protecting nine students, one who is seriously injured and needs the power of Olympus. Send Apollo urgently."

Within seconds a portal opened, and Apollo stepped through. He reached the boy and without saying a word, took him into his arms and brought him to Olympus.

"Where have you taken him?" Screamed the boy's distressed girlfriend, watching him disappear into thin air.

"Be happy your friend is in the care of Apollo," replied Maximus, trying to keep an eye on the Shadow Riders coming down from the ridge opposite, "he'll be fine, death cannot enter the realm of Olympus."

He then left the protection of the boulders and moved to stand alongside Viktor prompting the commander to say, "Now we wait for the third one."

Drayce listened from the nearby high bank of rocks, hoping his invisibility unsettled Shadow. While waiting for the signal to attack the only sounds to be heard were the low whimpering of the terrified students, and the gentle fluttering of capes. There were no birds chirping, or animals baying, roaring, or bleating. It was an eerie silence.

Drayce finally materialised, sending terror through the ranks of Shadow. In their eyes he presented as very powerful dragon, one they knew was angry and itching for revenge. He stood there, his scales glistening in the afternoon sunlight, his neck glowing and his flame primed and ready for release. The commander laughed even louder when he saw who it was but didn't seem to be overly confident. "Ah," he sneered, "a dragon Lord! Oh wait; it's the big brother. Your little brothers tasted delightful."

Drayce showed signs of reacting but thankfully he picked up on a restraint signal sent by Viktor, he calmed and continued waiting.

A few moments later what looked like a dragonfly landed on the boulder shielding the students. He crouched for a moment before transforming to stand as a six-foot tall, winged sprite. It was Finn and he too was angry. "Soldiers of Shadow," he yelled, while storming towards them, "you have defiled the realm of a Celtic Goddess for the last time. You are not welcome. Leave my mother's homeland or feel the wrath of an angry prince of the Fair Lands."

Again, the Shadow Riders laughed before this time, attacking. They moved in two waves forcing Maximus and Viktor to retreat and assist in protecting the students. Finn covered them by releasing his arrows in rapid succession but was horrified to find his arrows were just passing through the soldiers without having any effect. "What magic is this?" he yelled.

A third wave of riders attacked, but this time Drayce took to the sky, swiftly flapping his wings to increase his speed. His plan was to deceive shadow into thinking he was a coward. He soon went out of sight, then turned back to silently glide just above the tree line. On coming into view, he released a continuous stream of fire, destroying many riders. His actions only had a minimum effect, many other riders survived, and this troubled him. He circled around, but this time he released a conflagration so powerful it did a lot more damage to all in its path, but it still wasn't enough. The remaining riders regrouped to continue their attack on Viktor, Maximus, and Finn, leaving no choice for Drayce, he took his human form and stood next to Viktor.

All four immortals now stood together, and they certainly looked formidable. They were fully aware that this fight was destined to be vicious, with many casualties, possibly even amongst them. They were all master swordsmen, and their prowess showed when they went into action, but they were up against so many adversaries they soon wavered. The continuous clashing of steel grated on their nerves as they fought off attack after attack, but it was the noxious odour rising from the quickly congealing black blood-spatter that really sickened them. As the battle progressed Finn got great pleasure in confusing the riders, he continuously used the magic of the Little People, at times, standing as a six-foot winged warrior and then suddenly appearing as a four-inch-high sprite. Like Drayce, he sought vengeance for the attacks on his homeland, he was determined to drive Shadow from his mother's lands.

Drayce was inspired by the actions of Finn and decided to take to the sky again. This time he recommenced his onslaught by releasing a constant stream of a more devastating flame, successfully destroying the rear ranks of Shadow. After rejoining Finn and Maximus he retook his human form. "Your flame has certainly been devastating," said Maximus, "but still they keep coming. Are we dealing with a new and evolved Shadow Rider?"

"Maybe!" replied Drayce, "but we've reduced their force by almost half."

"Don't be deceived by those you've killed," said Finn, "I've been trailing this army for the last few days. They get a visit every night from an entity that appears out of nowhere, getting stronger after each visit. Have you noticed how when you destroy one, more appear?"

"I'm not sure you're right, look at their dead," said Drayce, pointing towards the damage he did, "there's definitely only about half left standing."

"Wait and watch," replied Finn.

This time Finn was wrong; the Shadow Riders moved back onto the ridge and were again getting more confident; they seemed to have a different plan. From beneath their legs a very thick black mist wafted, it was a mist that soon turned into a sinister and foul-smelling fog bank, a smell not that unlike poisonous methane. The fog was so thick it completely camouflaged the riders, but the gods knew exactly where they were, the chattering and screeches of terror never ceased, betraying their location. Maximus placed his hand into the fog only to be seriously mauled, then burned. When he retracted his arm it was blistered and oozing blood. Drayce released his fire, but it too was repelled. Finn tried his arrows, only for them, on impact, to fall to the ground without reaching their target.

While waiting on the next attack Viktor closed his eyes and lowered his head. On opening his eyes, he was heard to say, "Yes, My Lord."

"I've just received a plan from the Ancient One," he whispered, hoping the Shadow Riders couldn't hear what he had to say, "Drayce, take to the sky, and fly behind the lines of Shadow. Burn everything and when done, don't allow anything, no matter what, cross the cleared lands."

He then turned to Maximus and Finn, instructing them to back away and protect the students from what he suspected was going to be a 'do or die' attack.

Drayce immediately took to the sky and did as requested. Within moments he released his flame, burning every tree, shrub, and blade of grass, blackening them before turning them to ash. He then intensified his flame to disintegrate the surrounding boulders or rocks, ensuring nothing survived the flame of a dragon.

Viktor in the meantime had removed his armour and tunic, revealing his muscular and toned torso. He tightened the amulet around his neck before moving closer to the fog bank. "Soldiers of Shadow!" he yelled, "reveal yourselves." There was no response.

"Soldiers of Shadow," he yelled again, this time much louder, "do not try my patience, you should know better. Ignoring the command of an Archangel will make it worse. Show yourselves and I'll make it quick."

A volley of arrows shot out from the fog bank to no effect, Viktor was ready and as they approached he did a serious of swift pirouettes, using his staff to deflect all arrows. A second and third volley arrived and met the same fate. "You have defied me for the last time," he yelled, "prepare for my wrath."

Stepping back from the fog bank he ensured everyone saw what was about to happen. As his anger grew his upper body muscles flexed, allowing two enormous white wings to appear and by the look on his face it was obvious he was no longer interested in talking. His patience had run thin. He approached the fog bank, then spread his fingers before placing them on the rim, releasing a continuous flow of blindingly bright lightning bolts that spread in all directions. The lightning was followed by extremely loud peels of thunder, so loud they shook the very heavens. The bolts were relentless and as they penetrated the fog, they ignited the methane, clearing the fog, causing the evil, cold, and indifferent eyes of the riders to reveal their terror. For the forces of Shadow this was a disaster, many were killed, their corpses turned to dust. Those that survived now had to face an archangel who was wielding his sword without mercy, slashing his way through their ranks. Blood flowed, innards spilled, limbs shattered, and heads rolled. There was no clemency or compassion, those at the rear who tried to escape, were incinerated by Drayce who was patrolling the higher slopes. Finn successfully captured three riders, subdued them, then secured them to a nearby tree, awaiting Drayce's return. Drayce was eager to interrogate them and report his findings back to Jacob.

For the students, witnessing a battle between demons and armed warriors terrified them, but their fears were slightly allayed when a new portal opened and their injured friend reappeared, completely healed, and accompanied by what looked like two goddesses. "Apollo believes our powers are required," said one of the goddesses. It was Helena, and she was shaking her head while observing the damage done by Drayce.

"Such devastation," said Sagal, "the scars of battle are everywhere. You really know how to make our work difficult. You've burned everything, not even a seed has survived."

Gasps were heard coming from the students as Helena and Sagal passed, they had never before seen women of such beauty. Another who was in awe was Finn, his face betraying his feelings. He had noticed Sagal when he was last in Olympus and since then, couldn't get her from his mind, having her so close was sending exciting sensations through his body. When she passed she gave him a fleeting glance, he then knew she felt the same way.

She made her way to the ash scarred landscape and waited for Helena to join her, while waiting she wondered if their powers would be enough, such was the damage. When Helena arrived, they knelt, closed their eyes, and allowed their hands to reach deep into the sub-soils to call upon the Earth Mothers, and they answered. They announced their arrival by sending tremors, then wild winds carrying all kinds of seeds, they followed this with a localised rainstorm. Within seconds green shoots appeared, growing to conceal the scars of battle. The landscape became a grass and wildflower covered meadow, interspersed with fast growing shrubs and trees. Their job was done.

Helena approached the students, sensing their fear, she used her powers to put them at ease. "What you've witnessed is too much for you to bear," she said, still trying to calm them, "it's best I erase all memory of what happened here. No human should have to carry such memories of Shadow, such a burden. Nothing will remain."

She clicked her finger and before the students had time to react their memories were erased leaving them looking very confused and wondering how they arrived in that part of the mountain. They were no longer afraid; they just shrugged and made their way along the lakeshore towards their hostel. Little did they know that they were being escorted by four Children of the Gods.

Drayce and Finn remained behind, determined to interrogate the three riders, hoping to get information Jacob so dearly needed. Drayce extracted his dagger and used it to intimidate his captives, but they weren't afraid.

"Tell me demons," he asked, "do you fear the fire of a dragon?" There was no reply.

Drayce transformed and began releasing a very targeted flame. He narrowed its trajectory to travel in a straight line towards the first soldier. When it reached the soldiers toes, he held it firm for a moment and when there was no reaction he slowly moved it up his foot towards his ankle, but the soldier still never flinched.

"It seems friend you're wasting your time," said Finn, "they come from fire and fear no flame. I wonder, as they come from darkness will they fear the Light?"

Drayce also wondered; he retook his human form and then gripped his amulet; he closed his eyes and called on the Light and when it came it shot across to incinerate the rider.

"Now that Viktor is an Archangel," whispered Finn, "is it possible for him to be in two places at once, just like Maximus and Magnar? If it is, can his spirit appear, not as white light, but as dark light?"

"You are one devious fuck," replied Drayce, "I know where you're going with this."

When Viktor returned he wasn't given time to catch his breath. Drayce insisted he attempt Finn's suggestion and when he did, he found he had the power, all he needed to do was learn to master it. He made several attempts but each one failed, it was a white mist that kept appearing beside him. Drayce was losing his patience.

"You are some prick!" yelled Drayce, hoping to rile him, "a useless excuse of an Archangel. Think of the attack on Thora and the attempted abduction of your baby. Will that not bring the darkness out in you."

It did. This time, after leaning against a tree and closing his eyes, a black mist appeared, and as the minutes passed, the mist took the mist-made shape of a Dark Angel, tall and winged, with the face of a demon wearing the horns of a devil.

Viktor made his way over to where the two riders were being held. To them he appeared as an entity that had no clear definition and to his delight the two riders assumed him to be Shadow, especially when he expanded his black wings. He prayed his deception would work. "Tell me, riders of Shadow," he asked. "Have you betrayed me?"

"No, My Lord. We told them nothing," replied one of the riders, delighted he was in the presence of his master. "They know nothing about your vast army gathering at the rim of the universe."

"Nor your plans to destroy the gods," said the other.

"What else haven't you told them?" asked the entity. The soldiers looked confused.

"There's nothing else," said one.

"They don't even know that you have spies in all realms," said the other. The entity then disappeared, leaving the riders to their fate.

Viktor rejoined Drayce and Finn. He told them of what he had learned and insisted Drayce urgently contact Jacob. Drayce didn't, he wanted his revenge. He approached the two riders, his face getting darker and more sinister as he took each step. He extracted his dagger and used it to slowly tear into their flesh, painfully bleeding them. He seemed to be getting pleasure as their black blood flowed, he intended making them suffer for as long as possible before sending them back to where they came from. His hatred risked taking him to the side of The Darkness.

"Friend," said Viktor, trying to prevent Drayce from going any further into a rage, "don't go there, you're better than that."

Drayce acknowledged Victor's concern and apologised. He turned back to the riders and said, "Tell your master of us, tell Shadow of the power wielded by the Children of the Gods." He then, without mercy, dispatched them both.

When Maximus, Helena and Sagal joined them, it was suggested they return to Olympus and report on what they discovered, but Helena had other ideas. "You four have eliminated the immediate threat of Shadow," she said, "Sagal and I have restored any damage done. There's no threat here and I feel very safe with you War Gods protecting me. I've just seen for the first time this beautiful place and I want to see more." She looked across the lake to the mountains on the far side of the valley, "I want to see why my father always says, 'Earth is worth fighting for'. It's so beautiful. Surely we can stay here until tomorrow?"

Viktor and Maximus weren't in favour, they knew Magni had plans to search for the Elves and they were also very aware of how important the trips to Africa and America were, but most importantly, the information they had garnered was so important it needed to be delivered; especially the news about spies operating in all realms.

"I think that's a great idea," said Drayce.

"Of course, you think it's a great idea," replied Maximus, "we all know what you're after,"

"So?" said Drayce, looking across at Helena, "a young dragon has needs."

"A Goddess of the Light also has needs," replied Helena, crossing to take Drayce's hand.

Drayce placed two fingers to his forehead and went quiet for a few moments. "Jacob is aware of what we have found," he said, "I've just told him everything, I also told him we won't be back until tomorrow."

Sagal in particular was delighted they were staying; she had admired Finn since their first meeting and wanted to get to know him better. She was determined to use what little time available to that end.

Helena and Drayce also manipulated the situation so they too could get to know each other in ways that Jacob wouldn't approve, especially now that they were away from the prying eyes of Olympus. Maximus was still uneasy; he knew his father too well and didn't want to be on the receiving end of his wrath, he insisted they return to Olympus first thing in the morning. The fact that Drayce had informed Jacob of what they had found made no difference.

It wasn't long before the two couples drifted away, moving in different directions, both heading higher up the mountain leaving Maximus and Viktor alone.

"Drayce has been through so much," said Viktor, showing his concern for his safety now that he and Helena were going to spend the night alone. "Did you see his face when Helena arrived, his hormones took over and his grief disappeared: I'll never understand a dragon."

"If I was him," said Maximus, "I'd constantly be looking over my shoulder. Uncle Jacob is very clever; he could be anywhere and ready to pounce. I'd hate to be Drayce if he pounced at that very special moment."

Sagal and Finn, in the meantime, reached a ridge higher up the mountain, giving them a panoramic view across the many lakes and forests in the valley below. There they waited for the sun to set.

Finn was uneasy, never having been alone with a girl before. He felt he needed to impress her, and being a natural show-off, he decided to show what he can do. He used his skills to leap and somersault from one high rock to another, while at the same time allowing the setting sun to penetrate his fully opened wings to send brightly coloured beams of light in all directions. At one point he stopped and asked her to listen.

"Can you hear it," he said, "it's the music of the 'Little People'." He backed away and began dancing, bringing a wide smile to her face, she joined him and after a while she embraced him.

"You're amazing," she said, reaching up to kiss his cheek, "your dance makes me feel like I'm walking on the clouds. How you can dance so perfectly using just the music set deep in your head, is amazing."

"How can you not hear the music," he said, stopping his dance and looking confused, "these lands are a favourite place of our nation, the music is everywhere."

"Finn," said Sagal, getting concerned, "do you not know? There are no 'Little People' left in the Fair Lands. The Lady Danu and Lord Faer led your people into the meadows of Olympus. They sought the protection of the gods. The Fair Lands have been emptied."

"How is it I still hear the music?" said a shocked Finn.

Sagal placed her hands on his cheeks then closed her eyes. "Ah," she said, "you do hear the music, but isn't from here, it's coming from Olympus and it's calling out to you."

"Jacob must have spoken with my father," he said, getting emotional.

"If Jacob said he'd speak with your father," she replied, holding him closer, "trust me he will. In fact, if you can hear the music, be sure he did."

"It seems," said Finn, "you and I will be going to Olympus in the morning. This time I won't be wearing a blindfold."

It was soon dark, and both Drayce and Finn lit fires. Drayce used his flame, while Finn caused sparks by scraping two arrow heads together. It was an exciting night for both couples and as their passion grew Viktor and Maximus got very uncomfortable.

"Can you sing?" whispered Viktor.

"Not a note," replied Maximus.

"Well, you better start learning," said Viktor, "things are about to heat up and get very noisy."

"Can we not just stuff our ears?" asked Maximus.

They needn't have worried, the love making wasn't noisy; it was quiet, sensuous, and very passionate. For both couples it was their first time, and it was real love. They quickly became one, sending two birth lights shooting out across the universe.

In Olympus Jacob and Eala were sitting on the patio enjoying the calmness of that particular night. When they saw the lights they both knew what was coming. Jacob cringed but knew to say nothing, he glanced across at Eala and saw her staring back, she was ready to pounce if he opened his mouth. He did attempt to open his mouth.

"Don't even think about it," she snarled, "if Helena is responsible for one of those lights I for one will be very happy, and I expect you to be as well."

Jacob stood and walked away; he wasn't happy. On his way he met Fafner and Faer.

"Did you see the lights?" asked Fafner. Jacob just nodded and continued walking away.

"Leave him," said Eala, calling them to join her, "he'll get over it. He knows Helena is alone with Drayce and is now likely to be pregnant."

"And the other light?" asked Faer.

"That is the question?" replied Eala, "Sagal! Was she with Maximus or Viktor?"

"If it's Maximus," said Fafner, "Magni will have great difficulty keeping me away from killing him."

"If it's Viktor" said Faer, "there'll be a queue starting with Thora, followed by Odi. Not a nice place for him to be in."

"Somehow I feel all is not what it seems," said Eala, taking both of their hands. "We'll know soon enough."

The following morning Drayce and Helena were first to arrive at the campsite to find Maximus and Viktor still asleep. At some stage during the night Viktor had turned and ended up with his head resting on Maximus's chest while his leg was across his waist, Maximus's arm was wrapped around Viktor's shoulder.

"How I would love Obelius to be here," whispered Helena, "he would have so much fun. He'd never let them live this down."

"Never mind Obelius," laughed Drayce, "I'll never let them live this down: Especially Viktor - Mister Macho Man."

"Hello boys," said Helena, reaching down to shake both of them, "wakey, wakey. Time to head home."

Maximus woke first and looked down at Viktor. Viktor woke and was afraid to move. They slowly moved their heads to look at each other and then suddenly leapt up, both said at the same time, "What the Fuck?"

"I bet," said a hysterical Drayce, trying to talk between his bursts of laughter, "last night you both learned something new about each other."

"I'm comfortable in my sexuality," said Maximus, not rising to the bait, "so I don't care who you tell: Viktor and I will always have last night, are you jealous?"

Drayce placed his arm around Helena and with a beaming smile said, "Do I look jealous."

Sagal and Finn then arrived, and they were glowing. Finn's wings refusing to retract; such was his delight.

"About time," snapped Maximus, "we best make our way back to the temple."

Helena and Sagal raised their arms to open a portal. When they looked through, they were surprised to see that the portal had opened at the steps of the temple, and there was a reception of very stern looking gods waiting for them.

First to walk through was Helena and Drayce.

"Your dad looks as though he's going to kill me," said a very worried looking Drayce. Helena gripped his hand tighter.

Next through was Maximus and Viktor. "I knew it," said an anxious looking Maximus, "we shouldn't have stayed the extra day, they really look pissed."

Last through was Sagal and Finn. "Wow," whispered Finn, "they look as though they all need a chill pill."

Eala reached into hug both Helena and Drayce. "I'm so happy for you both," she said.

Jacob coolly kissed Helena on the cheek but totally ignored Drayce. Drayce looked up at Fafner who just shrugged.

Magni summoned Maximus and Viktor. "Never leave me waiting again," he hissed, "I want a full report, and I want it now. Jacob told me what you discovered. Don't you think I too should also have been informed?" Maximus attempted to argue but was silenced when Magni just raised his hand.

"You are some dark Horse," said Eala, kissing Sagal on the cheek, "Finn! Who would have thought? I'm so happy for you. I will look after you until your mother arrives." Sagal was confused; she wondered why she would need extra care.

Jacob warmly greeted Finn. "Your return to Olympus is most welcome," he said, "I've spoken with your father and would now encourage you to go seek him out."

"Finn," interrupted Magni, "I too welcome you back into Olympus but before you go I need you to join with Maximus, Viktor, and Drayce I want a full report on the battle."

Jacob and Magni placed their hands on each of the boy's heads and soon learned of all that happened during the battle. Magni was pleased by how they conducted themselves.

"Everything you did was exactly as I and Ares would have expected," he said, "I'm proud of you. What you've shown gives us insight into what we are up against. Go and rest, tomorrow new tasks await." The boys then left.

"Now we know how Shadow takes the realms," said Magni, "the rest we should always have assumed."

Drayce kissed Helena's cheek and backed away to greet his grandfather, he bowed and was surprised to see Fafner bow to him. "Grandfather," he asked, "why bow to me?"

"Drayce," said Fafner, while embracing his grandson, "you are now King of the Dragons and will soon be their Emperor. All dragons must see me bow for them to understand they must follow you."

"I don't want to be King or Emperor," said a shocked Drayce, "I'm in love and want to spend eternity with Helena. Osian should be King; he's more deserving, he's wiser and just."

Jacob was still within earshot and decided to intervene.

"The Kingdom of the Dragons does indeed need a wise and just King," said Jacob, "the crown has landed on your head, and you must accept it. Your grandfather will always be known as Emperor of the Dragons, but that will only be in name. You are destined to one day be known as Emperor, and that will be in reality. Today it is you who is King, anointed by the Ancient One. You will have the guidance of your grandparents, the support of Olympus, and just think about it, you will have the expertise of your uncles and aunts as well as the assistance of Andras, Galyna, Isidra, and Osian. I need to know my daughter and grandchild will be safe, and I can't think of anyone more worthy than you Drayce, King of the Dragons."

Drayce got emotional, only partially grasping what Jacob had said. "I thought you hated me?"

"I hated the idea of any boy being near my daughter," replied Jacob, "you arrived under the radar and got her pregnant, so I have no choice."

"Pregnant!" gasped Drayce, falling back against the wall in shock, "When? How?"

Jacob bit his lip. Fafner rolled his eyes. "The light announced it across the cosmos last night," he said.

Drayce looked down towards where Helena was talking with Eala; he noticed a slight bump and then ran to be with her.

"Why didn't you tell me?" he asked,

"What are you talking about?" she quizzingly replied.

"The Baby," he said, lifting her off her feet.

She looked at her mother who just nodded; she then felt the bump.

"Is that's what it is?" she said, "I woke this morning, and I felt something, but twenty-four hours and already showing?"

Drayce placed his arm across Helena's shoulders and ushered her out towards the meadows. "Your father told me of the baby," he said, taking her hand and kneeling, "he wants me to accept the throne of the dragon lands. I will accept but only if you will agree to become my Queen. Will you be my Queen?"

All watching from the temple saw him stand, sweep her off her feet and swing her around. They knew she had accepted.

In the meantime, Finn and Sagal made their way towards the Fair Land encampment, and it was noted how nervous he was, especially as the whole nation was watching. It was a long walk that seemed to go on forever. Finn used this time to acknowledge many of his friends as he passed. He soon reached the royal enclosure and was greeted by his two brothers who showed by their excitement how they had forgiven him. When he entered the royal tent he was greeted by Aoife who above all was the one who really missed him.

He looked towards the throne and saw his mother, showing signs of emotion, something she seldom revealed. She raised her arms, encouraging him to run to her, but before he did, he looked around, and was disappointed not to see his father.

"My beautiful boy," she said when he reached her, "how I've missed you."

"I see father hasn't forgiven me," he said trying to contain himself, "what is it I have to do?"

"You've already done it," she replied, "you've come to see him, now seek him out. Always remember how he is the kindest, wisest, and most loyal man I have ever known. He placed his life on the line so many times just to protect me. Don't judge him too harshly."

She turned to Sagal. "I can't thank you enough for bringing my son back." She then noticed a slight bump. "It seems not only have you brought Finn home, but you've also gifted us a grandchild."

"A baby," said a shocked Finn, "really! How?... Last night?"

"We only got together..." she said, stumbling backwards, "now I understand what Eala meant."

"The Gods certainly work in mysterious ways," said Danu, "so be happy."

"I'm shocked," said Finn after thinking for a moment, "but I'm really happy." He reached over and hugged Sagal. "Let's be happy together,"

"My father is going to kill me," she said, "he thinks like Jacob and assumed I'd be safe under his protection.

"Leave Jahiri to me," said Danu.

It was then when Finn left the encampment and made his way through the meadows towards the lagoon. He crossed the dunes and soon reached the beach where in the distance he saw the lonely figure of his father sitting on the sand, firing stones into the waves. He cautiously approached him.

"Father," he softly said, "I miss our fights."

Faer didn't respond, he kept firing stones but at a much slower pace. Finn tried again.

"I've been so lonely, I need you and the Fair Lands in my life. I met a Goddess of the Light. Her name is Sagal, and she is of Africa, a daughter of Jahiri and Jamilah. Father, she carries my baby, and because of that I understand how important family is. I need you in my life; my family will need you in their lives. Please forgive me. Please."

Faer still didn't respond so Finn slowly backed away, but he didn't get very far.

"I forgave you a long time ago," said Faer, "I hoped for this day and still I find it overwhelming. I was too proud to go searching for you so if anybody needs forgiveness it's me. I should have gone after you."

Finn turned back and was delighted to see his father's arms outstretched; he ran to receive an embrace he sorely missed.

From the temple many were watching, Eala said while snuggling closer to Jacob, "I look on Finn, resting his head on his father's shoulder and can see how it's not only the Light we protect. It's Love. When this is over we should always remember that."

Chapter 7

The next morning the sun had barely risen when Jacob arrived back from his morning run. He thought it odd that there were so many stewards in attendance, but what intrigued him the most was the aromas wafting from the kitchens. He summoned the chief steward. "What's different this morning?" he asked, "why are so many toiling today?"

"Worry not, My Lord," replied the steward, "everything is under control. Breakfast for the people of the Fair Lands, and those of the Dragon realm, is already prepared. The chefs are now making ready for the arrival of more visitors."

"Who are you expecting?" asked Jacob, looking bewildered.

"We're expecting visitors from the south. listen carefully and tell me what you hear." He did and soon he heard the beat of the Djembe drums.

"There's more," continued Jacob, "I hear the loud rumble of galloping horses."

He left and made his way to the main door just in time to witness a portal open near the tree line. Chiron immerged leading all Centaur nations. It was a continuous flow, indicating there were thousands coming through.

"I had no choice," said Chiron, on reaching the temple steps, "Pelion has fallen, the Russian realm is in disarray, and as for the centaurs of Cyprus; they've been decimated. With the assistance of the Light, I rescued as many as I could."

Jacob was numb; overwhelmed by the depth of their despair and grief. When he saw their injuries, he recognised the shredded flesh, torn muscles, and gnawed bones as the work of Shadow, the same type of injuries already described by all those who have encountered Shadow to date.

Jacob called on the Goddesses of the Light and when they arrived they formed a line along the south side of the temple and from there they used their Light to send its healing waves across the meadows. The centaurs slowly recovered, but they were still subdued, their spirit broken, and they were showing a lack of interest in reclaiming their homelands.

Lord Polkan approached Jacob. "For days," he said, itching to lambast Olympus, "the centaurs of the Russian realm fought, we alone faced the on-slaught of Shadow, and many of my most formidable warriors are lost. No allies came to our aid, why was that? The other thing is, and please forgive me if my fears are misplaced. Why are we being watched by fully armed, and ready to attack, temple guards. Why does Olympus treat us so?"

"Fear not, friend of Olympus," replied Jacob, "those temple guards were put in place before we became aware of the attacks on all Astral realms. We knew something bad was happening, but it was shielded from us, that's why you fought alone, we weren't aware. The guards you speak of are war-rior immortals, born out of the beating heart of Mount Olympus. When they sense aggression, they awaken and prepare, when swords are drawn they move, they don't differentiate between friend and foe. They are few, and because of them, nothing has ever breached the security of this temple. Even if I ask them to stand down, they won't, especially if they sense danger, and today they sense danger."

Obelius arrived. "Father," he yelled, without acknowledging the pres-ence of Lord Polkan, "all this is too much. Can't you see how something is wrong? Very, very, wrong."

"Not now," said Jacob, brushing him aside, embarrassed by his disrespect, "I need to calm the centaurs."

"Father," insisted Obelius, "look around, too much is happening, and my head is spinning. For crying out loud, what is that infernal drumbeat?"

Jacob raised his hand requesting silence, then he too heard the drumbeat. "More visitors," he said, "we're getting more visitors. Ask the kitchens to prepare."

"Father," yelled Obelius, this time getting aggressive, "are you serious? There'll soon be no room in the meadows. Do you know these people?"

"Obelius," said Magni, trying to calm him, "look on the face of your Asgard uncles, see how relaxed we are. Look at the wizards, they too are relaxed. There's no anxiety showing on the faces of Ares, Eris, Athena, or Apollo. There's nothing to fear, Olympus can cope. I respect your concerns but today, there is no danger." Obelius still wasn't happy.

Jacob joined Chiron and together they went to speak with those centaurs who were still very agitated. They sought out Queen Zephyra of Pelion, and when they found her they listened with compassion to the story she had to tell. She spoke of an unimaginable savagery, of how her people were torn limb from limb before their bones were gnawed on for every last scintilla of flesh. She shed a tear while remembering the initial attack and how her people were so unprepared, distracted while celebrating the festival of the First Horn, that most important time in a centaur's life when horns first appear on the heads of their younglings. Her heart was breaking telling them about how Shadow wiped out a whole generation in just a few minutes. She then moved away, wanting to be alone.

What happened to the Pelion centaurs was bad enough, but when they reached the Cypriot centaurs they were shocked by how so few were left. Almost all younglings were killed; no elderly were left and well over half their adults were slaughtered. It was them who suffered the most. The cruelty meted out knew no bounds and no age group was immune. Painful removal of horns was where the cruelty started, this was followed by shattering of upper leg bones and then genital mutilations. Jacob didn't know what to say, he just offered the assistance of the goddesses, hoping their powers could break through the unbearable suffering.

There was no more to say so Jacob made his way back to the terrace, there he was met by a very excited Zane and Sagal. They understood the drumbeats and announced that the African gods would soon request entry into Olympus. They continued staring out towards the shield, occasionally looking back at Jacob in anticipation of him opening a portal.

When he did, over a thousand African deities stepped through. They were led by a number of lesser-known gods from the Orisha pantheon. Walking just behind them was Oba, Jomo, Jahiri and Jamilah as well as their children. Zane could wait no longer; he summoned two stallions, so he and Sagal could ride out to greet their kin.

Jomo soon reached his siblings and after much hugging and kissing he ran to embrace his mother who was shocked at how tall and broad he had become. He then embraced his father who seemed much smaller in comparison. Sagal shed many tears on reaching her family.

The arrival of the African gods was beyond spectacular; it was the magnificence and variety of their garments that helped them stand out. The mesmerising colours were not only dazzling; they were also spellbinding. The assorted shapes and sizes of the head-dresses drew gasps from those watching.

When they reached the steps of the temple it was the god Oko, and the goddess Mawu, who represented the Orisha.

"Forgive us this intrusion," said Mawu, "I am one of the Creator Goddesses of Africa, tasked by the Orisha to seek sanctuary in these sacred lands for what's left of the gods of our homeland. They believe Olympus is the sanctuary of the gods, we seek sanctuary."

"I too am a God of Africa," said Oko, "our War Gods remain behind; they stand guard over Man, but fear the new threat is more powerful and ruthless. They seek the identity of Shadow, but all efforts have failed. They will soon be joining us."

"You're right," said Jacob after acknowledging them, "Olympus is your sanctuary, you are all most welcome into my domain. The kitchens are prepared, and the stewards will assist in setting up your encampment. Go now and rest, there'll be much to talk about later."

It was then when a new sound was heard; it was the sound of trumpeting elephants and they weren't too far away, causing great excitement for Hemish, Gaia, and Aria, who made their way out into the meadows. Jacob soon opened a portal, allowing a caravan of majestic bull elephants to enter. They were carrying deities from India, Japan, and China, and included in the caravan was Mulan, Manasa, Girish, Garuda, and Aria's twin brothers.

Mulan and Garuda became emotional when they saw their daughter, it was their first time to see her as a fully armed Warrior Goddess.

"Darling," said a very happy Mulan while giving her daughter a tight embrace, "I see my premonition has come to pass, you've found love, I'm so happy for you."

"He's amazing," replied Aria, "a God of Olympus. It's Obelius, Jacob's son." She then turned to greet her two brothers. "When I left I was looking down on you," she said, straining to look up, "now my neck is pained, you two have grown so much, you must be over six feet tall. Should I fear you?

You both look very intimidating." Li grabbed her and raised her above his head.

For Hemish and Gaia, they found it difficult to contain their excitement, they knew the customs of the Indus and initially tried to show no emotion. Their time in Olympus, where emotion was always encouraged, changed all that. They gave up and enthusiastically ran to their parents throwing their arms around them.

"Father," said Hemish while hugging Girish, "it's good to see you, I really missed you." Girish tried to be excited but seemed listless.

"Is everybody here?" he asked, showing a degree of anxiety.

"Yes," replied Hemish, "all four messengers and all eight guardians are back together."

"And that's what worries me," said Girish, shaking his head showing more concern, "take me to Jacob."

They quickly made their way to meet up with Jacob and Odi, and after embracing them Girish whispered in Jacob's ear, "Lord Shiva is awake, after having a troubled sleep. He fears a trap is set and into it, you are falling."

"There is a trap being set," said Jacob, showing no concern, "I too have seen it. I know we face a new threat, but I cannot see from where it comes. Olympus is the best defence for all Astrals and that's why I'm happy for you all to be here."

Obelius heard everything that was said and was so apoplectic he was fit to be tied. "I don't believe this," he yelled, "we've heard the trumpeting of hundreds of elephants and the beat of the drums, so too will have Shadow. How many more are coming? Girish is right, a trap is being set."

He stormed off but Jacob followed him and when he caught up he wedged him against the wall using his extended left arm. "I've had enough of your whinging," he yelled, "don't you think I know what I'm doing? I expect you to stand by my side; advise me but don't question or undermine me again." He then punched his son on the shoulder. "Pull yourself together, and be the god you've been trained to be."

Jacob briskly walked away then stopped; he called Obelius to join him. He raised his hand against Obelius's face and entered his head. "Son," he said, "I love you more than life itself, but you have got to trust me. I know Shadow is coming, and will enter Olympus, I don't know how or when, all I know is; it will be soon. Right now, my biggest worry is the elves. Where are the elves?"

Chapter 8

Jacob went to sit on his throne, surrounded my many of the senior gods. He was distracted, he knew the wizards were upset and as time passed he felt their concern grow. When they arrived at the Great Hall it was obvious to all those present that they were now more distressed.

"Throughout history there were many constants," said Apollonius, after reaching the throne and bowing, "the gods are always primary. But the elves, they are the watchers, the artists, and the guardians of the timeline. Shadow it seems, has worked out how to undermine the natural order. We must seek out the elves and mount a rescue."

Magni agreed, he had already summoned those he had chosen to begin the search. He chose Tristan, Zane, and Lovisa as guardians. Hemish, Sunniva, and Sofia were to be the seekers. When they arrived he said, "In two guardians I see cunning and stealth, a trait that can only have come from the power of Asgard and in the other I see a brute strength that I believe will be necessary before your journey is done. Your task is to protect a wizard and three mystic gods." He then turned to the mystic gods.

"I look on you three," he continued, "and I see gods with the power to break through any obstacle placed before you. Hemish, the ways of the Indus will be your refuge. Sofia, make sure nothing can happen without your wisdom, and Sunniva, remember you are a Goddess of the Sun, fear not its power. Use it."

Ares had one minor concern. "God of Asgard," he said, calling Tristan aside, "you worry me. During your training you showed how great your abilities are, but you also showed some insecurities and that's unsettling. You never took the lead, always a millisecond behind. Lord Magni has great faith in you, he's you uncle, I'm not, and whereas I do trust his judgement, my concern forces me to ask you to accept Lovisa as your commander for this mission. She's most powerful and has the same ability as Magni when it comes to planning. Do you accept my concern?" Tristan nodded and then bowed.

The task ahead was then laid before the six young gods. They were also informed that Lovisa was in command, and that Merlin would be travelling with them. Before they left, Lovisa approached Tristan. "I had no idea," she said, "I don't understand why they picked me over you."

"No worries," replied Tristan, "I never liked taking the lead, this suits me. I will have your back."

The time for departure arrived when a portal opened, one that took them close to a concealed entrance within a folly built near Stonehenge. It was then when a second portal appeared, giving them access into the realm of the Elves. Merlin led the way.

From the highest step of a masterfully crafted stone stairwell, they had a wide view over the unroofed Elven throne room, a room surrounded by cloister style arches. From their vantage point they were captivated by the beauty of the light shining through the stain glassed windows set between those same arches, creating the most amazing spectrum of colourful light, colours that enhanced the many imposing sculptures depicting long gone elves.

They remained on the stair for a few moments, taking in what was before them. They then made their way down, bringing them into what they were told should have been a most enchanting land. They reached the Elven Tree of Life, one that had been growing in the centre of the hall for over five thousand years. They found it fire damaged, scorched along one side, and devoid of all leaves. The surrounding flowers were no longer in full colour and those that were, drooped as though unloved. In the gardens the stands of once majestic trees were bereft of all leaves. Unfinished carvings were scattered and broken. All this so alarmed Merlin, he needed the support of the nearby stone balustrades.

"Once there were eight doors," he said, pointing around the walls, "each leading to the Fire, Forest, Ice, Meadow, Mountain, Storm, Water, and Woodland realms. Today I see there's a new door: it can only be the one that should lead to the realm of the Fire Islands but who knows? This should be the domain of the Spirit Elves led by Lord Kalen, but where are they?"

Hemish walked across the room and placed his two hands on the wall, he closed his eyes to call for the assistance of the Earth Mothers. "There's no response," he said, "something blocks my powers, we should leave this place and leave now."

Merlin didn't want to leave; he felt something but couldn't figure out what it was. Zane, Tristan, and Lovisa drew their swords, preparing for an attack, but none came. Sunniva called on the sun to send its brightest beams and what arrived was very subdued; she began to feel afraid.

Her fears were well founded. Out of nowhere came six terrifying soldiers of Shadow, they were so swift there was no time to react. They grabbed

Hemish, Sofia and Sunniva then disappeared. It was a raid that completely undermined the War Gods.

Tristan went into shock, falling backwards against the Tree of Life. His heart violently pounding while thinking of the last image he had of his beloved sister - her terrified face as she was being dragged away by winged demons. When he composed himself he placed his fingers to his forehead. "Mother, mother!" he pleaded, "can you hear me? Mother, please answer."

Eris was in the Great Hall with Modi when she received her sons panicked message. "Yes son," she replied, slightly moving away, "I hear you. Why do I sense terror?"

"We've been attacked," he replied, struggling to get his breath, "They came out of nowhere, demons that match the description we have of Shadow, but these ones are winged. They have a speed that makes them almost invisible. Mother, they've taken Sofia, Sunniva, and Hemish. We can hear their screams but can't figure out where they are. We need you."

Lovisa was also panicking, not knowing what to do. She used her powers to call for her brother. "Vik, Viktor, do you hear me?" she said, "please answer, we're in trouble, Sofia, Sunniva and Hemish have been taken, come quickly."

"I hear you sis," he replied, racing towards the temple. He reached Odi and Panya and after catching his breath said, "there's no easy way to tell you this - Hemish, Sofia and Sunniva have been taken. Shadow seems to have a new power. It must have been waiting for them."

Odi looked across to the far side of the temple just as Eris collapsed into Modi's arms, he knew then she too had just received the bad news. He was aware an attack on any of her children would see her reverting to her old ways. Modi backed away knowing that even their great love for each other wouldn't be strong enough to contain the unleashed power of the

100

Goddess of Chaos, especially when she was in a rage. He tried to intervene but was too late. Eris disappeared, to reappear in the throne room of the elf realm.

Manasa arrived and said when she joined Odi and Panya, "There's a tightness in my chest, I keep getting images of my son, something's wrong with Hemish."

"Everything is wrong," replied Odi, while Panya embraced Manasa, "Hemish, Sofia and Sunniva have been abducted by Shadow. I'm following Eris to the Elf Realm in a few moments, come with me."

"Try stopping me," she said.

"I promise to bring her home," said Odi, wiping away the gathered tears from Panya's eyes, "then watch me release the wrath of Asgard."

Odi gripped Manasa, blinked, then arrived next to Eris who, even in a rage, was trying to comfort Tristan.

Odi grabbed Zane and Lovisa, he was having difficulty controlling his anger. "How could you," he yelled, "how could you allow this happen, there's not a mark on any of you. Where you asleep?"

"My lord Odi," intervened Merlin, standing between the War Gods and Odi.

"What?" he snapped.

"Your anger is misplaced," continued Merlin, ignoring the aggression, "the War Gods were fully armed and always on guard. They stood no chance and cannot be blamed, there's a new magic at play, it also deceived me."

Odi wasn't interested; he was too angry. He insisted on blaming the War Gods and kept looking for reasons to make them suffer, that was until out from the shadows stepped a hunched figure, a shrouded being, wearing a torn and putrid smelling hooded cloak. A sinister atmosphere also arrived, as black and as terrifying as the darkness of a stormy night. The being was scrawny with withered hands protruded from below his drooping long sleeves. From beneath his hood came his true terror, two yellow and piercing eyes, rotting teeth, pointed chin and pock-marked nose. His rasping laugh sent shivers through all who were present. It was Shadow.

"My strength returns as each day passes," he said, continuing his sinister laugh, "but this day just keeps getting better. Not only have I abducted three children of the gods, but I also now have in my presence a wizard, three senior gods, and three more children of the gods. My hunger will be quieted this night."

Eris was first to react. "Release my daughter," she demanded, while lunging forward, "or you'll feel the wrath of Chaos."

"Oh No," he responded, raising his arms, pretending to recoil, "release the daughter of Chaos?" He moved closer. "Never!" He sneered, enjoying his taunting and teasing.

Odi and Manasa joined Eris and together they continued demanding the release of their children. This was the opportunity the young gods were waiting on; they came from behind with their swords drawn, and their hands resting on the amulets they acquired the first night they became Gods of the Light. They used the amulets to release an aureate and blinding light, a light so bright it sent Shadow crashing against the wall. They maintained the flow of light long enough for him to disappear.

Eris and Odi were furious and let their feelings be known but Manasa was raging. "Idiots," she screamed, "how are we to get our children back, we've no idea where he has taken them."

"We are not Idiots," responded Tristan, standing up to her, "we are War Gods, sent to protect the Mystic Gods. Trust us; we will find and rescue them. I insist you three leave and let us do our jobs."

"Son," said Eris, placing her hands on his shoulders, surprised at how assertive he had become, "I love you dearly, but we are the Ancient Ones and have far greater powers, we will deal with this."

"Enough," said Lovisa, getting angry, "I was appointed by Lord Magni to lead this group, and I will. If you three are staying you will follow my lead, and I say this with due respect to you, my King." She respectfully bowed to Odi then continued, "While you were arguing I noticed to where Shadow disappeared. Look at the lintel above the second stained-glass window and see the crack in the masonry. He travelled through that crack. Be quiet and listen."

They all listened, and soon they heard the muffled, yet tortured screams of both Sunniva and Hemish. There were no sounds coming from Sofia causing Eris to panic. "He has already killed her."

"No Mother," said Tristan, trying to reassure her, "she's alive, she's trying to reach me. I can feel it. They're nearby."

Lovisa climbed towards the crack and on reaching it, she recoiled in horror. The overpowering stench of death was wafting through from the other side. She used her dagger to prise and chip away at the crack but was getting nowhere.

"I was told of how your powers allow you to call on Chaos," she said, turning to Eris, "now would be a good time. Undo what binds this stone and open a way for us to enter."

Eris was there at the beginning of Time; she watched the 'Big Bang' and observed its Chaos. It was her home, and right now, she was determined to use its power. She raised herself towards the crack, she too momentarily recoiled on inhaling the sickly stench.

She wasted no time, closing her eyes and rotating her hands. Soon the molecules binding the lintel and granite violently vibrated before breaking apart, sending their electrons in all directions. Many shot out into the universe while others fell to the ground. Every impact causing mini explosions, releasing bolts of coloured lightning. The more she brought on Chaos the more the gap in the wall opened.

When it widened enough she stepped through followed by Lovisa. They were in another dimension, out of Space and Time. Tristan, Zane, and Merlin followed.

For them all, the grim, semi-darkness and swirling mist was unsettling but not frightening. They could hear dark voices, loaded with madness and menace; they sensed no empathy or remorse just pure vileness. All around them lay cold corpses, discarded, half eaten. They then went into invisibility.

Occasionally, as they made their way towards the source of the only light available to them, they heard the pitiful screams of Hemish and Sunniva. On entering one of the tunnels, they knew they were heading in the right direction when the screams got louder.

Moving along the passageways they passed archways leading to various caverns, the first ten partially lit by clouded lanterns. Each of the ten caverns held thousands of bodies, all hanging from hooks, as though in suspended animation. It was quickly established that the caverns contained the missing elf realms, one realm per cavern.

Lovisa turned to Zane, Tristan, and Merlin. "Avoid the elites," she said, "they would have been the first to be targeted, seek out lowly servants and waken them, find out what happened."

Zane, Tristan, and Merlin made their way into the lines of frozen-in-time elves, and reached two they felt sure were servants. Merlin used his magic to slowly bring them out of their deep sleep. He gestured for them to remain quiet while checking for guards, there were none.

"What do you remember?" he asked, "how did this happen?"

"We were in the kitchens" said one of the servants, nervously looking around, "and we noticed how quiet everything became. No sound of music, the birds had stopped singing. There was not even a sound coming from the workshops, it was an unnerving silence. We peeked through a slightly opened window, and it was then when we saw Shadow working his way through our realm. He seemed to be using an ancient magic, a creeping mist that entered the mouths of our people. As each one fell his forces arrived and carried them away."

"I know of this creeping mist," said Merlin as Odi and Manasa joined them, "it's a most powerful magic, but I have the antidote."

He reached into his satchel and extracted a flask containing a thick, black coloured liquid. Using ten small vials he shared the liquid with the two servants, Odi and Manasa, instructing them to split up and sprinkle one in each of the caverns. He warned them to ensure those waking remained quiet, especially the babies and toddlers. This was to be done with stealth and cunning.

When the vials were opened and the contents sprinkled, the liquid quickly turned to a pale grey mist that rapidly spread around each cavern beginning a widespread awakening. While the rescue of the elves was under way, Zane and Tristan made their way towards a cavern where they believed Hemish and Sunniva were being held. On looking through the entrance they saw a wide platform containing three large stone stakes, from which was hanging a naked Hemish, Sunniva and Sofia. Surrounding the stakes were discarded bones and piles of putrid flesh. In the pit surrounding the platform hundreds of Shadow soldiers circled as though baying for blood, cheering each time Shadow appeared, pacing from side to side while piercing either Hemish or Sunniva.

"Look at my sister," said a horrified Tristan, "look at how stoic she is. Why is Shadow sparing her?"

"It is strange," replied Zane, "see how when he passes he gently fondles her; is it possible he has plans to impregnate her? Just like Lucifer, Shadow might want the baby of a goddess."

The thoughts of this was too much for Tristan and he began to react, preparing to mount a rescue.

"No," whispered Zane, holding him back, "we're only to observe and alert if anyone approaches. Lovisa will need more time to safely rescue the elves." Tristan wasn't happy.

Back at the entrance Lovisa continued with her plan, she asked Eris to again use her power to widen the gap in the wall, wide enough to allow the elves pass through in larger numbers.

While Eris used her powers, Odi, Manasa, Merlin, and the two servants, continued working their way through the caverns, releasing the antidote, and ushering those who had recovered through the gap into the realm of the spirit elves. Only when the last of the elves was rescued did they rejoin Lovisa.

The last Elf to arrive was a most enchanting Elfena. "I am Ellaweise," she said, while bowing to Eris, Manasa, and Odi, recognising them as senior gods, "I was consort of Kalen, now I'm all that's left of our royal house. They skewered him and then ate him while making me watch. In my five thousand years I've witnessed many strange and wonderful things but never have I witnessed such evil, such terror, or such lack of empathy. We are dealing with a new foe, one that is so powerful I fear soon all will be lost."

"Lord Kalen was a true friend of Olympus," said Odi, attempting to comfort her, "he will be sorely missed but right now we need to find a way to rescue three young gods."

Ellaweise acknowledged his kind words then offered her power as an Earth Mother.

"The power of an Earth Mother will be much appreciated," said Lovisa, turning back to face Eris, Odi, and Manasa, "you three need to leave, go assist the elves when the portal into Olympus opens."

Lovisa saw they weren't happy, and she attempted to reassure them. "You've all heard Hemish and Sunniva scream in pain," she said while backing away to join Zane and Tristan, "and because of that I can't trust you to act rationally. You must have faith in us, especially now I have an Earth Mother by my side."

She had more to say, pausing for a moment, then turning back.

"My lady," she said on reaching Eris, "when all elves are safely delivered into Olympus, return and take up position at the entrance to this domain. Will you do this for me?" Eris agreed. She then turned to Manasa.

"My Lady," she began, "do you think Hemish would appreciate you to see him battered, bruised, and beaten? Will he be able to face you seeing him naked and severely abused?"

"My Lord," she continued, after turning to Odi, "Sunniva is one of my closest friends and I know her really well. She wouldn't like her father to witness her humiliation. I too can hear her screams, and it breaks my heart. I promise we will rescue her, now please go."

Odi backed away followed by Manasa and Eris, they made their way to the realm of the Spirit elves to find a portal had already opened allowing Jacob, Obelius, Maximus and Viktor to assist with the rescue of the elves.

Jacob acknowledged all members of the elf supreme council while not allowing normal formalities delay the rescue. He then joined Odi. "Where is Lord Kalen and the Lady Ellaweise?" he asked, "are there more to come through? What of the young gods?"

"There are no more elves to come through," said an embarrassed Odi, "Lovisa sent us away; she said we couldn't be trusted, she has a plan, and it didn't include us."

"What?" yelled Jacob's, his face priceless, his jaw dropping and his eyes widening.

"I respect Lovisa," interrupted Eris, "I watched her grow into a most beautiful goddess and a powerful Warrior of Asgard. She asked me to return to the entrance, but I'm not so sure that's the right decision. I should be the one to rescue my own daughter."

"If Lovisa said she didn't need you," said Obelius, "trust me, she doesn't, but she will need me and Maximus."

He began walking towards the hole in the wall, calling Viktor to join him. They went through and made their way along the tunnels to join up with Lovisa.

"It took you long enough," she said.

"What is it you want us to do?" asked Maximus.

She just pointed, saying nothing. They followed her direction and soon they were met by a sight they'll never forget.

"What the fuck?" cried Obelius, falling back against the wall. Maximus raised his hands to cover his face, and Viktor just stared.

"They are the same ones who tried to take my baby," said a visibly upset Viktor, "we slew all of them, how can this be? Is he creating clones?"

"Now we implement my plan," said Lovisa. She called Ellaweise, Tristan and Zane to join her.

"My Lady," she said pointing Ellaweise towards a high ridge, "Zane and I will be your guardians. From up there, you must use your powers to bring on the tremors. When the rumbling and falling rocks distract Shadow and his army, Maximus, Obelius, and Tristan will blink across to the platform and release Sunniva, Sofia, and Hemish. They will then use their powers to take them to Olympus before returning to continue with my plan."

"And what about me?" enquired Viktor.

"Brother," she said, pointing to a grotto higher up near the ceiling, "up there you will wait, and when the time is right, become the Archangel Viktor. Conceal yourself until then by hiding your Light, make ready to swoop down and slay Shadow."

"There will be four of you left and only three of us," interrupted Maximus, showing signs of concern, "it means one will be left alone and at the mercy of Shadow."

"This is my plan," replied Lovisa, "it's I who will be left behind; I'll be fine."

"Sister," said Viktor, "it's better I stay, and you go, I'm an Archangel and they fear me the most."

From out of the shadows stepped Jacob. "Lovisa," he said, "I'm impressed; even I wouldn't have produced a plan as simple yet as daring as yours. Now, just to reassure me, show me what you are up against." He then slightly bowed to Ellaweise.

Lovisa took him to the edge of the tunnel, and they peeked out across to where the three torture posts stood. When he saw the condition of the young gods he stumbled, such was the shock. His suppressed memories of his own torture at the hands of Lucifer returned and his anger grew.

"Lovisa!" he said, when he recovered, "Go for it. With one small exception. Viktor will be last to leave. You will be rescued, and I will remain to take Viktor from here."

Ellaweise, Lovisa and Zane discretely made their way over to the ridge while Viktor climbed higher to reach the grotto. Obelius, Maximus and Tristan got ready while Jacob observed.

When all was in place Ellaweise crouched and placed her hands on to the ledge, she closed her eyes. "Sisters," she whispered, "hear me, send your power and help me bring on the tremors."

Within seconds the tremors arrived, dislodging boulders, and causing loose rock to tumble towards the cave floor. They achieved what Lovisa intended, Shadow and the soldiers were distracted, but there was an added bonus, many soldiers of Shadow were crushed. Those that survived quickly realised what was happening and rushed towards the ridge. Shadow too re-alised what was happening.

"Earth Mother," he yelled on seeing Ellaweise and while moving to-wards the edge of the platform, "he tasted divine, will you taste as good?"

While Shadow was distracted, Obelius, Maximus and Tristan blinked to appear roughly ten feet behind him. Obelius quickly reached the post holding Hemish, he cut the binds while at the same time covering Hemish's mouth trying to prevent him from screaming. "It's me, it's Obelius," he said, trying to prevent himself retching from the amount of torn skin and con-gealed blood, "I have you, friend."

Maximus was also covered in blood and loose skin; he too had the same problem. "Cousin," he whispered, as Sunniva collapsed into his arms, "hang in there, Apollo is waiting."

"Please tell me Hemish is still alive," she managed to quietly whisper, "I don't know what I'd do without him. He lights up…" she fell unconscious.

"Obelius has rescued him," replied Maximus, hoping she could still hear him, "he'll be in Olympus by now. Trust Apollo, he will heal him."

Tristan was also gone; he had rescued his much-traumatised sister and had her safely back in Olympus.

Obelius, Maximus and Tristan quickly returned to join Jacob where they watched Lovisa and Zane continuously and successfully fight off all efforts to capture them. Ellaweise remained on the ridge waiting to be rescued.

"Right," said Obelius, "let's get them out of here." At the blink of an eye all six disappeared to arrive back at the entrance where Eris was waiting.

Back in the cavern Jacob received a vision while watching Viktor transform into an Archangel. The vision was of Shadow surrounded by hundreds of clones, and it was a vision that alarmed him. He realised the possibility existed that they were not looking on the face of Shadow but an imposter, or another clone.

The soldiers of Shadow now had Viktor in their sights and began moving towards him, but he was too fast for them, he just kept leaping from one level to another. It was then when Shadow realised his prisoners had escaped causing his screams of rage to echo all through the tunnels and caverns.

"I think the penny has dropped," sniggered Zane.

Meanwhile Viktor saw his opportunity to attack and without hesitation he prepared to propel himself towards the platform. His wings opened and spread out to allow his Light to shine so bright, it blinded the approaching soldiers. He focused again on Shadow and then he crouched, drew his sword, before flying higher while preparing to dive at great speed towards his target.

It was at that point when Jacob noticed another figure hiding near what looked like a secret entrance into another dimension. The figure looked exactly like Shadow confirming his hunch was right. He was looking at clones, and Viktor was diving into a trap.

Jacob acted immediately, blinking to materialise above the now speeding Viktor. He gripped him and pulled him closer before blinking again to rematerialize at the original entrance.

"It was a trap," he said, "Shadow wasn't there; we were looking at a clone." Viktor accepted his word.

Tristan approached the entrance and noted how hundreds of Shadow Soldiers were rapidly approaching. "Mother," he yelled, "it's time you did your worst. Bring Chaos to this place and let all memory of that accursed realm be forever erased. Split the atoms and let the protons, neutrons and electrons shatter his universe. Let Chaos be his destiny."

Eris took great pleasure in obliging; she released her power, swirling then bringing forth the winds before sending her lightning into the darkness of Shadow. The universe knew her anger was unleashed as the caverns began to disintegrate; they were turning into Chaos and what was left was sent away to be placed among the distant clouds of primordial elements. She ensured it was all sent back to where temperatures were so high nothing could possibly survive.

When finished she and Jacob used their combined magic to permanently seal the entrance, ensuring no other crack could develop to be a future threat to the realm of the elves.

Jacob exhaled a sigh of relief, but it was not to last. He watched Ellaweise go into grief and fall to her knees.

"We didn't see or hear them coming," she said, "it was so fast no one escaped. They held me back and made me watch them bleed and skin my Kalen. They ate him before my very eyes." She bowed her head again as her tears reached the floor. "While feasting, they smashed through the nine doors and within an hour it was all over. They had taken all realms."

When she composed herself she made her way to the scorched tree and using her magic she opened a secret compartment. She recovered an amulet which had at its centre a green gemstone. "In this is the repository of all elf knowledge," she said, placing the amulet into Jacob's care, "apart from it containing all elf memories, its Light assists all of nature to stay in balance. Thousands of years have passed since last its power was called upon."

"Come, My Lady," said Jacob, taking her by the arm, "walk with me into the safety of Olympus."

They stepped through the portal to find the stewards were assisting the elves in building a vast encampment suitable for such esteemed quests.

"My Lady," said Jacob, "Lord Kalen would want you to give hope to your peoples. Walk among them and give them that hope."

She was nervous, she had never seen so many elves in one place. When she found her courage, she moved among them to be greeted as their queen.

Just as Jacob was backing away he noticed Jomo talking with some of the Storm elves and was curious. He joined them and was immediately presented with a special request.

"Over the years," said Jomo, "I've learned how the elves bring order to the chaos of nature but to do that, they need order in their lives. I spoke with Lord Cassiel, and he has suggested we create a circle of ten stone thrones, one for each of their realms. I've agreed to use my stone-mason skills, but I need to get the granite blocks here, and that's something I need you to do."

"It seems I'm not king in my own realm," said a bemused Jacob, trying to be funny, "everyone is making decisions without consulting me."

"Jacob," reacted a taken aback Jomo, "I'm not undermining you; we're friends. All I was doing was taking one dilemma away, allowing you to concentrate on the bigger issues."

"And your efforts are really appreciated," replied Jacob, "I can definitely help with this one."

He used his magic to guide ten large granite boulders from near the workshops into the centre of the elf encampment. When the boulders arrived, he arranged them to land in such a way so as to form a perfect circle. In the centre of the circle, he placed another boulder, one that was to be used to create a four-foot pedestal. The plan was for ten pathways to be dug from the pedestal out to each boulder.

"Now I get to work," said a pleased Jomo.

"Father," said Zane, who felt he was needed, "remember how you showed me the ways of the stonemason? Can I help?"

Jomo was thrilled to have his son working with him and together they worked through the night. By early the following afternoon they had created ten very ornate thrones fit only for the most powerful among the elves. Each throne exuded a timeless charm that harked back to the time of the great Elvan sculptures. Each had an imposing presence, made for comfort with intricately carved arm and back rests, all carrying symbols depicting important events from each realm. The thrones were finished off using painted gold accents on each leg and armrest, and for extra comfort, embroidered cushions and plush back rests were designed.

The pedestal didn't take too long to complete; it was a simple structure consisting of a lined column with four carved hands holding a round tray. While Jomo completed the pedestal, Zane finished the ten pebbled pathways.

It was late afternoon when Ellaweise arrived, and to say she was delighted would be an understatement. She was followed by Lords Evander, Azreal, Aeson and Cassiel as well as the ladies Lirrisa, Elvina, Ariella, and Thalia. They were then joined by a very reluctant elf who said, "Never before have I seen such a gathering of elf-kind, it overwhelms me. I am Lord Tadakki of the Fire Islands; they say I am of the faithful light." Ellaweise welcomed him onto the supreme council and gestured for him to take a seat.

It was then when a lone musician began strumming on the strings of an Ash-wood carved harp, sending the saddest melody out across the Olympus meadows. While she was strumming Jacob and Ellaweise approached the centre of the circle and placed the rescued amulet on the pedestal. Then all went quiet.

The council sat on their thrones, upright and still, waiting on the now rising moon to reach its highest point. Its beams crept slowly towards the pedestal to eventually place its light into the amulet's very heart. For a few moments, the amulet pulsated before sending its luminous green light all across the meadows. When the light reached all elves was when their grief really showed. It was a grief made more poignant when from the terrace of the temple was heard a voice that sounded like an angel. It was Drayce, accompanied by the harpist, and he began singing a sorrowful version of 'The song of the Elves.' bringing tears to the eyes of his friends as well as the Olympian and Asgard Gods, even Magni.

All across the meadows the Dragons, the Centaurs, and the Fairy Folk, as well as the Gods of the East, and the Gods of Africa, all stood with reverence to the suffering of the elves. It was a scene the gods will never forget, never before had so many Astrals gathered together under the protection of Olympus. The centaurs all stood in large columns and bowed to the elves. The wings of the Little People changed colour as the green light shone through them, creating a most magical scene, even the spectacular colours worn by the various Eastern and African gods were highlighted by the magical light shining that night.

Jacob, after joining Eala on the steps of the temple, said, "I wonder as to why so many Astrals stand before us, nothing makes sense, but I must trust that the Ancient One has a plan. This Shadow is more cunning and more prepared than Lucifer ever was, and it's a worry."

Chapter 9

Jacob had difficulty sleeping that night; his mind was in turmoil and all he wanted was to stretch across and seek comfort from Eala. Sensing his unease she immediately snuggled closer helping him to remember all the reasons he does what he does. He drifted into sleep, but his sleep was broken by a light flickering from beneath his door. He left his bed with Eala walking cautiously behind and, on opening the door, the light got brighter. They quickly dressed, then hesitantly followed the light. They moved through the candle-lit corridors to arrive at the Great Hall where Magni, Modi, Odi, and Panya were already waiting.

"Did you see the light?" asked Odi.

"I did, I noticed it flickering and felt it was calling me to follow."

Odi wasn't happy; he paced the Hall and checked behind the columns finding nothing. While walking behind the statues he said, "It feels as though we've all been summoned."

"Four War Gods and two Goddesses of the Light," said Jacob, "strange how we all felt the same thing."

"Who is Shadow?" asked a voice coming from the rear of the temple, "that is the question!"

"Mother?" reacted Jacob, "is it really you?"

There were gasps when from behind the statue of Zeus an amazing blast of white light shot in all directions. It lit up every corner and crevice; then she appeared. She just drifted into view, not touching the ground.

Jacob thought back to that time when he arrived at the temple, the time when he first saw his mother as a goddess. This was different, he saw how much more powerful she now was. While drifting towards him her light grew brighter bringing her calmness to all those present. On reaching him she said while raising her hand to rest on his cheek, "My beautiful and handsome boy, I see you still suffer. I too feel the pain. I never wanted this for you but when the Ancient One speaks, we as gods, have no choice but to listen."

She joined Odi, and just like for Jacob, she placed her hand on his cheek. "That fateful day, two of you came into this world," she said, leaning in to kiss his forehead, "in my womb you were his guardian, his protector and even now you're still on guard, your eyes are never far from him." She kissed his forehead again, then continued, "I held you the most because I knew you were the one to leave. I whispered in your ear just before your father took you away..."

"I remember that whisper," interrupted Odi as his mother's tears gathered, "in my dreams I still hear it, 'A mother only has one heart. Room for all her children; take half with you and when we meet again return it to me.' It was then when father took me away."

"Mother," asked Jacob. "Why are you here? Where's father?"

"Your father is in Asgard," she replied, "he wishes to meet with his brothers."

"I must leave for Asgard immediately," said Odi, "it's my place as King to be there to greet him."

"No!" said Maria, shaking her head, "remain here: your father will soon be with us."

She raised her right hand and using her magic she manoeuvred five chairs into the centre of the hall. She gestured for Magni, Modi, and Jacob to sit. She sat opposite them, while Odi, Panya and Eala stepped aside.

"The empty chair," asked Jacob, "who's it for?"

Just then Helena arrived, "Grandma," she excitedly screamed, running towards her, "when did you get here? I've really missed you."

Maria was delighted to see her, but her task was more pressing, in fact all present noted the sense of urgency. She guided Helena to sit on the vacant chair alongside her father.

"Son," she asked, "the day you were rescued; tell me what you saw."

"No. Never!" replied Jacob, shaking his head, "Mother! It's too difficult, I've not spoken of that day; even Eala knows nothing of what I suffered."

Eala went to hold him but was gestured away by Maria. Odi also went to interfere, and he too was ushered away.

"Jacob!" she repeated, slightly raising her voice, "please try. Tell me what you saw."

He started fidgeting, folding, and then unfolding his arms; he crossed his legs and then began shifting from left to right. "Mother," he whispered, "it's too painful."

Maria raised her voice even higher. "Tell us what happened then Tell Me What You Saw," she yelled, showing her agitation.

"No!" shouted Jacob. He went to rise only to be pushed back into the chair by a new and very powerful force used by his mother. Everyone present was shocked and then she turned to Magni.

"Tell me what you saw," she demanded.

Magni looked at her with one of his well-known angry stares trying to unnerve her, but she didn't flinch. He mumbled for a moment and then his voice got stronger. "I was beaten by a more powerful foe," he said, looking a bit ashamed, "I'm one of the greatest War Gods yet couldn't bring him down. I saw my youngest brother, naked, bloodied, and bruised, even near death his dignity was being trampled on. I saw him fall into sleep; I saw the sickly grey colour of death take him. I saw his true age come and turn his body to just shrivelled skin and bone and wondered why Helena brought us there when all we did was hasten his death. I still feel my head impact the flowstone. As I fell into sleep I was happy we hastened his death, we took away his pain and ended his eternal torture."

"I also wondered," interrupted Modi, "and then I called on father to send me the hammer. Something entered my head; it was like I felt his love travel across the universe. The hammer came and my strength grew. I looked at Jacob wasting away, then I knew he was gone. I comforted myself knowing we would bring his body to rest in the tombs of Elysium. I then watched Magni being crushed against the flowstone walls. I still remember the flow stone, how it was everywhere, it seemed to seal the floors, the walls, and the ceiling.

"Father, pappa," said Helena, as her tears flowed, "I was a two-year-old, I remember now, I never saw you, you were hidden from me, shielded by uncles, Magni, and Modi, but I heard your screams, and I felt your pain. I saw his power and felt his anger. I heard the clashing of swords and watched the sparks reflect off the flow stone. I felt a hand rest on my shoulder protecting me, it was an old man, and he stayed by my side; his power surrounding me. Then my hand just moved with my palm facing upwards, I felt something small, very small, it rested in my palm and then something made me blow it towards you."

"That was the speck of dust," said Odi, taking her hand to reassure her, "it was blown by the Ancient One at the beginning of time. It was also the spark of life."

Eala by now had rested her hands on Jacob's shoulders, she moved closer to rest her lips on his cheek where she felt one of his trickling tears. She passed her calmness into him then said, "It's time you spoke; it's time you released the pain."

Maria was pleased to yet again see the power of the love Eala had for her son; she then tried again. "Jacob, my beautiful son, now it's time to tell me what you saw."

He left his seat and paced back and forth across the hall. He was in turmoil and resented the pressure being put on him. He eventually sat down and placed his head in his hands before lowering them to his knees, just staring at the floor. He really didn't want to talk but knew his mother wouldn't give up and will ensure he remained in the Great Hall until he told his story.

"My powers were gone," he mumbled, having difficulty letting the words out, "they were stifled by the flowstone."

"I can't hear you," said Maria moving closer to encourage him, "you must gather your strength and tell me what you saw."

"The plan should have worked," he said as his mumbling got stronger, "it was a good plan. Odi was to strike first, I was to come from behind and decapitate Cain, but he seemed to know our plan, how could this be? My armour didn't protect me; do we have a traitor among the shield makers? I remember the White Mist, it gathered in my mouth, it was about to leave when 'He' arrived, then I felt my teeth break. His fist entered my mouth to reach my throat preventing the White Mist from leaving. Using his fist, he raised me high, as though in triumph, then he shook me like a rag doll. He had me and took me through the portal into the vastness of the universe. I too remember the flowstone; his torches lit his way, and the shiny walls reflected my pain as he dragged me and bound me to the torture post. He said my terror would begin immediately, destined to go on forever, no hope of rescue. I can still smell the stench of his putrid breath; it continues to make me sick. Where did such hatred and bitterness come from? Mother, mother, he took the last of my dignity, he stripped me naked and did things to me; he used his extended fingernails to tear into me. The worst was when he used his full weight and strength to land blows on parts of my body, enough to crack my bones and stun me. Then he'd gag me, preventing relief if the White Mist should escape. It never escaped; he intended to keep it there, keeping me alive for eternity."

He paused for breath while laying his head to rest on Eala's shoulder. She just cradled him saying nothing. He looked at his three brothers and prayed they wouldn't think less of him.

Magni left his seat and knelt before him; he then placed his hands into Jacobs.

"You've just described exactly what happened to me, then I was res-cued," he said, hoping to reassure his brother, "feel the love coming from Eala; hear the sobs of your daughter and look at your mother, Panya, and us, your three brothers. We're here for you and will always be by your side. After this day, your healing begins."

"Magni," said Jacob, reaching over to embrace his hardman brother, "the memories of his rage won't go away. I never thought a rage could be so potent it allowed bitterness grow in me. I can't forget the blows that rained down on me, or how the impacts would cut each breath short."

"Son," said Maria, taking his hand from Magni, "please tell me what you saw."

"Mother," he shouted, while leaping to his feet, "for crying out loud, what do you mean?"

"Tell...Me... What...You...Saw?" she yelled back.

He paused for a moment, shocked by how loud his mother could shout.

"I saw a tunnel," he said, "there was a bright light. I travelled towards it and felt at peace, but then there was a shield, I couldn't get through. I looked back and saw the hammer, I saw it crush him, I heard his bones break. I saw Magni and Modi dismember and then burn his remains."

"You've got to tell me what else you saw," Marie replied, this time using her softer voice.

"Mother," pleaded Jacob, "please. Enough! What else could there be."

Magni and Modi almost together, raised their hands to their heads and in unison said, "The Black Mist, where did the Black Mist go?"

"While listening to all your stories," Maria said as her voice faded, "the one thing you all mentioned was the flowstone. Flowstone is porous yet in this place nothing penetrated it. It hid his chamber from the gaze of the gods using an ancient magic; that very same magic must have prevented the Black Mist from leaving while you were all there. It must have found a place somewhere in the cave to hide, a place hidden in Shadow."

Odi grabbed a chair and sat opposite Jacob, they placed their hands on each other's heads, allowing them to travel back in time. They soon reached the cave, and Odi began reporting on everything he saw.

"I feel Jacob's pain," he said, occasionally wincing, "it's taking my breath. I see the tunnel and the light; I can hear the sound of battle." He went quiet and continued looking around, "I see the hammer; it has crushed Lucifer. I see Magni and Modi burning his dismembered body. Oh. I see it, the Black Mist. It has risen, unseen and rests near a bend in the ceiling; it cannot get through the flowstone. Mother! How did you know? I know now, he still lives and is a spirit. He is in Shadow."

"My work is done," said Maria as she disappeared.

Chapter 10

Maria gave them all something to think about; the idea that Lucifer was still alive never entered any of their heads including Jacob's. It was agreed not to discuss Maria's suspicions with anybody other than Athena and the Wizards until more evidence was gathered. Odi was still disturbed at being prevented from travelling to Asgard and let his feelings be known. Jacob called him aside.

"Trust me brother, you don't want to be there. Leave what is about to happen for father to deal with. I know your heart is going to be broken but because of what's coming your place is with me."

"Why do you always speak in riddles," said Odi, getting more annoyed, "what's about to happen?"

He broke their long-standing agreement and entered Jacob's head without permission and found out what lay ahead.

"Can we not prevent this?" he gasped, "why aren't you sending your army to assist?"

Jacob was furious with him and pushed him away, "Every time you enter my head without agreement we end up in a fight. This time I should send you out across the universe so as to shut you up. If you open your mouth I swear I will cut your tongue out."

He sensed Odi was about to go against him and discreetly clicked his fingers creating an invisible shield around the Great Hall. Odi blinked and attempted to travel to Asgard but rebounded off the shield. He tried again and this time he was bounced back into the centre of the hall. He leapt to his feet and using his momentum he sent Jacob reeling back towards his throne. He continued his attack by raining down a succession of punches on his brother. Jacob allowed him vent for a few more moments.

"One more punch," he said, raising his arm to strike back, "and you won't be attacking your brother you'll be attacking the God of Gods."

Eala, Panya and Helena were sobbing while Magni and Modi were dumbfounded, such was the viciousness of Odi's attack. Modi went to intervene but was prevented. "I think I know what it is Jacob has seen," said Magni, "and we're not going to like it. I hate saying it, but Jacob might be right in preventing Odi from leaving."

"What in the name of Odin are you talking about?" exclaimed Modi.

"I think Jacob has seen the fall of Asgard," replied Magni.

⊰⊱

The royal palace of Asgard was a vast and very ornate building. It had many spire-like towers with pointed roofs and gold painted window frames. From the spires flew flags bearing the emblems of the royal family, and along the numerous surrounding turrets stood solitary soldiers tasked with watching all entrances. Every hundred meters, tall towers stood, permanently manned and ready for any disturbance. Civic buildings and mansions were dotted all across the cityscape, surrounded by thousands of smaller houses. At night, torches provided sufficient light to ensure the safety of the citizenry.

This particular night was one that was unusually calm and balmy. The senior Asgard gods were struggling to sleep but managed, all except for

Prudr who was so restless she chose to sit on her balcony and take in the quietness. It was then when she noticed her blind uncle Hodr leaving one of the nearby houses to make his way toward the city wall. He was moving as though he could see exactly where he was going. She watched him use a key to open a trapdoor and stand back. She thought this curious and decided to investigate. When she reached the house she found the door ajar, and when she peeked inside she saw the body of another uncle, it was her uncle Balder. She concluded he was murdered by Hodr. She prepared to raise the alarm but stopped when she thought she heard movement beneath the trap door. She hid behind some nearby barrels and waited.

The trapdoor opened and three agents of Shadow immerged. They met with Hodr and then made their way back to where they came from. The trapdoor wasn't secured so when Hodr went out of view Prudr moved to secure it. She was concerned and for a moment had difficulty trying to decide what to do. She concluded that she had found the traitor Odi had warned her about, so chose to keep secret the death of Balder.

It was while making her way towards the palace when she felt a slight wobble, a wobble so light she decided to ignore it. Within seconds another more pronounced tremor was felt, and she knew this wasn't right, it was an earthquake and never before had the ground shook in the realm of Asgard. She ran to one of the gate towers and looked across the Bifrost Bridge to find it unguarded. Lord Heimdallr wasn't there, his plinth empty, she knew then that Asgard was unprotected and in serious danger.

Heimdallr had fallen to a new magic, a magic never before seen. He had been overcome and taken into a hidden dimension where he was totally incapacitated.

Another much more powerful earthquake arrived, and this one ensured all of Asgard awoke. Then came what sounded like a sonic boom, followed by two more. There was a brief respite, then the booms became more regular. Their sound was sharp yet hollow, just like the ponding of a base drum, and the closer they got the more threatening they became.

Prudr recognised the booms as sinister and knew a terrible calamity was coming. She last heard those sounds just before her beloved Sol Invictus fell to the forces of Hell. She raised her Gjallarhorn and in a panicky burst summoned the army. She was joined by Thor, Hermod and Vidar.

"Where's Balder?" enquired Hermod, "he's needed here."

"He won't be joining us," replied Prudr, "he has fallen to a traitor."

"Who is it you accuse?" asked Thor.

"I accuse Uncle Hodr," said Prudr, "I saw him open a trapdoor and speak with what looked like three soldiers of Shadow, caped and hooded beings with gangly arms and scrawny hands. When they departed he left the trapdoor open, I secured it." No more was said.

Just then over three hundred Oseberg ships, supported by well-armed Long Ships, arrived to take up defensive positions each side of the bridge, each one carrying over a hundred warriors. All ships not only had the ability to move rapidly through water, but they also had the ability to float meters above the surface.

The Oseberg's positioned themselves near the city walls, and the Long Ships were placed where it was believed any attack on Asgard would begin. The Long Ships were always placed at the frontline, their long and narrow shape giving them an ability to move quickly and at high speeds.

Over four thousand horse drawn chariots then arrived to form a protective force completely surrounding the city. Each chariot was manned by a charioteer, two bowmen and a swordsman.

For some time, the booms continued, then they stopped. There was no enemy on the bridge, no waves rippling across the water, no flags flapping.

There were no children crying or dogs barking, it was absolute silence until, over two hours later, a sudden and extremely loud boom was heard. Soon the pitiful wailing of a distraught family reached the ears of the gods telling them of grief as one family mourned the sudden death of their loved ones. Another boom led to more cries of terror, this time coming from the outskirts of the city, an area where the least defences were built. As the moments passed, more and more citizens fell.

Thor was usually assertive but this time he showed signs of panic. "What are we fighting?" he yelled, pacing back and forth, "where are they hiding?" When the palace guards failed to find the source of the booms, he became more agitated.

He raised his hand, calling for his hammer, and within seconds it arrived. He took to the sky, searching above the clouds, but found nothing. He then flew below the clouds only to see his city in flames, with panicking citizen's scurrying in all directions, seeking shelter. He still couldn't find the source. The violent booms kept coming, getting more frequent, bringing death and widespread destruction everywhere. The palace in particular was targeted, bringing down column after column causing the roof to collapse. Civic buildings and places of worship were next to be targeted, bringing on the greatest destruction ever meted out on any civilization. Throughout the city many of the intricately carved spires were ablaze with some already beyond repair. The destruction of the palace continued with the flames becoming so intense they burst through the once amazing stained-glass windows, shattering them beyond all recognition.

"We're fighting an invisible force and will soon be annihilated," said Thor after rejoining Prudr and his brothers, "we need to evacuate the city."

The booms intensified and this time they were targeting the ships. Many were sunk, suffering massive loss of life, while others were so damaged they were rendered useless for any form of defence. The ships were like sitting ducks with no chance of escape.

"Who would have thought," said Thor, getting more despondent, "that I would be the one to order the abandonment of Asgard, today I see no alternative. Odin protected this realm under worse threats, and we survived, but this is different."

He looked for support from his brothers and his daughter, which he got. He also sought guidance from the ancient Asgard gods, but none was forthcoming. The booms got much louder and more relentless, more and more of the city fell.

"How do we fight a foe we cannot see," he asked, "where is the honour, where is the valour in such treachery." He was pained and then announced as he opened a portal, "There's only one place we can go and be safe. We must leave now. Get the children, the elderly, the injured into the portal and until they are all safely through, all others remain."

❧⨀❧

In the meantime, it was another troubled night for Jacob causing him to rise earlier than usual, but this time he didn't go for his normal training regime. He sat on the patio looking at the various encampments set up across the meadows hoping that offering them his protection was the right thing to do. He was joined by Odi. "I'm sorry," he said, "you know how much I love Asgard, I felt my place was there, not with you."

"You are my brother," replied Jacob, "and if you feel about Asgard the way I feel about Olympus, I definitely understand, I think I would try to do the same. Somehow I think your task will be to rebuild, and that's what you will be remembered for."

"Be gentle with me," said Odi, "it's already happened, hasn't it? Asgard is gone."

"For hours now I've been sensing something foreboding," replied Jacob, "I'm certain it's Asgard. I'm bewildered by the strategy of Shadow, or should we now call him Lucifer?"

They then sat watching the hustle and bustle out in the meadows saying very little to each other. Odi finally changed the subject. "Oh! By the way, this is the first opportunity I've had to tell you something important, I think you're going to really be pissed with me, I completely forgot about this."

"You've got me intrigued," said Jacob, getting very interested, "don't keep me in the dark."

"There's only one way to tell you and that's to be blunt," replied Odi, cautiously backing away, "you have an older sister, her name is Prudr,"

"I have a sister!" exclaimed Jacob, tightening his lips and clenching his fists, "and you're only telling me this now? Why has nobody told me before now? Is there more family secrets been kept from me?"

"You've got to understand," said Odi, hoping to get the story straight, "I put her from my mind years ago. One morning, when I was about three years old, I woke, and she was gone. Before that she was everything to me, she brought me everywhere, looked after me. She was like a mother to me, but I always understood she was my sister. It took me years to recover and as time passed I just forgot about her. When I returned to Asgard as King she was there on the steps with our uncles. Even Modi shied away from warning me of her return and when he did tell me he asked me to treat her with compassion. When I met her I saw she was a broken goddess, and I found out why. She had lost her greatest love; he was a powerful Sun God, killed in the last battle against the forces of The Darkness. On top of that, her two children have been kidnapped. She searched and is always searching, believing them still to be alive. She feels their life force and won't give up. She returned to Asgard to make her peace, hoping we'd help. Panya nearly killed me for not telling her, shit, I never want to get on Panya's bad side again."

"I have a sister," repeated Jacob, "I always wanted a sister. Tell me more about her."

Odi was about to speak when Thora arrived, she was carrying Astrid. "Father," she said, "will you look after your granddaughter please? There's something bothering me, a few moments ago the Hammer vibrated and left my shoulder. It could only have been called by grandfather. Something bad has happened and I want to investigate."

"We all sense something," said Odi, "I'm sure we're about to discover what it is." He reached across to take Astrid into his arms. "The great thing about minding someone else's baby," he said while kissing her forehead, "is they don't answer back. Better still they can always be returned."

Just as he sat down, he received a sudden jolt, a vision, Thora also received the same vision. It was showing them the fall of Asgard and the terrible plight their people were suffering. He leapt back on to his feet, handing Astrid to Jacob, "I understand why you prevented me going to Asgard, but now, I've no choice. My people need rescuing and it's the duty of their king to make sure a rescue happens." Jacob didn't object this time.

Odi raced to his room, knocking aggressively on the bedroom doors of Magni, Modi, Thanases and Baldor as he passed. They were already in their armour, their instincts had earlier warned them to prepare for something, they just didn't know what they were preparing for. Odi, after leaving his room, used his Gjallarhorn to call for his imperial chariots and when they arrived they showed all those in the meadows the awesome power of Asgard.

As the Asgard army passed the temple, Jacob entered Odi's head. "I suspect all in Asgard has gone wrong," he said, "I'll have the meadows ready for the arrival of any survivors. Olympus will be their sanctuary."

"Asgard has never fallen," snapped Odi, not impressed with Jacob's lack of faith in the abilities of Asgard's defences, "it will not fall while under my watch."

"I will say no more," replied Jacob before returning back into the temple.

Magni and Modi were ahead of Odi; they were approaching the shield when a portal opened allowing a procession of Asgardians to enter Olympus. There were thousands coming through, mainly the wounded, elderly, and the children, all distraught and terrified. Magni approached the lead soldier "Tell me!" he asked, "how bad is it, what happened?"

"Asgard has fallen," replied the soldier, "our armies were no match, we are being annihilated, and the city lies in ruins. The last of our warriors fight alongside the royal family but they too will soon fall. We were attacked by an invisible force; there was no defence."

Odi arrived and was devastated to see his people so traumatised. After spending a short while with them, he joined Magni and Modi. "I'm leaving for Asgard and will be going alone," he said, expecting a reaction but there was none, "you two must help prepare the defence of Olympus. You must also let our people see you as their god protectors.

Just as he was about to enter the portal, another opened allowing through a vast column of horse drawn carriages, chariots, and floating vessels, as well as the remnants of the Asgard army. The carriages were carrying what remained of the history of Asgard, artifacts rescued from the museums, libraries, and archives. They were followed by the royal family, and finally Thor, who was still frantically swinging his hammer deflecting any booms that entered the portal. Only when the portals closed did Thor collapse to his knees, letting out a most mournful roar.

Thor remained on his knees for quite some time until he was assisted back to his feet by Prudr. "Father," she said, gripping him tightly, "stand, show our people your strength. Let them see that it'll be our family who will rebuild Asgard. Let them see you stand among your children, who are all together for the first time ever. There will be another time to grieve."

Thor looked around and was shocked to see the different Astrals camped all across the meadows. "Has Jacob lost his mind?" he asked, turning back to Prudr, "has he made a mistake allowing such a gathering of Astrals? I fear he has endangered Olympus?"

He was about to speak again when he felt a hand rest on his shoulder. It was Magni. "Fear not, father," he said, "Jacob knows what he's doing."

Thor lit up and felt overwhelmed. "I've missed you so much," he said when he found his voice, "I heard what happened to Marduk, and I worried. Are you well?"

"Only for my sons," replied Magni, "I think I'd be resting in the tombs of Elysium."

"Sons?" exclaimed a bemused Thor.

Magni called for Maximus and Magnar to join him. "This is your grandfather," he said. The boys bowed and then embraced him.

"Remind me," asked Thor. "How many grandchildren do I actually have?"

"You have eleven," replied Modi, "six grandsons and five granddaughters."

Prudr lowered her head as tears gathered, Odi noticed and embraced her. "It's too painful," she said, "he has eleven grandchildren but two are missing, my two."

"We all promised to search" replied Odi, holding her tighter, "and we will. I won't rest until we find them."

"What are you talking about?" asked Magni.

"Prudr's children, son and daughter, were taken by The Darkness many years ago," Odi replied, "their life-force has not diminished, so we know they're still alive, somewhere out there, living in shadow."

Thor reached across to embrace his daughter. "That morning," he said, "when I returned to Asgard to find you standing on the steps, I was so excited. Then my heart broke on finding out about my missing grandchildren. I promised you then I'd search for them, I promise you again that no stone will go unturned. We will find them." They then made their way to the temple.

Jacob was still cradling Astrid when the first reports of Asgard arriving at the meadows reached him. He knew it was going to be bad news so just sat and waited. He looked around the Great Hall, it was bursting at the seams with the number of gods and Astrals who had arrived earlier. He watched Obelius and wondered why he was standing in the centre of the Hall. A slight smile crossed his face when Obelius pounded his staff off the tiles seeking silence. "For those who don't know, I am Obelius, God of Olympus, guardian of the God of Gods, and today I'm taking control of the defence of this realm."

No one gasped, no one questioned his decision, they were all impressed at this assertiveness. He was about to announce his plans when the main doors opened and Thor entered, followed by Odi and the remnants of the Asgard royal family. Obelius in particular was thrilled to see his grandfather.

Thor made his way to meet with Jacob and on passing Obelius he paused, "My grandson, how you've grown. I see you're now a most powerful Greek God. I hoped you would be of Asgard, but Olympus will no doubt be safe in your hands."

He looked around for the rest of his grandchildren and was pleased to see Demetrius. "Ah, thanks be to the All Father that one of my grandsons is a Mystic." He kissed his forehead and then continued, "Now. Where are my granddaughters?"

Helena, Sofia, Thora, and a still injured Sunniva joined him. "I'm so proud, I'm grandfather to three Goddesses of the Light, and a War Queen of Asgard." He especially paid attention to Sunniva, "I promise 'He' will pay for what he did to you."

He looked around and was perplexed. "Where's Tristan?"

Tristan stepped out of the shadows; he was the shy one and hated being the centre of attention. "Aah, there you are," said Thor, "so like your father, you even act like him. He too was shy, and still he became the God of War he was meant to be. In you I see a great warrior; you too will be a King of Asgard."

He then approached Jacob. "I offer you my Hammer," he said, "and the power of the storms. Your mother will soon be with us and together we all deal with this Shadow or, to be more precise, as your mother suspects, we will deal with the spirit of Lucifer?

Jacob was still cradling Astrid. "Before we talk business," he said, "look into the peaceful face of your great granddaughter, she's Thora and Viktor's baby."

Thor took Astrid into his arms and quickly became besotted. "Daughter of an Archangel, and a War Goddess. You, my darling, are one who will, one day, wield much power."

He then turned to the gathering and raised Astrid above his head. "Look upon the face of this beautiful baby. Look at all our children and see it's them that we fight for, not the land, the buildings, or the wealth. We fight for their lives. I am the God of Thunder, bringer of the storms, a War God, and today the fight-back begins."

There was an uneasy shuffling among the younger gods, wondering how Obelius was going to react. They didn't have to wait too long. "I'm pleased I now have the greatest War God by my side," he said, looking very confident, "I am the God Protector of Olympus, nothing happens without my knowledge."

Thor was taken aback; he looked at Jacob whose face didn't betray his feelings; he then looked at Magni and saw him shrug his shoulders. He faced Obelius. "How things have changed, a sixteen-year-old in command of the armies of Olympus. If this is so you have my allegiance. What is your command?"

"My command?" said Obelius, "all I need is for you to hold my hand and make sure I make no mistakes."

Jacob was never as proud of anything in his life as much as he was of Obelius at that moment. He stood and walked over to Prudr. "I believe you're my sister?" he said, reaching in to kiss her cheek, "there's something important I really need to do, but when I get back we'll talk properly. I sense the pain of your great loss and promise that I too will assist in your search."

He then called Odi to join him.

"Please don't say 'I told you so'" said Odi, "I don't think I'd cope."

"I'd never say that!" replied Jacob, "we both know what we must do. Let's leave together and see what awaits us."

They blinked and disappeared to re-materialise in the shattered city only to be taken aback when two more gods arrived. It was Obelius and Thora, and they were furious.

"When will you two ever learn?" snapped Obelius, "I just announced to the temple that nothing was to happen without my knowledge and what do you two do? You cannot travel without the protection of the War Gods. If I had more time I would have brought Maximus, Tristan, and Magnar as a precaution." Jacob and Odi ignored him; they were too engrossed in looking around at the devastation before them.

The dust covered, shattered remains, of Asgard's beautiful buildings lay fallen and unloved. The streets that once bustled stood covered in debris and devoid of all life. Gone were the market traders and dealers who brought a character unrivalled anywhere else in the universe. Gone were the children who teased and played amongst the stalls and along the alleyways. There was nothing left; all they heard was a dust laden wind, winding its way along the desolate and cracked passageways.

They made their way towards the palace and looked upon the remains of the smooth sandstone walls that gave Asgard its beauty. Odi had tears in his eyes. "Once there were buildings in this city that were so beautiful and loved," he said, wiping his eyes, "to see them destroyed is breaking my heart. I cannot believe how, under my watch, all that was built since the beginning of time lies ruined at my feet."

"Father," said Thora, gripping his arm, hoping to support him, "this is only bricks and mortar, it can be rebuilt. You have given Asgard all that's good, we are the survivors and will return."

"They even destroyed the statues and the library," said Odi, "how are we to remember the heroes and the blessed dead of old? How can we come back from this?" He turned to Jacob. "Every step I take makes me want to retch, the decay, do you smell it? This once great city is now a graveyard with many unburied dead. The least I can do is use my powers to assist them into Valhalla, I must try and preserve the last of their dignity."

"I agree," said Jacob, as he moved further out on to the Palace terrace.

Just then a new portal opened, and more young gods arrived. "It took you long enough," said Obelius. There was no response, they were all in shock.

Jacob summoned Odi and the young gods to join him. He placed them in a semi-circle, facing out over the city. In unison, they bowed their heads and arced their right arms.

"Hear us, fallen of Asgard. Your toil is over. Go now and seek your reward. Let the power of the Aesir assist your bodies to find your place in Valhalla. Listen on to us, rise up and go in peace."

From below scattered masonry and toppled trees, at first the spirits, then the bodies of fallen Asgardians, in their thousands, began rising up to drift towards the north. It was a solemn sight, one never to be forgotten.

No sooner had the last body gone out of view when Thora got agitated. "Father," she yelled, breaking the circle, "they're still here, I smell them. It's that very same smell I got when on the folly."

She held her amulet, closed her eyes and within seconds her Light travelled across the ruins, highlighting creatures of shadow watching them. She was joined by the other war gods, they too held their amulets, sending their Light in many directions. Their combined Light was much stronger, driving Shadow from Asgard. It was then when the revenge of the Children of the Gods was born.

When sure it was safe, they spread out among the ruins searching for survivors, but none were found. They listened carefully for the least sound, but none was heard, they then returned to join Jacob and Odi.

"Uncle," said Maximus, as he watched Odi picking up debris and trying to put smashed pieces back together, "I lived for the time when I'd arrive in Asgard as the son of Magni and I still long for that day, but it's not today. The rebuilding of Asgard will have to wait, and I promise to use all my powers assisting you in the rebuilding. We must leave and prepare the defence of the last bastion of the gods."

Tristan was alongside Jacob. "Uncle," he said, "don't you think it strange how Olympus now houses the remnants of all Astrals? The Dragons, The Yeti, the Centaurs, the Elves, the Fairy Folk, the Wizards, the Eastern Gods, the African Gods and now Asgard, they all dwell in the same place. Is this his plan?"

Odi ignored Maximus and continued putting pieces of debris together, that was until he and Jacob felt another portal opening. It was the arrival of Aria, Drayce, Galyna, Finn, and Zane. "It's strange how we five received a calling," said Zane, "a voice telling us to go to the folly. When we got there, an open portal was waiting. We looked through and saw you on the other side. The voice is still in our heads. What's going on?"

"I too hear the voice," said Jacob, looking around at all the worried faces.

He raised his hands and called on the Light to create a cocoon. An opaque coloured cocoon quickly formed and when he clenched his fists, it strengthened so no eyes could gaze upon them, no ears could hear them, and no minds could sense them.

"We've been caught short yet again," he said, "we are up against a more lethal adversary than the one we fought during the war of the End Times. You War Gods were called together by me to be schooled, but really it was the Ancient One who called you. His plans are for you to lead the fight against Shadow, but it's obvious there aren't enough of you. The Ancient

One knows Olympus is where the battle between Good and Evil will finally be decided. The arrival of the Astrals in Olympus is the bait, they will always be safe, Olympus has many secret hiding places, but there is one that will protect them all. Even Shadow will never find it."

"Father," asked Obelius, "what about the Mystic Gods?"

"Fear not for the Mystic Gods," replied Odi, "it's likely they will be the ones to vanquish his army; they will have the assistance of the Sun Gods, the Wizards, and the Earth Mothers. They will be led by Demetrius."

"Uncle," said Magnar, turning to Jacob, "you said there's not enough of us, how do you know? And who do you have in mind to be trained?"

"Your brothers and sisters," replied Jacob, "some of them are already sixteen, those that aren't, will go to bed tonight and wake up in the morning as sixteen-year-olds.

Jacob closed his eyes and sought out Athena. "My Lady," he began, allowing everyone to hear his conversation, "it's time. You know what to do."

He turned to Magnar. "The lady Athena is in charge of the temple security while I'm away, she's aware of the plans to protect the realms and she's working with Ares and Magni to put in place the training of your brothers and sisters."

"Which brothers and sisters are to be trained?" asked Aria.

"Aodh, Aoife, Amma, Cetan, Hai, Lir, Li, and Osian, are to be trained as War Gods," replied Jacob, "and Aja, Isidra, Kitake, and Yeshe, are to be trained as Mystic Gods."

Odi then turned to Finn. "Olympus recognises your prowess as a Warrior God of the Fair Lands, but wonders should you too train with Magni. He's one of the ancients, one who has vast knowledge. There may be things he could teach you." Finn bowed and agreed to go into training.

Back in Olympus there was a great deal of activity with preparations being made for the defence of the realm. After the training regime for the young gods was put in place Athena placed herself at the main entrance to the temple with Apollo by her side. She re-created the metal shield, last used when Shadow's army first attacked. She again ensured the only entrance would be under her control. Apollo provided extra protection by using his powers to create a Light barrier across the entrance ensuring only those bathed in the Light could get through.

Out in the Asgard encampment there was a lot of tension. Prudr had informed Modi, Baldor, and Thanases about Hodr's betrayal. She insisted he be watched at all times. When she was happy Hodr was under control she went to meet up with Magni whom she hadn't seen for many years. He was her younger brother and when they met, all watching could see the affection that once existed between them. They hugged and then sympathised with each other.

Prudr took the opportunity to tell Magni about Hodr betraying Asgard, news that really upset Magni, Hodr was always one of his favourite uncles. It hurt him more when he saw fellow Asgardians step aside or turn their backs as his uncle passed, but he understood; it's the way of Asgard when a traitor walks among them. When he saw Modi, Baldor, and Thanases shadowing Hodr, with their swords drawn, he decided to intervene. He looked across at his father and uncles and saw the pain in their faces.

"No need for others to draw their sword," he said to Prudr, "it'll be me who brings him down. It's time I continued with my revenge on Shadow, and no better place to continue than here."

Magni approached Hodr. "Tell me uncle," he yelled for all to hear, "how much did it cost for you to betray Asgard?"

Hodr waved his walking stick around, he didn't answer, he just continued walking towards the steps of the temple. Magni moved to block his way while at the same time preparing to swing his sword. "Do not ignore me," he said, his voice getting louder, "you'll pay for what you did."

Just as Magni was about to strike, Hodr loudly laughed, looked around, it was obvious to all watching he was no longer blind. The laugh became more sinister and then he spoke.

"Imbecilic son of Thunder," he said, "Marduk tasted so good, maybe needed a little marinade but salt and pepper sufficed." Magni froze for a moment then Hodr roared, "I am SHADOW, beware my wrath."

Instantly Shadow shot out through Hodr's mouth, and raced at great speed towards the temple but was repelled back out into the meadows by the power of the Light-shield created by Apollo. He made a second attempt and again he was repelled. His anger grew and he responded by firing molten fireballs in all directions, terrifying the refugees. He then disappeared.

Back in Asgard Jacob went very quiet before falling back against a wall. He was in shock. "Shadow has again found a way into Olympus," he said, trying not to panic. He urgently opened a portal near the temple and raced through just in time to see Shadow disappear out through the shield.

On the steps Magni was still standing over Hodr, unsure of what to do, especially as Hodr was sobbing uncontrollably. He was heard to cry out, "I killed my brother; I killed my brother. He made me do it, help me."

"Magni," said Athena, showing a little bit of compassion, "bring him to the shield. If he's still possessed the Light won't let him through."

Magni did what was asked and brought Hodr to the shield. He ushered him through and then joined him on the other side. Hodr was no longer possessed but he had to submit to probing by Thor, Ares, and Magni. They entered his head and found that he had betrayed very little to Shadow, what he did betray was insignificant.

Jacob made his way into the temple and sat on his throne. All saw his disquiet over how a lone wolf attack by Shadow succeeded in compromising the defences so meticulously put in place. He called Athena to join him. "Is everything ready?" he asked. Athena just nodded.

"What's he up to?" whispered Modi.

"I've no idea," replied Magni, "he is the God of Gods and it's not our place to question him. He will tell us in his own time. One thing I am curious about though! Why is he confiding in Athena and not his brothers?"

Thor was still devastated over the destruction of Asgard and had difficulty speaking with all those who approached him. Jacob saw how upset he was and joined him. "Father," he said, "I really missed you. Where's mother?"

"Your mother has been having nightmares, she refused to tell me what they were about, she just suggested I travel to Asgard. She was supposed to travel here, she had suspicions, and thought you had the answers."

"She was here," said Jacob, "she sought the answers and then quickly disappeared. I wish she were here now and under our protection."

"Trust me son," said Thor, "she'll be here soon."

Obelius arrived and asked Jacob to walk with him. "Father, don't you trust me?" he asked. "You seem to have arranged secret plans with Athena and again you've excluded me. I heard you call on Athena and say to her 'My Lady, it's time. You know what to do.' What did she do?"

"She placed the metal shield around the temple and with the help of Apollo she placed the Light-shield across the entrance and she......." Jacob stopped talking and allowed Obelius to enter his head. Obelius read his father's mind and then said, "I will say no more. When you're ready for me to do my part, I'll be waiting."

What Jacob had shown him was a network of tunnels and caverns deep below the cellars of Olympus. Places built as a secret refuge only to be used in times of great need. Their location is only known to Athena as the Goddess of Wisdom.

The difficulty for Jacob was how to get the children and elderly into the tunnels without being detected by Shadow.

Chapter 11

Two days had passed since the fall of Asgard, and everyone was settling down and getting used to their new circumstances. At the temple doors Athena remained on alert, refusing to let her guard down, her sole purpose was the absolute protection of the temple. In the meadows the new recruits into the ranks of the young gods were continuing with their daily training regime and it was obvious to those watching that they were becoming powerful warriors, eager to learn.

At the end of the third day when the dinner bell tolled those same young gods made their way to wash and change, except for Aodh. He was a bit of a loner, preferring to swim alone in the lagoon just to enjoy its life-giving waters.

That day, while making his way across the dunes towards the beach, he was confronted by a spectacular burst of light causing him to shield his eyes. He had just witnessed the appearance of a most stunning lady. He watched her leave an injured girl at the water's edge before disappearing.

He ran to assist and when he reached the girl, he was struck by how beautiful she was. He took her into his arms, planning to run to the temple. It was then when a second burst of light arrived and this time the lady brought a very dishevelled youth who, when he opened his eyes, went on the attack. "Leave my sister alone," he screamed.

The lady tried to reason with him, but he was having none of it. Aodh sensed danger and placed the girl back on to the sand and prepared to defend himself. The fight that ensued was one of the most vicious fights ever fought on the beach. There was no reasoning with the youth, he was blinded to any efforts to calm things down. Aodh used every skill taught to him by his father and by the War Gods, but he was losing, leaving him with no choice but to seek a breather. After expanding, then flapping his wings, he took to the sky and hovered ten feet above the ground before launching an aerial assault. He found that even those attempts failed, such was the power of the youth.

The lady had no choice but to grip the youth and blink him into the temple where she hoped an Earth Mother was present and able to use her calming powers. Her gamble paid off when she materialised close to Panya and Eala, both somehow knowing they were to help; they did and within seconds the youth fell asleep. What was interesting was that Apollo's shield didn't prevent him from entering the temple, suggesting he was a God of the Light.

The lady returned to the beach to find Aodh carrying the girl towards the temple.

"It's said that death cannot enter this sanctuary," he said, "Apollo will assist her back to health." The lady agreed and walked with him.

From the patio Odi and Jacob saw Aodh approaching and became concerned when they saw him carrying what to them looked like a body. They also saw the lady walking alongside him. Jacob was first to react and blinked himself across to join them. "Mother," he yelled, "how? Why?" He hugged her showing how much he missed her. Odi then appeared and he too was emotional. It was a heart-warming moment, but it was soon interrupted when Aodh said, "Excuse me; I could do with a little help here."

Jacob took the girl from him and blinked into Apollo's rooms and was taken aback to see Eala cradling a very handsome young man.

"He's sleeping soundly," she said, "but deep down he's very troubled and is fighting our calming ways. He seems to have taken some kind of horrific abuse just to save his sister."

Odi and Aodh arrived. "Who are they?" asked Odi, looking very confused, "he looks familiar, come to think of it so does she!"

"Leave," said apollo, "all of you leave, I'll call you when I wake them."

"My Lord," said Aodh, "I'd like to stay, she was happy in my arms, I felt something, and I sensed she'd like me to be here when she awakens." Apollo wasn't happy but agreed to the request.

"Who are they?" asked Panya, "how did they get through the shield?"

"All I remember is the boy being dropped before us by a very fast-moving lady," said Eala. "Jacob, I'd swear it was your mother, but I can't be sure. She was too fast."

Jacob smiled knowingly across at Odi, then said, "It was our mother, she's outside."

Eala and Panya excitedly ran out to meet her. "You really know how to make an entrance," said Eala, on reaching her. "Who are they?"

"I have no idea," replied Maria, "I was drawn to them by an overpowering force. I found them being dragged across a foreboding desert by agents of Shadow. I sensed they were special and knew I had to rescue them. Shadow had no idea what hit it, everything happened so fast. The boy is very protective of the girl. I'm sure they are brother and sister."

Odi and Jacob arrived. "Enough of them," said Odi, "mother, I need a proper hug." He reached in and was delighted to be held firm. "I'm getting more like Jacob," he said, "there's tears gathering in my eyes. I'm the bloody King of Asgard, or at least I was, and I'm about to cry. I don't believe this."

"Here, get lost," said Jacob, pushing Odi away, "we're too big for our mother to hug both of us, it's my turn."

"You're like two little boys," said Panya, gently punching Odi, "instead of two powerful Kings." Eala and Panya then left to spread the news of Maria's return.

It wasn't long before Thor arrived, then Obelius, Demetrius, Thora, Helena, and Sunniva. There was great excitement, it was one happy reunion especially when Viktor joined them, cradling Astrid.

Several hours later Aodh arrived at the Great Hall. "My Lord Thor," he said almost apologetically, "you should come with me and meet the boy; he's awake and has a story to tell." He then whispered but was overheard by Jacob and Odi. "He is the son of Prudr."

Thor and Aodh rushed back to Apollo's rooms. Aodh immediately went and sat with the girl, he held her hand and it was noticed how the Light was using his strength to assist with her recovery.

The boy was sitting on his bed with his head resting against the wall. When he saw Thor approach, he gasped. Never before had he seen someone so tall and broad.

"You have a story to tell?" said Thor, "but before you do, tell me, who are you?"

"I am Arum," said the boy, trying to straighten up, "son of Sol Invictus and the Goddess Prudr of Asgard." He looked across at the girl. "She's my sister, Eliana. We were taken many years ago. We know Shadow killed our father; we saw their savagery when they attacked our home. We don't know what happened to our mother. It's strange, but there are times when we feel her love reach us, we think she still searches for us, but Shadow seems to be always one step ahead. We fear she has forgotten us."

"Your mother never gave up," said Thor, getting very emotional, "your mother is my daughter, she sits in the meadows all day, and she spends every night looking out at the stars hoping that one day she will find you. She's a broken goddess."

"You're my grandfather?" reacted Arum, struggling to stand, "You are Thor, the God of Thunder?" He tried to bow but was still too weak, it seems Aodh did a lot more damage during their fight.

"There's no need to bow before me, we're family," said Thor, gently assisting him to stand.

Arum struggled over to sit with his sister, he gently rubbed her forehead and hair.

"Hi sis," he whispered, "we're safe now, please wake up, mother's here." There was still no response.

"She's gathering my strength," said Aodh, "she will soon waken."

"Thank you," replied Arum, "I tried to protect her. The things I had to do. Oh, you are some fighter. Where did you get your skills?"

Aodh offered his hand. "I am of the Fair Lands," he said, "we might be slight of frame, but we have strength and speed."

"You certainly have," replied Arum.

"Come," said Thor, taking his grandson by the arm, "it's time you met your mother."

They walked through the corridors and arrived in the Great Hall. For Arum it was overwhelming, he had never seen such grandeur. The statues of the Greek Gods were impressive but the sight of all the assembled Asgard gods frightened him.

"Continue holding my arm if you still feel weak," said Thor trying to reassure him.

"Why are they looking at me?" whispered Arum, "who are they?"

"You will know them all soon enough," replied Thor, "they are your kin, your uncles and aunts, your cousins and see that one over there, that's Odi, your King. Look who stands beside him, that's his twin, Jacob. He is your uncle, and the God of Gods."

Arum parted from Thor and moved to bow to Odi; he was limping and showing his pain, especially by the way he held his chest. He stumbled and Odi said while leaping forward to save him, "Nephew, there's no need to bow, you're with family."

Jacob joined him. "We can help you with your pain," he said, "we are Gods of the Light and are here for you."

Arum nodded and lowered his head. Jacob and Odi then called on the Light and when it came, it entered Arum to begin its healing ways. Within moments he grew in strength and height. His sparse clothing changed into the robes and armour of an Asgard Warrior God. When an elk-skin cape appeared, it was full length, draping to touch the ground. His weapons were equal to those of the War Gods. When the transformation was complete he turned to face his family and said, "I am Arum, grandson of the mighty Thunder. I'm the charioteer of the Gods and Bringer of the Dawn. I am of Asgard."

At the back of the hall, Aodh had arrived with Eliana gripping his arm; she too was struggling to walk but insisted on joining her brother. Aodh helped her reach Odi and said, "My Lord, this is Eliana, sister of Arum." With great difficulty, she curtsied.

"No need to curtsey," said Odi, "you are among family."

Eala and Panya approached her and offered to bring the healing which she accepted. When the Light came it changed her raggedy clothes into the most exquisite silk gown of an Asgard Goddess. Her soft and cascading hair framed her high cheek-boned and perfect face, hair that was held in place by an intricately designed sun disc. It was obvious to all watching that they were looking at a now powerful Sun Goddess. Aodh too was watching and although he was already besotted, he was now in awe of her.

Thor gestured for them to join him for a short walk and as they were walking through the hall, Arum asked, "Is that Lord Magni?"

"Yes, it is," said Thor grinning from ear to ear, "are you telling me his reputation even stretched out to the farthest suns?"

"Nowhere has escaped the legend that is Magni. He's spoken of everywhere," said Eliana, "the universe is waiting on his revenge. Our captors joked and partied when they were told of the fall of a Sun God. They mentioned the fall of Bel Marduk." Thor was speechless.

When they reached the ornamental gardens they saw a lonely figure sitting just staring at the stars, they immediately knew it was their mother. Her head was slowly moving from side to side as though listening carefully, hoping to hear a calling. Thor encouraged them to hold hands and make their way to banish their mother's pain.

Thor remained close by and got very emotional when his grandchildren sat each side of their mother and then buried their heads into her chest.

"Is this real?" he heard his daughter say, "is it true? Are you really here?" They sat all night, sharing harrowing stories, never breaking each other's embrace.

Just as dawn broke, Eliana and Prudr left for their bedroom to rest. Arum wasn't tired, he chose to walk around to the front of the temple where he sat on the steps, watching the sunrise.

When Jacob arrived to begin his morning workout, he noticed Arum sitting alone and invited him to join him. Arum agreed and after removing his robes and completing a few light warmups, they made their way out into the meadows from where they jogged towards the mountains before making their way back to the lagoon.

It was there when Arum stopped and fell to his knees, he was having flashbacks and became distraught, his tears freely flowing. "They did things to me," he said, bending forward to hide his face, "they made me do things. I did; I did. I had to save Eliana. Each time they came to take her I offered myself just so they wouldn't touch her. I discarded my dignity to protect her, now my head won't banish the memories, they're always there."

Jacob knelt before Arum and, without permission, entered his nephews head to find the bad memories everywhere. He walked through the memories, making sure he missed nothing. When he finished, he sat back and tried to comfort him. "I saw everything," he said, "and I know you can't be blamed. You did what you had to do; there's no dishonour." Jacob then insisted he stand. "I recognise the cave where you were held captive. I've been there." He then pulled Arum closer and whispered, "He did the same to me; I know your pain. Although only two years old, it was Helena who saved my life."

"I thought I was the only one," said Arum, trying to stop his tears, "I fear Asgard will reject me when they find out the things I did."

"Who cares what others think" replied Jacob, "I'll never reject you,"

"Will the pain ever go away?" asked Arum.

"You will soon be walking among the Goddesses of the Light," replied Jacob, hoping to reassure him. "Trust me, they'll quickly take your pain away."

He thought for a moment then asked, "Do you want revenge?"

"The thought of ever travelling back to that horrible place terrifies me," replied Arum, "but yes, I definitely want revenge."

"Come," said Jacob, deciding not to swim today, "let's return to the temple."

They ran through the Yeti encampment, then the Elf encampment, and soon reached the steps of the temple. They entered through a side door and while Arum made his way to wash and prepare for breakfast, Jacob summoned Obelius, instructing him to make sure Odi, Maximus and Tristan prepared for a journey. When he was satisfied everything was in place he too made his way to freshen up.

It was still early when he and Eala arrived down for breakfast, and they were delighted Prudr, Arum and Eliana were already there. They joined them, hoping to use this time to get to know the newest members of their family before everyone else arrived. They spent a good hour together and were very comfortable in each other's company. Odi then arrived followed by Maximus, Obelius, and Tristan.

"Good, you're all here," said Jacob, "have a quick breakfast then join me out in the meadows. I want you all fully armed and ready to assist in an act of revenge. Arum is coming with us, and he will be in command. Whatever action he chooses to take, don't question it. Do I make myself clear?"

"Is there anything I can do?" asked Eala.

"Yes," replied Jacob, "I need the Earth Mothers to create six spheres, each one must be big enough to carry a War God. I intend leaving as soon as the War Gods are ready."

"Father," said Obelius, after calling Jacob aside, "you're at it again, you are supposed to run everything by me?"

"Obi," replied Jacob, "I'm bringing you with me, is that not enough? What I'm about to do has nothing to do with Olympus, it's all about Arum. He needs closure and I intend helping him find that closure. But I do need you to have my back, that's why I'm bringing you."

"My Lord Jacob," said Apollonius, who was within earshot, "far be it for me to question the decision of the God of Gods, but need I remind you that it's not the way of the gods to seek revenge."

"I'm sure the Ancient One will forgive me one small indiscretion," replied Jacob.

Out in the meadows Eala and the Earth Mothers spaced themselves roughly ten meters apart allowing them the space required to create the six spheres. When the War Gods arrived, there was no delay, they quickly entered the spheres and within seconds they levitated, at first slowly and then at speed. When they reached the stratosphere their momentum increased to a speed that was so fast they were gone in a nano-second.

On reaching their destination they found a cave large enough to conceal the spheres. They then wasted no time in entering a nearby dark and sinister tunnel that took them to an entrance reeking of evil. From that point on they were accompanied by the pitiful cries of captives, pleading for their lives, cries that churned their stomachs. Odi went ahead to investigate and when he saw what was going on he fell back against the wall, horrified. Arum also looked, reigniting his fears, totally unsettling him. Visible shivers raced through his body as he too fell back against the wall.

"I'm sorry," he gasped, looking for comfort from Jacob, "I can't do this. Look what they're doing to those poor souls. I feel their pain. I feel him inside me; he's hurting me again."

"It's ok to be afraid," said Jacob, "remember what I told you, the same thing happened to me, except, in my case it was Lucifer, one whose lust for pleasure knows no bounds. You can do this."

Jacob was furious with himself when he realised he had inadvertently revealed to others what had happened to him. He looked across at his son and could see the shock written across his face. He had no choice but to just shrug and say, "I had, and still have, the best wife, mother, and an amazing family."

Arum found the courage to again look down at the torture chamber, this time he didn't shiver. Watching the jailers brutally abuse the captives, gather their souls, and then dump their bodies into the pit, reinforced his need for revenge. He counted twenty soldiers of Shadow, and he recognised their commander to be his worst torturer and abuser. He began developing his plan.

"It's too far," he said, "we won't be able to take them by surprise." He began removing his armour, and then his tunic and skirt."

"What are you doing?" asked Odi, showing concern.

"He likes us naked," replied Arum, still trying to hold it together, "He particularly liked my body, I'm using it to distract him." As he walked away he turned back to Jacob, "when I get close, you know what to do."

Arum walked down the ramp to the sound of loud and continuous wolf-whistles that got louder when he stepped on to the platform.

"Ah," said the commander, licking his lips, "it seems my favourite plaything can't get enough of me. Coming back for more, are we? This is so unexpected; you must really love my touch. Did you miss me?"

Seeing the commander leering and licking his lips was too much for Arum but he continued to hold his nerve, inside he was cringing remembering what had happened. He continued walking until he was within smelling distance.

"Look on my naked body, see how it has matured," yelled Arum, "no longer am I a twelve-year-old boy, now I'm a God of War, and you're going to pay for what you did to me."

The commander and his soldiers thought what was happening to be amusing until Arum raised his hand to catch a sword that Jacob tossed across to him. They knew they were in trouble when a ball of light arrived and grew to be a cocoon, large enough to completely surround and protect Arum. In the few seconds, as the cocoon grew, Arum used the sword to pierce the commanders armour and with a quick flick he castrated him. He wasn't finished, he used the sword to slice his nemesis from his groin to his neck, before rapidly swinging the sword to decapitate him. He quickly leapt into the cocoon and watched as the commander's innards tumbled out into the pits below to be devoured by the hounds.

The Soldiers of Shadow then attacked but couldn't break through the cocoon. They were so engrossed in their assault they didn't hear the gods approaching from behind, but when they did, it was too late. The soldiers didn't stand a chance; such was the onslaught they suffered. They were eliminated one by one, leaving two senior soldiers to be dealt with by Arum.

Arum stepped from the cocoon and walked over to where the two soldiers were on their knees. He teased them by sliding his sword down each of their bodies, gently prodding so as to cause trickles of blood to flow. He stopped and thought better of it.

"I'm better than this," he said as he raised his sword.

"Look on me," he shouted, "a God of Asgard. I'm the last face you will ever see." He then slaughtered them.

"Your healing starts now," said Jacob, placing a cape around his shoulders.

"All the years, being abused," said Arum, getting emotional, "I longed for this day. Why does it feel so hollow?"

"Killing, no matter how just," said Odi, "always feels hollow. Trust me the pain will go away. Get dressed, we need to leave."

"Ahem," interrupted Maximus, "Uncle, look around."

They all looked around and were taken aback at the number of wretched souls that were stepping out of the shadows, there were at least fifty. Arum recognised some of them and ran to assist. He looked back and was surprised to see the gods hadn't moved.

"We need to help them," he said, looking confused.

"We can't interfere," said Tristan, "we have no choice but to leave and allow nature take its course."

Just then a young boy walked out from behind a boulder. He stared at Obelius "I know your face," he said, "your photograph, one belonging to my grandfather, has your face, it still hangs in his study."

"I'm afraid you're mistaken," said Obelius.

"Who was your grandfather?" Asked Jacob, still wearing his helmet.

"My grandfather," said the boy, "he was a friend of the God, Jacob. His name was Shane. I'm named after him."

Jacob gasped; he was shocked. Shane was never far from his thoughts; he never forgot his promise to look after his family. "Your grandfather is revered in the realm of the gods," said Jacob, "he fought bravely and was involved in the defence of the Fair Lands. He was my greatest friend."

"It's true then," said Shane, his eyes widening in shock as Jacob removed his helmet, "you really existed?"

"Uncles," interrupted Arum, "these people are victims of a terrible evil, they've been taken millions upon millions of miles away from earth, is it not our duty to right a terrible wrong? What happened here is not like a conflict between two armies on earth. They had no chance against such pure evil. It cannot be seen to win, we must assist."

"He makes a strong case," said Odi, taking Jacob aside, "the law is clear, but it only applies to earth, this is not earth."

Jacob agreed. He asked Obelius to produce a plan, then walked among the victims. He used his powers to heal them of their injuries while Odi assisted by lessening the impact of the bad memories.

Obelius left the cave and went through the tunnel to look up at the stars, he paced while trying to develop a plan. It was then when he noticed a sinister cloud approaching from where the Nothingness was said to be. He hid and watched the bulk of the cloud drift by, his anxiety growing when he concluded it was heading in the direction of Olympus. He kept watching and soon realised it wasn't a thick mist or a heavy fog, it was a murmuration of Shadow Riders, and they were travelling at such speed he worked it out they would reach earth within two weeks. As soon as it was clear, he ran back to the cave.

"Shadow has shown his hand," he said, "millions of Shadow Riders have just passed over us, I believe they're travelling towards Olympus. I estimate they'll be there within two weeks."

"Have you come up with a plan?" asked Jacob.

"Father," he replied, "we cannot use a portal, too easy to detect. Even if we split the captives equally between each sphere they wouldn't fit so I'm wondering - you have always told us of how both you and Uncle Odi have the ability to tap into the powers of all gods. If that's the case, can you tap into the power of Finn and the Little People?"

"Obelius," said Odi, "brilliant, brilliant, brilliant."

He ran over and gripped two of the men, he thought of the Fair Lands and all three shrunk to no more than six inches. He had the power, which meant Jacob also had it.

All captives were quickly shrunk and moved to one or other of the spheres and when everybody was safely on board, the six spheres levitated, then shot out into the cosmos at such speed they were undetectable when passing the Shadow Riders. What troubled Jacob was how obvious it was that the Riders were actually travelling towards Olympus.

During the journey it was established where each of the captives were from and when the spheres landed portals opened allowing each one to return to their respective homelands. That was, all except Shane, Jacob wanted to spend time with him and learn more about how his family was coping since the great battle. Before taking him home, he broke another rule, he took him to Elysium to visit the tombs of his grandparents.

Chapter 12

Jacob enjoyed his short time with young Shane but was very aware of the impending arrival of the Shadow army. He arranged for him to be safely delivered home before visiting the realms that were now under the protection of Olympus. Everywhere he went he sensed their fear and apprehensions, he also became aware that each realm was even training their elderly and younglings, and it troubled him that the sick and injured couldn't escape the ways of war; they too were being trained.

When he reached the realm of the elves he was met by the council who informed him of the visions reported by their oracles. He confirmed that he too had the same visions, he then informed them of what was witnessed by Obelius while out in the far reaches of the universe. At all times he showed his stoicism, but the senior elves sensed his fears, and when he was leaving he was approached by the oldest elf of them all, the one known as the 'Elderone'.

"Word has reached the oracles, my Lord," she said, "that man's astronomers have also detected a cloud, dark and sinister. Its travelling across the expanse of the universe. They've seen how it spreads and grows as each day passes. Star after star is shaded by its vastness. They fear it's coming to visit on them revenge for the death of Lucifer. Man is beginning to believe he has been betrayed by the gods."

"I can't worry about what man believes," replied Jacob, "what's coming is far more dangerous. Today the gods returned fifty abductees back to their homes, including children. When they speak of what they saw while travelling through space, any rumours about us not caring will be countered." While walking away he continued, "let me assure you of how aware I am of what we have to do."

He continued his walk and when he reached one of the higher dunes he turned back to look across the grasslands, and into the far meadows, were he saw many younglings being trained in the art of conflict. He believed he was watching the extinction of childhood and wondered was it right to allow that happen, this to him was one of the most painful things about war.

While walking along the beach he was startled to hear his name being called from beyond the waves. The sea was troubled, its waves showing a raging anger never before witnessed in the peaceful realm of the gods. He continued walking the sandy beach and soon reached the pebble slopes next to the deeper pools and was shocked to meet with a very dishevelled and distressed Lord Toyesh.

"Tell me my Lord," Jacob asked, "what brings the Emperor of the Mer-People into my presence?"

"All has changed," Toyesh replied, "the oceans are dying, and our food is disappearing. Creatures of the deep are no longer breeding, those that do, find their eggs are infertile. There's an extinction event happening and everything we try has failed, we need the protection of Olympus."

"And you have our protection," replied Jacob. "But I fear to ask this question, even though I must. Tell me my lord, how vast are the nations of the Mer-People?"

"Apart from the Mer-People, all aquatics have sought my protection," said Toyesh, "over the last few days they arrived at Mer city and there are now over three hundred thousand."

Jacob was shocked, and for a moment he wondered what he could do. He didn't wonder for too long, as the God of Gods he knew he had the power to do things that seemed impossible. He entered the water and placed his hand into the waves, calling any passing whale into his presence, he was soon answered. He mounted the whale that arrived and guided it towards the horizon, next to the rim of the Olympus shield. Those near the beach witnessed an amazing sight, Jacob gliding across the sea just like the Whale Riders of legend.

On reaching the shield he noticed a hint of redness drifting through the water and concluded the attack on the seas had now reached Olympus. He summoned more whales and sent them to collect Apollo, Ares, Obelius, and Demetrius, with instructions to transport them out to join him. He then directed Demetrius to use his powers to invite all creatures of the deep to make their way to Olympus.

Demetrius crouched and placed his hand on his whale's head, the whale slowly submerged allowing him to then place his hands in the water and send out his Light. It travelled to all oceans and reached the deepest trenches, but it wasn't strong enough. Back in the temple Gaia, Helena, Hemish, and Sagal sensed what he was doing and rushed to assist, their combined power got so strong all creatures answered, and they came from everywhere.

The spawn of all fish, crustaceans and molluscs led the way. They were followed by the few remaining shoals of endangered species. Then came the larger fish - the cod, salmon, tuna, and sharks. They were followed by the mammalians - the dolphins and whales.

Jacob was joined by a now very concerned Toyesh. "The lagoon is full," he said, "there's no room for my people, what have you done?"

"Fear not my friend," replied Jacob, "watch."

He instructed the gods and their whales to exit the shield and assist in the protecting of the Mer-nations. He then called for the assistance of the Titan, Oceanus.

"How can I be of assistance?" he asked, on arrival.

"It's time the oceans went to sleep," replied Jacob.

Oceanus knew exactly what he had to do. He called on a primordial, yet very potent magic, and sent it out across the lagoon into the open seas. Within seconds creature after creature fell into sleep, all floating while waiting on Oceanus to provide their place of rest.

He began by descending to the depths to move his hands along the sea-bed, disturbing the sands, and churning the oceans into a murky and dark seascape. By the time he was finished all sea life was gone, safely buried, and protected deep beneath the ocean floor. When the churned-up sands had settled and the sea floor was pristine again, the absolute protection of all sea life was now complete.

Jacob looked towards the beach and was delighted to see Sunniva had arrived, she was with Amma and Eliana and they were preparing to do their part. Sunniva and Eliana used their powers as Sun Goddesses to direct the healing rays of the sun into every part of the lagoon. Amma was an untested Creator Goddess, but her powers were getting stronger since she arrived in Olympus. She used those same powers to assist the germination of any floating seeds so that sea grasses could grow, marine algae could return, and the kelp forests could find their place. She then woke some of the sleeping spawn and assisted them to rapidly mature to quickly begin reproducing. Soon the lagoon was clear and again teeming with life.

Jacob was pleased but he knew the hardest part was yet to come; he was still concerned that the lagoon was too small for the thousands of Mer-People waiting to enter. He told Oceanus of his plan, and he agreed to remain and assist. Together they opened a portal and stood guard as the nations of the seas entered.

When all were through it soon confirmed that the lagoon was in fact too small, forcing Jacob to modify his plan. He placed Apollo, Ares, Oceanus, Obelius and himself in a straight line roughly five hundred meters apart and together they used their powers to push the rim of the shield further out to sea, creating a much larger sea area ensuring the Mer-nations were more comfortable. When this was completed Oceanus bade his farewell and returned to Elysium while the gods made their way back to the beach.

The arrival of the Mer-Nations caused great wonderment and excitement among the teenage Astrals from all realms. The legendary beauty of the Mermaids and the handsomeness of the Mermen sent hormones racing. Soon the beach was almost empty as most of the teenagers entered the water to mingle among the new arrivals. Jacob saw this as an opportunity for him to leave and continue his walk back to the temple. When he neared the gardens he was pleased to see Eala waiting for him.

"That was a beautiful thing you did today," she said, snuggling closer to him, "the Sea Gods will forever be in your debt."

"No," he replied, enjoying her embrace, "there will be no debt. Without life in the seas nothing on land can exist, all will be extinct. I wonder is that his plan. If it is, we have thwarted it and with a bit of luck he will never know."

These were his most favourite moments, he loved sitting alone with Eala in his arms, he could tell her everything and know she'd always use the right words to cheer him up, but he never expected the reaction he got when he whispered, "I've achieved so much during my short time as a god, why then do I feel such a failure?"

"In all my years I've never met a god so insecure," she yelled, while getting to her feet and pointing her finger, "you need a good kicking. You're getting on my nerves, and if I stay I'll only say something I'll regret." She began walking away.

"What did I say?" responded a shocked Jacob.

"You said," she replied, as she turned back to be almost face to face with him "'Why do I feel such a failure' that's what you said, I've listened to you time and time again question yourself, I've had enough. You're the God of God's. You were the beacon of light that rallied all armies to win the war of the End Times. You sent the goddesses to give Earth its next age. You are father to three powerful Gods of the Light. You are a son of the most powerful God of Thunder and brother to three War Gods. Need I go on? Just go and grow a pair." She stormed off and left him with his mouth open.

From behind a nearby wall Odi stepped out, and with an 'ear to ear' smile said, "Who's in the doghouse now?" He sat with Jacob and then inched closer, Jacob moved away, and Odi again inched even closer.

"What are you up to?" he asked.

"I'm just trying to see what it feels like to be sitting in your spot after that roasting," replied Odi.

"She didn't hold back," said Jacob with a nervous laugh, "she must be getting lessons from your other half."

"It seems we've both landed two tough ones," said Odi, "but do you know what I like the most about my rows with Panya, it's the making up. Phew, every time I think about it I always end up breathless sometimes even a bit sore."

"Eh" laughed Jacob, moving away, "too much information."

"Don't knock it until you try it," retorted Odi. He then said, "On a serious note, Eala is right. As one king to another, you really should be more self-assured. You have a new crisis coming and all pantheons are depending on you being assertive. Let's break our deal, the next time you feel unsure, nervous, or even scared, enter my head. Together we'd be formidable. I will be a great help to you." He sniggered then continued, "The only thing to remember is, I'm still quite young and have thoughts I prefer to keep private; you must keep them to yourself."

"You forget," replied Jacob, enjoying the conversation, "remember that time I entered your head uninvited, I saw things that scarred me for life. Pervert."

"Ah, but just think of the things you learned," responded Odi, "I bet if the truth be known, you were jealous."

"I love you brother," replied Jacob, slapping Odi across the back of the neck as he got up to leave, "I don't know what I'd do without you?"

Jacob left, and again had doubts, no matter what Eala and Odi said he was still unsure. Nothing seemed to lessen the fears he had about letting Olympus down. He arrived at his room, washed, and changed, then made his way back to the Great Hall to sit upon his throne. He was alone, wanting time to mull over all what had happened over the last few days.

The stewards were very considerate of his feelings and always discreetly checked on him. "My Lord," said the chief steward, "once before I stood here and watched a powerful king sit on that very throne, he was troubled and didn't seem to know what to do. That king was Zeus, I encouraged him to wear his crown and cape, sit up straight, and allow what troubles him fade. He did what was asked and soon he began feeling the power of the Light. I ask you, allow me to fetch your crown and place it upon your head. You will feel that same relief and I promise you will then know what to do."

Jacob nodded and waited for the steward to return, and when he did he placed the crown on Jacob's head, and the cape over his shoulders. He then placed an amulet around his neck, stepped back, bowed, and left.

Jacob closed his eyes and waited for relief. It was slow in coming but when it did he felt his strength and confidence grow. He kept his eyes closed, seeking out all that was bothering him. In his mind he compartmentalised everything and then a pattern emerged. He saw the attack on Isidra, then the probing against the Titans, he saw Drayce being tracked into Olympus and how Shadow used him to breach its defences. He then saw the seeds being sown beginning the search for Thanases and Modi and how it was a ploy to remove the senior gods from Olympus allowing the attack on Thora. He still couldn't see who was leading the attacks but knew it was someone using old magic and who was well concealed. Every now and again he saw a mist, a black Shadow and wondered, he felt he saw that mist once before but couldn't quite remember. He thought of Shadow's abilities and how it was able to locate Olympus even while hiding out in space, confirming his decision to move Olympus back to earth was the correct one. He then thought of his mother and how, in his mind she dragged him back through the dungeons to see the stake that held his tormented and naked body. How she showed him that Shadow was in fact Lucifer reborn. He worried if his brothers really didn't think less of him, but he quickly dismissed those thoughts when the memories of his earlier banter with Odi bounced into his head.

His mind took him back to his time living in Dublin and he remembered how happy he was. He loved the way his friends, especially Shane, always kept him grounded, causing a tear to form when he thought of his best friend lying in the tombs of Elysium. He thought of earth before the war of the End Times and wondered was it there where Shadow dwelled. He opened his eyes and felt he could see clearly again.

He stood to leave for the meadows but stopped. There was a presence, and it was getting more forceful. The amulet lit up, emitting a muted glow. It was the Light, and it was giving him a new strength, a strength he only felt once before. His cape fell from his shoulders and his robes changed to a pure white before they tightened around his body. Golden armour appeared, covering his chest, torso, and hips. His two hands stretched out and then retracted after gripping a Light created sword and staff. A brilliant white cape appeared and rested over his shoulders, while at the same time his crown tightened around his head, its gems glowing, sending their light in all directions.

He, only for the third time, stood as the most powerful Warrior God. His aura brightened as his amulet continued to attract the brilliant white source light. It became so bright the temple failed to contain it as it burst through the main doors attracting the attention of all in the meadows and along the seashore.

When he reached the doors he acknowledged Athena who was still doing her duty as guardian of the temple. He continued walking until he reached the highest step where his light was now blinding. Those watching from across the beach, grasslands, meadows, and woodlands, shielded their eyes before going to their knees and bowing in homage to their God of Gods.

"I see my little rant worked?" Eala said as she joined him.

"You never told me you had started taking lessons from Panya," he replied.

"Poor Odi," she said, moving closer to place her hands on his hips, "Panya really does have him under her thumb."

Jacob turned his head to his right; he was listening to pleadings and sensed terrible despair. He opened a new portal allowing a very distressed party of once powerful deities emerge. They were the remnants of what was left of the mighty Mesoamerican pantheon and their escorts. Many had great difficulty going to their knees, or even bowing, but Jacob didn't expect them to. He hurried them through and then used his powers to begin their healing. He continued using his powers to clean them and restore their robes and brilliant coloured head dresses back to their pristine best.

"So few of you remain!" he said, offering his sympathy, "why didn't you call for help? Olympus is in your debt; we would have answered."

"There was no time," replied Cizan, "everything was so sudden, we were ill-prepared, overwhelmed by a more cunning and vicious foe. We had no chance and as you can see, many fell."

"My lord Cizan," said Jacob, "I fear even Olympus is unsafe, but I have a plan. Work with my stewards and build your encampment, wait for my call." He then called a steward to escort them to a location near the Yeti encampment.

"I need you to walk among the realms," he said to Eala, "arrange for the young and infirm to prepare for a big event in the temple. They'll know it's time when they hear the trumpet of the Archangel." She left and made the arrangements.

Chapter 13

Jacob re-entered the temple and was joined by his brothers, his sons and all the young War Gods. Ares and Apollo were last to arrive. He said nothing for a while, he was waiting on the oracles, the wizards as well as the council of the elves. When they arrived, he telepathically began revealing his plan for the protection of the realms. "Apollo, Ares," he said, summoning them to the lowest steps, "open the gateways."

They each located stone effect caps that were so well concealed they went unnoticed for millennia. It took all their strength to extract the four-inch diameter steel ropes, hidden within. When enough was retracted they began tugging, and then pulling, causing the surrounding steps to part, revealing a wide passageway leading down to vaults hidden deep beneath the temple.

When the entrance was fully opened, and wide enough, Jacob turned to Viktor.

"Go to the terrace," he said, "Let an Archangels trumpet blare and send its sound out into the heavens."

Viktor immediately left and stood at the rim of the grass terrace where he was sure all realms would hear his call. From his back, magnificent and brilliant white wings unfurled allowing his Light to illuminate out into the meadows, transforming him to be an Archangel. When he blew his trumpet, its sound was so loud, no one failed to hear its call, in their thousands they answered.

From the various realms columns of children as well as the elderly began moving across the meadows, escorted by their warriors. They processed into the temple to make their way through the Great Hall towards the entrance to the vaults. They bowed while passing Jacob, never having seen him so close and in all his glory, they were awestruck. He was their God of Gods and with his Light shining so brightly they knew that, wherever he was sending them, they would be safe. There were to be no delays, each realm was instructed to quickly make their way down the passageways into safety.

The first to arrive were the centaurs led by Queen Zephyra and Lord Polkan and they quickly made their way into the vaults. When they were all through Jacob turned to Chiron. "You are their God," he said, "go with them, they're still suffering, and will need your calming ways." Chiron then left.

The centaurs were followed by the Little People led by Danu and Faer. Young and old, their translucent wings were spread wide, at times flapping, bringing a cool breeze into the temple. They, like the Centaurs rapidly made their way into the vaults. Aoife, Lir, and Aodh moved to join them, but were stopped by Jacob. "The cunning, speed and power of you three will be required for the battle against the armies of Shadow, I need you here, fighting by my side."

Next to arrive were the ten realms of elf kind. When they reached the throne they bowed before entering the passageway. They were joined by Ellaweise and the council. When the last elf went out of view, Jacob turned to the Wizards and the Oracles.

"You carry great power," he said, "you are the ancients, the guides, and hold within you the wisdom of the ages. You will be needed to assist in the rebuilding of all realms if what's coming goes wrong." There was no discussion, the wizards and oracles immediately entered the passageway.

The elves were quickly followed by those from the Indus, the Asian, the Mesoamerican, and the African Pantheons. They were led in by Jomo, Jahiri, Garuda and Girish, accompanied by Oba, Jamilah, Manasa, and Mulan. Watching this procession was the most difficult for Jacob, this time he was watching eight of his closest friends take on the responsibility of protecting four ancient pantheons, and they would have to do it alone. He knew where he was sending them was safe but he still worried, Shadow seems to know his every move.

Jacob looked across at Drayce and nodded, prompting him to extract his Lyre and begin strumming. Soon the footsteps of thousands of dragons was heard. Drayce began singing the 'Song of the Dragons' when the lead dragon entered the temple and for him, it was very emotional. Tears filled his eyes while watching his people being led by his grandparents, followed by his aunts and uncles. He acknowledged his close friend, Galyna, when he saw the sad and lonely figure of Andras, her father, walk by. He continued singing and repeated the song time and time again until all dragons had entered the vaults.

Next to arrive was the Yeti nation who were still in their human form. Their pure white hair draped down beyond the collars of their robes and capes. Their pale blue eyes were all that broke their sad faces. They were still deep in grief for all those they lost, but no matter how sad they were they acknowledged the gods, especially Cetan and Yeshe, the sons of Yaz.

At the rear of the procession was a young Yeti boy, no more than thirteen or fourteen years old. He seemed very distressed and unsure about following his people. Drayce noticed and joined him. "Tell me young Yeti," he said, "why so scared? You look as though you're about to run away."

"I am Yasna," said the boy, "grandson of Yaz. I'm a weakling, my power and strength never came to me. My brothers, sisters, cousins, and friends, all walk up ahead as warriors of the Yeti nation. I'm so ashamed."

Drayce attempted to comfort him, "I too was left behind when my powers failed to show," he said, "but now look into my eyes and feel my power. I'm King of the Dragons and believe me when I say, you are in the realm of Olympus, the God of God will answer your prayers. Bow to him as you pass, and soon after your powers will show themselves to be your friend."

The boy briskly moved to catch up with his people. On his way he acknowledged Cetan and Yeshe, his uncles, he then bowed to Jacob. What he didn't notice was Jacob raising his right index finger and sending a beam of light towards him. The boy continued his walk and entered the passageway, unaware he had been given his powers.

The sound of a slow drumbeat was then heard; it was Asgard. The drumbeat maintained its steady rhythm, growing louder as it approached. The procession was led by Prudr, Vidar and Hermod, and on arrival into the temple, they were joined by Thor, Maria, Thanases, and Irina. Jacob turned to Thora. "It's time for your daughter to leave, pass Astrid to Irina. It's for her own safety."

Thora was upset but knew her daughter's safety was more important. She looked out the doors in the hope of catching Viktor's eye, but he was too busy monitoring the shield. She felt very alone.

Jacob left his throne to watch Asgard pass into the vaults. He was particularly watching out for Baldor. "Magni insists you stay," he said on meeting him, "something about your beacon being needed before this day is out."

"My beacon?" asked Baldor, his face getting red.

"I know," whispered Jacob, "I think he's after a bit more than your beacon." The redness in Baldor's face intensified.

The Asgardians continued their walk into the vaults and soon it was only the stewards, servants and the palace guards that were left. They had earlier gathered at the rear of the temple while waiting for the last of the statues to be covered and all torches extinguished. When ready, and as one mass movement, they made their way into the vaults.

Jacob left the temple to view the meadows; he was happy to see them cleared. Other than the ten stone thrones used by the Elves, all traces of the encampments had gone, but he was concerned when he saw the white horses still grazing and the Mer-Armies still patrolling."

"Summon the Mystic gods," he said as Viktor joined him, "their powers are required to protect the herds as well as the Mer-People."

Viktor soon returned with Demetrius, Hemish, Gaia, Amma, Kitaka and Aja, and after explaining what was required, they immediately went into action. They stood at the edge of the terrace and together sent out their Light, opening a portal at the far side of the lagoon. The portal allowed the Mer-People pass through into safety, taking them into another dimension, hiding all traces of their existence.

At the same time the horses cantered, then galloped towards the lagoon. They raced into the waves, turning into a raging white foam as they submerged, before totally disappearing. Jacob was now satisfied the meadows were completely empty, he returned into the temple and again sat on his throne.

The Great Hall was empty except for Apollo and Ares; Jacob asked them to leave and wait on the terrace. He remained on his throne as though waiting on something else to happen. Something else did happen; the strange light he witnessed and wondered about some weeks earlier reappeared. This time it had split in two and instead of being behind him, it was now before him.

The two lights changed and took their human form; one was male, the other female. "It takes a lot to waken us," said the male, "we sense fear everywhere and the coming desolation disturbs us. We are not happy."

"We are the First Ones and from us came the Titans," said the female, "from them came the Olympians, and from them it seems comes the end."

"Why speak of the end," asked Jacob, "when you know we've already fought off The Darkness and won. Man, and the Gods lived on."

"What's coming," said the lady, "is out of space and time, living in Shadow. You will need us before this battle is over. We are here to offer our services."

"I've been chosen by the Ancient One," said Jacob, while at the same time, accepting their offer, "this Shadow, or shall we call him Lucifer?, must have a weakness. We just haven't found it yet."

"Tell me young god," said the male, "do you know who we are?"

"I do," replied Jacob, "when you said, 'out of us came the Titans' that was the clue. You can only be Uranus, known as Father Sky." He turned to the lady, "And you can only be Gaia, Mother Earth. My great, great, grandparents." He then bowed to them.

In the meantime, on the beaches of Elysium, the twelve Titans were on alert, standing guard, protecting the tombs. At night they never took their eyes from the approaching Shadow Riders that were now coming from different regions of the universe. As the hours passed they were getting more alarmed by the vastness of the army Olympus was soon to face. For Cronus, the protection of Elysium was his number one priority, but he was very aware that the protection of Olympus was far more important. He decided they should all travel to assist in the defence of the temple but before they travelled he asked Oceanus to churn up the seas and use its power to deposit vast volumes of sand and pebbles on the beaches.

Oceanus instinctively knew what Cronus was planning and arranged for a raging tempest to stir up the sea. Within minutes tons upon tons of sand and pebbles were deposited on the beaches. A violent wind arrived to blow the deposited sand and pebbles further inland, covering the tombs and headstones. Even the mausoleum was completely engulfed. When the winds abated Rhea used her Earth Mother powers to call on Mother Nature to send the seeds of the sturdy Marram grass and they came. She also requested a selection of flowering shrubs. They quickly germinated and soon the grass grew, the shrubs sprouted, and the camouflage was complete.

Back in Olympus the gods were now out on the terrace, others on the steps. They were waiting on Jacob and getting anxious. Those gods with acute hearing got more alarmed as the sound of hooves, although still faint, were getting closer. When they heard the slow pounding of footsteps they became even more alarmed, not knowing where the footsteps were coming from. They needn't have been feared, it was the Titans, and they were making their way through the shield. They were in their colossus form but as they approached the temple, they shrunk to take their human form. Drayce, having met them in the past, stepped forward to greet Cronus and Rhea, he welcomed them and then introduced them to those he knew were related to them.

Obelius was watching the arrival of the Titans and decided to alert his father. On entering the Great Hall, he was shocked to see two menacing looking strangers. He drew his sword and ran towards the throne ready to do battle.

"There's no threat here," said Jacob, gesturing for Obelius to put his sword away, "come and meet the First Ones, they're your three times great grandparents."

"Aah," Uranus said, "a fiery one, strong and brave. I see in you a guardian of Olympus. This pleases me." He rested his hand on the side of Obelius's head. "I see Shadow fears you, he intends destroying you; he sees in you the one who will bring him down."

Gaia approached him. "I give you a gift that will shield you from his gaze," she said, before pausing, looking troubled. She then placed both hands upon his head. "He knows of your babies, he knows Aria is pregnant and plans to target her. He hasn't forgotten how, in the past, he failed to capture you when you were unborn; he believes you are a favourite of the Ancient One and will not rest until you're dead, your babies are in danger."

"My mother suggested Lucifer still lives," interrupted Jacob, trying not to be distracted by the news Obelius was going to be a father, "what you've just said confirms her belief. Lucifer lives, now we know for sure whom it is we fight."

"There is no more to say," said Uranus while backing away, "I sense the Titans have reached the terraces. It's time I made my peace before the Shadow Riders arrive." He and Gaia then left.

"Do I congratulate you or call you a careless prick?" asked Jacob, showing his annoyance.

"I don't know how it happened," replied Obelius, still in shock.

"We did tell you about the birds and the bees," continued Jacob, sarcastically furrowing his brow. "Remember when we had the 'Talk'? You obviously weren't listening. It was careless of you considering you knew Shadow is everywhere."

"Father," asked Obelius, "what'll I do?"

"What will you Do? You're asking me? How about 'God Up,' take responsibility."

Obelius was in turmoil, he was concerned and started backing away. "I'm going to take her away," he said, "she doesn't deserve this. It's our family Shadow hates."

"No!" said Jacob, firmly laying down the law, "you will stay and protect Olympus; that's your duty. Aria will be protected; she's not the only goddess who's pregnant, but she is the one who is most in danger. Trust me."

Jacob sought out Eala and asked her to use her Light to identify all those who were pregnant. She did as requested and after sending out her light she called Helena, Aria, Sagal and Lovisa to follow her.

Jacob's face was priceless, he already knew Helena was pregnant and had just found out his son was to become a father. Having the girls stand before him brought it home how life in Olympus just moves on. "In the past," he said, when he composed himself, and speaking directly to Helena, "my instincts would have told me to go for Drayce and kick him across the universe, but I need him. How am I supposed to deal with this?"

"What are you talking about?" said a confused Helena, "Drayce has done nothing wrong."

"It's not about Drayce," said Eala, "it's the fact Aria, Lovisa and Sagal are also pregnant."

Sagal was first to react, "I found out a few days ago and I'm so happy, Finn and I love each other, our parents are thrilled knowing all our children will grow together as Children of the Light." She turned to hug Aria and Lovisa, and knew by the looks on their faces that it was best to say no more.

"I'm about to send you away," said Jacob, standing from his throne and showing he wasn't impressed, "your new task is to protect your babies, they will be the future of the gods if all goes wrong."

He asked Eala to summon Drayce, Obelius and Finn. "Who were you with?" he asked, turning to Lovisa.

Lovisa was still shocked and had difficulty answering. "I'd prefer not to say," she eventually said.

"Tell me now," he asked again. "Who is the child's father. Who is he?" Lovisa again refused to answer.

"I have no time for this," said Jacob, starting to get angry, "I need to know now." Lovisa still refused to answer so he broke one of his own rules; he entered Lovisa's head and quickly established who the father was. He turned to Eala. "Summon Zane."

Aria, Helena, and Sagal put their own situation aside while trying to process this latest news. They slowly turned their heads to stare at Lovisa. "You dark horse," said Aria, "I'm impressed. Zane? You were with Zane? Where? When?"

"Never mind the where and when," said Helena, "how did you snare him, he's the most stand-offish and private of the War Gods. He's never shown any interest in girls. What have you got that the rest of us don't? He's the brute of Africa; you have to tell us everything."

Eala arrived back with the four very confused looking War Gods in tow. Obelius immediately went over to embrace Aria. "The 'First One' told me you're pregnant," he said, "he said babies but didn't say if they were twins or triplets. Please tell me you're happy." She just nodded.

Finn hugged Sagal. "What's going on?" he asked.

"Two bits of news," she said, "we are not the only ones expecting a baby. The other will upset you: they're sending me away."

"It seems I too will be sent away," said Helena, while embracing Drayce. He went to react but thought better of it when he looked up at Jacob; he thought he saw fire in his eyes.

182

"Shit," he said, "I think he's going to kill me."

"Don't worry," replied Helena, squeezing his hand, "he'd have to get through me first, anyway he said he needs you,"

Obelius and Drayce joined Zane, both placing their arms across his shoulders.

"You dirt bag," said Obelius, "when were you going to tell us. You and Lovisa together! Who would have thought?"

"What are you on about?" said Zane, still looking very confused, "why am I here?" Lovisa broke the news. "It seems you got me pregnant!"

"No, no, no, no," replied a horrified Zane, while pacing back and forth, "we only...once, in the dunes? My first time." He placed his hands to his head. "This can't be," he continued, "I don't really know you...no, no."

"In that case," said Lovisa, "there's no need to worry. If that's how you feel; I'm quite capable of raising a baby on my own. When this battle is over I'll be helping rebuild Asgard and you can go 'find yourself' in Africa.

"You don't understand," he said, gently gripping her, "since the first time I saw you, that day we all arrived, you stood on the steps, so striking, so beautiful, you took my breath away. You never showed any interest in me, so I stayed away, afraid I'd lose you as a friend. They call me a brute, look at the size of me, why would you be interested in someone like me?"

"A brute?" she said, taking his hand, "that you are, but you are a brute who is tender and loving, two nights ago it was you who took my breath away."

"The size of him," sniggered Drayce, "I'd bet he did." He got a clatter from Helena.

"Ladies," interrupted Jacob, "there will be no battle for any of you, it's time to go, enter the passageway and seek out my mother, she will help. Your babies are all of the Light and will soon be born."

The boys began to react, but one stare from Jacob and they knew they were to keep their mouths shut. They remained in the temple until the girls went out of view and Apollo and Ares had sealed the entrance, leaving no trace of its existence. They then left to take up their positions out in the meadows.

Jacob watched them leave and looked around at the now covered statues and wondered how it all came to this. He sat back on his throne, listening carefully to the gathering of Shadow Riders out on the rim of earth's star system, he just wanted to scream. He worried for mankind but was convinced that this time the coming battle was nothing to do with Man; it was to do with the destruction of the gods. He knew he had to hold it together and show those outside how he was in control.

He decided to put in place the rest of the sleeping Olympus army knowing it was an army created to defend the temple and to protect the God of Gods when all seemed lost. He tapped three times on his throne's right armrest and said, "Wake up, soldiers of Zeus, your time has come."

He made his way out to the terrace and was pleased to see all gods lined up and ready for action. Looking back towards the door he saw that Ares, Apollo, Athena, and Eris were well prepared and looking formidable, they were the ancient gods, the ones entrusted with the absolute protection of the main entrance to the temple.

Standing several meters ahead of them, on the top step, stood Sofia, Sunniva, Aoife, and Eliana as well as Eala and Panya, six powerful Goddesses of the Light. The six Mystic Gods - Demetrius, Hemish, Amma, Gaia, Kitaka and Aja, were six steps lower: each one levitated, and sitting in the lotus position, hovering three feet above the steps, their eyes closed, in deep meditation. The War Gods - Hai, Li, Zane, Finn, Aodh, Lir, Cetan, and Yeshe, were at the base of the temple steps alongside six grandchildren of Odin

- Obelius, Maximus, Magnar, Tristan, Thora, and Arum. He was pleased to see the four Dragons, Drayce, Galyna, Isidra, and Osian, standing upon the portico and ready to take to the sky.

He looked out into the meadows to see that the First Ones, and the twelve Titans, had put aside their differences, they had formed a protective perimeter around the temple. What surprised him was they had all turned to stone.

From his position, standing alongside his three brothers, he saw Viktor climb to the roof of the folly, his wings spread, and his sword drawn. It was then when he saw Baldor standing at the centre of the meadows with his staff raised towards the heavens.

Jacob's curiosity was noticed by Magni who said, "Trust me, what Baldor is about to do is necessary."

Baldor called on his light and when it came it shot out through the shield into the realm of man. "Wow," said Magni, "Baldor certainly knows how to use the Light. He stands there as a God of Asgard, the beacon of light that will lead us home. Who would have thought he'd be the one who takes my breath away."

Baldor remained where he was until the light disappeared, he then returned to take his place next to Magni.

Jacob was satisfied all plans were now in place, especially with the arrival of the Titans, and the First Ones. He was still wondering why they had turned to twenty-foot-high stone statues but surmised there had to be a good reason.

"All I'm waiting for is the arrival of the soldiers of Zeus."

"The Who?" enquired Modi.

"Watch!" said Jacob.

When they arrived, it was nothing short of spectacular. Two rectangular shaped openings appeared, fifty meters away from the lowest step. Both openings had steep ramps that travelled beneath the temple and were wide enough to allow large columns of soldiers to quickly exit.

A slow rhythmic drumbeat was heard coming from deep in the caverns, getting louder as company after company, each consisting of two hundred fully armed soldiers, marched out to take up strategic positions all around the temple grounds. As soldiers, they looked impressive, each one wearing bright white tunics beneath body hugging silver armour. Even their capes made them stand out, heavily embroidered using silver threads highlighting the symbols of a warrior of Olympus. Their helmets were designed to give absolute protection to their heads and necks, but it was their shields and weapons that made them formidable.

When the emergence of the soldiers of Zeus ceased, it was followed by platoon after platoon of airborne warriors, each one riding fearsome flying griffins that immediately took to the sky, taking up positions near the rim of the shield; they were to be the first line of defence.

When all was in place the openings closed, and an eerie silence descended across the meadows. There was a palpable uneasiness in the air and the atmosphere was so tense a pin dropping would easily be heard. Magni's anxious eyes glanced back towards his sons, and he was reassured when he saw they were well prepared, both looking unafraid.

Modi uncomfortably shifted from leg to leg while his sweaty, nervous hands continuously grasped and un-grasped his sword. Odi shuffled his feet against the soft grass showing how rattled he was. It was the calm before the storm, and this coming storm was destined to be one that will never be forgotten. It will be written about for all time. Jacob just stood, didn't move, and said nothing.

Several hours had passed when Jacob looked back towards the temple, seeking reassurance from Eala, he slightly nodded and smiled when she blew him a kiss.

"She really is the love of your life," said Odi, "what would you do without her?"

"How lucky have I been?" Jacob replied, "she's the one who makes my life worth living, makes me feel on top of the world, and is the keeper of my heart."

"Are you OK brother?" asked Modi.

"Leave him be," snapped Magni, "can't you see how the divine gifts, given to him by the Ancient One, have helped him put together the greatest defence of this realm; even I cannot see any flaws."

"My mouth has never been this dry," said Jacob, looking across at Modi, "it reminds me of a child's sand pit during a long and hot summer. I'm surprised you cannot hear my heartbeat; it feels as though my chest is about to burst."

"Strange how no sound comes from the meadows," remarked Odi. "Where are the birds? Are they so wise that they too have left? Even the waves have stopped crashing against the shore. Strange."

Chapter 14

Several more hours passed, and the quietness got more unsettling. A light breeze developed, changing the atmosphere. The Soldiers of Zeus maintained their readiness, not flinching, not moving, even when the approaching wind caused their capes to flap gently before getting wilder. Hidden among them were the griffins and their riders, they had earlier changed their strategy and left their positions near the shield, choosing to hide among the ground troops, they were primed and ready to launch at a moment's notice.

On the terraces, the gods showed they were ready to defend the temple, each one now fully in tune with Jacob's thoughts knowing everything entering his mind was immediately being shared. Still the only movement was the flapping of their capes.

In the line of the War Gods, it was noticed how Arum was agitated and fidgeting.

"Cousin," said Obelius, "hold it together, it won't be long now."

"There's something bothering me," responded Arum, "I need to speak with Jacob. Will he be annoyed if I break rank?"

"If you think it's important," replied Obelius, "you must speak your mind. I can help" He raised his finger to his head and telepathically contacted Jacob.

"Father," he said, "Arum is troubled; he needs to talk to you."

Jacob summoned him and asked what was bothering him.

"Uncle," he said, "that time, while in the spheres, and travelling across the cosmos, we saw the size of the approaching army and none of us remarked on how light they were travelling. No baggage or satchels, wearing just the clothes on their back, and they carried only the weapons we could see. Remember the planets we passed? Those planets didn't sustain life so there was no food available to them. The Shadow Riders will be ravenous and the only food available will be….?"

"What are you suggesting?" interrupted Modi, getting more concerned.

"They need to feed," replied Arum, "In the past I saw them tear flesh from the bone and then grind the bone until nothing is left. Look out beyond the shield; see how the only food available is here on earth. What is coming is such a vast army they will pick earth clean in a matter of hours. They will feed on every human and every creature; then we will be dealing with a well-fed army."

"We put in place the greatest Astral Army since the battle of the End Times," yelled Jacob, trying to contain his anger, "one that may not be as vast as what's coming, but is far stronger. Look around and see how we've thought of everything. How in the name of Zeus did we miss this? I don't believe it." Magni said nothing for a moment, getting pleasure out of Jacob's reaction. He then said, with a wide smirk on his face, "O ye, of little faith. Brothers, brothers. Tell me, who am I?"

"For pity's sake," yelled Jacob, "I've no time for games."

"Magni," said Odi, "there are times I could kill you; this is too serious to joke about."

"As Magni said, 'O ye, of little faith'," interrupted Baldor, "he asked as to who you think he is? Well, let me remind you. He is Magni, War God of Asgard, known as the greatest tactician and strategist. Be assured he has acted."

"'O ye, of little faith'" said Jacob, trying not to explode, "that's a term my friend Shane always used when we were in school. What the fuck? What have you done?"

"There's an old Magic only known to the ancient gods," said Magni, turning to face Arum, "I too am one of those ancient gods." He embraced Arum. "I'm so proud to have you as a nephew," he said, "I too thought of how, when, and where the Shadow Riders would feed. I saw their ravenous appetite and remembered how they savaged my beloved Bel Marduk, and I wondered." He walked over to Jacob. "You didn't question when I sent Baldor to the meadows, you trusted me. When Baldor sent out his light it was laced with the old magic I spoke of, and because of Baldor it's now dispersed throughout earth, there is no life to view, all is gone, protected, and shielded by that same magic."

Jacob and Odi blinked and disappeared, they travelled to London, Moscow, Brisbane, among other cities, before visiting the Serengeti and Yellowstone. They quickly established that what Magni said was true. They returned to Olympus and retook their place out on the terrace.

Soon after they returned, the sun faded, its light diminished. The forces of Shadow had arrived, and they were a force of many millions. They completely surrounded Olympus and their incessant pounding off the shield became grating. Then everything quietened, allowing a rasping and sinister voice to be heard, at times it was a booming voice, so strong it shook the walls of the temple.

"Boy King," it yelled, "I see and feel your fear."

For Jacob to be called 'Boy King' again confirmed he was dealing with a re-born Lucifer, and this troubled him. Memories of his torture and defilement rushed back and rattled him. Odi entered his head. "Brother," he said, trying to reassure him, "put those thoughts from your mind, you are God of Gods, be that God of Gods." Jacob appreciated Odi's words of support.

"My friend Lucifer," he said, using a sneering tone, "our paths cross again. Be aware, this time you don't frighten me. You might have deceived me up to now but no more. Tell me, how is it you are still so devoid of sympathy? How is it you are the bringer of so much brutality, ferocity, horror, and savagery? What makes you think you can get away with crushing peaceful worlds, peaceful nations, and slaughtering all before you with impunity?"

"Crushing peaceful nations?" replied Lucifer, "Slaughtering? Can't you see I have an army to feed and what better place to quell the pangs of hunger then using the bounty earth has to offer? So many creatures, so many men, women, and children: Oh! The children; the children so young and tender: A meal to relish."

Jacob crossed his arms and teasingly smiled, while at the same time, he was scouring the shield looking for the source of the voice. He counted seven possible sightings but wasn't sure. "Did no one tell you?" he said, hoping to identify where the voice was coming from, "your spies must have been sleeping."

Lucifer remained quiet for a moment before demanding to know what Jacob meant. He wasn't left wondering for too long.

"Earth has been emptied; the gods have outsmarted you. There's no flesh for your minions to tear, no bones for them to crush. All that's left is a vast and empty wilderness. Your army will starve this day."

There was a sudden burst of anger, but it was quickly suppressed when a pitchfork appeared and scraped against the shield before skewering the nearest riders.

"No matter," said Lucifer, trying to quell his anger, "we see your army, there are many, and they'll be enough to feed us this coming night."

Jacob raised his staff and used its power to raise the shield by two meters, allowing many thousands of Shadow Riders to enter Olympus from all directions. He timed it perfectly before quickly closing it again, incinerating about a thousand riders in the process. Those who entered didn't wait to catch their breath; they were ravenous and quickly attacked. Many others took to the sky expecting to feast upon any flying creature they found.

Odi turned to Drayce and signalled to him that it was time for the dragons to take to the Sky. From above the portico Drayce, Galyna, Isidra, and Osian transformed from their human form into magnificent dragons. They leapt out over the meadows before flying closer to the shield and acting as though they were clumsy and inexperienced giving a false sense of security to the pursuing riders. Their ruse worked by drawing the riders closer to the shield, distracting them long enough for the Griffins to leave their hiding places and attack. The griffins were ruthless in pecking away at the underbellies of the Shadow Riders, quickly bringing on their demise. Those not vanquished by the Griffins were quickly incinerated by the combined flame of the four dragons.

In the meadows, the army of Shadow continued attacking, not accepting that they were up against a formidable and close-knit fighting force, one that was totally united in the defence of the temple. What was driving the Riders was their hunger; they were so ravenous; the stabbing pangs of starvation forced them to lose their cohesiveness. They attacked the forward ranks of the temple soldiers so as to immediately feed without checking their surroundings. They were so distracted they didn't see or hear the swishing sound of the approaching broadswords; they didn't even feel the cleaving of their heads; such was the intensity of their gorging. Those vanquished quickly turned to ash.

The rear ranks of Olympus, while waiting to act, split into two large columns, one went left and the other to the right. Their objective - to create a pincer movement, completely surrounding the invaders. Their plan was so effective, the overpowering of the first wave of Shadow quickly came to pass.

Although overpowered, it didn't come easy, many Soldiers of Zeus fell, and their bodies were in danger of becoming a hindrance towards the total defeat of the next wave of Shadow. It was then when the Griffins returned to form a protective perimeter around the temple.

On the terrace Jacob looked pleased with himself, until Magni said, "That was a very conclusive battle, but my instincts tell me our victory was just a bit too easy. I fear Shadow is playing games with us."

"Magni," said Odi, "for Zeus's sake, please stop referring to him as Shadow, his name is Lucifer. We now know who we are fighting."

Jacob again raised the shield, this time a little higher. Thousands more Shadow Riders passed through and immediately attacked. They were a more agile and focused force, suggesting Lucifer had now unleashed his elite troops. This force targeted the Griffins, using the Griffins inherent weakness – their penchant for gold and shiny objects. Every Shadow Rider attacking the Griffens wore necklaces made from gold or silver, each one encased with all kinds of precious stones. Although distracted by the gems, many Griffins resisted and used their vice like beaks to rip the heads from the closest attacking Riders, but ultimately the precious stones got to the Griffins making them powerless to resist, causing a major defeat.

When the griffins were routed, the Riders turned their attention towards the four dragons who initially had difficulty defending themselves, such was the number of Riders attacking. With the rout of the Griffins the Shadow Riders split, some remained to continue the attack on the dragons, the majority descended to join the attack on the ground forces. That was a mistake, the odds now favoured the dragons, odds on which they were quick to capitalise. They increased their speed after taking up positions at different levels. They then released a continuous and sustained flame that quickly incinerated any Shadow Riders that came close.

In the battle below, the ground forces put up a stoic defence, soon getting the upper hand. The gods watching chose not to intervene; they were happy Drayce, and the dragons had everything under control, motivated by revenge for the murder of their family and friends as well as the destruction of their homeland. Their determination was unmatched, and they were ruthless in the pursuit of this enemy. Even the remaining Griffins and the soldiers of Zeus recognised their power and bowed with respect. The second wave was now defeated.

Modi suggested Zeus's army be rested, he was concerned by how many that had fallen. He believed they needed time to regroup. Jacob agreed and decided to hold the shield firm until the following morning.

Under the cover of darkness, Jacob again opened the vaults allowing thousands more Soldiers of Zeus to awaken, this time he insisted on a silent exit. On reaching the meadows they took up positions among the already depleted army. From behind them came thousands more Griffins, ones that looked more fearsome than those already in the meadows.

When dawn broke the full devastation across the battlefield was revealed, bodies lying everywhere, bringing on a stench that was sickening. What surprised the gods was the lack of Shadow Rider bodies.

"It seems that after being vanquished, a few hours passes, then the Shadow soldiers turn to piles of black ash," said Odi, turning to Magni, "we must remove the bodies of our soldiers, they will become a distraction. Should we use our magic?"

"Don't waste your magic," insisted Jacob, "the Soldiers of Zeus are soulless, their genesis was out of dust, and to dust they will return. Trust me, they will be reborn to fight another day." He raised his staff and sent out his Light. All across the meadows the deceased soldiers turned to dust, and when he summoned the winds, that same dust was gone. The black ash remained in place.

"It hurts me to see how they come to our realm and take away its beauty," said Jacob, turning to face his brothers, "no flowers, no shrubs, not even a blade of grass has survived, The Sprites and the flower Nymphs, where are they? Did they escape? Why didn't we think of them?"

"Brother," said Magni, losing his patience, "enough of this, you know what to do."

Jacob looked back at the temple and got an encouraging nod from Apollo and Ares; he then looked at his son and the young War Gods. He nodded to Demetrius and acknowledged the Mystic Gods. He saved the longest glance for Eala, then turned to Magni. "Tell me again, why do you believe I should completely drop the shield."

"We can continue allowing groups of several thousand in at a time," replied Magni, "we will eventually weaken, and they know that. If we allow them all in at once, there will be too many for them to be effective."

Chapter 15

"Today we have before us the army of Shadow," said Magni after turning back to address the gods, "forgive me, from now on, we call it the army of Lucifer. They're here for one reason and one reason only - the complete annihilation of the gods. In a few moments, the shield will be removed allowing the war proper to begin. Everyone prepare."

He summoned the dragons and suggested they go rest in the temple, a suggestion to which they didn't object. Transforming into their human form showed the effect the battle had on them. They looked wretched, their clothing scorched and marked, ripped in many places. They carried the scars of battle, and it seemed they really did need time to recover. Drayce worried for his sister; he thought about the way the Shadow Riders particularly targeted her. He thought about his brother and was proud of how he fought and knew as time passed; he would become his greatest ally. When he thought of how Galyna so ruthlessly led the charge, he believed that between the four of them the Dragon Realm would be rebuilt and in safe hands.

When leaving, Isidra slightly detoured to brush off Maximus before reaching in to steal a kiss. He lit up, the tension of war diminishing just for those few seconds.

Galyna, in the meantime, struggled to climb the steps and needed to be assisted. On reaching the top step she collapsed into Osian's arms, no longer able to walk. It was then when he saw a trail of blood, left behind after ooz-ing from a gaping wound. She passed out just as he laid her on the ground.

"Take her to my plinth," said Apollo, unable to assist, the protection of the temple still his priority, "she's of the Light and in need of its healing powers, she'll be fine. Trust me."

Osian did as was asked, taking her into the temple and placing her on Apollo's plinth. He fetched water and linen bandages, preparing to wash and clean her wounds. Isidra joined him and after assessing the situation she felt Galyna wouldn't appreciate her dignity being compromised by being washed by a male dragon. She sent Osian away before removing Galyna's armour and clothing, making it easier to clean away the dust, grit, and con-gealed blood. After cleaning and dressing her wounds, she assisted her into more comfortable robes.

Osian stood nearby, never taking his eyes from the plinth. "Brother," asked Drayce, "have you something to tell me?"

"I look at her and only now realise I should have spoken up years ago," he replied, "she's the only one for me and she doesn't even know it. My heart sunk when I saw the seriousness of her wound and I feel ashamed I wasn't there to protect her. I've decided that when this war is over I'll ask her to leave with me. We'll find a place where we can be together forever, a place where no evil can enter."

"Osian," said an unhappy Drayce, "when this war is over I expect you to be by my side. I am King of the Dragons and will need you, there's no other I would trust more than you. You will be required to be my counsel, my emissary, and my confidant. The rebuilding of the dragon lands will take years, and you will be needed for your calmness, and more importantly, your negotiation skills."

"I appreciate what you're saying," replied Osian, "but it's not what I want, the paths we walk go in different directions. Anyway, why would you need me? You'll have Helena by your side, a Goddess of the Light, one who is carrying your baby, first in line to the throne of the dragon royal house."

"What of Galyna?" asked Drayce, "I see her as a supreme general of the dragon armies. She may not want what you're planning."

"Osian," interrupted Isidra, "she's asking for you."

Osian, without hesitation, rushed to be with her, and on looking down at her, in his mind, she was more beautiful than the goddesses of Olympus. He was delighted when she reached up and touched his face. "Strange," she said, "how at my weakest I get the one thing I always wanted."

"What did you always want," he asked.

"Your attention!" she replied, "but you never noticed me. I always wanted to rub my hand along your handsome face, but being a warrior-dragon meant there was no time for romance. How do we always get the important things so wrong?"

"We always get the important things wrong because of who we are," he replied, "but no more, from today everything changes." He started sniffing, then yelled, "What is that ungodly smell?"

"How romantic," said Galyna, trying to suppress a smile, "it's you!"

He looked at his torn clothing and saw the stains of battle, he raised his tunic and saw the congealed black blood covering his legs and arms, it was even in his hair. He was so embarrassed he ran out the main doors, forgetting Olympus was at war, but he didn't care. He ran to the ornamental gardens to sit under the overflow from the ponds, using his dagger to scrape the blood from everywhere he could reach. He then ran to his room, with Drayce running close behind, filled a tub, and used his fire to heat the water. He stripped and climbed in, scrubbing as he slid into the water. When he felt clean enough, he dried himself, then looked into a mirror and was horrified by the number of scars and bruises he was still carrying.

"Apollo!" he pleaded, hoping he'd answer, "please remove the scars of war. Help me Apollo."

Apollo, although guarding the main entrance to the temple, heard the plea and sent his magic. Within seconds, Osian's body shuddered as though invisible hands were electrifying him. His body became that of a god, all tanned and toned with no scars or blemishes of any kind. While dressing, he asked Drayce to go to the kitchen and find flowers that can be made into a bouquet.

"When did I become your slave?" asked Drayce as he was leaving.

"Oh!" yelled Osian, making sure Drayce heard him, "while you're at it. That scent Jacob always wears, the really strong one, go to his room and fetch it for me. He won't mind."

"You expect me to raid Jacob's room?" said a very bemused Drayce, who had returned to the door. "Are you mad?"

"Just go and do it," replied Osian, throwing a sandal at his brother, "Jacob's a romantic. He won't care."

While waiting on Drayce to return, he chose the gunmetal grey robes of a dragon lord, he also chose a stiff collared, gold braided, cream coloured cape, knowing it would perfectly frame his handsome face and long flowing hair.

When Drayce returned and saw his brother dressed as a royal dragon lord, he was impressed. He handed him the flowers and while spraying Jacob's scent he got emotional. "I wish father was here to see you like this," he said, as a tear gathered, "he would be so proud. Can you imagine mother? She would be fussing. I bet she'd tell you you're not quite ready yet."

"Oh, come on," said Osian, "I can do no more."

Drayce opened a nearby wooden chest, one that belonged to his father, and extracted a thin gold banded crown with the horn of a dragon at its centre.

"You are a son of Derwyn and Isabella," he said while placing the crown on Osian's head, "you are also a grandson of Fafner and Heulwyn. It is proper you wear the crown of a Dragon Prince."

Jacob was seen to be smiling. "What are you smirking at?" asked Modi.

"In the middle of all this tension," he replied, "I've just remembered something Eala said about how we are not just fighting for survival. We're also fighting for LOVE. Drayce has just raided my room and taken a bottle of scent. He sprayed it on Osian who's finally going to tell Galyna how he feels."

"For Odin's sake," cried Magni, folding his arms, showing his exasperation, "we are fighting for our lives, nothing else matters."

"Well," said Odi, "I don't agree, I'm fighting for Panya and my daughters, I'm fighting for Jacob, Eala and his family. I'm fighting for Modi and his family. Believe it or not brother, I'm fighting for you, your boys, and Baldor. That's love."

Osian made his way through the corridors and soon reached the Great Hall. "Do I still smell?" he asked on reaching Galyna.

She smiled as he presented her with the flowers. He reached in and kissed her for the first time before embracing her. She responded snuggling closer.

"You robbed Jacob's scent?" she said. They both laughed.

Isidra was at the back of the temple watching. "My baby brother is in love," she said, turning to Drayce, "I won't have to worry about him anymore."

Back on the terrace Jacob took a deep breath, listening to the incessant pounding and screeching coming from all around them, it was becoming unbearable. He looked around one last time, exhaled, and then fully opened the shield.

From the north and the west, columns of Shadow soldiers marched into Olympus; they split, with one heading towards the temple, and the other, a very large column, setting their sights on the folly guarded by Viktor, who saw the danger. He looked back towards his beloved Thora and winked; she then knew he had a plan. When he turned back to face the advancing army, he puffed out his chest just as his Light enhanced, illuminating him, his armour tightened, and his pristine white wings unfurled. Although alone, there was no fear, he knew something else was about to happen, and it did. From the sky above seven shards of light came to land in a wide circle around the folly. Each shard carried one of the seven Archangels, and immediately behind them came the vast armies of the heavens. The last time this army went into battle was during the first war. "You have our swords," said Michael, bowing to Viktor, "we are at your command."

Viktor acknowledged his brother Archangels and then together, they prepared to unleash the power of the heavens. The nearby Soldiers of Zeus withdrew and made their way towards the temple to assist in that battle leaving the angels free to re-enact the first war. The power of Michael, Gabriel and Raphael was unmatched but when added to Viktor's they looked invincible. They didn't wait, they took to the sky to direct such an attack, they conjured up images of a dance of destruction that soon became devastating to the Shadow army. There was no emotion, just sheer vengeance, the faces of the angels couldn't be read, they were so impassive and totally focused. The Shadow Riders had no chance, the angels unleashed on them the full fury of Heaven, darkening the battlefield with smashed bones, torn flesh, and a torrent of black blood. Their targeting of the Rider's jugulars was so precise the demise of this army surely was in sight except the Riders just kept coming. It soon became obvious that this battle was destined to last for days; Lucifer was throwing at it everything he could muster.

Those angels fighting the ground forces had great difficulty. Every effort by Uriel, Selaphiel, Raguel and Barachiel to secure Victory was thwarted by the continuous flow of blood and guts from the battle above, creating a sticky sludge as they fought, causing them to lose their balance and making them vulnerable to the now precise sword cuts of the elite riders who had arrived. The pleasure on the demonic faces of the Riders as they spilled the blood and innards of the angels was unnerving, especially in those few moments just before an angel passed away. The Riders made sure to slice their wings from their backs, taking away the last of their dignity.

From the south and the east thousands more Shadow Riders were approaching, they stopped in the meadows to allow several battalions of Riders to separate from the main body and fly towards the temple.

Demetrius, Gaia, and Hemish anticipated this attack, they called on the wind by rotating their arms, creating a figure eight. As they increased their speed, mini tornados formed, and after a few more moments the tornadoes increased in size, intensity, and power. Amma, Kitaka and Aja then used those same winds by waving their hands from left to right to increase the speed, pushing the tornadoes higher into the sky. The tornadoes grew to be so violent they soon spun their way through the ranks of the Riders who were targeting the temple. They sucked the Riders high into the sky, propelling their bodies out into space towards the sun to be incinerated.

The Mystic Gods were not finished; all six turned their attention to the lagoon by using gentle movements of their index fingers to begin creating ever increasing waves, then larger more threatening ones. Soon they brought four-meter-high tsunamis, bringing terror to the forces of Shadow. For the soldiers of Zeus near the beach, there was no danger, they went on one knee, plunging their swords deep into the hardened sand. They turned to stone and anchored themselves to the ground. When the waves passed the shadow army along the seashore was no more.

The rear of the temple was the least protected area of Olympus; there was nothing of value there. The rear doors were completely sealed and protected by old magic. Even so, four Titans were earlier placed there. It was a wise decision, thousands more Shadow Riders were approaching, bringing grappling hooks and battering-rams. The sleeping Titans sensed their approach and awoke, surmising that the hooks were to be used to tear into Athena's protective shields, making the temple walls vulnerable. They quickly released their fury, sending fireball after fireball rolling across the meadows. The fireballs burned and scorched their way towards incinerating the Shadow Riders.

At the front of the temple, the First Ones and the remaining eight Titans awoke and immediately went into action. They too released fireballs, but for every Rider they killed, several more appeared, they just kept coming.

The Goddesses were watching, preparing to play their part. They raised their arms and brought their hands together by linking their thumbs. They called on their Light before releasing it as intense beams not dissimilar to a Super Trooper. As their Light shot across the sky, it sliced its way through any Shadow Rider it touched. Their power was so potent it quickly cleared the skies.

From the rim of the meadows, close to the tree line, seven beings immerged and as they walked towards the temple it became clear as to who they were. They were the Princes of Hell, and the one in the middle looked to be the most powerful; he had no horns and with his chiselled good looks and strikingly muscular appearance, he looked to be a creation of the Ancient One. Jacob wondered was he Lucifer or was he another clone. As they approached they cleared the way by using their magic to aggressively disperse the crammed Shadow Riders.

Modi turned to the War Gods and just nodded, it was his signal for them to go into action, their task was to take command of the Soldiers of Zeus that had by now split into fourteen different armies, they were also to maintain a clear passageway for Jacob to alone take on Lucifer.

Obelius requested permission to temporarily break rank, which Jacob granted, knowing his son could be trusted. Magni wasn't happy.

Obelius rushed to meet with the First Ones, he was seen to be gesticulating while whispering in their ears. He then ran back to the temple to meet with the Mystic Gods, before returning to take up his position at the head of the twelfth army.

"That little prick," said Magni, "whatever he's doing is not part of my plans."

"Brother," sniggered Modi, "I think you've met your match; that one has skills even you don't possess. Let's trust him; it seems he's now working with the First Ones. That has to be good."

"Don't worry about the plan," said Jacob, "it's still in place. All he's doing is ensuring a prophecy is fulfilled, a prophecy given many years ago, it said his face will be one of the last faces Lucifer will see."

It was now time, Jacob moved forward with Magni and Odi on his right, and Modi to his left. Baldor was walking ahead, using his powerful Light to shield them from the gaze of the Shadow army.

They made their way through the clearing created by the Soldiers of Zeus, led by Thora and Yeshe, giving them a clear view across the battlefield. It was then when they saw Hai, Aodh and Tristan fall, followed by Zane.

"Stay focused," said Magni, turning to Modi, "I know he's your son, you did know there would be losses."

"Fear not," said Jacob, hoping to reassure Modi, "I have a plan."

He raised his staff and sent his Light to form individual cocoons around the four fallen gods, protecting them from becoming fodder for the Riders. There was no time for grieving.

"Which one is Lucifer," asked Odi.

"Any one of them," replied Jacob, "the one in the centre has grown horns, now they all look alike. They walk in unison, notice how when one lifts a hand, all others do the same. Credit, where credit's due, it's an effective way to deceive us."

"Garuda once told me of that tactic," said Modi, "he and Girish noticed how it was used when they were attacked in India. That strategy is well known as hard to maintain, mistakes will eventually be made."

"He won't be the one in the centre, too obvious," said Jacob, intently watching all seven. "He's unlikely to be on the extremes, too dangerous." He turned to Magni. "Watch the two who are left of centre," he said, "I'll watch the two right of centre."

As luck would have it, the Soldiers of Zeus were engaged close by, they were under the command of Finn and Lir. Finn in particular was very alert to the approaching Princes of Hell and decided to break away using a pile of bodies as cover. He targeted the Riders as he passed, using his speed to take them down in their hundreds. When he was joined by Lir, the power of the Little People kicked in, at times they shrunk to the size of a dragonfly, then, at the blink of an eye, they were the size of a man. At first they released single arrows, then a torrent. Eventually they managed to get close enough to target the prince on the extreme right, bringing him down.

"Finn and Lir," said Odi, in awe of their fighting abilities, "they're using an ancient Celtic magic. It's said that the Little People dip their arrows in a spell filled cauldron, one that was created five thousand years ago by our friend, the Sun God Lugh. Amazing how his magic still works."

"Got him," interrupted Magni, still watching the approaching princes, "the one second from the left grimaced when Finn's arrow struck. Lucifer is second from the left."

Finn and Lir continued their barrage and successfully took out two more princes leaving four still moving forward. Again, the same Prince grimaced confirming which one was in fact Lucifer.

Suddenly the priorities of the Shadow Riders changed; they moved in their thousands to protect the four remaining princes. There were now two battles in progress, the main body of the Riders continued their relentless assault on the temple, and even with the power of the First Ones, and the Titans, they were beginning to make progress.

"Ah!" said Lucifer on catching Obelius's eye and preparing to throw a spear, "the heir to Olympus; chip off the old block and favourite of the Ancient One. This, my friend, is for you."

He fired the spear, a spear with the ability to split into thousands of smaller shards. Each shard seemed to have a mind of its own, some soared to attack from above, others increased then decreased their speed, more had the ability to bore through all kinds of shields and it was these that penetrated Obelius's armour, rendering him unconscious and as they continued targeting him, his white mist began to rise. Magnar, then Arum, met the same fate, leaving the four sons of Thor as the last hope of destroying Lucifer once and for all.

Odi felt his three brother's hearts break, watching each of their sons fall. He worried about his sister and her reaction when she discovers Arum had died. He hoped they'd all remember their sons are warrior gods, and that they should only grieve when the battle was won. Little did he know that very shortly it was to be him who would attempt to break rank. He looked across at his fallen nephews and used the power of his Light to create cocoons protecting each of their bodies from further attack, or decay. His action stopped the white mist from leaving. Jacob acknowledged his action, nodding his approval.

The four brothers continued walking towards the remaining princes, while the War Gods were slowly making their way to protect Jacob. Lir was first to reach, and then attack the Riders who were targeting the gods, launching himself from behind a mound of bodies only to be skewered by a more alert adversary. He had fallen and was about to be eaten when Jacob sent his Light to cocoon him.

It was then when Cetan and Thora fell. Odi was devastated and attempted to break rank but was stopped. "Brother," said Modi, "this is Olympus, when the battle ends we will revive all of them."

"She's my daughter," screamed Odi, showing his despair, "there's no worse pain. What if Olympus can't bring them back, there are so many?"

In the meantime, the angels were being decimated by the overpowering numbers of Shadow Riders attacking them. The Archangels were beginning to count their losses and soon realised Lucifer was a lot more prepared than they anticipated. Michael was horrified to see Uriel and Raguel fall, the savagery that was meted out on them sickened him. Viktor saw an even greater danger, his visions showed him the four princes becoming more powerful, each one gaining their wings, using a three-meter span to deflect all incoming arrows. He decided to join the War Gods and assist them in targeting the remaining Princes of Hell.

He landed alongside Maximus, Li, Finn, and Yeshe. "This is not going well," he said, "for us to prevail we must take out three of the remaining Princes leaving Lucifer as the last one standing. The battle will then not be ours; it will be between the God of Gods and the Prince of Darkness. I've seen it. Finn, you know what to do. Li, target the one on the left, he's definitely not Lucifer; look at his face, it shows fear. Kill him now."

Li had difficulty taking out the prince on the left but eventually made his way to use his sword and decapitate him.

Finn made his way among the uncountable bodies close to where the princes were passing, he concealed himself from all prying eyes and then unleashed his power. Another two princes fell.

It was then when Magni and Modi fell to an attack not anticipated. From behind them, a column of Riders and vicious flying demons appeared, sending volleys of poison tipped arrows that had the ability to penetrate Baldor's powerful Light. Maximus was nearby, still struggling with the death of his brother, but to see his father fall was too much to bear. He collapsed to his knees but wasn't given much time to grieve. "Get off your knees," screamed Yeshe. "You are a War God of Asgard, and your battle still rages. Our task is to clear a path for the God of Gods. Rise now. Too few of us still stand."

Odi was getting scared. "Brother, this is the first time I've ever felt fear. The two brothers who always had my back are gone. I know you are by my side, but I also sense your fear and that's not good."

"Hold your nerve," replied Jacob, "you will not be the one to end this, I will. And I intend surviving."

Odi was about to speak again when blood began trickling from the sides of his mouth. His eyes widened then closed as he fell to his knees, the tip of a spear showing just below his ribcage. It was a spear similar to the one that took Obelius, and no one saw it coming. Jacob had no time to react other than ensuring a cocoon was placed around his fallen brother, he also secured Modi's body but couldn't protect Magni's. He rushed to join Baldor, each temporarily enhancing the others Light. "Go to Magni," said Jacob, preparing to face Lucifer alone, "his is the only body my Light hasn't reached. He needs you now more than ever. He also needs you to tell him how you feel, I knows he knows, but he needs you to say it!"

Baldor did as instructed. He reached Magni, knelt, and created a cocoon to protect both of them. He then used his Light to revive Magni.

Magni soon responded and immediately tried to go and assist Jacob but was held firm. "Your war is over," said Baldor, "Jacob has spoken, he intends to bring Lucifer down before the sun sets this day." Magni at first resisted, but was held firm by Baldor's Light, he conceded and rested his head against Baldor's chest.

"Remember that first time when you walked into the Great Hall?" said Baldor, holding him tighter, "we were behind the columns, I felt something then. Remember that time when I was impaled to the tree in Georgia? Remember again when I led the exodus from near St. Petersburg? They were some of the many times when I so wanted to be with you, not as friends, I wanted us to be together as lovers, but I saw you only had eyes for another, and I chose not to reveal my feelings to anyone. Panya knew, she hinted over the years, she even prophesied where my love path would take me. Well today I'm holding in my arms the one I want to spend eternity with. I pray this cocoon will hold; I don't want this to be our last time together."

"This cocoon will hold," replied Magni, stretching up to grip Baldor's neck, "it has been built out of your love for me, the kind of love that will always triumph. Isn't it strange how all around us is death and destruction, and all I want is to stay in your arms and maybe bring your lips closer to mine. Can you do that for me?"

Baldor lowered his head and for the first time he felt a passion long missing from his life. He felt sensations radiate through his body, the very ones the boys spoke about, but he never understood. He knew by the way Magni turned to take him into his arms that his dreams were now coming true. They both closed their eyes and waited for rescue.

Meanwhile, Jacob continued his walk further out into the meadows. "Protect the goddesses at all costs," he yelled, after dismissing the remaining War Gods and sending them back to deal with the Shadow Riders attacking the temple. "Let me deal with the Prince of Hell."

All across the meadows the battle raged on. There was no reprieve for the angels or the Soldiers of Zeus. Both armies were falling at such a rate, the security of the Heavens and of Olympus was now in doubt. The Mystic Gods continued to do their best, but the Shadow Riders just kept coming, so much so that the ancient gods, Apollo, Ares, Athena, and Eris, changed their strategy. They all saw the danger. They melded together to become an impenetrable solid wall that sealed the main entrance, further ensuring no evil could enter. Before they turned to stone, Eris was seen to be weeping, she was grieving for her son, Tristan, and her beloved Modi.

The goddesses never gave up, they continued sending their beams in all directions, slicing through any Shadow Rider that got too close even though it was difficult for some of them to stay composed, Panya had watched Thora fall, then her beloved Odi. Eala had seen Obelius fall and was watching Jacob make his way towards Lucifer for a battle that could end with the loss of her husband.

Jacob called on his Light knowing that Lucifer could possibly stand against it. It was the most powerful Light of them all and was so bright anything it touched was incinerated. Its sheering power terrorised the Shadow Riders forcing them to retreat onto the swords of the remaining Soldiers of Zeus and the suffering angels.

Then it happened, Jacob reached a clearing where Lucifer was waiting. Nothing was said, they just lunged at each other, and within seconds the battle of the ages began. It was fast and vicious, no punches were pulled, no daggers or swords were retracked, it was full on. Each attack was met by taunts hoping to bring mistakes, but no mistakes were made. Lucifer continued sneering and laughing, rushing back and forth while each time attempting to cleave Jacob's head, but Jacob was faster, ready for all eventualities. On his counterattack he'd get great pleasure each time his sword landed flush against any part of Lucifer.

It was at those times when the sneering increased. "Still the actions of a decrepit boy," snapped Lucifer, "I'll test your body armour to its limits and will look forward to your roars of pain. This time my resolve is so strong even my rage will not break through. There will be no mistakes."

"Look again at me, Idiot," replied Jacob, "I'm no boy. Just like the last time, your arrogance will betray you. Be warned, it will be over my dead body that you will take Olympus."

Lucifer backed away towards a much wider clearing, he realised it was too difficult to continue the fight in such a small clearing surrounded by so many dead and mutilated bodies. Jacob followed him and while making his way he was pleased to see more and more Shadow Riders being picked off by Finn and other arrow-firing snipers. It troubled him seeing so many disembowelled bodies of the loyal Soldiers of Zeus, it really hurt seeing them being fed upon by ravenous Riders, all gnawing into their soft tissue and shattered bones. This was distracting and becoming too much for him especially when he looked out further into the battlefield. He felt ashamed by the carnage all around him, blaming himself for failing to protect Olympus. The only solace he got was when he looked back at the temple and saw Demetrius was still alive, his heart lifted while watching his remaining son using his magic to save so many lives. He then turned back to continue his battle. He never tired, remaining focused and determined to finish Lucifer off once and for all.

He decided to make his next attack the last one but misjudged the effects the pools of congealing blood and internal organs, lying all around him, would have on his plans. He slipped in the sickly sludge and lost his balance, giving Lucifer an opening to show his prowess with a sword. He attacked using impressive fore-swings, followed by a series of back-swings which eventually made contact, but did no damage, Jacob's speed again came to his aid. During one very close encounter Jacob's face was so close to Lucifer's, he saw the real hatred, and blood lust of the Prince of Darkness.

Seeing such an evil looking face, Jacob's resolve increased, and he forcefully used his sword to push Lucifer out of the clearing into a nearby pile of bodies. He was determined to win and even though he was determined, he worried about how many more would fall before this day was over.

He needn't have worried, as twilight approached the First Ones decided to end the battle, they had had enough. Gaia, as supreme Mother Earth, encouraged the Mystic gods to use their powers to soften the soil and when they did, she dived in and travelled deep beneath the meadows to where

Jacob was fighting. Jacob was aware she was coming and worked to distract Lucifer while the meadows undulated as she approached.

Uranus, as Father Sky knew exactly where she was, he then made his move. He raised himself high and then floated to hover above where Gaia lay. He dropped at speed, and when he neared Jacob he brushed him aside so as to continue his fall. Lucifer had no time to react, he looked up and to his horror he didn't see the face of Uranus, at first he saw the face of the Asgard oracle, Fitch, then he saw the sneering face of Obelius. The prophecy was fulfilled. Uranus fell upon Lucifer crushing him into oblivion; he and Gaia then melded into one, permanently holding Lucifer between the Earth and the Sky and this time there would be no escape.

Chapter 16

To all the gods it looked like Lucifer being crushed between Father Sky and Mother Earth was the end of the battle, especially when they saw how quickly his army fell into disarray. The forces of what was once known as Shadow lost their cohesiveness and began to panic.

Jacob decided no mercy was to be shown and instructed the remaining armies of the Light to annihilate any agents of Shadow they met. They did and were relentless in their pursuit of every last Rider and demon. Just to be sure and to ensure there were no escapees Jacob ensured the shield closed all escape routes. As each Rider fell, this time they exploded into black ash, but unfortunately for the gods, it was some time before that ash settled.

When the last of the Shadow army was destroyed the full horror of their attack became obvious. The black ash was in excess of a meter deep and covered every part of Olympus. Nothing that grew had survived.

Jacob looked around at what were once his beautiful and pristine meadows and went into total shock. He stumbled in despair only to be caught by Maximus who said, "Uncle, not now, you must show your strength. Let the survivors see your power. We'll rebuild, and we start now."

They were soon joined by Finn, Yeshe, Viktor and Li, and together they walked with great difficulty towards the temple. The black ash was so deep, each step they took disturbed the ash for it to become asphyxiating. Their attempts to scramble through the mounds got more arduous as they got closer to the steps causing clouds of ash to rise and clog every orifice so much so that they were chewing grit and becoming more agitated.

When they reached the portico Jacob turned to Viktor. "There are so few angels left, they must be protected, or the very Heavens will be in danger. Ensure all of them reach the safety of the temple and are given what they need to recover." Viktor did what was asked and soon the temple was brimming with thousands of angels.

Jacob made his way over to where Demetrius and the Mystic Gods were gathered and was pleased none had fallen. He saw they were shattered and were showing their despair at the loss of so many of their friends. He tried to comfort Demetrius in particular but failed. There was no consoling him; he was despondent over the loss of his brother. When he looked across at Viktor he saw that he too was devastated over the loss of his beloved Thora.

He continued walking up the steps to meet up with Eala who was softly weeping. He reached in and hugged her only to listen as she whispered in his ear. "My beautiful son is gone," she said, "he might be a man but it's his baby cries I still hear. I cannot feel or see him yet there are fleeting glimpses in my future. I think he waits for you to release him; Jacob, they all wait for you to release them. Oh, the Ancient One has awoken and he's not happy. Even in his anger he has sent the sparks of life."

Jacob softly kissed her cheek before making his way to sit on his throne. While there he stared out over the crest-fallen gods and couldn't think of anything to say. It was then when he gasped and was seen to take a deep breath. He froze for a moment before looking around: he stood and seemed confused before becoming very unsettled. "It's not over!" he exclaimed, showing his alarm. "I can still sense him. Something's wrong."

He ran back out on to the steps and looked up at the stone statues of Athena, Ares, Apollo, and Eris. "Guardians of Olympus," he yelled, "don't let your guard down. He still lives. I feel and smell him. He's the great deceiver and I fear he has deceived us yet again."

In a panic he ran out on to the terraces and called on the twelve Titans. "My lords, my Ladies," he yelled, "you must return to Elysium. He thinks the gods are decimated and will now target anything that bears our names; he will destroy all books, codices, engravings, and repositories that speak of us."

Rhea gently caressed his face. "Young God," she said, trying to calm him, "we too sense his presence, his deception knows no bounds."

"It's so unfair for so much to fall on the shoulders of one so young," said Cronus, "but somehow I feel it's the young who have what it takes to bring peace back to these sacred lands. We will leave now but I promise we'll always be ready to answer your call." The Titans then disappeared.

Jacob extracted his staff and sent its light out over the meadows in the hope of dispersing the ash cover, but all he did was cause a dust-storm. He tried to locate the cocoons, planning to revive the gods but something was blocking his power. He called on the First Ones but got no answer. While the ash was settling he thought he saw figures moving about causing him to become more alarmed. "Did you see what I just saw?" he asked Maximus, who was close by.

"I did," replied Maximus, "and I know what to do."

He raised his spear and prepared to send it out into the meadows. He was cautious for fear of hitting the cocoons but was assured by Jacob that no damage can be done as the cocoons were heavily protected. He then released his spear with such force that it travelled deep into the meadows. He watched it land and was shocked to see a Dark Angel rise up only to collapse in agony as the spear retracted so as to return into his hand.

Drayce and the dragons had arrived, they offered to take to the sky and use their fire to disturb the ash, but Jacob decided it was too risky. He ushered them back into the temple, telling them to wait with the Mystic gods and the Goddesses of the Light.

In the meantime, Finn, Li, and Yeshe fired their spears, and they too hit several Dark Angels proving that some kind of deception was in play and the battle wasn't over. Jacob made another attempt to clear the ash but found it very resilient and it bothered him that everything he tried failed; he was now certain something sinister was holding it in place.

"What if you took Olympus out into the cosmos," suggested Finn, "and lowered the shield? What if you allowed the solar winds to do what they do best? They should be strong enough to disturb and then blow away the ash?"

"You are certainly your father's son," said Jacob, "you five, stay on guard until I have everything in place."

He called Apollo, Ares, Athena, and Eris to awaken so that he could discuss the plan with them. They listened carefully and agreed Finn's suggestion was sound. They also indicated that their place was to remain at the entrance of the temple, they retook their stone form. Just as they were about to transform they and Jacob felt a presence, soon all the Gods felt the same presence. It was Uranus.

"Listen on to me," he said. "Gods of the Light, Lucifer still lives and is using clones to deceive us. Gaia and I have left to begin our own search. Olympus is safe for now. To the God of Gods I say, create a sphere, allow it to take you deep into the cosmos, don't stop until you reach the end."

Jacob called the five War Gods into the temple and secured the doors. As in the past he moved to the centre of the hall, raised his arms and using his magic he moved Olympus.

At first the temple moved slowly and then made its way beyond the moon before gathering speed and shooting out into deep space. It travelled over four billion kilometres taking it beyond Neptune, where Jacob felt it was safe for him to lower the shields. As Finn suggested, the speed and the winds, dislodged, then blew the accumulated ash out into the cosmos.

Maximus had earlier climbed into the rafters to reach the only window not completely covered by Athena's shield. He reported the ash had been cleared and then counted the cocoons. "Three cocoons are missing," he cried out in despair.

Maximus barely had the words out of his mouth when Jacob ran to check for himself. He too counted and could clearly see the three empty spots where the cocoons should have rested. He rushed towards the doors, out into the meadows where he ran from cocoon to cocoon and soon his worst fears were realised. Obelius, Magnar and Odi were missing. He ran back into the temple, and immediately arranged to return to earth.

While travelling back he joined Eala. "Please," he said, "please tell me you can see Obelius in our future, because I can't. He's hidden from me."

"I can't sense Odi," he said, turning to Panya, "I searched; he hasn't entered my head. I've tried to reach him, there's nothing?"

"What about my brother" asked Maximus, "is Magnar gone? I can't reach him. Please uncle, tell me he's not gone." Jacob just shook his head.

Eala quietened, entering some form of trance as she made her way out on to the terrace. She was joined by Panya and together they raised their arms. They used their light by allowing it travel out from them to grip the remaining cocoons. They magically levitated each one before guiding them towards the temple. They then manoeuvred them, one by one, into the Great Hall where all ten were laid out near the statue of Zeus. There was much relief among the young gods when they saw their brothers and sisters safely laid out, knowing they were soon to be resurrected but when they realised who was missing, despair set in.

Magni and Baldor were sharing the largest cocoon and because their cocoon was created by Baldor, he was able to quickly open its lid. Magni leapt up and looked around for his sons, he lit up when he saw Maximus, but his relief turned to pain when he saw Maximus's face, he knew then Magnar didn't make it. He looked across at Panya and Eala's tear-streaked faces and surmised that both Obelius and Odi didn't make it either. He joined Jacob. "How long was I gone?" he asked, he didn't get an answer.

For the first time ever, he was stuck for words, he couldn't even see the formation of a plan to begin a search, his skills had deserted him. When he felt the low rumbling beneath his feet and asked, "Where are we travelling to?"

"Back to earth," replied Jacob.

Maximus's patience grew thin while waiting for a rescue plan to be prepared, he challenged his father to do something only to get more agitated when no response was forthcoming. He felt nobody cared as his grief clouded his judgement. He then accused his father of not being the War God they all knew, and suggested he was no good to anyone. Magni didn't respond, he too was grieving.

Maximus was having none of it; he paced the Great Hall, getting more agitated, especially by the rumbling sound of the travelling Olympus.

"When will this infernal temple land?" he yelled, but again got no response. He stomped over to where Jacob and his father were sitting demanding they do something. His disgust grew when there was still no response, but he should have had more faith because his father had already worked out what needed to be done, and it didn't include him or the young Gods.

When the Archangels Michael, Gabriel and Raphael joined Jacob and Magni, Maximus's anger got out of control, but what hurt him the most was when Eala and Panya joined them. "How could you?" he screamed, "one of you grieves for your son, and the other for your daughter and husband, yet you stand behind two burnt out gods who don't seem to know what to do."

Baldor attempted to calm things. "Maximus," he said, showing his well-known compassion, "say no more or you'll live to regret this day."

"Just because you're sleeping with my father," yelled Maximus, unable to contain himself and gripping Baldor by the collar, "it doesn't give you the right to treat me as your son. I'm not your son and never will be, so shut it and mind your own business."

Baldor was dumbfounded and backed away but those watching Magni could see he was biting his lip and ready to explode.

Olympus had no sooner landed when the doors opened, and the four ancient gods entered announcing their belief that there was no presence of Lucifer or Shadow Riders.

Maximus threw his arms into the air still showing his frustration. "Four ancient gods and they too decide to do or say nothing," he said, making his way back towards his father and Jacob, "I don't believe this. Uncle, if you or my father are not prepared to do anything, trust me, I will." He glared at his father. "Seeing that you are incapable," he sneered, "I'm taking control! I have four War Gods, four Dragons, six Mystic Gods and four Goddesses of the Light and together we will be a force to be reckoned with. Our magic will assist us find the missing cocoons. We're leaving now, and there'll be no stopping us."

Magni was still seething as he left his seat. He walked over to Maximus and gripped him by the neck. He leaned in so as to be out of earshot of those around. "I love you son," he whispered through gritted teeth, "but today you crossed the line. What you said to Baldor is unforgivable. When this is over I'm going to kick you from one end of the universe to the other and you are going to regret the day you were born."

Maximus was sick inside and doing everything in his power to show no fear. "I'd love to see you try!" he yelled, hoping everyone heard.

Magni just pouted his lips, walked away. "They say the apple doesn't fall too far from the tree," said Jacob, trying to stifle a smile.

"I know," replied Magni, "I'm really proud of how he stood up to me, and I'm delighted he has taken control, but I'm so angry at the way he spoke to Baldor. I still think I'm going to kill him."

Chapter 17

Maximus puffed out his chest and made his way towards the doors, calling for the young gods to follow. They were slow in moving until Hemish and Demetrius walked to the centre of the hall, looked up at Jacob and bowed, they joined Maximus, prompting all other young gods to do the same.

As Demetrius exited the temple he felt his father in his head. "Son," he said, "find your brother and bring him home. Also, look after Maximus, he's developing the skills of his father but hasn't reached ten steps ahead. He's grieving and will need you before this day is out. Viktor, Li, and Finn are also suffering, they too have lost family, so allow Drayce to be your ally."

Magni entered Finn's head. "Prince of the Fair Lands," he said, "you are the bow master, teach the War Gods your skills, they're going to need those skills before your battle is over. Distract the remaining armies of Lucifer and leave what's left for us to deal with."

Demetrius was aware Magni had entered Finn's head. "Uncle," he said, "Maximus is angry, and I worry about his judgement. I'm going to insist Drayce takes command, he is Emperor of the Dragons and the most senior among us."

"That's a strategy for you to decide on," replied Magni, "he's my son and I love him, beware his temper."

"Worry not uncle," said Demetrius, "I fear no War God."

"Son," interrupted Jacob, "this is not a time for arrogance. I'm depending on you to use your powers wisely, assist the War Gods and bring Odi, Obelius and Magnar home."

Viktor then felt Jacob in his head. "Archangel," he said, "the Goddesses are of the Light and are now in your care. Be strong and be prepared to make decisions that might lose you your friends." Viktor acknowledged his guidance.

Jacob then stood and addressed the angels. "The gates of the Heavens are compromised; such is your losses." He turning to Michael, "Lucifer still lives; he believes he has decimated the gods and is growing in arrogance. He thinks we believe him to be dead, crushed between Father Sky and Mother Earth. You must leave, rebuild the defences of Heaven."

He turned to Magni. "Brother, I need you to protect Eala and Panya. I'm leaving for deep space."

"You forget," replied Magni, "I too am one of the ancients. I heard what Uranus said so I will be travelling with you. Baldor will be their guardian."

In the meadows all nineteen of the young gods reached the section of the meadows where the cocoons had rested, there they began their investigations. They quickly identified which cocoon lay where and concentrated their efforts on the area where Odi, Obelius and Magnar fell.

Gaia plunged her hands into the soil and detected tunnels still being created. She identified various sounds - boring tools, shovels, and chisels. She also detected heavy objects being dragged, and concluded the heavy objects can only be the missing cocoons. She stood and with Hemish by her side, they used their powers to burst through the soil, creating an opening. The War Gods leapt into the tunnel where up ahead they saw twelve Dark Angels dragging the cocoons through a portal into a dimension that looked like what Jacob once described as Hell. They pursued but were too late, the portal closed, and all went quiet, the cocoons were now out of reach.

This turn of events troubled them, to be so close and now so far away was something they didn't expect. They exited the tunnel and reported what they found, only to be greeted by the sight of a large sphere leaving the temple. They watched it make its way high into the stratosphere before shooting out into the cosmos. It was carrying Jacob and Magni. Demetrius joined Maximus and both were heard to say, "Safe journey father."

"Do you know what they're up to?" asked Maximus.

"No," replied Demetrius, "I don't, my father asked me to look after you; he said you are developing your father's skills, but you are not quite there yet; he also said you will need me before this day is out." He then placed his hand on Maximus's arm. "They're not burnt out, while you were venting they were listening to something; some of us sensed it. Did you not feel a presence? Didn't you notice my father's face change and then there was calmness? I saw the same calmness in the faces of Apollo, Ares, your father, and Eris. I couldn't see Athena's face, but I bet she felt the same. Something big is about to happen and both our fathers will be in the thick of it. Somehow I feel they have been summoned."

"Deme," said Maximus, "I felt nothing, I just sensed they didn't care, that's why I was so angry. If what you say is true I really made a fool of myself, didn't I?"

"Of course they care," replied Demetrius, "but right now, and because of your outburst, we are stuck with the task of finding the missing cocoons and trust me we are going to find them." He pulled Maximus closer and whispered. "Your rant in the temple shows how volatile you are and suggests you can't fully be relied on. I love you cousin, but your judgement is clouded by the loss of your brother, just like mine is, so I have a suggestion."

"What is it?" asked Maximus.

"There's one War God among us who has suffered greatly in the past, but he has learned to control his anger, so I'm going to suggest we allow him take command. Drayce is powerful and will not make mistakes."

"That's a brilliant idea," said a relieved looking Maximus. He then called Drayce to join them. "Demetrius has suggested you take command, and I agree, will you take control?"

"Yes," replied Drayce without hesitation, "I will." He stepped away and thought for a moment, he then said to Maximus, "Your father is renowned for being able to think ten steps ahead in all conflict situations. How many steps ahead can you think?"

"I, I, I, I can't think at all," stuttered Maximus, showing his insecurities, "Magnar was all I ever had growing up and now he's gone and it's breaking my heart. Its distracting me and I don't know what to do."

"It seems you need me a lot sooner than my father thought," said Demetrius, "pull yourself together, come on cousin. Think!"

"I haven't got the tactical skills of my father," said Maximus, trying to calm himself, "but I've his determination and strength. I'm my father's son and I know a plan will come because of my brother, I know he's still alive."

"I too see images of him, and he's with Obelius," said Demetrius, "my images show them causing havoc across the cosmos. The prophecies also show Uncle Odi spear-heading the rebuilding of Asgard."

Drayce called Finn to join him, and it was agreed that they alone would re-enter the tunnel. He instructed Finn to send a flaming arrow the length of the tunnel and count the seconds as it travelled. The arrow only took a few seconds before slamming into the wall where the portal last appeared.

After exiting Drayce asked the Mystic Gods to space themselves along where he surmised the tunnel ran. Finn then launched another flaming arrow while Drayce counted. Using this method, he was able to calculate where the portal should be if it was above ground. Gaia and Hemish again used their powers and shifted the soil to reveal the exact location of the sealed portal.

"Drayce," said Maximus, looking more confident, "A plan has suddenly formed, and I believe it will work." He waited for a reaction and when none came he continued. "To begin, the Mystic Gods will use their magic to open the portal. Secondly, you and the War Gods will take the lead and cautiously enter his domain. Thirdly, two dragons will patrol the sky, watching for more portals. Next, the remaining dragon will guard this portal and be ready to release its fire. Fifthly, the Goddesses of the Light will follow while using their powers to protect the War Gods. Sixthly, Viktor will make himself known by spreading his wings and sending out his Light. Then I, Li, Yeshe, and Finn will release our arrows in continuous volleys while the Dark Angels are distracted by Viktor's light, hopefully killing as many as we can. After that, the Mystic Gods will use their invisibility to search for the cocoons. When found one goddess will tap into Eala's and Panya's powers, raise the cocoons, and float them towards the exit. Finally, when done, we use our combined powers to collapse the cavern."

"It seems you have inherited your father's skills after all," said an impressed Drayce, "it sounds like a good plan and well thought out but, what if we are outnumbered? What if they are not there? What if your plan is foreseen by Lucifer and he's waiting for us?"

"My plan will work," said Maximus, getting more assertive.

The Mystic Gods used their magic to reopen the portal allowing Viktor to make his way through to investigate. When satisfied it was safe he called the Goddesses and the War Gods to join him. Together they made their way towards the edge of what seemed to be a deep crevice. They managed to cross the crevice to reach a series of passageways, each one equally as dark and dank as the other. They chose to enter the largest passageway, the only one illuminated by dimly lit lanterns. This passageway led them towards a much wider cavern where they stumbled across the three cocoons only for their hopes to be dashed, the cocoons were empty.

They continued searching, and soon reached a long and wide tunnel with no hiding places and from there they saw another portal closing, they assumed it was through there Obelius, Odi and Magnar had been taken. When they reached the portal Demetrius and Gaia placed their hands on the cliff-face in the hope their powers would inspire them, but they didn't. What they felt was the terror and abuse being suffered by Obelius and Magnar, they had no sense of Odi still being alive.

"Once I dreamt of such a place," said Amma, moving her hands along the cliff-face, "for weeks I've had the same dream and every time I tried to break through something stopped me. This is the place I dreamt of, there is a way through, but I can't remember."

"I too had those dreams," said Aja, "in them I got through. Why is it, I too can't remember?"

"I too had the same dream," said Yeshe, "there are cliffs, just like these, except they're white, camouflaged by centuries of ice. The dream showed me the way. We must go to the highlands. My dream showed me a portal being there."

Demetrius was unsure, without discussing his concerns he contacted Jacob. "Father," he said, hoping for guidance, "the cocoons are empty, we're out of options. Yeshe feels we must go to the Yeti lands. His visions show him a cliff-face where he believes a portal will open allowing us through to the Underworld. Should we go?"

Jacob said nothing for a few moments. "Magni and I are too far away," he eventually said, while processing the news that the cocoons were compromised, "there's nothing we can do to help. Trust your instincts son, they'll see you right?"

"But father," replied Demetrius, "I can't trust my instincts, Obelius is in and out of my head, his screams of pain are clouding my judgement."

"Yeshe's vision is sound," interrupted Magni, "it's the only course of action open to you. You will find his instincts are guiding him."

Demetrius said while looking towards the northern mountains, "They are so far away, but needs must. It will take too long if we walk so can I suggest something? There are seven here who can fly! Viktor and the dragons can each carry two of us, Finn and Aoife can carry one each." It was agreed, and all nineteen took to the sky to quickly arrive at the outskirts of the Yeti village.

On landing Yeshe's face showed how shocked he was. He stood there just staring, his mouth slightly opened, his eyes widened, his hands resting each side of his face. He was trying to take in the damage, every hut, every monument, every semblance of this once peaceful village was either partially or totally obliterated There was a stench still permeating the air, a stench left by the departing army of Shadow. The bodies of the few guardians, caught off-guard, still lay where they fell, and this was the worst thing for Yeshe especially when he recognised some of them to be his friends. He insisted on giving them the dignity of a proper burial before leading the gods higher up the mountains.

On climbing higher, they soon reached the white cliff face. "This must have been how the army of Shadow entered my homeland," wondered Yeshe aloud.

"It is" said Finn, "My father is known as the God of Travel, and I have many of his powers, I can confirm this is in fact how the forces of Hell entered the realm of the Yeti.

It didn't take too long for the Mystic Gods to open the portal; such was their combined power. The war gods cautiously led the way through the tunnels, passing many caverns filled with discarded bones. Yeshe, being the most sensitive, found the foul smell of decay overpowering making him retch and it wasn't long before they all sensed the rising toxicity. The deeper they travelled the more obvious it became that they were in another form of Hell, but they had no idea where it was. All contact with the Gods of Olympus was now lost suggesting they had also entered another dimension.

"I know you are the strong one," Viktor discreetly said to Drayce, "but I see the fear in your face and can hear your elevated heartbeat. You seem terrified, would you like me to take the lead?"

"You're right," replied Drayce, "I am terrified, are you not?"

"I've never known fear like this," said Viktor, "the power we nineteen share is formidable and that's what is keeping me going. I'm confident we can stand up to whatever is thrown at us. So, I ask again, would you like me to take the lead while you prepare an attack strategy?" Drayce just nodded.

Viktor walked ahead while Maximus made sure they all knew what they had to do. It was agreed no mercy would be shown and no prisoners taken. He also made sure that Li, Finn, and Yeshe shared in his power of being in two places at once. He placed the dragons on each side of the Mystic Gods and with Viktor's agreement he personally took responsibility for the Goddesses of the Light.

On leaving the tunnel they had a panoramic view across what was a vast valley, confirming they were in another dimension. Across the valley they observed numerous bonfires surrounded by what looked like very drunk Shadow Riders, what surprised them was the number of demons and Dark Angels in the vicinity. They continued observing and quickly found what they were looking for. It was a wooden structure containing three x-shaped crosses, each one holding a battered and bruised naked body. Drayce, using his dragon eyes, focused, and then gasped. "I've found them, they're spread-eagled between two thorn laden stakes and are being used by every passing demon as living punch bags. They're inflicting punches, whippings and doing other things, they're relentless in their depravity."

"I too see them," said Viktor, "They are causing just enough pain to take Obelius and Magnar close to their threshold, then, they back away. It looks like their plan is to keep them alive as long as possible. King Odi seems to be dead."

Viktor summoned Demetrius, suggesting he seek a link with Obelius not knowing that Demetrius was way ahead of him, he had already reached out. While in his brothers head he recalled every happy memory they shared trying to raise his spirits. Even with his intervention the power of Shadow continued to grow causing Obelius to fall in and out of consciousness, when he partially revived he pleaded, "Deme, help me; please help me. They're doing things to me." He gasped as another impact caused him to retch. "I think Uncle Odi is dead, he hasn't moved in hours. His body is wilting." He retched again, this time struggling to stop his whole body from violently jerking. "Magnar is defiant," he continued, "but I wonder how much longer he can hold out. He keeps calling for Aoife."

"We're working on a rescue plan" said Demetrius, trying to bolster him, "I promise this day will not be your last."

Aoife and Maximus were nearby, concerned that no attention was being paid to Magnar. Aoife tried to reach him, and when she did, she was shocked by the horrendous treatment he was receiving. She tried to encourage him, reminding him of their love for each other, reminding him about their walks through the misty walkways of the Fair Lands, the majesty of the Olympus meadows, their time swimming and making love in the lagoon, but more especially, she reminded him of the magic he found in his mother's realm. Soon he was at peace basking in her soothing words. Her connection was then broken, she was being blocked and didn't understand why.

Maximus attempted to help but he too was being blocked causing his patience to wear thin, he prepared to challenge Viktor who, at that moment, was transfixed by a new Light. "Magnar is safe," he said, "the spirit of your mother has arrived, she's protecting him." He kept staring and after turning to Maximus announced, "It's the very same spirit who visited you, that time in the meadows. She's invisible to Shadow and is cushioning the blows reigning down on your brother."

Demetrius then found himself suddenly blocked from protecting Obelius, but Maximus saw the danger and sent his spirit, wrapping his arms around him, encouraging him not to give up.

At the same time, the Mystic Gods slowly drifted into a trance, they were hearing voices. When they regained their consciousness, Aja announced, "The Ancient one has spoken. A Spark of Life is on its way; it will be here soon; it's intended for King Odi."

On hearing this news Viktor announced a change to the plan. He sent the War Gods to a ledge set close to the wooden structure; his plan was for the War Gods to create a distraction. He moved himself to a higher ledge hoping he'd create more confusion when shining his Light, expanding his wings, and blowing the trumpet of an Archangel. He instructed the Goddesses of the Light to remain where they were.

Gaia and Hemish moved to protect Maximus, while the remaining Mystic Gods awaited the arrival of the Spark. The dragons continued to guard the portals, planning to incinerate any agent of Shadow that tried to escape.

Aoife was by now distraught, sensing the deteriorating condition of Magnar and moved to break ranks. She didn't trust the spirit of Medeina to protect him, so she shrunk to her miniature size, preparing to fly to his aid. Demetrius pleaded with her to wait fearing any premature action would give the demons the advantage. With difficulty she agreed, but her heart was telling her something different.

In the meantime, Sunniva got more frantic, unable to feel the life force of her father. She also knew by the way Drayce and Viktor reacted on returning from the ridge, that he was indeed dead.

Before Viktor left he moved to comfort her. "I may not be an Archangel for very long," he said, trying to reassure her, "but one thing I'm sure of is, the Ancient One never allows anyone of the Light die without a fight. Aja has given you hope, the Spark of Life is on its way, and I promise he will be revived."

"How do you know the Spark of Life is for my father," she asked, still showing her concern, "could it not be for one of us if this rescue goes badly."

"Enough of this speculation," interrupted Demetrius, "the Spark of Life is for King Odi. This rescue will take no more than ten minutes to complete; there will be no time if it were for any of us."

"Look," said Kitaka, "here it comes, see how it travels towards us."

Demetrius, Amma, Aja and Kitaka went into invisibility before escorting the spark towards the ridge where Demetrius raised his hand, and just like Helena did all those years ago, he allowed it rest for a moment. He then gently used his power to guide it into Odi's now skeletal mouth.

Several minutes passed with no signs of life showing. "It's not working," said Sunniva as she turned on Demetrius, "look at him. There's still no sign of life, he's gone."

"You must have patience," replied Demetrius, while reaching in to embrace her, "the Ancient One never sends hope just to take it away. There will be a reason why he's not reviving."

Just then a portal opened, next to the still bound Obelius and Magnar. It was Lucifer and he appeared as the true Prince of Hell, he stood there wafting smoke and surrounded by flickering flames. Gone were his renowned chiselled good looks only to be replaced with the most hideous face of a demon. His wings spreading to over twelve feet.

Those sitting around the bonfires leapt to their feet and cheered while watching their beloved leader move to inflict more torture upon his captives. It wasn't to be, his attempt to bite into Magnar's neck failed, he was repulsed, and sent tumbling towards the nearby wall by a sudden burst of Light. Medeina's protection of her son was working.

When Lucifer recovered he saw an opportunity to taunt. "Ah, the whore of Magni," he sneered, "still trying to protect her little boy. Lady, don't you know? This is my domain."

He summoned the wraiths, the only entities with the ability to see spirits. When they arrived, they went into a frenzy, such was their hunger. The light emitted by the spirits of both Medeina and Maximus was so bright, it acted as a beacon, immediately drawing them to attack. Medeina and Maximus's spirits had no choice but to withdraw, leaving both Magnar and Obelius to suffer more of Lucifers debauchery. Medeina disappeared and Maximus woke up; the wraiths had completed their task.

Lucifer then continued with his torture by menacingly whispering his acidulous words before slowly sticking his unnaturally long tongue into

Magnar's ear, attempting to erase every happy memory he held. He then extended his nails.

At first it was the pitiful wince of a low groan, but then was heard groans that got louder and more constant to become heart wrenching screams as the nails dug deeper. For Magnar, the searing fiery bursts of pain pulsated around his now crimson wounds becoming unbearable as the slow methodical tearing of flesh intensified to become jarring and brutal. Each tensing of his muscles didn't bring relief only an amplification of pain that no god could ever be able to withstand. His natural and well-toned skin had now changed colour to take on the sickly and lifeless shade of death.

Viktor was watching and itching to act but knew he had to wait until everything was in place. He used his Archangel power's to telepathically reach Magnar. "Friend," he softly whispered, "remember I too have been in as dark a place as you, I too have suffered the unbelievable pain you're experiencing. Please, please hold on, we'll be with you soon and I promise, we'll take away the pain. Let the tide of consciousness ebb and flow and then when it ebbs again he will get bored."

Lucifer did get bored and went over to where Obelius was hanging, he gripped him by the hair to raise his head. "Look across at the spawn of Magni," he said while slowly turning Obelius's head, "see how he struggles to breathe, his innards are now a mess. See how his blood slowly oozes from his gaping wounds, watch it congeal and then, as he takes a deeper breath, watch how they reopen and relentlessly weep. Look on to his broken body and see how his abdomen has changed colour and is now lumpy, where once it was toned and smooth."

In all his pain Magnar managed to enter Obelius's head. "Cousin," he gasped, "my heart's breaking and no longer knows if it should keep beating. There'll be no more walks in the meadows for me, no more racing the white horses, or swimming in the soothing waters of the lagoon. The pain is erasing every happy thought I once had and is now paralyzing me. Let my last memory be of Aoife holding my hand before her soft lips reaches in to kiss mine." Magnar then fell back unconscious.

Viktor also managed to enter Obelius's head. "I just heard everything Magnar said and it's breaking my heart. Try bear the pain for just a short while longer. We're close, very close, and about to attack, but we must wait for all to be in place."

Lucifer relished the thoughts of what he was about to do, his anticipation of the pleasure he was about to get caused his breath to rapidly increase. He paced around the posts taking in the sight of the hapless, naked, and spread-eagled body before him. "Son of the Boy King," he said, licking his lips as he got closer, "the one who claimed to be one of the last faces I will see. Strange how the tables have turned, strange that now it will be my face to be the last one you will see."

Obelius managed to turn his head and spit, only for Lucifer to just extend his tongue and lick the spittle away. "Ah, very tasty, but not half as tasty as the blood I am about to drink."

"How is it?" gasped a now very weak Obelius, "how is it you are so bereft of empathy and so empty of love? Where is your compassion and conscience?"

The only answer he got was the excruciating pain of fangs penetrating his neck. "I don't need weapons to hurt you," Lucifer sneered after extracting his fangs, "just my nails, my teeth, but most importantly my words. When I'm finished I will have known the satisfaction of watching you squirm as your real pain begins, but my greatest thrill will be watching your eyes darken as the Light fades." So began the torture of Obelius.

It was long and harrowing, filled with a raw cruelty designed to last for days. At times he went quiet, trying to suppress the pain, then he'd just pant so as to garner further brief moments of relief. The scratch marks now reached all parts of his body and felt like a thousand paper cuts being delivered. For him, the constant pain felt like a vice-grip, choking the very air from deep within. His bones felt as though they no longer supported him, and his brain felt like an icy wind had arrived to freeze all the memories he cherished. He knew it was futile to hope for rescue and being so proud he chose to bite his lip so as to keep from crying out. He went unconscious, about to give up his spirit. Rescue did come, and it was from an unexpected source. It was Odi, the Spark of Life had finally revived him.

From the ridge Finn and Yeshe were so intent in watching the torture of Magnar and Obelius that they failed to notice the resurrection of Odi. When Finn finally noticed he leapt to his feet and hurled a sword in Odi's direction. This was the cue for Drayce to launch the planned attack beginning with Viktor revealing himself for all to see; he loudly blew his trumpet then spread his wings, transforming into an Archangel. He sent his light across the valley, blinding the demons and attracting the attention of Lucifer. It was then when the War Gods released their arrows bringing down a rain of death upon many of the Riders, demons, and Dark Angels. Maximus joined in the attack while fighting his way towards the platform, planning to rescue his brother. Demetrius went into invisibility, and joined by Hemish, they quickly made their way to rescue Obelius.

Lucifer raged; he hated being interrupted while torturing any victim, especially a victim whose father was the God of Gods. When he turned he was met by a naked and armed Odi who immediately went on the attack but unfortunately he wasn't fully recovered and was no match for the master of deceit. He did get a few blows in but was very much at a disadvantage until the goddesses materialised. They were led by Eliana, and they let loose the most dazzling light ever emitted. It was so strong it repelled Lucifer, sending him violently crashing against the valley walls. He was outwitted again, but everyone knew his revenge wouldn't be long in coming.

The battle wasn't over; there was still danger. Many Riders, Demons, and Dark Angels, attempted to escape through three portals hidden around the valley but for them there was no escape. The portals were identified earlier by the dragons, and they were waiting. Without mercy, they released their flame with such ferociousness nothing stood a chance of surviving. The dragons were ruthless in their attack and didn't stop until all demons were vanquished, and when they were sure none survived, they then moved to bring down the portals. Osian, although in the throes of battle, did catch a glimpse of a very dark wispy black mist escaping and he wondered.

On the platform Magnar and Obelius were untied and laid on the ground, both so seriously injured their survival was in doubt. Sunniva removed her cape and said while wrapping it around her father, "I can't have a King of Asgard walking around naked, especially when that king is my father." She then left him and went to join the other goddesses who were with Demetrius and the Mystic Gods. All ten formed a large circle around Odi, Magnar, and Obelius, lowered their heads and brought forth their Light. When it came it was so bright it penetrated deep into their souls, beginning the healing process. It didn't take long, all breaks, tears, scars, and bruises, began healing.

Aoife reached in and took a still naked Magnar into her arms. "I too want to hold your hand," she said, holding him closer and whispering in his ear, "I too want to kiss your lips while walking in the meadows of Olympus."

"You read my thoughts?" he replied, still numb and having difficulty trying to talk.

"It seems our love for each other is stronger than we thought," she said, reaching up for a kiss, "of course I read your thoughts. You better get used to it."

Demetrius held Obelius only to find that he too was numb. He assisted him to his feet. "I thought we lost you," he said, "I've never been so devastated."

Obelius had difficulty standing but when he did, he felt the power and warmth of his brother surround him.

"In the last few hours," continued Demetrius, holding his brother even tighter, "I received visions, showing me twin boys, future Warrior Gods. Obelius, they're your boys, you're a father, and soon you'll meet them. Find your strength and prepare to become the great pappa you are destined to be."

Obelius was still shattered and had difficulty taking in the good news, it was slow to sink in but when it did the old Obelius began shining through.

Finn and Li located the discarded clothes and assisted Odi to dress, while Demetrius and Maximus assisted Obelius and Magnar. Demetrius helped Obelius fasten his belt and secure his armour. "You definitely have a fat ass!" he said with a cheeky smile.

Obelius didn't respond but Viktor did. "After what you've just been through," he said, "I wouldn't worry about a fat ass. I too saw a vision and it showed you carrying two little boys, that's what I'd worry about. You, being a father, just doesn't go together? Odin, help them." Obelius managed to smile, nodding his head in agreement.

Odi had regained his strength and asked to be updated on all what had happened since the attack on Olympus, and when he was fully briefed he asked Drayce to lead the way back to the temple.

Drayce led them from the valley and through the tunnels, to exit back into the Yeti realm where the dragons were waiting. Odi was last to exit and when he joined Drayce he said, "It's time you did your worst."

Drayce, Galyna, Osian and Isidra lined up and retook their dragon form. They released their fire and sustained its power until the entrance collapsed. They weren't finished, they released a second burst and this time the cliff-face melted and flowed before forming into solid rock, completely sealing the entrance, protecting the Yeti Lands against any further attack. Odi thanked the dragons and apologised to Yeshe for leaving a dark reminder of the devastating attack so close to his home.

Osian joined Odi. "There's something I need to report, I know we destroyed every Rider, demon and Dark Angel that tried to escape, none got by our flame, but, through the corner of my eye, I thought I saw a swiftly moving wisp of a black mist. It was dark and sinister. It then disappeared."

Odi stopped, thought for moment, then said, "If you, as a dragon lord, think you saw a dark and sinister mist, even if it's through the corner of your eye, I'll act as if it's true. We are dealing with the greatest deceiver, and every bone in my body tells me this is not over."

They continued their journey and quickly reached the meadows. On the way to the temple Odi attempted to contact Jacob but failed to reach him, he turned to Demetrius. "Your father's unreachable, any ideas?"

"I don't really know," replied Demetrius, "before we entered the tunnels a sphere left the temple, it was carrying father and uncle Magni. I sensed their urgency; they weren't going to stop." Odi said no more.

They soon reached the terraces and quickly climbed the steps, all except Obelius. He hesitated before turning to Drayce and Viktor. "I can't do this," he said, "I need some time alone. Please give my apologies."

He made his way through the remnants of the ornamental gardens and reached the seat near the statue of David, where he sat staring out towards the mountains. He wasn't destined to be alone for long, his mother arrived. "Once you heard your father speak of how we split our hearts into three," she said moving to embrace him, "the thought of almost losing one of those parts nearly killed me."

Obelius lay his head on her shoulder, he was still suffering and took his time finding the words. "I'm a War God of Olympus and here I am crying in my mother's arms, should I be ashamed?"

"Ashamed?" she whispered, "why would you be ashamed? I'm your mother and no matter how old you are, you'll always be my baby. My shoulder will forever be there for you. Now, come on, speak up, have you not got something important to tell me?"

He wondered for a moment, then realised what she meant, he lit up. "Deme had a vision, it told him my babies are born, two little boys, mother I can't believe it. Aria is amazing. I wasn't with her, and that's bothering me. I hope she wasn't alone."

"Congratulations son," said Eala, "I'm so proud of you. Now, pull yourself together and into the temple with you, it's important for all gods to be present when King Odi opens the cocoons."

With his mother's support Obelius made his way into the temple and was pleased to see Viktor sitting close by. "I can't thank you enough for entering my head when you did," he said, "I lost the will to live until you encouraged me. There's no better friend."

"You would have done the same for me," replied Viktor.

Just then Odi loudly cleared his throat, indicating he was seeking quietness. Before using his powers, he walked among the nine cocoons hoping none were breached and when he satisfied himself all was well he returned to the steps. He looked around at the anxious faces then raised his staff, lowered his head, and spoke a few magic words, "Lux saeculorum, venit ad me. Ostende mihi virtutem ad eos liberos." (Light of ages, come on to me. Show me the power to set them free.)

The Light came and soon the cocoons cracked open revealing the dead gods. Seeing the condition of each god shocked everyone, especially those directly related. Their injuries included severed muscles and tendons, crushed faces, broken bones as well as widespread bruising. All caused by swords, embedded arrows, and spears, as well as medieval-like spiked chain maces.

Odi got anxious when nothing seemed to be happening, he prepared to repeat his spell fearing his intervention was too late, but he should have had more faith. In the meadows a violent wind blew, then all quietened. The main doors burst open, and nine specks of dust arrived, each one glowing, showing they were the sparks of life. They drifted towards the nine cocoons, and as they approached, their Light intensified before entering the now emaciated mouths of each body. Very quickly, the arrows and spears turned to dust and fell away, torn flesh healed, bruises faded, and bones knitted back together. The cocoons then disintegrated.

The first stirrings happened almost immediately when Modi leapt to his feet, looking very confused. He knew his son had been killed and worried his daughter may have also fallen, his face lit up when he saw Sofia race the length of the Great Hall to embrace him. He then looked around for Tristan, who was beginning to stir.

Zane was next to awaken, he was the least injured, but his spirit seemed broken, that was until Aja and Kitake assisted him to his feet. Aodh and Lir were next to open their eyes, and both struggled to stand until they were assisted by Finn and Aoife. Aodh couldn't relax until Eliana came into view.

There was a gap of about twenty minutes before Cetan sat up, he was very shaky until Yeshe arrived to assist him to his feet. Hai then awoke, he was full of life, a smile from ear to ear, especially when he was greeted by his brother, Li. Thora took longer to revive and when she did it was her baby she asked after, forgetting her baby was safely in the vaults. Her face lit up when she saw Viktor racing towards her.

Another hour passed before Arum began to stir and when he did finally stand, he looked shuck. "I reached the tombs," he said as Eliana and Aodh helped him to his feet. "They turned me away saying it wasn't my time, they showed me the last battle but not its end." He stumbled again, still weak, then said for all to hear, "Before the sun sets this day, the last battle between good and evil, between Uncle Jacob and Lucifer will be fought. I wasn't shown how the fight ends."

Chapter 18

Meanwhile the sphere containing Jacob and Magni continued travelling across the universe, its destination still hidden. Their journey began slowly, only increasing its pace after passing Mars, Jupiter, and Saturn; it was there where they witnessed the first of many spectacular cosmic displays, beginning with Saturn's colourful light filled storms and the way they swirled while roaming its violent atmosphere. They passed Uranus and then Neptune after which they gathered speed and made their way deeper out into space.

"Not far from here Marduk and I found a sun that suited our needs," said Magni, trying not to get too upset. "See that," he pointed to a star two left of Alpha Centauri, "that's where we built our home. One day I had hoped to show you what I'd built using my own hands, but now, all I want to do is avoid it. Too many bad memories."

"You're too hard on yourself," replied Jacob, hoping to make him feel better, "remember, good memories also came from what you built, look at your boys. Always remember the good things." They went quiet while taking in the beauty all around them.

"I'm always amazed at what's before us," said Magni, "billions of glistening stars just staring back.

"Did the ancients ever try to count them?" asked Jacob.

"There was a time," replied Magni, "just after the creation. Some of us asked that very question and were laughed at. We tried to work it out. In the Milky Way galaxy alone, there are over a hundred billion stars, can you imagine how many planets surround them? The Ancient One laughed at us because apparently, in the visible part of the universe there are in excess of two trillion galaxies, that's a figure a normal brain would have difficulty in comprehending, let alone the brain of a god."

Their speed increased as they passed four supernovas, one that was so big its light was bent into an arc by the gravity of a passing galaxy.

"Helena," remarked Jacob, "from an early age, could bend light. It's one of her greatest powers."

"That one has more powers than you can imagine," said Magni, "she will be formidable: my heart goes out to Drayce. I hope he's strong enough."

They continued their journey and soon passed a most colourful sight. It was the Crab Nebula and to them it was awe inspiring, it was so vast its gases swirled in all directions.

"Look to your left," suggested Magni, "there's another Nebula you should see, it's known as the Bubble Nebula, and at its centre is a star, forty-five times the size of earths sun. There are many things a god should see in their long lifetime and that star is certainly one of them. Watch the solar winds, see how they guide the interstellar gases to form a giant bubble. Truly that's an impressive sight."

They moved on, zigzagging in different directions, for fear they were being monitored. They encountered rogue planets, the ones that wandered the cosmos without the gravitational pull of a star to tie them down. "Some of those planets defy physics," said Magni, "they create clouds filled with molten metals."

They then passed quasars and more supernovas, a colourful and primal beauty, holding their gazes for many hours before they moved on to reach a neighbouring galaxy.

"Ah," said Magni, "it's many years since I last visited this amazing place, it's known as the large Magellanic Cloud, made from thick cosmic dust, concealing numerous comets, and shooting stars. Look further ahead, you will see two further galaxies. They always make me smile, look at them, they seem to have what looks like a smiling mouth. The two galaxies look like eyes, and the smile is caused by what's called, strong gravitational lensing. The gravitational pull of all the nearby galaxy clusters is so strong it warps space-time around them. The light from distant galaxies gets caught in its pull, distorting it to present as arcs or circles."

"I never knew you to be an astronomer," said an impressed Jacob, "I'm speechless. I can't think of anyone so least likely to be a scholar, and I mean that with the greatest respect."

"Brother," he continued, after not saying anything for a while, "I've never been as comfortable with anyone as I am right now. I can't thank you enough."

The journey across the cosmos, although relatively quick, was special for Jacob. He worshipped Magni, and spending such a long time with him was one of his dearest wishes. He felt they were really bonding. He listened to, and enjoyed all his amazing stories, before asking question after question. It never dawned on him that Magni, being a War God, would be so knowledgeable.

They passed many more amazing sights, none more so than the galactic light shows. They felt shockwaves, and watched reservoirs of gas, emit the most spectacular beams of light, but nothing prepared them for the spiral galaxies, especially the ones with the extra arms spiralling out to the edge of the Nothingness. They remained close by just for a short while enjoying the stunning, dazzling, and colourful galactic displays generated by the enormous black holes at their centre.

Their enjoyment was not to last, they both showed a new sense of purpose and changed direction taking them into a vast Nebula that spanned such a distance, a thousand light years would normally be required to cross. There was no danger from the swirling winds or the toxic gasses wafting all around them, so they continued their journey into its centre where, up ahead, they saw a thicker cloud bank. Arriving at the base of the cloud bank was uneventful; even so it was a bit disconcerting, there were no visible platforms or breaks in the cloud.

"Just steer into the clouds," suggested Magni, with a snigger, "and place your faith in the gods."

Jacob was unsure but always trusted Magni, so he turned the sphere and just as he reached the cloudbank a wide platform appeared.

They stepped from the sphere, cautiously investigating what was around them. They soon located a narrow stone stairwell that seemed to wind its way up and out of view. It was set between two rugged, moss and vine-covered walls, and was just about wide enough for one God at a time to climb. The vines at the base were bare but the higher they climbed they found the branches to be in full leaf. It was an arduous climb and seemed to take forever but they persevered and eventually reached the top. On reaching the highest step they were breathless, something that was unusual for War Gods.

They stepped on to an even wider platform that had a number of stone benches set each side of two ornate pillars holding heavy metal gates. The gates were unguarded and open, encouraging them to walk through. When through they found themselves standing at the edge of a pristine meadow not that unlike the meadows of Olympus, but they knew it wasn't Olympus. There were no galloping horses, no chirping birds, there was no crashing waves, no sound of chattering children or boisterous teenagers. Even the wind failed to blow. It was absolute silence, so calm it was unnerving. They soon felt they were in a place that was transcendent, full of wonder.

In the distance they saw a high jagged rock formation, one that was bathed in golden sunlight, reflecting its beams in all directions, creating an image not that unlike a halo. At the base of the formation was a large stone trestle style table placed on a perfectly manicured lawn. Five ornately carved stone thrones sat at the back of the table, each one identical, reminded them of Zeus's throne back in Olympus.

They made their way across the meadows. Eventually reaching a canyon so deep they'd no way of crossing. Jacob linked Magni and attempted to blink only to fail. "My powers are gone," he said, looking around in surprise. "What's happening?"

"No idea," replied Magni, "at least we can still enter each other's heads."

"That was sneaky," said Jacob, wondering how much private information Magni had accumulated on all the gods, "I didn't know you had that power."

"It's the one power I kept to myself," he replied, "having that power gave me a great advantage. The best part is I can do it undetected."

Magni realised they had lost their powers much earlier, he noticed how they both struggled to climb the steps, and his fears were confirmed, judging by how long it took them to recover after they reached the top.

"Where are we?" asked Jacob, hoping Magni knew.

"I know exactly where we are!" replied Magni, "it's where the first war was fought. This is the domain of the Ancient One."

Why would the Ancient One want to see us?" asked Jacob, "did he not decide to give all of creation the right to choose their own destiny?"

"He did," answered Magni, "but always remember, where there's light there's darkness, where there's peace there's war, where there's good there's evil, need I go on. Is it possible your battle against Lucifer isn't balanced? Is it possible that where there is the Ancient One there's always Lucifer, and your battle is one of those battles that can never be won, unless by the hand of the Ancient One?"

"You're not making sense," said a confused Jacob, "if what you say is the case, why would he bother to create us gods to carry out his 'Will' when all the time he knew we can't win? Why would he give us our emotions and allow us fall in love or have children just so Lucifer could use it against us?" Magni just shrugged his shoulders.

"See how the thrones are now occupied," said Magni, pointing towards the table, "look upon the pure white robes and the light that surrounds them, see the golden crowns and how they hold their sun halos in place, look who sits at the table. I feel you are about to get the answers to all your questions."

They waited a few more moments as a light created, magical bridge materialised, one that was held in place by the wings of twelve angels. Their excitement grew as they crossed and made their way into the presence of the Ancient One. They found it difficult to avert their eyes and when they did they were thrilled to see Shango and Zeus sitting to his right, and Dione and Odin sitting to his left. There was no armour, no weapons, no guards. There was no need. This was the safest place in existence.

"What do I do now?" whispered Jacob as he bowed, "all the questions I wanted to ask are gone, I've no memory of them."

"My amazing grandson," said Zeus, "welcome to the domain of the Ancients. Your journey from being born in Crete to today has been really

250

impressive, you've been really tested and still you survive. Truly you are our God of Gods."

"My dearest Grandson," said Odin, getting up to greet Magni. "We felt your pain and hope the one we sent will help take it away."

Magni looked confused and wondered who was sent. Jacob entered his head, "Its Baldor, idiot."

Odin then placed both his hands on Jacob's shoulders. "When first I met you I knew you were special, your humanity made you different and that's the greatest gift your mother gave you. You are the God of Gods, but I'm afraid your battle isn't over. We brought you here to prepare you for what's coming. You are the bait."

The Ancient One stood and used his intangibility to walk through the table. He reached Jacob and took him by the arm. "Come, young god," he said, "walk with me."

They walked through the meadows for many hours, the Ancient Ones hand permanently resting on Jacob's arm. During this time Jacob was being shown everything that was to happen, spanning the next ten thousand years. He was also being shown what was happening to Odi, Obelius, and Magnar, as well as the rescue that was taking place. He tried to be strong, but his humanity betrayed him while watching the murder of Odi, and the abuse of his son and nephew. He fell to his knees in despair, covering his ears trying to drown out Obelius's painful pleas for rescue. He attempted to blink his way to help, but found his powers were still suppressed.

The Ancient one assisted him back to his feet. "You now know every-thing," he said, "and even with that wealth of knowledge it is I and I alone who will have to end this war. As Odin said, you will be my bait. Every word you speak and every action you take won't be yours; they will be mine. When you face him, he won't know until it's too late. When he grasps what's happening will be when I appear. It will be his end and only then will peace reign for the promised ten thousand years."

The Ancient One gathered a few specks of dust and gestured Jacob to follow him. They made their way towards the canyon where a very wide portal opened showing them a passageway towards Earth. The Ancient One then raised his hand and blew. "There goes the Sparks of Life," he said, "they will travel for ten thousand years and it's you who will be there to receive them. It's you who will still rule Olympus."

He then raised his hand again and this time when he blew, only one speck was seen to leave. "That is another spark of life," he said. "It will travel much faster and will reach its destination soon after you return to Olympus. It's my gift to you, a gift I believe you really want."

"I seek nothing for myself," said Jacob, "other than getting home to be with my family. If the truth be known, all I want is to restore peace to all realms." He thought for a moment before continuing. "Even though you have shown me the future, it's what's happening to my son that's really upsetting me."

"Take my gift," said the Ancient One, placing his finger over Jacob's lips, "you will love it. That Spark of Life is a part of your future I've hidden. Trust me; it's a gift you really want."

Jacob looked through the portal, taking in the beauty of the universe, and when he turned back to ask another question, the Ancient One was gone, and by the time he reached Magni all the ancient gods had disappeared.

"We're alone," said Magni, "I guess we should travel back to Olympus?" Jacob just slowly nodded.

They returned to the sphere and used the still open portal to lessen their journey. They travelled through several more portals at a speed that saw them arrive near Neptune in less than ten minutes. There was no time for a full conversation, but Jacob knew Magni was itching to know what the Ancient One said. He left him wondering choosing to keep what was about to happen to himself. He felt invigorated knowing the full power of the Ancient One was now by his side. He continued to say nothing even though he sensed Magni's curiosity was getting the better of him. Magni eventually could take it no more. "Well," he demanded, "are you going to tell me?"

Jacob deflected the question, looking out at the stars. "In every direction the stars shine brighter. I feel they know what the Ancient One has decided. One more chance he has given me, one more battle to end all battles."

"Does he not know how depleted our armies are," asked Magni, "does he not care?"

"Enter my head and tell me what it is I must do," said Jacob, raising his hands and placing them on each side of Magni's face. Magni then witnessed the plan of the Ancient One; he backed away looking really upset.

"Brother," he said, trying to find the right words, "I don't know what to say."

"I ask you again," said Jacob, "tell me what it is I must do? Tell me, Lord of Asgard. Ten steps ahead, who wins?"

"This time there are no ten steps," replied Magni, "this time the War God of Asgard has no plan. My powers have deserted me and I've no idea what to do, or what to say." He went very quiet, staring out at the stars. "Strange how we fly through the universe not sure about what it is we face, yet the Ancient One knows, he always knows. Brother, tilt your head and gaze upon just one star, the brightest one, look at the planet to its right. Keep staring, how is it we can see their souls, all at once? Is that what makes us gods and guardians of creation?"

"Brother," said Jacob, leaning across and taking Magni's hand. "It's definitely what makes us Gods. Stop worrying, this day, before the sun sets on Olympus, it'll finally be over."

They travelled passed Uranus, Saturn, Mars and then the moon. They then reached Earth and made their way towards the Middle East, landing close to the steps of the temple. There was nobody there to greet them. All, including Eris, Athena, Apollo, and Ares were in the temple listening to stories about the rescue of Odi, Obelius and Magnar.

When they entered the temple all present bowed as Jacob made his way to sit on his throne.

"Son," said Magni, checking on Magnar, "the Ancient One showed Jacob what happened, Jacob then showed me. It broke my heart knowing the same thing happened to me. You will recover and go on to have a happy and long life with Aoife. Cherish her, she really loves you." He then stood next to Jacob.

Jacob still said nothing; he stared across at Eala who was seen raising her hand to cover her mouth. Those watching then knew she had just telepathically learned something upsetting and was having difficulty dealing with it. Odi also picked up the troubling news, he tried to enter Jacob's head but was prevented.

Jacob stood and was assisted by Magni to remove his tunic and outer skirt. He then removed the scabbard from below his knee. A steward arrived with a narrow headband, securing his tousled hair. All he was left wearing was a short loose wrap, and light sandals that were securely strapped to his ankles. He held his sword before him as though examining its sharpness, then he began walking towards the door.

On his way he was confronted by a troubled Obelius who had limped across to stop him. "Father," he pleaded, "wait until I'm fully recovered, you'll need me as your guardian, please don't go out there. Please don't do this."

Jacob still said nothing: he leaned in to kiss his son's forehead, then gently moved him aside and kept walking. He used his magic to open the doors and was soon standing alone out on the terrace. He looked towards the horizon, and sure enough, there was a solitary figure walking towards him. His flowing black robes showed his menace, his sharp horns, pointed chin and fiery eyes completed his demonic face. It was the occasional expanding of his massive wings that confirmed it was Lucifer. This was certainly to be the final battle.

Jacob watched him approach, wondering was the staff he was carrying the one used to kill Heulwyn. He felt it was a staff so dark it could only have been created by being dipped in the fires of Hell. It bothered him when the suns light bounced off the black gem set in its orb, sending dark beams in all directions, making it very difficult for him to maintain a clear view of Lucifers face. When he did get a clear view he saw the arrogance, the determination, and the confidence. He wondered why Lucifer believed he was so invinsible.

Jacob walked to meet him and when he was within twenty metres he stopped. "There will be no more questions, no answers. There'll be no more talking, only listening. I am Jacob, God of Gods - Guardian of Olympus. You will not leave these sacred lands alive; your time is up."

He raised his sword and tossed it a good distance away from both of them, an action that alarmed his sons who had arrived out on to the terrace to watch.

Lucifer began taunting him, starting with his almost naked body. He then teased him by telling him about the pleasure he got from tormenting his naked son. Jacob winced, trying to contain himself while thinking of his son being abused.

When the taunts didn't work Lucifer turned his palm towards the sky, and using an ancient magic he created fireballs. He then propelled the fireballs, in quick succession, towards Jacob, who just used a gentle motion of his hand to raise a light filled shield, casting the fireballs aside. Lucifer then pointed the tip of his staff towards the watching gods who had gathered on the steps of the temple, but his efforts were again repelled: Athena and Magni had anticipated this move and created their own invisible shield.

Lucifer then sent shock waves through the soil so as to upend Jacob, but he again failed, Jacob just raised himself six feet above the ground. He never said a word, never responded, he just allowed Lucifer attack and attack. More molten fireballs were produced, and Lucifer swung them above his head linking them using strings of fire. He released them and this time he made contact. The strings wrapped themselves around Jacob causing what looked like an explosion of violent light. The intense light and flame rose towards the Heavens suggesting Jacob was incinerated, causing a great deal of concern among the gods, especially Obelius. For a while there was no sign of Jacob, but he materialised behind Lucifer ready to continue drawing him out.

Lucifer then resorted to releasing his allies by opening a portal and called on the ferocious Hounds of Hell as well as a nest of Wraiths. His patience was wearing thin, his determination to destroy Jacob, then take the temple, was clouding his judgement. His temper was really being tested by Jacob's silence and stoicism.

All the Gods now gathered on the steps were watching the conflict between what seemed to them to be two equals, they failed to understand why they were not being called into action. Magni encouraged them to hold their nerve but didn't tell them that the battle was skewed in favour of the Light and it was to be the final battle between the forces for good and the forces for evil.

Modi and Odi didn't listen and made moves to attack but were forcefully stopped by Magni. "Brothers," he yelled, "you must have patience. Jacob is protected and is just playing with him. Keep watching, something, unseen since the beginning of time is about to happen."

At the very same time Obelius and Demetrius were getting more upset, and they too started making moves towards assisting their father. They were also stopped by Magni. "This is one battle you cannot be part of," he said, trying to calm them, "it's the last battle. The Ancient One has spoken."

The hounds circled Jacob, but he didn't flinch, they snapped at his feet and legs but never made contact. The wraiths attempted to possess him, flying towards him at speed, but all that happened was they were repelled back through the portal. Jacob allowed the hounds attack for a few more moments, then finally he had enough, he waited until they were within ten feet of him, he clicked his fingers, and the hounds turned to dust. He had difficulty in preventing a smile from crossing his face, but he allowed it. Even so he still said nothing, just kept staring.

Lucifer had boundless energy, and the stand-off seemed to go on for an age. He was not going to give up now that he was so close. He opened another portal and this time he called his demons to drag out the latest captured souls, those that were of the Light.

There must have been a thousand of them, he stood back and allowed his demons systematically savage the souls by tearing them limb from limb. They used every form of torture imaginable, but Jacob still didn't react. The goddesses on the temple steps were about to, until Magni convinced them to do nothing. "Jacob is playing a blinder," he said, "he knows Lucifer is conjuring these scenes, what's happening isn't real."

Lucifer didn't realise his days were in fact numbered and they had now reached zero. Not even when the atmosphere changed did he detect danger, or when the light drastically dimmed did he sense that something was wrong. Even when a violent wind crossed the lagoon, causing waves to flow over the meadows, he didn't feel a threat. It was only after a vibrant beam of light streaked across the sky when he became alarmed. His alarm intensified when the light turned back to form a flaming pillar alongside Jacob. It arrived with such force every nearby planet felt its power. It was a different light, pulsating, radiant and angry. Jacob kept staring and was not affected by its radiance, but Lucifer was. He was being blinded, causing him to back away to cower behind some boulders. He was visibly shook, knowing he was now out of his depth. He knew he was going to be subjected to the wrath of the Ancient One.

From the pillar of light stepped a very elderly man, white haired and bearded, wearing the most brilliant white robes and carrying a staff bearing at its tip a repository of the First Light. He immediately used a quick flick of his hand to roll the boulders away, revealing Lucifer on his knees and showing real fear. The Ancient One then used a slow movement of his hand to raise Lucifer up into a hanging position. "Will you ever learn," he said, loud enough for the universe to hear, "I created the gods to guard my creations while I slept. You caused the first war and lost; you continuously use your wily ways to bring chaos, but no more. Your arrogance reached into my dreams, forcing me to awaken and when I'm awake you know how agitated I get. I will not make the same mistake, I'm again going to place you into a cocoon but this time, no incantation, no prayer, no magic will penetrate its power. Your cocoon will not be in a cave but will be encased in one of the many rogue planets of solid rock, and only I will know which one, and where it is."

There was no more discussion, he clicked his finger, and a cocoon arrived to surround Lucifer. He clicked his finger again and a barren planet appeared as a second moon circling earth. He clicked his finger for the third time and the cocoon shot out towards the planet.

The Gods watched the cocoon explosively plunge into the surface of the planet before being completely encased, to be concealed deep in its core. The Ancient One clicked his finger for the fourth and last time, and the planet was gone.

"Now," he said, turning to Jacob, "for the next ten thousand years, go and enjoy the peace gifted to all realms."

"What happens after ten thousand years?" asked Jacob.

"Still the worrier, your greatest strength," said the Ancient one as he slowly faded, "you have the power to slow down time, making my gift possibly one hundred thousand years. Worry about The Darkness, Shadow, Lucifer, whoever, at another time, but always remember, dark magic is everywhere. It will interrupt peace, but it'll be vanquished easily. At the moment it's in retreat. Your task, and that of the gods, is to keep it at bay." He disappeared.

Chapter 19

For Jacob, the battle was truly over, and he was looking forward to the peaceful times ahead. He made his way back to the temple where, on reaching the steps, he was greeted by Magni. "Truly my brother," he said, while draping a cape across Jacob's shoulder, "truly you are the God of Gods."

They climbed the steps and on reaching the doors they were met by Demetrius, and a still struggling Obelius. Jacob immediately sensed the mental struggles Obelius was suffering, and offered to help. Before taking him aside he spoke to Demetrius. He deliberately embraced him, remembering their conversation some months back. "Son," he said, "I'm so proud of all you achieved while Olympus was being attacked, but right now and just like in the past, your brother needs me more. Trust me, he really needs me. Go with Magni and prepare for the opening of the vaults." When Magni and Demetrius left Jacob rejoined Obelius. "Do you want me to show you what happened went I was being tortured?"

"I already know, you don't have to show me," replied Obelius, moving his head to rest on his father's shoulder, "I still feel his claws tear into me, and the shame won't go away. While using my body as his plaything he shared his memories of what he did to you, he kept comparing us, saying, 'like father, like son.' Father, your arms around me is helping, but the memory of what he did is like a mist building up to cloud my view of this once peaceful land. How can I look on the faces of my sons knowing what he did to me? Today, I should be the happiest god in the universe, but I'm broken, a War God who's beaten. "

Jacob looked confused. "Sons?" he said.

"Yes, twin boys," replied Obelius, "Demetrius had a vision showing the birth of my babies."

"All the more reason to open the vaults right away," said Jacob, showing his delight. "Come, pull yourself together and begin learning to be a father."

"I'm not ready to enter the Great Hall," said Obelius, still wanting comfort from his father, "I can't get the shame from my mind, it's eating away at me. The only thing that got me through was Demetrius reaching out to me, giving me hope. I was the one who always watched out for him, and in the end it was he who rescued me. I'm so proud to have him as my brother."

Jacob tightened his grip. "Your pain will soon be gone," he said, "and the bad memories will lessen to drift away into the mists of time. Peace will soon be yours and trust me, you'll need it with all the sleepless nights coming your way. I insist we make our way to the Great Hall, are you ready?" Obelius reluctantly nodded.

Jacob paused. "Change of plan," he said, looking back out across the meadows, "there's no way I'll allow the realms leave the vaults into a wilderness that smells of death and has no beauty. Olympus must be restored to its former glory. Summon the Mystic Gods and ask your mother and Panya to join us."

While waiting, Jacob used his powers to restore the folly by magically removing the smoke stains and blood spatter from the white marble columns, allowing it to once again, gleam in the bright afternoon sunlight. He then went to the ornamental gardens and used his magic to cleanse the pond waters, bringing them back to be clear and pristine, awaiting the return of the lilies, grasses, and exotic fish that once dwelt there. He wasn't finished, he worked to repair and cleanse the many statues and benches damaged during the attack, bringing them back to be bright and white. All that was left was for the flowers and shrubs to bloom and soon they did.

Demetrius and Hemish were first to arrive and without being asked they knew what to do. They went to the edge of the terrace and plunged their hands into the soil, summoning the assistance of the Earth Mothers. All across the meadows, out as far as the treeline, the soil violently vibrated.

Aja, Amma, Gaia and Kitaka arrived and used their skills to turn the soil making it receptive to new growth. They then raised their hands and separated their fingers, pointing them into the meadows. From their fingers the seeds of grasses, wildflowers, shrubs, and trees shot out to nestle into the softened soil.

Next to use their magic was Panya and Eala, they created the clouds and from those clouds came a soft and gentle, yet continuous rain, bringing all that was needed to moisten the soil encouraging the seeds to quickly germinate.

By now all gods were out on the steps witnessing the rebirth of Olympus. Not only were they taking in the many shades of green that stretched from the temple all the way to the distant woodlands, but they were also enjoying the burst of colour that pleasured their eyes as all across the meadows the flowers and shrubs exploded into bloom.

Jacob was pleased, even though he knew there was still more to be done. He looked across at the lagoon to see it was still struggling. The reeds hadn't returned, unable to flourish in the still murky and heavily polluted water.

"You may be the God of Gods," said Odi, after joining him, "but I think even you will have difficulty sorting this one. It's a good job I'm here."

"It certainly is," replied Jacob. "At the beginning of time the Ancient One blew a speck of dust out into the universe, it travelled for millions of years. It was the Spark of Life, and it revived me after Helena blew it towards my body. He sent another and it was destined to revive you. When Demetrius blew it towards you, was when you and I became equal, so yes, it's a good job you are here, together we will restore all realms, and it starts now."

They both raised their arms and called on the Light. When it came they focused it on a single spot creating a violently rotating whirlpool that sucked the sludge and murky water away revealing the cleansed sand of the seabed. Odi picked up a number of nearby rocks and fired them high into the sky. They reached a great height before turning back to puncture the sand on impact, to reach the water table causing geysers to erupt. What was erupting was clear and pristine water that quickly refilled the lagoon. Soon after the waves came and then the beginnings of the white foam.

"You know what to do," said Jacob turning to Hemish.

Hemish and the other five Mystic Gods made their way down to the shoreline. They set themselves thirty feet apart, and after a few moments of deep meditation they used their magic. As the gentle waves crashed, the white foam increased in height then thickened until one large wave rolled in to push the foam onto the beach. When it touched the sand, it transformed into the herds, the white horses had returned.

Demetrius then reopened a portal allowing the Mer-peoples swim through. On the western side of the lagoon the reeds reappeared and soon the dragonflies returned followed by the mayflies. On the far side of the lagoon the ancient forests burst into leaf bringing on the return of birds. The Mystic Gods had completed their task. When Jacob was satisfied everything in the meadows was back to where it should be, he gestured for all to return into the temple for the opening of the vaults.

Chapter 20

On opening the vaults, the first group to exit were the temple guards, stewards, and servants. They immediately moved to take up their positions both inside and outside the temple. Some opened the kitchens, others removed the statue coverings before cleaning the temple, another group went out on to the terraces to assist the various realms to their designated encampments. The oracles followed and took up positions close to Jacob.

The Yeti Nation was next to arrive; they were being led by a very young warrior. It was Yasna, the young boy who initially had great difficulty entering the vaults. While in the vaults he grew to stand at over six feet tall, and his handsomeness didn't go unnoticed. He stood out and looked very striking. His white hair, tied back into a ponytail with long strands hanging loosely on both sides framed his perfect face. His pale blue eyes and unblemished sallow skin completed his handsomeness. His flowing robes failed to hide the muscles that lay beneath and when passing the goddesses he was pleased to hear the whispers of admiration. This helped him feel good about himself especially when he noticed Sofia staring at him. Jacob too was impressed and gestured for him to join him.

"When first you entered the vaults I was concerned, I heard what Drayce said and hoped his words helped. I too helped, with the raising of one finger I sent to you your powers, and they certainly show today. It pleases me to see how you are now in command." He stretched in and whispered, "Your nation has been devastated, and will need your power and that of the other younglings. Cetan and Yeshe are the true heirs of Yaz and God Kings of the Yeti Nation, they will need your counsel. They have the full support of Olympus and will always have me as an ally. Bide your time, my visions show me your destiny. You will become Emperor of the Yeti but not yet, your task is to take control of their armies by becoming their supreme general."

Yasna bowed and made his way to meet his uncles who were amazed at how he had grown in size and strength, he now stood taller than all around him. All three made their way out into the meadows to where the stewards had created an igloo village big enough to house their entire nation. They raised the emblem of the Yeti and began putting in place plans to return and rebuild their homeland. When ready, Yasna, Cetan, and Yeshe, made their way back to the temple. Before climbing the steps, they stopped and looked back at the Igloo village. "How relieved our people look," said Yasna, "yet their faces still betray their sadness, so many gone. It worries me when I think of how Shadow destroyed our elderly, killing the repositories of all our knowledge. What they did is unforgivable."

"We'll recover," said Cetan, "Most of that lost knowledge can be recovered, the Olympus library stores much of our history, all is not lost."

"It's strange when I think about that day when I first walked into the vaults," continued Yasna, "I was a scared boy, a Yeti with no powers. I will be forever grateful to the Lord of all Dragons, and the God of Gods. Because of them, I left those same vaults a most powerful Yeti." He again looked around at the grandeur of Olympus. "Four years have passed," he said, "and yet here in Olympus it has been no more than a few days. This certainly is a strange and wondrous place."

He and his uncle's returned to the temple just in time to witness the arrival of the Centaur nations led by Chiron, who was followed by Queen Zephyra and Lord Polkan. Between them was a very boisterous young centaur, her name was Rhiannon, and she was so lively she was a danger to herself. She cantered up to Jacob and nudged against him causing a great deal of laughter around the temple. Lord Polkan wasn't impressed and found his daughter's inquisitiveness embarrassing. He moved to usher her away but was stopped by Jacob. "My Lord," he said, "she's brought life back into the temple, leave her be. I see she's a princess of the Greek and Russian realms; I'm so pleased for you both. Long live the houses of Zephyra and Polkan."

Eala approached Queen Zephyra. "The temple is a more appropriate place for such esteemed guests as yourself and Lord Polkan. It doesn't feel right for you to stay in the stables." Zephyra acknowledged Eala's concern but insisted the stables were fine.

The centaur nations then made their way out into the meadows close to the stables. They were led by Lord Polkan while Queen Zephyra remained behind, doing everything in her power to control the princess. Rhiannon continued galloping around the temple, kicking, bolting, and neighing, providing great entertainment. She then stopped and before the god's very eyes she began to grow. There were several spurts in the space of just a few moments and then she changed, she took her human form causing gasps among those watching. They were looking upon a goddess of great beauty who could only be a creation of the Ancient One. Her ink black, soft, and silky hair, cascaded in layers to rest on her delicate white skinned shoulders. The way her hair framed her face created soft shadows under her cheekbones; enhanced her amazing smile, and the pink hue of her lips. Her eyes were so pale, the blue of the afternoon sky paled into insignificance. She was a free spirit. one who would be hard to tame. She was stunning and she knew it, especially when she saw the way all the young gods were staring at her. She noticed one God in particular, one acting shy and bashful, and this attracted her more. It was Tristan, and she sensed he was besotted by her; she deliberately brushed off him while passing.

"When a son of the Goddess of Chaos and a free-spirited centaur princess get together all Hell will break loose," whispered Jacob to Magni, "I think our beloved brother is going to have his hands full."

"Trust me," sniggered Magni, "'That's my Boy' is all Modi will say."

A short time elapsed before the sweet song of the elves was heard. On exiting, they were being led by the wizards. Ellaweise and the Council of the Elves followed, and when they reached the young gods, they stopped to express their gratitude. It was then when a troubled Zane approached Jacob.

"My lord," he whispered, "I believe you should delay the elves from entering the meadows. They only accept perfection and trust me; they will be upset when they see their damaged thrones. My father taught me the ways of the stonemason, and I can repair that damage. I'll need some time to restore and ensure all will be perfect for them." Jacob nodded in agreement.

Drayce was nearby and heard what Zane whispered. "My Lord," he said, while extracting his lyre from his satchel, "if you slow Time, and I sing very long versions of elven songs, especially 'Song of the Elves', that should give Zane enough time."

Jacob did slow Time and Drayce began strumming. His haunting voice lit up the temple, stopping the elves in their tracks. Listening to Drayce was very emotional, it brought back the bad memories and the sense of loss the elf realms had suffered, but Drayce wasn't finished, he had verses unheard of for millennia, and it was those verses that gave the elves hope. Drayce's plan worked and he only stopped singing when he was sure Zane had completed his task.

The elves thanked Drayce and recommenced the journey towards their encampment. There they were met by a beaming Zane who had just brushed the last of the dust and rubble away.

"Drayce's delaying tactics worked," said Ellaweise, looking around at the perfectly restored thrones, "what you've done for us will never be forgotten. Your skills have restored the thrones, giving them great beauty, how can we ever thank you?"

"There's no need for your thanks" replied Zane as he bowed, "the gods of my homeland will never forget the sacrifices made by the ten realms of elf kind, or the assistance the tribes received during the great battle." He again bowed and returned to the temple.

Ellaweise moved to the centre pedestal to place the amulet carrying the green gem of knowledge into its cradle. She, alongside the lords and ladies of the other nine realms, took their seats. It was then when the harpists came together to create more beautiful and haunting music, songs so calming, they helped with the recovery of, not only their realm, but also all other realms.

Back at the entrance of the vaults the Little People had arrived, and they were greeted by Finn, Aoife, Aodh, and Lir, who were taken aback by the number of younglings that had been born. Everyone, young and old, wore ankle length robes, all tailored using different shades of green, their translucent wings were fully opened and shimmering as they walked. All stood over six feet tall, except for the preteens and younglings. The constant flapping of their wings captured the rays of the afternoon sun creating the most amazing colours, sending their radiance deep into every nook and cranny of the temple.

Finn got excited on seeing his parents and called for them to join him. They didn't hesitate; they quickly reached in to embrace all four of their children before turning back to acknowledge their people as they passed out into the meadows. When all had passed Faer turned to Finn, "I've never been as proud, Jacob entered my head and told me what you did for Olympus." He turned to his other children, "And that sense of pride extends to all of you. You've done the House of Danu proud." Danu and Faer then went to meet with Jacob.

From deep in the vaults the slow rhythmic drumbeat of the beat-maker was announcing the approach of Asgard. For Thora and Viktor, they found it difficult to contain their excitement while awaiting the arrival of their daughter. When Asgard did arrive, it was a massive procession, broken into several sections. It began with the magically shrunken carts, chariots, and ships, followed by thousands upon thousands of Asgardian citizens who were being led by lords Vidar and Hermod. They were greeted by Odi, Magni and Modi who remained close to the entrance until all their countrymen had left for the meadows. When Prudr arrived she was so excited, she greeted her brothers than quickly joined Arum and Eliana, she was pleased to see they were uninjured and looking so well.

Much to the disappointment of Thora and Viktor there was no sign of their baby, and they weren't happy until they were assured by Jacob that their wait was nearly over.

The Asgard procession went on for some time and when the last section finally reached their encampment, meetings were held to put in place plans for the rebuilding of their city. For those on the steps of the temple it was amazing to watch the ships, chariots and carts magically return to their normal size. This happened with the assistance of Fitch who was now the greatest Asgardian oracle.

Back in the temple there was a short gap before the next realm arrived and this time it was the dragon realm. The procession was led by Fafner and Heulwyn who held between them an oversized banner bearing the emblems of their royal house. Drayce, Isidra, Osian, and Galyna were waiting, and just as their people appeared, Drayce extracted his lyre and began singing a haunting version of the 'Song of the Dragons'. He continued singing until all his people had reached their encampment and what was surprising, he was singing for the longest time, he then realised there were many more dragons leaving the vaults than what entered. Fafner and Heulwyn remained in the meadows until all their people settled and then, with Andras, they returned to the temple to meet up with Jacob and Eala.

On reaching the temple Heulwyn noticed Osian quickly withdraw his hand from Galyna. She joined them and said while placing her hands each side of Osian's head, "My beautiful and handsome grandson, never, ever hide love. Take Galyna's hand and show the world how much you love her. Her father isn't blind, see how his heart bursts with excitement, that's because he too saw you holding hands. He's happy his daughter has found love and even happier it's with you."

In the meantime, the Indus, Mesoamerican, Asian, and African Gods arrived, and their exit was nothing short of spectacular. They knew how to put on a show and when they did their colour and flamboyance was awe inspiring. Jacob and the ancient gods lined up and greeted each one individually, and this took a while, much to the annoyance of the young gods who were still waiting to greet their babies for the first time. Jacob invited them to remain in the temple, but they declined, they all wished to go to their encampments and begin planning the restoration of their realms. They too were assisted by their oracles. Jacob respected their decision to leave.

Chapter 21

It was now late afternoon and the tension among the young gods was unbearable, that was until finally, a low rustling sound was heard coming from deep within the vaults. When they arrived, it was led by the God of Thunder, carrying the hammer and resplendent in his imperial Asgard robes. For Odi, seeing his father brought tears to his eyes, he was so excited; he adored his father and couldn't wait to greet him.

Behind Thor came Maria, Thanases, and Irina with Astrid cradled in her arms. Thora and Viktor's excitement exploded when they saw their daughter hadn't changed, she was still a baby, and they were now going to have the pleasure of rearing her themselves.

Helena was with them, and she too cradled a baby, she searched around for Drayce and when she found him, she mouthed, 'It's a boy.' Drayce couldn't contain himself; he broke ranks and ran to join her before taking his son into his arms. "Can I name him?" he asked. Helena just nodded.

He moved to the centre of the Great Hall and raised his son above his head. He slowly spun around, ensuring all gods saw his baby. He then faced the ancient gods. "Before you I name my son, Derwyn - Prince of all Dragons."

Jacob looked across at Fafner and saw him struggling to hold back his tears.

Lovisa was next to appear, walking slightly behind the first group; she too was carrying a baby. She searched for Zane and on finding him she saw he too was bursting with excitement. He also broke ranks and ran to be with her.

"It's a girl and I named her Adira," she said when he reached her, "I hope you don't mind."

He didn't, he took his daughter and raised her above his head. "My daughter Adira," he announced to the gods, "just like me, she is of noble birth, and she is destined to be a goddess of great power."

He forgot his manners; he had ignored Thanases and Irina and when he realised his mistake he quickly joined them. "I've adored Lovisa since the day I first set my eyes on her," he said, looking nervous, "I live in hope you will accept me into your family."

Thanases embraced him and Irina kissed his cheek. He knew then he was accepted.

"And what about your parents?" a voice he recognised said. He turned and was greeted my Oba and Jomo. "Son," said Jomo, "we are so happy for you."

It was then when he saw four very large youths who were so tall they looked down on him. They were his brothers.

Amma intently watched the entrance as her excitement grew, she knew her parents had to be next, and they were. She too broke ranks and ran to greet them only to find herself, greeting two babies. Sagal was carrying one and Jamilah the other.

On seeing two babies, Finn went into a shock that didn't last too long. He found the strength and moved so fast he was with Sagal in less than a second. "Two babies? Two babies?" he kept repeating, taking one into his arms. "I've two babies!" His excitement caused his wings to spread out

274

across his back and as they captured the light, the temple was again lit up with a very radiant and colourful light. "Are they boys or girls?" he excitedly asked.

"You've a son and a daughter," she replied, "I hope you're happy with the names I've chosen?"

"I will always be happy with anything you do," he said reaching in to kiss her.

"I named our son, Senan," she said, hoping he approved, "I believe he's destined to be the wise one, the bearer of all 'Little People' knowledge."

Finn did approve, he took his son and like the other fathers, raised him high above his head. "Before you all," he announced, "I raise up my son. He has been named Senan by his mother. We believe he's destined to walk among the wizards. He will be a miracle worker and will forever be known as the wise one."

He then took his daughter into his arms. "And tell me my beauty," he said whispering into her ear, "what name have you been given?"

"She is of Africa," said Sagal, "so I named her Zahrah. My vision shows me her destiny. She will become a Goddess of the Sun, and a guardian of the tribes."

He lifted her above his head and again turned to the gods. "Here I raise before you my beautiful daughter Zahrah, one who is born to be a guardian of Africa. See the halo; it tells the world she is of the sun and from her the sun will always shine."

He looked for his parents and when he found them, he mouthed; "Now I know." All saw the pride written across Danu and Faer's faces. He was then formally greeted by Jahiri and Jamilah and welcomed into their family.

Girish and Manasa were next arriving, and they made their way to join Hemish and Gaia. They greeted Jacob and moved to wait for the final arrivals.

The excitement in Jacob's family was now reaching fever pitch, they had already met Helena and Drayce's son and were about to meet Obelius's sons. Jacob left his throne, "I'm so happy for you," he said, whispering in Obelius's ear, "and trust me, this is when your life really begins."

Obelius acknowledged the comments then began pacing, his nerves getting the better of him. He couldn't take his eyes from the entrance. When he saw Girish and Mulan exit his heart nearly missed a beat especially when he saw Mulan was carrying a baby. When Aria appeared, his heart was bursting, she was carrying the second baby.

Li and Hai were first to break ranks, they ran to greet their parents, Obelius was close behind. He didn't run to see his babies; all he wanted was to kiss and tightly embrace Aria.

"Be careful, be careful," she yelled, slightly turning, trying to protect her baby from being crushed, "he's very fragile, only born yesterday." She reached in to kiss him then said, "I didn't name them: That's something I wanted to share with you."

"Names are something I've no knowledge of," he said while taking his son into his arms, "give me my sword and shield and I know my place."

"Rub their cheeks," said Aria, "smell their breaths and touch their foreheads, their names will then come." He did as she suggested.

"I'd like to call my first son Aegeus," he said after thinking for a moment, "I see him stand with me as a protector of Olympus." He waited for a reaction and when none came he said, "And if you agree, I'd like to call my second son, Ulric. I sense in him the power of the wolf."

"They're the same two names that came to me," said Aria, with a wide smile.

They then stepped out into the centre of the Great Hall, each holding one of their babies. Together they raised them above their heads.

"Look upon this baby," said Aria, "he is our son, and we name him Ulric. He will be known as the Wolf of Olympus."

"And this is Aegeus," said Obelius, "he will grow to be a god protector of Olympus."

The vaults were now empty and then sealed.

Jacob made his way to his throne and sat for a few moments before again standing and pounding his staff off the floor. He was now at his happiest, peace was restored, and seven new babies were safely in the temple. All talk stopped and everyone faced the throne.

"For the next ten thousand years we've been granted peace," he said, "so there's plenty of time to rebuild. I'm inviting you all to avail of the hospitality of Olympus for as long as needed. Tomorrow will be a better day because it's then when all images and thoughts of the evil happenings will fade out of all memory." He sat back on his throne.

Obelius joined him. "Father," he said, "I've never known a feeling like this, look on the face of my son. Tell me I did well."

"Oh, my Zeus," exclaimed Jacob, after taking Aegeus into his arms, "I don't believe it. No, no, no! It can't be. It's Obelius all over again."

"Just because you weren't able to handle me," snapped Obelius, "it doesn't mean I won't be able to handle my son."

He left and fetched Ulrich, brought him back and placed him in Jacob's free arm. "There's something still missing," said Jacob.

"What's missing is your other grandson." It was Drayce and he moved to place Derwyn into a comfortable cradle created when Jacob raised his right leg to rest upon his left one. He now had all three of his grandsons with him, and all he could do was just smile.

"The great thing about this," said Magni, while taking a seat, left of the throne, "is you can always hand them back."

"Right now," disagreed Jacob, "if I could run out the door with all three I would, I'd keep running and never come back. I'm so happy."

He momentarily turned to his right and stared at the floor.

"That feeling of emptiness is still there, isn't it?" asked Magni, "don't you think it's time you shared it with someone?"

"I've never been this happy," repeated Jacob, "there's nothing wrong."

"Well then," said Magni, backing away, "I'll say no more."

Eala was close by when Magni left, and she quickly climbed the steps to kiss her three grandsons.

"I take it I'm now fourth in line when it comes to getting a kiss," said Jacob.

"You will always be number one," she replied while reaching in for a kiss. She then sat beside him and took Derwyn into her arms. "I heard what Magni said, and it reminded me of those times when we became one, you opened your body and most importantly, you opened your mind to me, it was always unconditional, just as I always opened my mind to you. Sometimes while in the throes of passion I'd notice a door and it was always locked. I never questioned you but lately I noticed it a lot more and just like Magni, I see sadness. Is it not time to open that door?"

"There's no point in opening it," he said, reaching across and giving her a peck on the cheek, "nothing can be changed. Let's just be happy, look at our grandsons. Look around at our friends and see how they enjoy sharing their grandchildren. Look at Thanases and see how he will be forever linked through his grandchildren to Odi, Panya, Jomo, and Oba. See Faer and how delighted he is to be forever linked to Jahiri and lastly, look again at our grandchildren and see how you and I will forever be linked to Fafner, Mulan, and Garuda."

"Well then," she replied, "it's settled, I will ask no more. Let's give our grandsons back, I think it's time you and I went to our room and do what we do best."

"Are you suggesting what I think you are suggesting?" asked Jacob, furrowing his brow.

Within seconds Aegeus and Ulrich left Jacob's arms to join Derwyn, and all three floated across the Great Hall towards their parents. Eala was using her new power, allowing her and Jacob to quickly leave.

Chapter 22

The following morning, Jacob as usual was first awake and he quickly started his training regime. After his warmups he ran out into the meadows only to hear a torrent of footsteps approaching from behind. When he looked around he saw he had company, in fact he had nine runners closing in on him. On passing they got great pleasure in teasing him, but he didn't rise to the bait. He let them run ahead and enjoyed watching them disappear into the distance. He entered Odi's head. "Don't even think about it," he said, "we're not going to the lagoon. I'm a grandfather now and would rather spend my time with my grandchildren." Odi responded with his well-known single finger gesture.

Jacob chose to change direction, taking him high into the snow-capped mountains. When he reached the first peak he met up with Cetan who was out patrolling with a number of his warriors.

"You do know you're welcome to stay in Olympus," said a surprised Jacob.

"We do," replied Cetan, "but up here the wildlife is returning and it's our task to maintain balance. Our damaged homes will easily be repaired. Much of our belongings have been stolen but they can be replaced. We appreciate your hospitality, but our place is on the highest peaks."

"I'm glad we met," he said turning to Yasna, "You are a young warrior with much to learn. It would be good for you to learn the ways of the Gods.

You are destined to be a God of the Yeti. I intend keeping the school going and hope you will take up a place there."

"Don't worry," said Cetan, "he's definitely attending your school." Yasna was seen biting his lip.

Jacob stayed for some time watching them carve the ice blocks required for the repairs. He was amazed at how quickly they were progressing and felt the Yeti will be returning to their homes within days. He offered his magic to assist but it was declined, Cetan felt the young warriors had to learn how to quickly build an igloo the hard way.

Jacob bade his farewells and made his way back to the meadows. He was met by the Gods of Asia; they indicated their desire to return to their homelands as soon as possible. They were soon joined by the Gods of Africa, and the Americas, who also intended leaving. Jacob accepted their desire to return home and offered to create portals when they were packed and ready to go. It didn't take them long and soon they were all on their way.

The centaurs were next to express their wish to leave. They didn't have much to pack, so their exit was fairly rapid. Jacob met with Queen Zephyra and Lord Polkan; he suggested they should allow Princess Rhiannon to attend his school. They were delighted with the offer.

"There is only one fear I have and that is the number of babies being born to the young gods," said Lord Polkan, "who will keep the boys away from my daughter?"

"I've seen it," replied Jacob, "there is one who will become very close. He will be good for her and bring much happiness into the centaur realms. Look at me, I'm the God of Gods and feared for my daughter especially when the young gods began arriving. My worst fears were realised and now she has given me a grandson. I look on it as a blessing from the Ancient One. You too will consider any child born to her as a blessing."

Lord Polkan acknowledged Jacob's words and turned to lead his people home.

Jacob then reached the lagoon and after a short while he walked into its soothing waters. He called on Oceanus who immediately answered. "My Lord," he said, "thank you for your assistance. It's now time to release the spawn and allow the seas to come back to life." Oceanus instantly disturbed the seabed causing the sands to rise. The waters became murky then very milky, the spawn had arrived, and using the currents they floated out into deeper waters, quickly reseeding the oceans; they were followed by vast shoals of fish, schools of dolphins and pods of whales. The molluscs and crustaceans where last to leave, they began by expanding their calcareous shells before finding their homes among the rocks and reefs.

Jacob knew there was more to do, he dived into deeper waters and swam through the re-lit torch colonnade to meet with Lord Toyesh. There he was treated as a hero and made very welcome. After much discussion he encouraged Toyesh to send his people back to their home waters, a suggestion that was quickly agreed to. The movement of the Mer-Nations began immediately, some travelled towards the Suez Canal, but the majority made their way towards the straits of Gibraltar. Lord Toyesh acknowledged the support his people got from Olympus and promised to make his armies available in any future conflict. Jacob then swam back towards the beach.

He made his way to the temple where he got a clear view across the meadows only to be surprised at how quickly they were clearing. He noted how the few remaining craftsmen of Asgard were sharpening their tools, some already creating all kinds of furniture and wooden structures. He also saw the Little People were preparing to leave. He was joined by the lady Danu.

"I fear we might be moving towards outstaying our welcome," she said, "so I've decided to arrange for my people to return to the Fair Lands. It's time we re-created the beauty of our homeland and rebuilt what we lost. Your hospitality will not be forgotten."

"You and your people will always be welcome in Olympus," replied Jacob, "it's the safest refuge of the Astrals should your craftsmen not rebuild before the return of your peoples?"

"All Little People have crafts," she said, "when they are together they work at their best. They will be leaving shortly and ask that you escort them to the portal." He agreed.

She then said, "Faer and I will be staying a while longer, Eala has insisted. My family will also be staying; I suspect lessons will have to be learned so it's best they remain in your school." Jacob was delighted his school numbers were building.

He made his way back out into the meadows and joined the Little People on their walk towards the shield. The procession was led by Mug Ruith and a number of recently created druids. Jacob opened a portal and soon Danu's people were back in the Fair Lands.

On his way back to the temple Jacob stopped by the Elf encampment. The council was in session, and they invited him to join them.

"The council has decided we should return to the ten realms," said Ellaweise, "we've already sent a thousand craftsmen to begin the restoration of our homes and temples; others will be restoring our art and monuments. We have also sent two thousand warrior elves to secure our borders mainly to seek out any weakness such as the one that allowed the Shadow Riders to enter our domain. We will not allow such an invasion to happen again."

"The Ancient One has spoken," said Jacob hoping to reassure them, "ten thousand years will pass before having to put up our guard once again. I trust the Ancient One."

"In Olympus time moves at a slow and steady pace," said Lord Eason of the Forest Elves, "sometimes when the Elf realms sleep a thousand years can pass, all at the blink of an eye. Your ten thousand years to us could be no more than a few years."

"The Ancient One was very clear," insisted Jacob, "it will be ten thousand years for all realms. Time will align. You must have faith."

The elves weren't convinced and decided to leave immediately. They packed and made their way towards the portals. Jacob was disappointed but still offered them refuge if ever it was required.

Their exit was a long and solemn one; there were thousands upon thousands walking in what seemed to be an endless procession. Jacob remained to watch as they passed, then closed the portal.

While walking through the now fully blooming wildflowers he heard something he really missed. It was the flower nymphs and tree sprites, and they were continuously chattering and incoherently gibbering but this time he understood what they were saying. He acknowledged their return and told them he looked forward to teasing and harassing them as long as they didn't mind.

In the distance, the dragon realm seemed to be preparing to leave, and this shocked him. He felt they were the ones most traumatised and most in need of the calmness Olympus offered. He was wrong, they were a race that was resilient. While in the vaults many young dragons were born, and it was felt rearing them in their own homes was the best way for them to understand what it is to lose everything.

"Lord Andras will lead my people back to our homeland," said Drayce, "I've insisted that the palace, and the civic buildings, not to be restored until all dragons have a home to call their own. Osian and Galyna will remain in Olympus to continue their schooling, they will also use their time here to master the art of war. They will be my generals, and will be guardians of the dragon realm. Isidra will also be staying but I'm aware her future is not with us; she will become a Queen of Asgard where she will always be by Maximus's side. I'm staying in Olympus until I'm certain Helena is comfortable with the idea of becoming my Queen. Only then will I return as King of the Dragons."

"That day," said Jacob, placing his arm across Drayce's shoulder, "it seems so long ago. When first you walked into Olympus I saw how you carried yourself. I was particularly impressed by how you challenged Apollo. I then saw the way you held yourself while fighting Viktor, and then how you dealt with the terror of Shadow. I knew then I was looking on a King destined to become Emperor of the Dragons. You must God up and tell her that her place is by your side as Queen of Dragons."

"My Lord, you forget," said a confused Drayce, "My grandfather is Emperor of the Dragons."

"Your Grandfather is staying in Olympus with me," said Jacob, "he and Heulwyn will visit you, but they have chosen Olympus as their home. They want you to rule alone."

Jacob blinked to where Odi and the boys where resting. He placed his hand on Fafner and brought him back to the temple where they rushed to their rooms to dress in their imperial robes. On returning to the steps Heulwyn, and her extended family were waiting, they too were dressed in their imperial robes. Jacob stood on the lowest step with Fafner to his right and Drayce on his left. Heulwyn was beside Fafner. The other dragons stood two steps higher. Jacob then opened a portal to his extreme right and then the march of the dragons began. There were thousands, and like other realms they too had increased in numbers while in the vaults. There were many younglings, and they had already learned how to respect their King. Drayce never took his clenched fist from across his heart until the last dragon had passed. Evan, Afan, Glain and Aneira then followed, they were to run the dragon lands until Drayce was ready to return as their King. Jacob then closed the portal.

The only realm now in the meadows was Asgard. They too had increased in numbers and were taking up a large section near the lagoon. Since the attack they lacked craftsmen and warriors, so many were killed. The Attack on their city was decisive, leaving much to restore. Jacob was concerned; he feared civil unrest unless some major decisions were made. He decided to call a council of Asgard for the following morning.

Chapter 23

The next morning dawned as one of those bright and calm days the Gods had gotten so used to. Jacob prepared for his run and when he reached the steps he looked across at the dunes to see Odi and the boys, they had been partying all night. He was fuming and decided to blink across and tear Odi asunder. He was too late, his father got there ahead of him, so he remained where he was, just watching. Thor was heard to yell while passing Magni, "I'm going to break his neck! That little prick should be attending the council and preparing for the rebuilding of Asgard. What king parties while his people are broken? I swear to Odin, he'll regret the day he was born."

The closer he got to where Odi and the boys were partying the more his forehead veins wanted to pop, such was his anger. When he was within twenty meters he paused, stomped his foot, folded both arms and clenched his fists.

Odi was very drunk and in full party mode with his singing, dancing, telling jokes and just being boisterous. He wasn't aware his father was behind him, but the boys were, and they very quickly sobered up. They immediately gathered their belongings and made their way towards the temple. All except Thanases and Baldor, who were always very protective of Odi, they took up a defensive stance. Their support for Odi didn't last long; they crumbled under the threatening glare they received from the God of Thunder.

Odi turned to see where the boys had got to only to find his father approaching and quickly realised he was in real trouble. He tried to calm the situation. "Hi Pappa," he said, hoping not to be punched, "grab a tankard."

This was like a red rag to a bull. Odi soon found himself being tossed through the air only to land face down in a nearby dune. His father's anger was so acute his booming and thunderous voice shook the very foundations of the temple.

"Grab a tankard?" he screamed, "you want me to grab a tankard when our homeland lies in ruins. How dare you? Your grandfather ruled Asgard for thousands upon thousands of years and never once was our defences breached. You rule for sixteen years and now it lies in ruins. If you were not my son I'd have kicked you halfway across the universe. I'm so ashamed."

Thor never used violence against any of his sons, it was always his words they feared. He had the gift of choosing words that always packed a powerful and devastating punch.

Odi quickly sobered and attempted to defend himself. "How do you think I feel?" he yelled, still unsteady on his feet, "not only have I let you and Asgard down, but I've also failed to protect my beautiful daughter, he captured her and did things to her. I'm the one who is ashamed. I've lost the respect of my brothers and when I look at their faces I see embarrassment and contempt. I'm a failure so why shouldn't I get drunk and party? No one cares about me; I see them looking on me with pity. I don't want anyone's pity I've enough of my own."

Thor gripped him by the neck, raising him off the ground. "You are a stupid, stupid prick," he shouted, "this isn't all about you. It's about the trust your grandfather placed in you, and all you do is wallow in self-pity. Pull yourself together and be the King you were crowned to be."

In the meantime, the boys had reached the steps while Jacob was still watching Odi being manhandled by his father.

"You've got to do something," said Thanases, "he will kill him, he's really angry."

"This is one battle Odi is going to have to fight alone," replied Jacob, "I heard my father is unapproachable when he's like this."

"You're the God of Gods," interrupted Baldor, "and you can't allow Asgard see their King being beaten by his father. It will completely undermine him."

"I'm ahead of you," said Jacob, "I've already used my powers to raise an invisible shield, it rests between the Asgard encampment and their view of the dunes. It's a deception shield and all they'll see is the lagoon and the dunes, they cannot see or hear the fight. What Jacob didn't realise was Thor also raised an invisible shield; he too was very aware Odi's reputation needed to be protected.

Odi attempted to gather his strength but was unsettled by the cold anger-stare he was still getting. He resigned himself to suffering but never expected the pain that was inflicted when his elbow was twisted behind his back as he was being frogged-marched towards the temple. He had never experienced his father in such a rage and knew he had to find a way to escape. It was then when he felt a presence. "Blink," said Jacob, "blink quickly, before he does real damage."

Odi blinked and disappeared, saving himself from further humiliation. Thor was furious; on reaching the temple he approached Jacob, yelling, "I take it you helped him escape?"

"He's my brother and I love him," replied Jacob, "so I suggested he blink. I've no idea where he's gone. You were too harsh, and I think you might regret the things you said. Did you not sense his devastation or understand why he needed to drown his sorrows. I except it was irresponsible of him to get so drunk, and I too was angry, but I know he feels the fall of Asgard is his fault, we both know it isn't. Right now, I'm not the God of Gods who's speaking; it's me, your son and I feel you should listen to me. I think he needed you to validate him; he needed you to hug him and tell him how proud of him you are. He needed you to tell him everything will be all right."

"I don't agree with you," said Thor while backing away, "he's a God King of Asgard and should have known better."

❧❧

Odi had materialised in the ruined palace gardens of Asgard where he sat on the only undamaged bench. He felt humiliated and found himself falling deeper into despair, but he didn't get much time to feel sorry for himself.

"Somehow I knew you'd blink yourself to this very spot." It was Jacob. "I'm God of Gods after all." Odi fell into his arms and cried pitifully.

"You do know father loves you," said Jacob, trying to comfort him as best he could, "more than he does me, Magni, or Modi. He always looks on you with pride?"

"For fucks sake," reacted Odi, pushing Jacob away, "I saw his eyes and they showed how ashamed of me he was. He will never forgive me for the loss of Asgard."

"It wasn't your fault," said Jacob, trying to reassure him. He then said, "I've garnered new powers, and they will assist in rebuilding Asgard just by waving my arm. Would you like me to restore your Kingdom?"

"You would do that for me?" replied Odi, getting interested.

"I would do anything for you," said Jacob.

Jacob walked towards a clearing and gently moved his arm from left to right. All around him damaged columns, stones and rubble levitated and began floating towards were once they existed as part of this once beautiful city.

"Stop," yelled Odi, leaping to his feet, "stop. This isn't real, it's magic. Asgard can only be restored using my blood, sweat and tears. It's the only way I will redeem myself."

Jacob was thrilled; he was hoping Odi would stop him and commit to rebuilding the city by himself. He felt a great deal of pride when Odi moved to gather some rubble and began trying to put the pieces back together.

"This isn't going to be easy," he said, turning back to Jacob, "I never learned the ways of the wood carver, or the stone mason, but I promise you brother, I'll make this work." Jacob left him and returned to Olympus.

Odi was now alone and when he looked around at the task before him he felt daunted. He knew he had the same powers as Jacob, meaning he should have the same powers of all the other gods, so lifting the tumbled columns to great heights wouldn't be a problem. Soon he had the ten main columns of the palace back in position and this gave him the confidence he needed to put in place his plans to complete the palace in the next few weeks.

He was about to start rebuilding the next section of columns when he heard a familiar voice, it was Jomo. "Friend," he said, "you need the skills of the woodcarver and the power of the stonemason. My five sons and I are here to assist."

Odi's face lit up and he ran to embrace them. "How did you know?" he asked, "I thought everyone was ashamed of me."

"Are you for real," replied Jomo, "you're one of my best friends." He moved closer to whisper, "I didn't see what happened and neither Thanases nor Baldor would say. They are so loyal to you they haven't spoken of it. Your father seems to regret whatever he did, he's been asking everyone he meets as to your whereabouts. Jacob has denied all knowledge, but he did tell me, and I offered my families services so here we are. Between us all we'll make you proud. Oh, just so you know, Jacob slowed 'Time' in Olympus. He's hoping that if it takes us five years to complete this daunting task, only a week will have passed in the meadows. He believes no one will be the wiser."

"My Lord," said Zane, "Drayce instructed his dragons to rebuild the homes for his people first, then the civic buildings and lastly the palace. I think it would be wise for you to follow his lead."

"You're right," agreed Odi, "We'll start with the homes furthest away and work towards the palace."

Jomo, Zane, Wamai and Adric took control of the stonework while Lishan, and Deon dealt with the woodwork, Odi did all the heavy lifting. They began by repairing those homes only partially damaged, and within a year they moved onto the more seriously damaged ones. Within three years all homes were rebuilt, and all damaged furniture repaired or replaced.

At the start of the fourth year, they split into two groups. Zane, and his brother, Wamai took charge of reinstating all the toppled statues and iconic memorials throughout the realm. By the time they reached the end of the year they had made their way through all the royal parks, squares, and plazas. They had also worked halfway across the Bi-Frost Bridge where they saw the end was in sight.

294

It was while working on the giant statue of an ancient Norse God when they realised there was someone entombed within.

"From within this statue I hear a heartbeat," said Zane after calling Odi to join him, "its faint but the heart still beats."

Odi became alarmed and considered calling for Jacob but was stopped by Jomo. "Once I heard of a prison such as this," he said, "there's always a weak point and it's usually near the knee. Use the power of Pegasus and carry me up."

Odi placed his arms on Jomo's shoulders, gripped him tightly and levitated him to rest opposite a crack in the masonry just below the knee. Jomo used his hammer and chisel to widen the crack revealing the missing, and very injured Heimdallr, hidden within. Jomo continued chipping away and eventually created a gap wide enough for a rescue.

When rescued, Heimdallr collapsed on to the bridge in despair. "Never before have I seen such carnage," he said, "they came out of nowhere and were so numerous I had no chance. There was one who wielded great power, and he used that power to suppress mine. He knew everything about me and anticipated my every move. I heard the booming sounds and couldn't see where they were coming from, I knew then Asgard was about to fall. I have failed in my duty as guardian of Asgard and will now go into exile."

"Asgard was not alone to fall," said Odi, trying to reassure him, "Olympus fell as did all other realms. The Gods fought and lost many battles, but it was Jacob with the assistance of the Ancient One who won the war. Peace is now restored, and the rebuilding has begun. You are the guardian of Asgard, and I expect you to do your duty. After you've healed, assist with the rebuilding while at the same time prepare a new protection for the bridge. There will be no more talk of exile. Asgard needs you." Odi then bowed to him.

The restoration of all statues, and civic buildings were within days of being completed and when done, it was realised that almost five years had passed. All that was left was the palace and Odi indicated he wanted to finish it alone. He sent Jomo and his sons back to Olympus and requested they discreetly send Hemish, Demetrius, and Gaia to meet with him.

He didn't get what he wanted, he got Panya, and she was furious. "I don't know whether to hug you or break your neck," she yelled, "I thought you trusted me? I thought you loved me?" She did hug him, then continued, "Jacob didn't fool me. Slowing Time was a good move, but you can't fool a Goddess of the Light, I knew while looking at the positioning of the stars that five years had passed, not just seven days. When I challenged him he just placed his finger over my lips, and I knew he was up to something. Why would you leave for five years without telling me?"

He was shocked when he saw her but quickly remembered how every time she was with him his heart raced or missed a beat. She was everything to him, but his shame was so acute he had difficulty facing her. He looked down at his grime covered hands and realised she was seeing him at his worst. His hair was no longer fair; it was darkened by caked in mud and oil. His torso, face, arms, and legs were torn and blood-stained from scrapes and tears that caused scares all over his once perfect skin. His sweat-stained skimpy and tattered skirt was torn and ragged, revealing a lot of what was beneath, and it looked as though it had never been changed or washed. He turned his back on her so as to wipe away the gathered tears.

She softly asked him to face her and when he didn't, she moved to stand before him forcing him to look her in the eye. He said as she raised her hands to wipe away his tears, "I'm so ashamed, I've let Asgard down and what's worse, my father hates me. Why would you want to be with me?"

"I want to be with you because I love you," she said hugging him tighter, "and I know you love me. You're a pain, but you are also the most loyal, honest, loving man I've ever known. I love you because you've always put the needs of others before your own and I love you because you make me feel complete."

"Look at Asgard," he said while turning her to look across the city, "with the help of Jomo and his sons I've rebuilt it. Look at my hands and see the calluses. Feel the sharp and stinging pain shoot through me. I will not rest until I've rebuilt this palace to be fit for you and my family."

"I am a Goddess of the Light," she said while sliding her hand across his scars, "now feel your pain fade."

She moved closer and then; while hugging him, she continued caressing his body, easing his pain as his scars started healing. The gathered dust and grime fell away and then the calluses disappeared.

"My heart tells me to reach in for a kiss," he said, "I really want a kiss, but my head tells me to send you back to Olympus. My task is to finish what I started and you, by coming here, gifted me all I need to complete that task. Go back to Olympus and wait for the call of my Gjallarhorn, but before you go there's one thing I need you to do. Use the magic of an Earth Mother and bring back the grasses, flowers, scrubs, and trees, bring the beauty of Mother Nature back into the realm of the Norse Gods?"

Panya leaned in and kissed him then made her way towards the Bifrost Bridge where she acknowledged Heimdallr before turning back to face the city. She raised her arms and called on the Light. When it came, it sent its beams to surround the city, causing the dormant grass and flower seeds to germinate, the life force of the trees to burst through the charcoal coating surrounding them, allowing them to send new growth, bringing back the leaves.

All across the city the blooming flowers sent their scent, inviting back the sound of buzzing bees. Dogs barked, birds chirped, life was returning bringing a great joy back into Odi's heart. She waved goodbye and returned to Olympus.

When Panya arrived back at the temple she was met by Thor. "Jacob thinks he's fooled me," he said, "he forgets who I am, and it seems so do you. Need I remind you that I'm one of the old ones and time means nothing to me. I know just by looking at the stars that Jacob slowed Time and judging by the glow, you too know where he is. So, tell me, where's he hiding?"

"He doesn't hide," she replied, "he's where he should be, as King."

Thor instantly disappeared and materialised beside the Bifrost bridge. "When you see my signal," he said after acknowledging Heimdallr, "light the torches and raise the banners." He then made his way to meet with Odi.

While crossing the bridge he was in awe. He couldn't believe what Odi had achieved and was bursting with pride. Passing the restored memorials, he stopped and admired how perfect they were. He soon reached the palace courtyard where he heard what sounded like the chipping of a stonemason and went to investigate. He hid behind a pillar, amazed to see it was Odi working to restore the two damaged thrones. he then watched him stand back and lower his head. "I know you're behind me, father."

"Yes, my boy," Thor said, stepping out from behind the pillar, "I am behind you, as I always have been. I will now bow before the true King of Asgard, one who is the worthiest. I look around in disbelief because never before has any king rebuilt his realm using his own hands." He went on one knee and bowed to his son.

"My greatest wish is for you to forgive me," said Odi.

"Forgive you!" exclaimed Thor. "I never blamed you. I was angry listening and watching you partying while Asgard lay in ruin. I knew you were

298

suffering and using beer to hide what you thought was your failure. I sensed your loss of confidence and knew my anger would spur you on. It did and now look at what you've achieved?"

"No, no, father," replied Odi, "Jomo and his sons helped, they are the stonemasons and the woodcarvers of the gods. They took control and taught me everything."

"For Odin's sake," cried Thor, throwing is arms towards the heavens, "you're getting worse than Jacob. Take the credit. You started alone and you've finished alone." He then said, "Oh, three columns at the side of the palace are a bit wobbly, they need their bases adjusted."

Odi was perplexed, and went around to investigate, wondering how he missed them. He immediately began chipping. He used the strength of Heracles to adjust the damaged flagstones at the base of the columns before realigning them and cementing them into place.

While his back was turned, Thor signalled to Heimdallr to use his magic. He did, and all across Asgard the torches burst into flame, and the flags unfurled. Thor then opened a portal to Olympus allowing all of Asgard to view their king using a hammer, chisel and trowel while completing the final touches to the restoration of their homeland. They were astonished by how well their city looked considering what they left behind and their excitement grew when they realised they were about to be called home. Jacob was also watching and used his powers to widen the portal so Odi could be viewed, not only by the Asgardians but also by the Gods of Olympus.

When Odi was satisfied his task was completed, he backed away and turned to seek validation from his father, instead he found himself on full view. All across the meadows the citizens of Asgard were staring back at him. He was shocked, aware he was wearing nothing but the skimpiest skirt.

Worse still he was very aware that he again looked retched, covered in dust and grime, also a bit bloodied and bruised.

He moved to hide behind the nearest column, such was his embarrassment, but his embarrassment soon dissipated when he peeked out and saw all of Asgard, including his brothers, his sister, and his uncles, all on their knees, bowing before him. He looked across at his father and he too was on his knees.

"I think it's time you stepped through the portal," said Thor, "get cleaned up and put in place your plans to lead your people home. Now, my king, you've earned the right to party."

They stepped through the portal into the meadows and after greeting many of their friends and family, they made their way to the temple where they met with Jacob, Panya, and Maria. Thor then left to meet with Magni and Modi to arrange for a battalion of Asgard guardsmen to immediately secure the city.

After speaking with Jacob, Odi left for his room where the stewards had prepared a hot bath. He slipped into the tub not feeling the best. He found it difficult to wash, such was the overwhelming feeling of tiredness. Panya arrived and never having seen him so listless, she stretched in to embrace him, encouraging her Light to revitalise him.

"I didn't eat, never drank," he said, "I wouldn't rest until the city was restored, all this has taken a terrible toll."

"No doubt it took a terrible toll, but you need to find your strength, there are two tasks still to be completed, the first is for you to lead your people home."

"And the second?" he asked, feeling a little stronger.

"We must return to Olympus."

"Why are we returning to Olympus?" he asked, looking puzzled, "surely I should remain with my people until they recover?"

"Eala has requested we return as quickly as possible, something about a gift for Jacob and she wants you there when he receives it."

Odi nodded his agreement as he climbed from the tub. The stewards arrived just as he finished drying himself, they were preparing to dress him in the imperial robes of an Asgard King. While he was being dressed, Panya was being assisted into her robes.

When both were ready they left their room and made their way to the temple steps where they were met by an epic sight. All of Asgard had formed up, ready to begin their journey home. It was a much larger procession than the one that had arrived in Olympus. Young boys and girls who had escaped the attack had grown to be powerful teenagers and were now trained as warriors. Many babies had been born and were now boisterous toddlers. What surprised Odi was, his sister, brothers, Thanases and their families were also travelling, even though they too had been invited by Eala to return to Olympus.

Baldor, as the light-bearer of the north, was chosen to lead the procession, sharing his chariot with Odi and Panya. When the Gjallarhorn was blown, it was the cue for him to release his Light for all of Asgard to follow. After the royal family came the carts bearing the wealth of the treasury, they were followed by the contents of the library, the ancient books and codices, accumulated knowledge, built up since the beginning of time. Next, it was the turn of the carriages carrying the families of every household, no one was left to walk. Then came the ships, over three hundred of them. Before entering the portal many twelve-year-old boys and girls magically transforming from being children into strong fully armed, eighteen-year-old youths who instantly leapt from their carts to take control of the ships that were floating by the Olympus gods. The final section was what remained of the Asgard army, all twelve thousand of them.

Jacob, and the Gods of Olympus, never left their positions until every last Asgardian had passed through the portal.

On reaching the Bifrost Bridge, Odi and Baldor dismounted to meet with Heimdallr, before beginning their slow walk into the city. They took time to admire the grandeur of the enormous, restored statues as they passed. They were escorted by numerous flaming torches and the wavelike flapping of many flags. There was great excitement, partying, celebrations that went on until the early hours.

The following morning, Odi called a council of Asgard and instructed them to review all laws, he also asked them to put in place plans to ensure Asgard was never compromised again. He then informed them of his plan to temporarily return to Olympus and requested they ensure the smooth running of his realm in his absence.

Chapter 24

For Jacob, he was now at his happiest, looking forward to ten thousand years of peace, but most of all, he looked forward to spending most of his time playing with his grandchildren and teaching them the ways of the gods. The wizards, agreeing to remain and continue running the school, made him even happier. He was also really looking forward to centuries of boy's nights out.

During the quiet times one of the greatest pleasures he got, was watching the young gods find their way, especially those who were still single and looking for love. He enjoyed watching Tristan overcome his female related insecurities to finally feel confident enough to spend time with girls, especially when he started spending more and more time with Rhiannon. He warned Tristan not to get too close, even suggested they should stay away from each other. He should have known better and soon realised this to be one of the worst mistakes he ever made. Tristan was maturing and beginning to show he was certainly the son of Chaos and getting more like his father - impetuous and manipulative. Modi was first to recognise it and warned Jacob not to interfere because he knew his son better than anyone and had no doubt he would find a way to be with her. He was right.

Tristan arranged to return to Asgard under the guise of checking something that was bothering him, he said nothing when asked and just left. While in Asgard he met up with Fitch who was now one of the most powerful oracles ever to exist. They had become friends soon after all oracles were brought to Olympus. Fitch immediately picked up on Tristan's insecurities. "My friend," he said, "there's a way to deceive the gods and it involves you running with the white stallions, from among them there's one who will allow you use him to race all other stallions across the meadows. If Rhiannon feels the same as you and her being a Centaur Horse Goddess, she will use her powers to race against those same stallions. This will be her fitness regime but really she will be learning the ways of camouflage. This camouflage will be so complete, those in the temple will fail to see her running alongside you. I have seen it.

Tristan was thrilled with Fitch's guidance and immediately returned to Olympus where he faced many questions but never answered any. He discreetly met with Rhiannon and explained what needed to be done. Over the next few days his plan fell into place and when they were sure the deception was working, they made their way to the furthest reaches of the meadows where they encouraged the white horses to surround them, hiding them from prying eyes. This deception went on for many days until the day a bright light shot across the cosmos. It was seen by all the gods, but they thought they were watching the birth light of a foal; it was Eala who said, "That's no birth light of a foal. It's the conception light of a god." Jacob closed his eyes and immediately saw who was involved.

"This is one problem I won't be dealing with," he said, turning to Modi, "he's your son, you can tell Lord Polkan."

"What are you talking about," asked Modi.

"Congrats granddad," sniggered Odi.

"Will someone please tell me what's going on?" asked Modi, getting agitated.

"It seems, my love," said an unsurprised Eris, "our son has been hiding out in the meadows with Rhiannon and now there's a baby on the way."

"Thank Odin the warriors of Asgard, and the Centaurs, are friends," said Modi, slumping back into his chair, "it might help me convince Lord Polkan not to kill my son."

He left the temple and while pacing the terraces he met up with two very nervous looking figures, it was Tristan and Rhiannon, and they held on to each other as though it was for dear life. They too saw the Light and realised they had been exposed.

"How could you," he said, shaking his head, "you both know what Lord Polkan asked of Jacob? Your actions have forced me to travel to Pelion and smooth these happenings before he hears it from someone else and explodes."

On returning to the temple there was an awkward silence, especially when all saw the sudden bump.

"It seems my grandchild is racing to be born," said Eris while embracing both of them, "no matter, all life is sacred, and your baby will be welcomed into the realm of the gods." She turned to Rhiannon, "Lord Modi will leave for Pelion in a few days, he will arrange for your parents to visit."

"It seems your day is full of surprises," said Jacob, turning to Modi, "look up at the main doors."

Modi looked and saw his daughter kissing Yazna. He again slumped back in his chair while watching them make their way down the steps towards the thrones.

"My lord, my lady," said Yazna, pausing for a moment while gripping Sofia's hand tighter, "Sofia and I have been seeing each other since I left the vaults. We wish to spend our future together and for that we seek your blessing. When our schooling ends we plan to move to the Yeti lands and spend eternity there. He paused waiting for a reaction and when none came he continued, "I'm a grandson of Yaz and destined to be the God King of the Yeti nation. Sofia will become my Queen and Sun Goddess of the Yeti."

Modi slumped deeper into his chair; he didn't see this one coming. Eris was thrilled. "Never did I imagine my daughter with a God of the Yeti," she said, "as her mother I'm really happy that it's you who will cherish and look after her."

While Modi and Eris were getting used to the news about Tristan and Sofia, Jacob moved away to check on Arum. Over the last few weeks, he noticed him sitting alone in the dunes and sensed he was still struggling with the abuse he suffered.

His concern abated when he saw Arum's face light up every time Aja was close by, so he decided to manipulate situations allowing them to be alone together. Some days later he was pleased to see Arum and Aja in a deep trance where Aja was using her powers to draw out his demons. He knew she had succeeded when he saw Arum with a permanent smile on his face, not realising what the real reason for the smile was. He then became concerned when Arum began showing signs of enjoying himself a bit too much, especially after listening to gossip from numerous gods who had stumbling upon Arum and Aja in compromising positions out in the dunes, in the lagoon, or in many of the quiet corners of the temple. Their constant love making was loud, boisterous, and becoming the story of legend. The talk became so rampant Prudr had no choice but to tackle her son and instruct him to be more discreet. She wasted her time; his hormones were out of control.

The gossip got too much for Jomo, he felt he had to act. He hid near the folly and when Arum passed he pounced, he upended him before raising him by the neck. "I've no problem with my daughter being with a God of

Asgard but I do have a problem with the shame you are bringing on our families. Your mother asked you to be discreet and you've ignored her. I am now telling you that my knife will slice through your very special place, leaving you with a very high-pitched voice. Always remember, the far reaches of the universe will not be able to hide you if I have to act again."

Arum didn't care, he showed no fear, his mind was elsewhere. He was thinking of Aja and already planning where they were next going to meet.

Chapter 25

Although balance had returned to the universe and Jacobs friends chose to stay in Olympus for a while longer, Eala still sensed a sadness lurking deep within him. She tried again but just like in the past, he dismissed her concerns, insisting he didn't want to discuss it. Even so she felt whatever was bothering him was getting worse so decided to keep a closer eye on him, especially when preparing for his morning run. She discreetly followed him, watched him warm up then jog across the meadows.

While awaiting his return she made her way to sit beside the statue of David where she slipped into a trance. "Ancient One," she pleaded, "I've done what you asked, all those we love are now in the temple, what more must I do? What is the gift you speak of?" She got no reply. She then watched Jacob return, brighten up after taking a rugby ball into his hands to spend the next hour drop kicking that same ball. She watched him finish his training then sit hugging the ball and this troubled her even more.

The following morning, she again followed him but this time she planned to confront him on his return. She decided there was no point in talking to him about her concerns, so she chose to break their most sacred rule, and enter his head uninvited. She greeted him, then waited until he was distracted. On entering his head, she got a fleeting glimpse of what was missing from his life, confirming what she already suspected. He quickly tried to bury his thoughts, but it was too late, and although she knew he was disgusted with her, she didn't care, even when he stormed off towards the lagoon.

Several hours passed with no sign of him returning, so she went looking for him and when she found him he was still holding the ball.

"Why didn't you tell me?" she asked.

"What's the point?" he replied, "I'm God of Gods and the one thing I want, the one thing I really miss is something I can't have."

"I'm sorry for doing what I did, but I had no choice," she said leaning over to embrace him. "I had to read your mind. I was so worried, you've never kept secrets from me before. I only wanted to help."

"When it's you," he said, tightening their embrace, "I really don't mind. If it were Odi, I'd break his neck. Why didn't I use my powers at the time? Why didn't I give him immortality? What stopped me?"

"I too have a secret desire and it's time I acted on it," she whispered.

"Does it involve you and I doing things to each other in the lagoon?" he asked, completely misreading her, "I'm a man and have needs."

"Does everything in your life always revolve around sex?" she snapped, pushing him from her in a friendly way. "Anyway, as interested as I am, I'm afraid, not this time. I want to go to Elysium and visit the tombs of my parents; you've never brought me there; it's been two thousand years."

"Come," he said gesturing for her to stand, "I'll take you now. It'll also give me a chance to catch up with Cronus and Rhea."

"Not now," she hesitated, taking his hands into hers, "no offence, but I want to go alone. There's a few things I need to say in private and it's time I said them."

"Too many bad things have happened," he said, showing his concern, "and I'm not sure you should travel alone. I'd prefer if you had an escort, or better still, take Obelius and Aria as guardians, I'll look after their babies."

"Well then," she said, leaning in for a kiss, "it's decided, I leave in the morning."

❧❧

Obelius rose early and without delay he had a chariot waiting at the steps of the temple. Aria wasn't with him; she had decided to remain with her babies. Instead, it was Maria, she sensed what Eala was about to do and wanted to be there to assist.

As soon as Eala arrived Obelius flicked the reign, and they quickly reached the rim of Olympus where a waiting portal allowed them through to enter the Elysium realm. On arrival, they were greeted as esteemed visitors and made very welcome.

"My beautiful granddaughter," said Rhea, while embracing Maria, "we've been expecting you for some time now." She then turned to Eala. "Welcome, Queen of Olympus. We too have sensed the call of an immortal."

"Am I the only one who knows or senses nothing?" asked Obelius.

"Son," replied Eala, "you, Demetrius and Helena are a gift only I could give your father, but there's another gift I believe he really wants, that's why we're here."

"Mother," said Obelius, getting exasperated, "I've no idea what you're talking about."

"I checked his coffin," said Cronus, "there's no decay; in fact, his body is no longer that of an elderly man, over the last three days he has taken on the appearance of one whose age is no more than that of a twenty-year-old."

"Let's waste no more time," said an excited Maria, "Jacob's pain needs to be lifted and the sooner the better."

"Walk among the yew trees," said Cronus pointing away from the beach, "follow them to the Avenue of the Tombs. The light will guide you to the mausoleum where you'll find the doors are already open."

Eala and Maria excitedly set off towards the mausoleum, only stopping when they reached a very ornate tomb set among two well-manicured trees. It was the tomb of Eala's parents and for her, seeing it for the first time, came as a terrible shock. She lowered her head while raising her hands to cover her face as her tears gathered. Obelius was watching and became so concerned he raced to be with her. "It's just the shock of seeing your mortal grandparents engraved names," she said as he tightly embraced her, "it's been two thousand years and still it comes as a shock, that's something I never expected."

"One day mother," he said, still holding her tightly, "I will ask father to bring you back in time to your village so you can see them one more time. Grandma, if father won't help, will you?" Maria just nodded.

"Son," continued Eala, composing herself and ushering him away, "go back to Cronus, your grandmother and I must continue with the plan." His curiosity was killing him, but he knew better than to ask.

Eala and Maria arrived at the entrance to the mausoleum and as Cronus said, the doors were open. On entering, lanterns each side of the stairwell burst into flame, as did the lanterns that lit their way to the tombs of the celts. On reaching the Celtic tombs they approached an open sarcophagus, its lid resting against a nearby pillar. There they saw what they had come for, his body perfectly preserved and looking as though he was just sleeping.

From behind them they heard a voice, "Today is a momentous day." It was Lord Lugh. "I too heard the voice of an immortal, and it summoned me from the Fair Lands. It seems my sunbeams, and your Light is to be added to the Spark of Life." He then looked at the body. "Strange how alike he and I have become, he certainly is of my blood."

Eala lovingly placed her hand on the body. "He's exactly as I remember him," she said, "that time when Jacob first brought him to the temple." She paused as tears gathered. "This is possibly the greatest gift I can give my husband; please tell me this is not a mistake."

"This is no mistake," said Lugh, "theirs is a friendship so strong it has broken through the barriers of death, Jacob will love this gift like no other. It's time for Shane to rise."

Eala looked up towards the steps. "Here it comes," she said, getting excited, "this is really happening, isn't it?

"Yes," said Lugh, "it really is. We must now call on our Light to assist."

"The Ancient One showed Jacob a speck of dust being sent across the universe," said Eala, "he said it was a gift. Seeing Shane again, will be some gift."

Maria, Eala and Lugh raised their arms and within seconds their light lit up the passageway before shooting out of the mausoleum to light up all of Elysium. All three then stepped away and watched as the speck of dust approached the coffin before slowly making its way to disappear through Shane's slightly parted lips.

Out among the dunes Obelius and the Titans had gathered. "It's so long since last a resurrection light shot across the cosmos," said Rhea, "even now I still find its power awe-inspiring."

Obelius was now furious. "Will someone please tell me what's going on?" he said, slightly raising his voice, "is my mother in danger?"

"You young gods," said Oceanus, slightly shaking his head, "no patience. You need to wait, what has just happened is very rare, and let me assure you, your mother is in no danger."

Back in the mausoleum Shane's fingers jerked, then his arms. His eyes opened, continuously darting from left to right. He tried to raise his head but failed, his breathing got stronger. When he finally sat up he looked confused. He saw Maria and his face lit up.

"Hi gorgeous," he said, finally able to speak, "you look amazing. Where's Jacob and how long have I been asleep?" He looked around again, still trying to take in what was around him. "I wasn't asleep, was I? Explains why I'm in a coffin?"

Maria assisted him from the coffin and held him as he found his feet. She tightly embraced him, feeling the same way, she felt about him all those years ago - protective, and supportive.

It was then when he saw the identical sarcophagus next to his. "I loved her," he said, gently touching the engraving of her name, "she helped me recover after the great battle, never allowed me to feel sorry for myself. She was my rock, mother to my children. Are any of them still alive?

Eala reached in to hug him. "Time has moved on," she said, "your children did carry on your legacy, now it's in the hands of your grandchildren, and great grandchildren. Jacob met one of your descendants, one who bears your name."

Lord Lugh interrupted. "There will be a time for questions," he said, "but it's not today. Be happy you're alive and now an immortal."

Shane was still unsteady and indicated to Lugh that he needed assistance. Lugh held his arm and when they stood together, they looked so alike, they could have been mistaken for twins.

Lugh assisted him up the steps and out among the tombs, still holding him as they made their way along the avenue. The further they walked the stronger Shane got and when they reached the Titans his strength had fully returned. When he saw Obelius his excitement grew. "Hi Scobie," he said on reaching him, "you still look great, not a wrinkle or a grey hair."

"Eh," said Obelius with an embarrassed smile, "we never met; I'm Obelius, son of Jacob."

"It seems the apple didn't fall too far from the tree," replied Shane, looking around at the smiling faces, "this is going to take some getting used to."

"You have eternity to get used to all what's coming for you," said Maria, "and we'll all be there to help."

"Come," said Obelius, taking Shane by the arm, after finally realizing what was going on, "the chariot is close by, we need to prepare our return to Olympus." When out of earshot, he said, "Tell me everything, what was he like? My father. Was he a prick? A bully? Was he liked? Did he break my grandma's heart?"

"He was certainly liked, and he definitely broke your grandma's heart," replied Shane, "He was never a bully or a prick, he was the greatest. When he left for Olympus, I lost my one true friend."

"You really loved my father, didn't you. This is going to be some surprise, he has no idea." Shane just nodded.

They soon reached the chariot, and as Obelius was untying the horses he yelled, "Mother, the portal is open, we must hurry."

"Be patient young god," snapped Lugh, "Shane needs time to gain his strength. The portal will wait."

"I see nothing has changed," sniggered Shane, "he's still snarky."

Obelius felt chastened, this was the second time he had been put in his place by an ancient god, and he didn't like it. When Lugh announced his plan to travel with them, he wasn't a bit happy.

When all had mounted the chariot Cronus leaned in and placed his hand on Shane's face, "I was there at the beginning of time and can tell you that what has happened here today is the greatest gift bestowed on anyone by the Ancient One. Treasure it and enjoy your immortal life."

They said their goodbyes and then Obelius flicked the reign taking the chariot through the portal to arrive at the rim of Olympus. That was when Shane felt overwhelmed, he asked Obelius to pull over, saying he needed some time alone before arriving in the temple.

He dismounted and before the chariot departed he asked Maria for a favour. "Mrs B," he said, "please use your magic and fetch me a rugby ball."

The words were no sooner out of his mouth when Maria blinked, disappeared, and instantaneously returned with the ball.

"Mrs B?" she said, while handing him the ball, "it's some time since I was called that name."

The chariot left and made its way to the temple.

Jacob was standing near the lower steps just kicking his rugby ball against a low wall before catching it only to be kicked and caught, time and time again. When the chariot reached him he was surprised to see Lord Lugh but was delighted and made him very welcome. "My father is in the Temple," he said, after greeting him, "your arrival will make his day."

He then greeted Eala. "Did you find their tomb?"

"I'm at peace now," she said while enjoying his embrace, "we created beautiful flowers and now their tomb looks loved." She again kissed him. "I need to change," she said, "enjoy the rest of your training; I'll meet you later."

"Hey Paps," yelled Obelius as he made his way to the stables, "I challenge you to a game, seven a side? Create a pitch."

When he reached the back of the temple he met Zane and Magnar, in the distance he saw Finn, Aodh and Maximus. He called them together. "I need one more," he said, "I've challenged my father to a seven a side rugby match." Just then Viktor arrived. "Don't go anywhere," he said, "you're picked."

Jacob was thrilled by the challenge; he needed no persuasion. He magically created the pitch as requested and after meeting Fafner, Garuda, Odi, Jahiri, Thanases and Jomo, he knew he had a team to teach the young gods a lesson. Apollo took a crash course in refereeing and after calling the two teams together, he laid out the law. The most important rule was - no use of magic or powers. Jacob's team wore white skirts and Obelius's black.

No whistle was needed; one yell from Apollo and all knew to obey. It was an epic game between one generation, against what was supposed to be a younger and fitter generation. Obelius used his time to taunt his father, but his real strategy was to keep him distracted. He needn't have tried too hard for Jacob was so immersed in the game; he was totally focused. He ranted and raved, especially when balls were dropped or passes missed, but his team-mates didn't mind, they too were keeping him occupied. Word of the resurrection of Shane had spread throughout the temple.

In the meantime, Shane slowly walked across the meadows. Unlike when he last visited, this time he took in the eye-pleasing beauty, the magical scents, the chattering of the flower nymphs and the singing of the tree sprites. On reaching the odd dip in the meadows he'd drop kick the ball and run to catch it, drop kick again, never once allowing the ball touch the ground. There were times when Jacob caught a glimpse of that ball and he wondered, but when he focused there was no ball or player, he thought he was losing his mind. It was coincidental that Shane reached the dips in the meadows at the very time Jacob caught that glimpse.

All gods on both teams were now frantically trying to keep Jacob distracted by deliberately breaking the rules, or just targeting him, but their efforts were useless, they were up against one of the greatest, swiftest, and most tactical rugby player ever. He taunted them, so much so, that most of them eventually threw their arms into the air and left the pitch. Obelius didn't give up; he remained on the temple side, constantly throwing, or kicking the ball, intentionally putting his father's skills to the test.

Shane was getting closer, and the sound of him kicking the ball was now so audible Jacob turned just in time to see a drop kick, then a skilful catch. Obelius was still trying to keep him occupied when we yelled, "Paps, catch."

Jacob turned and instantly caught the ball, he flicked it back only for an equally swift return which he caught, and then he froze. He stared at Obelius bearing a look of confusion. "Only one player had the skill to do that," he said, still looking confused. He looked up towards the steps and saw that all the gods had gathered, making him suspicious. Obelius knew his plan had worked and there was no more to be done, he left the pitch and moved to sit with Aria, his babies, and his mother.

Jacob again looked at the gods and saw smiles on their faces, especially his children and his brothers, he then felt his emotions get the better of him. He saw a sense of pride on his father's face and then saw the tears gather in his mother's eyes. He looked across at Eala and saw she was bursting with excitement. He then looked at Odi who was using a little circular motion of his index finger, indicating he should turn around, and when he did he watched the player drop kick the ball yet again, sending it straight up above him for near on twenty meters before skilfully catching it. He watched the player repeat this exercise three more times and as each kick happened his eyes filled with more tears until eventually he couldn't see at all.

He wiped his eyes and turned to face Eala. "You really fooled me this time," he said, "you didn't go to your parent's tomb." He ran up the steps and said as he tightly hugged her, "You did this for me? This is the greatest gift ever."

He then ran as fast as his legs could carry him.

"Hi Scobie," said Shane.

"Hi Bud," replied Jacob, "For someone who died so long ago, you look really good."

"For someone who has lived for over two thousand years," said Shane with a smirk, "you look even better. Not a grey hair in sight."

They kept staring at each other until Shane eventually said, "Well, are you going to kiss me or what?"

"Not a chance, just a hug," said Jacob, trying to suppress a laugh, "but not yet. I just want to keep staring."

"Ah, for fucks sake," said Shane, losing his patience, "give me that fucking hug."

They hugged and after a while began walking towards the temple, both trying to get a word in edgeways. Maria's tears were now flowing freely as she made her way down the steps. She took Odi's arm, wanting him to walk with her.

Hi Odi," said Shane, reaching across to shake his hand, "you kept your promise, you looked after my bud."

"Ah sure," replied Odi, "someone had to, but trust me, he's your responsibility now."

The End

Jacob
Journey of A God
Eamon Blake
'Jacob - Journey of a God' is the first in a gripping series of five books. It chronicles the journey of a troubled youth who, since his twelfth birthday, has been haunted by disturbing visions showing horrific events set in the past. As the visions escalate he learns of a future filled with turbulent and violent times.
Its 2016, and although living the normal life of a Dublin teenager - school, studies, rugby and girls; he soon discovers his true identity. His mother tells him the story of his birth and her efforts to protect him from forces beyond his comprehension. He begins to understand his extraordinary abilities especially when he realises those abilities are actually the powers of a God.
Amidst the unfolding drama of his life, Jacob's visions show him to be leading a battle against two malevolent forces - one is 'The Darkness' and the other, the nefarious 'Prince of Hell'. Both have made him a target of their venom, they know he has been chosen to be the defender of the Light and they fear his power.
Why does The Darkness loathe the Light?
What fuels the Prince of Hell's hatred of Jacob?
In the face of these existential questions, will Jacob embrace his divine destiny and become the God he was born to be?

Jacob
Walk of The Messengers
Eamon Blake
Throughout the ages there were many heroes, and the common thread weaving its way through their lives was honesty, bravery, chivalry and the protection of the weak. Nothing exemplifies this more than the heroism the four Messengers of the Gods and their formidable guardians showed while delivering Jacob's message during their journey of eighteen hundred years.
Jacob - Walk of the Messengers - is the second in an exhilarating series of five books; and this one tells the story of those same messengers and guardians. How on every road they walked, every river they crossed, every mountain they climbed, they were met by an onslaught of brutality from the forces of Hell that was relentless. With each attack their confidence grew and their skills enhanced, and as the years passed they continued to mature to become powerful gods in their own right.
Will they survive the relentless attacks by the forces of Hell?
Will they succeed in their task of creating the mightiest army ever assembled?
Will Jacob keep his promise and intervene when all seems lost?

Jacob

For centuries, there've been epic battles fought across vast battlegrounds. There've been empires that rose and then fell to the sound of powerful armies using weapons designed for mass killing. None of that compares to what is put together for the battle between the forces of the Light and the servants of Hell.

Jacob - War of the End Times - is the third book in a riveting series of five and tells the story of a monumental battle that threatens the very fabric of all existence. Apart from open battlefields, it also takes the reader into villages, towns and cities to witness the destruction of all infrastructures that makes those cities function.

Defence of the Light is led by Jacob, and using the power of the Gods, he brings together those of myth and legend. He also calls upon the overwhelming might of the Carriers, the millions of Carriers assembled over the centuries by his messengers.

Opposing Jacob is a massive army of pure Evil led by Lucifer, the Prince of Hell and Cain, the first murderer. Both of whom are being manipulated by the stifling shadow of The Darkness.

Does Jacob possess the strength to successfully command the armies of the Light?

Will humanity survive the relentless onslaught from the forces of evil?

Will the well-planned tactics of the Olympus and Asgard War Gods be enough to defeat Hell?

War of the End Times
Eamon Blake

Jacob

There are no words to describe a parent's love for their children and it's no different for any race or nation. Even for the Gods it's a love filled with pride, always forgiving and forever evolving.

Jacob - Children of the Gods - is the fourth in a riveting five book series continuing the story of Jacob and his battles against the Dark side. In this instalment he becomes aware of a new threat that seems to live in Shadow. At the same time the children of the gods are rapidly changing from being preteens to be sixteen year old hormonal youths with untested powers that can easily get out of control, powers that need mentoring.

Very soon they become targets of Shadow and begin suffering as each day passes. After months of intensive training brought in as a result of growing sinister attacks, they fall into a trance so deep it takes them through the halls of Olympus into a waiting dark mist where, before exiting, everything for them changes. They transform to present as very powerful young gods ready to take on all comers.

Is the rise of Shadow connected to the fall of Hell?

Will their new found powers be enough to assist in establishing Shadow's identity?

Is there a new battle coming?

Children of The Gods
Eamon Blake